HARMONY SPRINGS SERIES

# AMY DRAPER

*To my sister... My first and biggest fan.*
*You're the best sister a big sister could ask for.*

# MOLLY

*I* tipped the wine glass towards my mouth as far as it would go, but it was empty. Again. How did that keep happening?

I eyeballed the two traitors formerly known as my best friends across the table. Their wine glasses were still full. Mine was dry. It must have had a leak.

I'd accepted their invitation to an emergency "wine it out" session after finding out that Jase Tugwater, aka the best baseball player ever to grace the blue skies of Colorado, was moving next door and opening up shop right next to mine. The same Jase Tugwater who'd ghosted me so hard I'd felt invisible.

But instead of giving me sympathy because he was back in my life after nearly a decade of being nothing more to me than a specter with a big fat Major League Baseball contract, my besties—*former* besties—had spent the last thirty minutes googling pictures of him.

"It should be illegal to be that hot," Jeff Fisher, aka Traitor Number One, said. They pulled up a gif of Jase's cringy commercials on their phone, fanning their face with one hand. "Look at him," they said, practically shoving their phone into their husband's face. *"Look. At. Him!"*

Tyson, aka Traitor Number Two, aka my other former best friend, smiled at his spouse and gently moved the phone away. "You're going to have to tone that down to about a four when you meet him."

"Meet him? Oh. Em. Gee. I'm going to meet him!" Jeff screeched, continuing to fan their face with one hand and flipping through images of Jase in uniform with their other hand. "Do you think he'll wear his costume? Because they are fire."

I was going to give myself a migraine from eye rolling. Jase did look like a blessing from the gods in a baseball uniform. But that was not the point. I needed to vent about the unfairness of it all, and Jeff and Tyson were not cooperating.

I needed more wine.

Standing, I straightened my Spock "Live Long and Prosper" tee shirt and walked to the kitchen to help myself to another bottle.

A gigantic pile of dogs that included my Great Dane, Atlas, and rescues of all shapes and sizes belonging to the Fishers lounged between the dining room table and the kitchen counter. I silently congratulated myself on a rare display of athleticism, deftly maneuvering around all the paws and tails.

I grabbed a bottle from the wire wine rack that hugged the corner of the dining room. The wine was probably more expensive than my attitude deserved. Jeff and Tyson had impeccable taste. Served them right for not having my back.

The label said it was a Pinot Noir from the Santa Maria Valley, wherever that was. It apparently had aromas of ripe cherries and raspberries with a hint of pepper.

The top untwisted without resistance—*a thousand bless-ings to the inventor of the screw top*—and I took a swig.

*Bottoms up, pretentious wine.*

I tasted grapes that had fulfilled their potential. Unlike me.

Tyson raised an eyebrow.

"What? The glass was slowing me down."

He gave me a small smile, and my face flushed as I struggled against the feeling of disappointment. Tyson had been my best friend since kindergarten. He was supposed to have my back tonight as I grappled with the thought of coming face-to-face with the reason I've never, ever followed the advice of my vagina ever again.

But instead of support, Tyson sat next to his spouse with a look of pity on his face.

Motherfucking pity.

When had I become the person other people felt sorry for?

Avoiding more judgmental eye contact, I kept my eyes down as I retraced my steps back to the table, careful of wagging tails and wayward paws.

Tyson finally spoke up. "I still don't understand why this is such a bad thing, Molls. I thought you said it was just a fling?"

It was. And it wasn't.

It had been almost ten years since that weekend. A weekend that started with a drink at a bar after a brutal college final and ended with a charming, insanely hot guy in my bed. Two days and nights full of bliss and orgasms and promises he never intended to keep.

Because a month later, there was Jase fucking Tugwater on my TV, a skinny model on his arm, wearing a Colorado Vistas uniform. Smiling like he had the entire world at his feet. All those sweet words he'd whispered to me in the dark seemingly forgotten in the face of fame and fortune.

And now the King of Baseball was opening a micro-brewery next to my animal shelter.

Awesome.

"It was." Maybe if I kept telling myself that, I'd believe it.

I couldn't look up from my hands, which were spread on the table as though I were trying to steady a world that was threatening to tip over on me.

"Hey," Tyson said, leaning over and putting a hand over mine. "It's been a long time, but it's okay to need some time to adjust to this news."

Lifting my eyes, I looked at my two friends, both white men but a study in contrasts. Tyson's neatly shaven face. Jeff's gangly beard. Tyson's short brown hair, framing a round and kind face, a perfect pairing to his polo shirt. Jeff's blond bun, square jaw, and flip-flops that were permanently affixed to their feet, even in the dead of winter.

I loved these two people more than my *Star Trek: The Next Generation* poster signed by the entire cast.

But tonight? Tonight, I hated them. Hated their practical-ity. That they could see right through me. I turned my worst glare on them.

Unaffected, Jeff shrugged. "What? It's not like you're in love with the guy, right?"

Right.

That weekend had been pure lust, sprinkled with a dash of optimistic hope that things might just work out. But I learned my lesson. Gone were the days of being the naïve and hopeful young girl who believed promises whispered to her in the dark. Nope. Now I was all grown up and bitter, punctuated nicely by the kitten poop in my hair from this morning's fiasco at the rescue. *Thanks for nothing, universe.*

I poured the wine into my glass to look less like a

deranged drunk woman and more like a woman with her shit together because I drank my fucking wine out of a fucking wine glass like a fucking lady.

No wonder Jase hadn't wanted me.

There wasn't enough wine left for blind drunk, but I might get lucky and get close to happy drunk.

Tipping the rest of the bottle into my glass, I took a deep breath and thought, *WWJLPD?* What Would Jean-Luc Picard Do? It was my go-to in moments of crisis. Captain Picard would do something clever. And probably mature. Hmph.

Where was a Klingon when I really needed one? Those guys shot first and didn't bother asking questions.

"You guys are going to be neighbors, hon. What are you going to do?" Jeff quietly massaged Tyson's knee as they both looked expectantly at me.

I watched the dogs to avoid their stares. It made me feel broken. And I wasn't fucking broken.

The dogs had rearranged themselves so that the four smaller ones were curled around Atlas and General, the Fishers' pit bull mix. They all looked so peaceful, like they didn't have a care in the world.

In my next life, I was coming back as a dog.

"Avoid him for as long as I can, I guess," I whispered, defeat squeezing the fight out of me.

"This is a small town, Molls," Tyson said, leaning towards me and putting his hands on my knees. "You can't avoid him forever."

I nodded, knowing he was right. But it didn't stop me from wishing things were different.

"Speaking of problems," Jeff said, far too brightly for this to be anything but a foreshadowing of my demise. "I ran into Candi at the Bean earlier today and she mentioned she was the shiny new chairperson of the Sunshine Festival."

"Oh," Tyson said.

"Oh, shit," I said.

Candice fucking Shoowater had been the bane of my existence since middle school. Unfortunately for everyone, Candice had only gotten worse as we'd gotten older. Helped by an obvious boob job she took perverse pride in showing off to anyone unlucky enough to make eye contact. Not that I cared one way or the other if someone got a boob job. Girl power, sister. Just don't shove it in my face, okay?

"She said, and I quote, she's got big plans for this small town and people better get in line or be prepared to be trampled by progression." Their falsetto impression of Candice's screechy voice was dead on.

"Holy Klingons," I muttered. "What she calls progression the rest of us call the death of small-town life."

"She won't be happy until she's turned this place into the next resort town, full of pretentious pukes who don't care about anything but money and shiny things," Jeff agreed.

Tonight just kept getting better and better. Not only did I need to actively avoid running into Jase Tugwater every time I was at the shelter—which was pretty much always. I now had to figure out what nonsense Candice fucking Shoowater was planning and how it would impact my own plans.

All I needed was my rescue goat, Larry, aka the Duchess of Destruction, to pull off the crime of the century and it would be the icing on the cake of catastrophe that was my life.

I swallowed the last of my wine and stood, suddenly needing some space. My head swirled for a second. Harmony Springs was as small as small towns came, which, after tonight's impressive wine consumption, was a definite bonus. I could easily walk the two blocks home, even with an impressive buzz that I would regret tomorrow morning.

As always, Atlas seemed to understand my intent as he

extracted himself from the Fisher pack and ambled over to me.

"I'm going home."

"You're welcome to stay," Tyson said, gathering up the empty bottles.

"We could stay up and watch *Sex in the City* reruns and cattily judge their fashion choices and shitty taste in men," Jeff said.

A part of me really wanted to say yes, if only so I wouldn't have to be alone tonight. I was so tired of everything feeling so hard. Absolving myself of responsibility, even just for a night, felt like a luxury.

Atlas stood next to me, leaning gently against my leg, his long tail swooshing slowly. He turned his big brown eyes up at me, waiting for whatever was next.

Sweet dog… I had no idea what was next.

"That's okay," I finally said, grabbing my sweatshirt off the back of the chair I'd just vacated. "I just need to sleep it off."

"If you need anything…" Jeff looked at me, mirroring the pity I'd seen on Tyson's face earlier.

I smiled at my friends as I opened the door and followed Atlas outside. They meant well, and despite my earlier irritation towards them, I knew they had my back.

"I know. Tonight, I just need a shower and a bed."

Everything else I'd figure out tomorrow.

# 2

## JASE

*You Klingon shit-eating mastermind. How the fuck did you even?"*

The string of swear words echoing through the doorway worried me. Not because I feared for my safety. My size was usually enough of a deterrent for most people to think twice about messing with me. If that didn't work, my famous face usually did the trick.

My concern was more for the unlucky bastard bearing the brunt of the verbal attack. And why they might do so in my unfinished microbrewery after dark.

I placed my tablet on the stack of cardboard boxes that served as a bedside table next to the barely long-enough-for-me bed, all tightly squeezed into the small room that served as my makeshift apartment. At least until my house was finished. What it lacked in space, it more than made up for in convenience, being right down the hall from the tank room.

I'd bought the redbrick industrial building on the outskirts of Harmony Springs, Colorado, a few months ago. A tenant occupied one side, the Happy Tails Animal Shelter. The other side had been empty and perfect for my new brewery, the Catcher's Box Brewing Co. The well-apportioned outdoor space in the back that practically shouted "patio seating" had all but sealed the deal for me.

The cussing sounded like it was coming from the direction of my brewhouse, a large room in the middle of the space. I'd hooked up the large stainless steel vats last week, but the rest of my space was basically empty, and would be for a few more weeks.

I glanced at the small alarm panel next to my door. The light for the back door flashed green. Weird. I was certain I'd locked all the doors before I sat down to watch the day's sports highlights, er, run through my business plan.

With a groan, I stood and stretched, my knees popping and cracking—a souvenir from my career-ending knee injury last year. Swiping my phone, I checked the time. Nearly midnight. *Shit.* I'd been sitting on the lumpy bed surfing the internet—sorry, reviewing my expense reports, for five hours. No wonder everything hurt.

And no wonder Colorado had let me go. Who wanted a catcher who couldn't even get off his bed without sounding like a drum line?

"Ow! You mother rock-hopping lunatic demon spawn. I will fucking *end* you. Do you hear me?"

The voice was female and definitely coming from inside the Catcher's Box. *Interesting.* If she was a burglar, she was a bad one. The only things to steal were the boxes of disorganized paper in my office, bags of hops stacked up in the brewhouse, and a few tools I had brought with me to tinker until I could get a general contractor hired.

Who was this trespasser? More to the point, why had she broken into my empty brewery?

I walked through the office doorway but was stopped cold by the most inhuman noise I'd ever heard. A scream, yet not a scream. Was the woman in labor?

A shorter noise, this one sounding more like a broken car horn, pierced the air. It was more animalistic and less child-birthy. Was she murdering a duck?

A duck murdering woman who may or may not be giving birth was burgling my business. *Cool.*

I forced my feet to move. Time to get to the bottom of this little Scooby Doo mystery.

"Damn it, Larry!" the woman yelled.

What the hell?

My long strides made quick work of the distance to the brewhouse, the pungent flowery smell of hops leading the way. Rounding the corner, I was nearly knocked off my feet by the impact of a tall, lanky white woman dragging a mass of ratty fur behind her.

"Shit!" the woman exclaimed as she hit the ground. A giant, tan-colored dog stood behind her, its tail wagging in a long, slow swooshing motion.

At least someone was happy. I hoped. It was hard to tell in the dim light.

The dog looked down at the woman, its ears flopping forward, while a black-and-white goat—*wait, what?*—bleated in misery.

"Shut your pie hole, Larry," the brunette muttered. "This is all your fault, you miserable—"

I flicked on the hallway light.

The woman stopped talking, eyes blinking at the sudden brightness, and looked up at me, a blush spreading across her face.

A face that looked familiar.

Long-buried memories flashed across my brain. The weekend I had signed a contract to play for the Colorado Vistas baseball team. Celebrating with a woman at the bar. Two days and nights of mind-blowing sex.

"Molly?"

Her eyes pinched shut. "What? No."

Was I wrong? Maybe she just looked like my biggest mistake.

"I swear you look just like this woman I used to know."

"Nope. Not me."

Those pouty lips pressed together as a steely determination took over. She'd had the same look at the bar when I asked her if I could buy her next round. I hadn't seen Molly in nearly a decade, but I'd spent the better part of that weekend mapping every part of her.

This was definitely my Molly.

Wait. No. Not *my* Molly. Just Molly. Molly Sanders.

"Was that you I hit or the wall?" she asked, rubbing her shoulder and sitting up.

*Heh.*

I'd had plenty of opponents ask me the same thing after trying to steal home. *Not the point, Tug.*

Molly, I was sure of it, moved to stand, but the goat—*seriously, why was there a goat in my brewery?*—was trying its damnedest to foil her plans by hopping over her. During one hop, it grabbed her ponytail and chewed as if it were a chunk of hay. Before I could reach out a hand to help her up, the dog grabbed the rope hanging around the goat's neck and led it down the hallway a few steps.

*Huh.*

Finally freed, she hopped up and slapped the dust off her jeans. Jeans, I couldn't help noting in admiration, that covered long, lean legs. Legs that I remembered wrapping tightly around my—

"*Ahem.*"

I looked up from her legs to find her standing in front of me. She was tall, not as tall as me, but it afforded me the full effect of her eyes, which were the same striking shade of golden amber I remembered. They were also currently narrowed at me in annoyance.

"Get your fill?" she asked, hand on one hip, emphasizing her subtle curves.

"Not even remotely."

"Classy, Tug."

I smirked. "Ha! So it is you!"

"Don't get your knickers wadded," she said, continuing to glare at me. "You're Jase Tugwater, former all-pro catcher for the Vistas. Everyone in Colorado knows who you are."

"Everyone may know me, but you *know* me, Molly."

I didn't ask it. I didn't need to. The blush reddening her cheeks told me I was right.

She ignored my comment and looked for the animals. The Odd Couple of the animal kingdom were hanging out behind her. Now that the lights were on, I could see the peculiar duo more clearly. The dog looked like it might be a Great Dane. The goat looked like... trouble. I hadn't seen eyes like that since my encounter with the blue octopus at the Shedd Aquarium in Chicago when I was nine and my older sisters had told me that octopi liked to escape their enclosures to torture little boys who looked at them too long.

I suppressed a shudder. I'd had nightmares about those eyes for a week.

The dog licked the goat's face, which resulted in a response that sounded like *blet*.

No way Sam and Fozzy were going to believe me when I told them about tonight.

Molly leaned down to take the goat's—*sweet Jesus, why?*—leash from the dog. "We'll see ourselves out," she said without looking at me.

Seeing her in the Catcher's Box tonight, after all these years, all those regrets, in this place where I was making a fresh start... it had to be a sign. *Didn't it?*

I had no right to ask her to pick things back up with me, not after I'd left her the way I had. But that didn't mean I didn't want to.

"Who's Larry?" I finally asked, desperate to keep her here, even if it was just for a few more minutes.

Her brows furrowed in irritation as she glanced at the animals. "Larry's the goat," she spat.

"You named your goat Larry?"

"My mom named her."

"Her?"

She sighed, the angry tension in her face smoothing somewhat. "Yes. *Her*. Don't ask."

"And the dog?"

"His name's Atlas." Her face softened when she said it. She clearly adored the dog. Lucky pooch.

She looked like she wanted to leave, but wasn't moving.

"What are you doing here, Molly?"

"Not Molly," she insisted. She met my gaze, jaw thrust out. God, she was beautiful when she was being stubborn. The light dusting of freckles that traveled from cheek to cheek made it hard to take her too seriously, no matter how hard she was trying.

The more I looked at her and the more I talked to her, the more I knew I was right. I was looking at my past. And maybe, if I played my cards right, my future.

"And mostly I was trying to avoid you, but thanks to the hooved agent of chaos here, that clearly didn't work."

Her words were like a punch to my gut. I steeled my face so she wouldn't see the hurt.

"Why is there a goat in my building?" I asked, irritation sharpening my voice.

"I'm sorry," she muttered.

I actually believed her.

"Larry got loose from next door," she continued, "and I

tracked her here. It was late, and I thought you'd be gone for the day, so I, you know…" She trailed off.

Next door?

Happy Tails Animal Rescue. I'd known my tenant ran an animal rescue next door, but my business partner, Sam, had only mentioned "some crazy cat lady" ran it. I'd pictured the owner as a middle-aged woman who knitted sweaters out of cat hair. Not Molly Sanders, the woman I still dreamed about on those dark, lonely nights.

Yet here she was, standing in front of me, picking what looked like bits of hops and goat hair off the front of her Starfleet Academy tee shirt. She was adorable. I shook my head and tried to keep the grin off my face.

"So you broke in," I finished.

"Technically, Larry broke in." She turned her glare from the goat back to me. "And I said I was sorry."

I nodded. I still couldn't believe it. Molly Sanders. Here in my brewery. What were the odds?

"You can make it up to me by having a beer with me."

Although the beer in my tanks was weeks away from being ready, I had a small advanced batch I brewed before moving to Harmony Springs, tucked into a corner of my office. I didn't share it with anyone, not even Sam and Fozzy.

But I'd share it with Molly if it meant she'd stay a little longer.

"I prefer wine." And with that, she turned her back on me and called to the dog, who promptly trotted down the hallway towards his owner, goat in tow.

I watched her ass sway back and forth before I followed the trio down the hall to the back door.

Molly paused, hand on the handle, turning those jeweled eyes on me.

"Good night, Tug."

I grinned.

"Good night, Not Molly."

Atlas nudged my hand with his snout on the way out the door as if to say goodbye. Larry just fixed those freaky eyes on me and kicked her back legs.

My new neighbors: my biggest regret, a badly behaved goat, and a Great Dane with better manners than them both.

*Cool.*

I gave her back end one last look of admiration as she slipped outside. This was shaping up to be the most interesting summer I'd had since… Well, since the last time I was this close to Molly Sanders.

*Heh.*

*Play ball!*

3

# MOLLY

*I* parked my silver SUV across the street from the Happy Tails Animal Shelter and let Atlas out. The parking lot was public, but usually used only by people visiting Happy Tails Animal Rescue and Kenny Rogers—the mechanic, not the singer—who now owned Jim's Garage across the street. The sign out front of the garage still said *Spring on in for an oil change*, even though it was almost June.

The garage used to belong to my dad. But after my mom died last summer, he'd sold it to Kenny and moved to Arizona, saying the town held too many memories for him.

It did for me, too. But unlike my dad, I was clinging to those memories like a drowning woman to a life preserver.

Blowing out a breath, I looked at the brick building. I'd been dreading work this morning. Seeing Jase face-to-face last night had been bad enough. But seeing him after he caught me breaking into his business… nothing like a little B&E to make an awkward situation even worse.

Fucking Larry. How the criminal mastermind had broken out of her pen was mystery number one. Mystery number two was how she'd then broken into Jase's brewery. I'd seen the connection for a door alarm when I walked in after Larry. If my goat now possessed the ability to disarm a security system… Worf help us all.

Thankfully, Jase hadn't seen fit to call the cops on me after he'd caught us. Whether that was benevolence on his part or luck on mine, I didn't care. I had enough problems on my hands without adding jail time to the pile.

Hitching up the worn canvas tote that declared space was the final frontier, I crossed the street with Atlas in tow, stopping when I recognized Jase standing outside the front of my —*our*—building.

He wasn't so much standing as he was… prancing.

Jase Tugwater, all-pro catcher for the Colorado Vistas, was strutting like a proud peacock up and down the sidewalk, grinning and chuckling and looking like a wet dream doing it.

Tan cargo shorts couldn't quite conceal thick muscular legs that showed the beginning of a summer tan on his white skin. The navy tee pulled taut across his chest, showing off shoulders broad enough to give Atlas—the Greek god, not my dog—a run for his money. His blond hair looked a couple weeks past due for a haircut, but somehow still looked yummy enough to want to run my fingers through.

I took my phone out of my pocket to dial 9-1-1 just in case he was having a stroke, but opened my camera app and snapped a picture instead.

"What?" I asked Atlas—my dog, not the Greek god—who was leaning against my leg. "It's for possible blackmail later, not because he's hot."

Atlas looked unconvinced.

"Who likes tall, blond, and muscly, anyway?" I groused.

*Not this girl.*

Atlas nudged my hand with his cold snout, not believing my words any more than I did.

Not that it mattered. Jase had made it crystal clear years ago that I wasn't good enough for him.

I tightened my ponytail and looked down at my own outfit. Jeans that looked dirty despite being freshly washed, a ratty tee shirt with the words *Make it so, Number One* printed under Jean-Luc Picard's face, and slide-in shoes that used to be maroon but now looked closer to the color of the sidewalk I stood on.

Hardly a wonder he hadn't wanted to pursue a relationship. I was a hot mess.

Lucky for me, the animals in my charge cared more about the food and shelter I offered them than how I looked. And that was just fine with me.

More than fine. It was exactly how I wanted it.

Atlas rested under the old cottonwood tree on the corner of the lot while I walked up to my new neighbor to see what all the fuss was about.

"What are you—" I asked before noticing exactly what the fuss was about.

Above his entrance was a shiny new sign that declared, in all its purple, green, and silver glory, that this was the new home of the Catcher's Box Brewing Co.

What. The actual. Fuck.

I'd spent three months trying to reach our new landlord to ask about a sign for my shelter. Apart from the name painted in my front window—a project donated by the high school art class—there were no signs that my redbrick building housed Morris County's only animal shelter.

How was I supposed to turn my basic little shelter from a place that rescued wayward animals into the state's largest animal adoption site without a little pizzazz? Like a new logo, which I'd asked the art class to design as their next project. And a new sign.

When I'd reached out to the landlord for permission to put a sign out front, they'd ghosted me. I'd sent half a dozen emails and voicemails over the last three months, each met with deadening silence.

Which made the garish sign Jase had just installed all the more infuriating.

"What on earth is that?" I asked, annoyance punctuating my words.

Jase stopped his jerky movements and looked at me, head tilted and lips pursed in confusion.

"It's called my happy dance."

My eyes narrowed.

"Not that." I jutted a finger, pointing at the front of his side of the building. "*That.*"

"Yeah," he replied, the grin returning to his face, head bobbing up and down. "Isn't it great?"

"It's hideous."

"Hey—"

"How'd you get it?"

"I ordered it from the Colorado Sign Company. They just finished installing it."

Mother. Fucker.

I took a long breath to calm down. But Vulcans be damned. I had tried for months to do what this man had done in a week.

"What's wrong? Don't you like it?" His face scrunched up like it pained him to imagine someone not liking his things. Well, he could shove his things up his—

"Molly? You okay?"

I unclenched my fists, willing the vein in my forehead to stop pulsing. Losing my temper over this wouldn't solve anything. It wasn't as though any of this was Jase's fault.

*Big breath, Molls.*

"Not Molly. And no, I'm not okay. I've been trying to get a sign hung on the building for months," I explained, keeping my voice even-keeled to hide my irritation. "But I haven't heard a peep from our landlord."

Jase's nose wrinkled as he scratched the back of his neck. "Huh," he said.

I shook my head. Of course Jase got a sign while I couldn't even get an email response.

"I guess he only responds if you're a professional athlete with oodles of money," I spit out.

So much for calm.

"I, um, I can…"

"You know what? Never mind. It's not your fault our landlord is a big fat jerk."

Jase swallowed hard and cleared his throat.

"Look—"

"I said drop it, Tug. I don't need a stupid sign, anyway." Which was technically true. Except I really, *really* wanted one. Nothing said *I'm a legitimate business owner,* like having a cool-ass sign hanging over your door.

Like Jase did.

That spoiled jackwhacker with his big dumb handsome face and stupid chiseled jaw. A breeze drifted across my face, blowing the scent of his aftershave towards me. Warm leather and amber. Why did he have to smell so good? Yum.

Wait, no. This jerk probably used his charm on the landlord. *Ugh.*

And… now I was angry again.

As my breathing ratcheted up, I closed my eyes and tried to picture my happy place—the shelter, with its oodles of ragtag animals I was helping to save and find safe, loving homes for.

The shelter, which was right next to a brewery run by a man who'd slept with me and then ghosted me after he'd signed a multimillion dollar contract to play for the Colorado Vistas. A brewery everyone would know about because there was a brand new fucking sign hanging out front.

Squeezing my eyes shut, I fought back tears of frustration. I really needed to get a grip. My temper ran too close to the surface on an average day. Lately, it had been on a hair trigger thanks to the man standing next to me and some pompous ass of a landlord I'd never even met.

Jeff's words flitted into my head—*You guys are going to be neighbors, hon. What are you going to do?*

What indeed?

I slowly opened my eyes, but kept them firmly pointed towards my feet. Jase was watching me. I could feel the heat of his stare. He didn't need to know how much this bothered me, so instead of meeting his gaze, I picked at a spot on my jeans. It looked like a grease spot, but was probably kitten poop. Or goat drool. Maybe my jeans weren't as clean as I thought.

Movement by the tree caught my attention. Atlas had rolled over, bearing his tummy to the warming mountain air. He looked carefree and happy, the way he'd looked every single day since I rescued him four years ago.

The thought made me smile. At least I was doing something right.

"You okay?" Jase repeated, his voice soft, hands shoved deep into his pockets.

Great. My friends already pitied me. Now I was being pitied by a man who had rejected me.

"I'm sorry for snapping," I said, finally raising my face and making eye contact. It was like looking directly into a solar eclipse, beautiful and painful all at once. But I was done feeling weak. "You're not the reason the landlord's ignoring me."

Jase's mouth opened and shut, like he wanted to say something but changed his mind.

"I'll leave you to your celebrating," I said, shaking my head as I glanced up at his sign. "Fucking landlord," I muttered on my way past him.

"He's not so bad." He scratched the back of his neck again.

I stopped. "You've met him?"

"Um. Yeah?"

"Figures," I replied, keying in the entrance code to the electric lock. The same lock I'd installed a few months ago after the landlord ignored my repeated requests to replace it. I'd contemplated doing the same thing with the sign, but figured a door lock was a lot less conspicuous than a six-foot sign.

"I could, um, talk to him for you," Jase said.

I looked over my shoulder at him. The sunshine made his blue eyes look like they'd been plucked from the perfect sky above them. He was perfection. And I hated him for it.

But Jeff was right, not that I'd admit it. We were neighbors now, and I needed to find a way forward or I'd end up more miserable than I already was.

He was watching me, head tilted, waiting for a response.

I couldn't rely on anything he said. He'd taught me that years ago. But maybe just this once, I could put a little trust in him.

For the animals.

"That would be… very neighborly, Tug. Thanks."

He nodded, a small grin appearing on his sexy face, before disappearing behind his door.

Atlas unfolded himself into an upright position and lumbered over to stand next to me.

"I can do this, right?" I whispered to my faithful companion, opening the door and following him inside. "I can be polite, neighborly, even, without getting hurt."

Again.

If only it were that easy.

*Make it so, Number One.*

4

# JASE

*C*ome on, baby. Open for daddy."

I wriggled the silver key I'd found in a box labeled "Tenant" when I first moved my stuff into the Catcher's Box. The key had been unmarked, but since this was the only door I hadn't been able to open, I hoped maybe they were a matched set.

The doorknob stubbornly refused to move. "So that's a no."

I had no idea what was in the damned room. It could be a dead body for all I knew. *Knock it off, Tug. You would have smelled it.* Ooh, maybe it was something more awesome, like a pirate treasure chest full of plundered gold doubloons and jewels.

My imagination went wild as I thought up bigger and better things.

Like Molly, and the way her legs had looked in those skintight jeans yesterday. Or the way it felt, once, as she wrapped them around my waist while I drove into her.

She'd been attractive when we'd met that night at the bar. Straight chestnut hair falling almost to her waist, golden eyes sparkled like honey when the light caught them. Tall and lean, with slight curves that fit all my sharp angles.

Now? Now she was stunning. Everything I'd remembered her as being, but… more. More confidence, more intelligence, more bite. Life had molded her into a harder, sharper version of herself.

Which is why I'd felt like the world's biggest jerk yesterday lying to her. I shifted my weight, the pressure in my pants now an awkward reminder of a missed opportunity.

*You didn't technically say you* weren't *her landlord,* a little voice with devil horns whispered in one ear.

*Lying by omission is still lying,* a haloed voice countered in the other ear.

The angel was right.

Lying by omission was still lying, and I was not a liar. At least not until yesterday, when I'd seen Molly in the daylight, looking like a dressed-down goddess, knowing I was probably the last person on earth she wanted to see.

Also knowing I could give her what she wanted.

She'd let me back in yesterday, just a little, when she'd accepted my help. Telling her the truth yesterday would have only served as an excuse for her to slam that door shut and seal it, probably for good.

I didn't want to risk ruining a second chance with Molly, so I'd stayed quiet.

Yanking the impotent key out of the lock, I marked an "x" on it with a black marker so I'd know not to waste my time if I came across it later. Maybe there was another set of keys somewhere I hadn't found yet. Probably locked inside the room with the decaying body, er, treasure chest.

The cargo pocket of my shorts buzzed. I pulled out my phone and tossed the key back in the box.

"Hey, Sam," I answered.

"So you're not dead. Looks like I owe Fozzy twenty bucks."

My best friend, current agent, and business partner, Sam Duncan, had a flair for business *and* drama.

"Remind me to write you out of my will," I replied.

"I'm in your will? Good for me. I deserve it, with clients like you ghosting me for weeks on end."

I cringed. I had been ignoring Sam's emails and text messages over the past week. Not intentionally, but I'd been a little preoccupied between trying to get my business up and running, and finding out a certain sexy brunette spent her days on the other side of my wall.

A sexy brunette who needed me to talk to our "landlord" to get a sign on her building. So I'd finally texted Sam last night.

"Gotta earn that fifteen percent somehow," I replied.

"Fuck off," Sam quipped. The dinging of a car door sounded through the phone speaker right before it slammed shut. "What's so urgent it couldn't wait until our state of the business meeting next month?"

The meeting was Sam's idea. It was code for *I'm coming to Harmony Springs to drink your beer.* Considering he'd put in twenty percent of the business costs to make the Catcher's Box a reality, I could hardly say no.

"I need you to send an email for me."

"I know my ass looks great in these jeans, but I'm not your fucking secretary, Tugwater. Send your own emails."

"I, um, I can't."

"Why the fuck not? Last I checked, you had a bum knee, but the rest of you worked just fine."

*Because I'm a big fat liar who doesn't have the balls to tell Molly I'm the asshole landlord she's pissed at.*

"Look. Would you just do it? I need to approve a signage request for my tenant."

"Not that it doesn't just delight me to do your fucking bidding, my Supreme Overlord, but again, why don't you send it yourself?"

I hesitated and immediately regretted it.

"*Ohhh*," Sam said. "This is about a girl."

Yes. "No."

"Then send the email," Sam replied, calling my bluff.

I walked out to the back patio. The furniture I'd put together yesterday after I'd celebrated my new sign was spread out, a mix of iron and teak, matching the interior design and bringing new life to the redbrick exterior. I needed to power wash everything, but wanted to wait until I got closer to opening day.

Sitting under an umbrella blocking the intense Colorado sunshine on this cloudless day, I ran a hand over my face, weighing my answer to Sam.

"I need it to come from you."

"Because…" Sam prompted.

Screw it. "Because she doesn't know I'm her landlord, and I'd like to keep it that way."

Sam laughed. And kept laughing. And laughing.

"Dude," Sam finally huffed, out of breath. "You slept with your tenant?"

"I didn't sleep with her." At least not in this decade.

"Why the hell not? Is she ugly?"

"She's gorgeous," I blurted out before my brain could catch up. Why the hell had I said that?

"So, you *want* to sleep with her?"

Abso-fucking-lutely. "No."

It was Sam's turn to hesitate. "Is she going to be a problem?"

I stood and ran my hand lightly against the wall where a local artist had painted my new logo—two frothy beer mugs clinking together over home plate—remembering the work I'd put into this business. Into making my dream a reality.

That Sam would think I'd risk our business to get in a woman's pants hit a nerve. I'd put everything on the line for this—risking my reputation, butting heads with my family for not hiring a business manager to run it—everything. No way would I ruin this shot. No matter how much I wanted the girl next door.

Sam was one of the few people in my life who understood all that.

"No. She's not a problem."

"Good."

Larry had wandered over to the fence, looking like she was sizing up the wire for an afternoon snack. *Not today, fence eater.* "Stay away from the fence, Larry!"

"Who's Larry?" Sam asked.

Before I could answer, Goatzilla made eye contact and let out an unholy scream.

"Holy shit, dude!" Sam yelled, forcing me to pull the phone away from my ear and put him on speaker. "Who's being tortured?"

"I am." Damned goat. "Look, will you send the email or not?"

"I don't know. You still haven't told me why you don't want her to know you collect her rent checks every month."

"Larry!" Molly yelled from next door. "Get away from the fucking fence!"

*Shit.* When had she come outside? I waved at her and quickly switched from speaker mode as I hightailed it back inside, praying she'd been too far away to hear anything.

"Is that the woman who's not a problem and you don't want to sleep with?" Sam asked.

I had seen her for all of ten seconds, but I'd noticed every-thing about her. She wore a cute pair of bright blue cotton shorts that showed off tan, lean legs, and a simple gray tank that probably had kitten poop smeared all down the front.

I smiled at that thought.

Holy hell. I had it bad.

I wiped the sweat off my brow with the back of my hand. My two gently used stainless steel tanks, named Rosita and Junior, judged me silently from behind the glass wall that showcased their brewing brilliance.

Well, everyone could just fuck right off today.

"What the hell does that mean?" Sam asked.

Had I said that out loud?

"Do I need to rearrange my schedule so I can come out earlier?" Sam asked. "You don't sound so good."

"No. It's fine. I'm fine."

I really needed this conversation to end before Sam realized I wasn't, in fact, fine.

"I'll send you verbiage for the email," I continued. "Just make sure you send it under your name."

"You've got it bad, my friend."

I did. I really did. But Sam didn't need to know that. And if I ignored it long enough, maybe it would go away. Like an itch in a place you couldn't reach.

"Just fucking do it," I growled.

"Don't get your panties in a twist. Consider it done."

"Thank you."

"Head in the game, Romeo."

*Head in the game.* Sam gave me that advice whenever I was heading towards a slump. And it always worked.

Hopefully, the magic still held. I needed all the help I could get.

"Head in the game," I replied before disconnecting.

I settled myself into my new chair, positioned proudly in front of my new desk—a sleek cherry number I picked out to match the exposed redbrick in my office. They had arrived yesterday with the patio furniture, along with a grumpy delivery driver who kept grumbling about the "goddamned hairpin turns" up the canyon.

What Harmony Springs lacked in accessibility from major city centers, it made up for in charm and fresh air. The delivery guy was not amused when I pointed this out but had perked up once he'd seen the size of his tip.

My phone buzzed in my pocket. Expecting a text from Sam, I was surprised to see Molly's name pop up. I'd given her my number in case she had any other trouble with the landlord. Yep, I did that.

> Molly: sorry about larry I put her in her pen

> Molly: hopefully the new lock holds this time it got 4.8 stars from locksmithsrus.com <fingers crossed emoji>

I smiled as I pecked out a reply.

> Me: No worries. If it doesn't work, the electrified wire I ordered for the fence should be here next week.

> Molly: nice try she'll probably eat it and start shitting lightning bolts then we'll both be fucked

I laughed out loud before I could stop myself, the sound echoing off the brick walls.

Sam was going to have me by the balls. And I just might be okay with it.

5

MOLLY

*I* checked the time on my phone for the forty-second time.

"It's been thirty seconds since the last time you checked," Tyson replied, the calm in his voice making me want to shout at him to stop being so annoyingly reasonable.

Instead, I counted to ten and reminded myself that Tyson was my best friend. We'd gotten coffee together every Saturday morning since I'd moved back home after my mom got sick two years ago. I loved this ritual. It was one of the few things that had kept me sane dealing with my mom's illness. And in the aftermath of her death.

Tyson didn't deserve my temper. The fucking goat who opened the fucking doors to the fucking kennels last night deserved my fury. The hoofed menace allowed eight kittens who'd joined Happy Tails straight from the bowels of hell to wreak havoc in my shelter overnight.

It had taken me over an hour this morning to wrangle them back into their kennels and another hour to clean up their mess. All while Larry bleated like she was being tortured because I had locked her in her pen.

That goat was going to be the death of me. But she'd made my mom happy, and allowed her to pass peacefully when I assured her I'd take good care of Larry.

As much trouble as Larry was, she was one of the last connections I had to my mom. Even on days when I wanted to murder her.

I shoved my beat up cross-body bag with the motto *Live Long and Prosper* up my shoulder.

"Where did all these people come from, anyway?" I grumbled, my forehead aching from the perpetual pinch in my brows.

I, of course, knew the answer. All that stood between me and the elixir of life was the tour bus of white-haired retirees on their way to the historic gambling town of Cripple Creek to gamble away this month's retirement check.

It was a rookie mistake, forgetting today was the first weekend in June. For the past decade, the first weekend of every month brought retired gamblers to Harmony Springs in flocks, like wrinkly birds on migration in search of the greatest coffee in the tri-county area before they tried their hand at Lady Luck.

My already kitten-addled brain had taken another shot when Jase decided he needed to plant bushes along the edges of his patio this morning. Shirtless. Showing off hot, over-worked muscles that made me want to lick the sweat off.

*Gah.*

When I'd gotten a mouthwatering peek at the top of his boxer briefs, I'd forgotten how to speak. Was it any wonder I'd forgotten about the senior migration this morning?

The line shuffled forward by one whole person.

"There," Tyson said. "We're moving."

*Whoopty-fucking-doo.*

All this waiting was giving me far too much time to dwell on the email I'd gotten last night from my landlord, whose name was apparently S. R. Duncan. Mr. Duncan had finally approved my request to put up a sign on my side of the building. It had only taken three months and an intervention from Jase.

I hated beyond reason that he'd been able to do what I couldn't. I hated even more for how grateful I was for his help.

After the landlord's email hit my inbox, I had wasted exactly zero seconds ordering a new sign from the Colorado Sign Company. It would be here next week. *Praise baby Spock.*

Looking around, I tried to focus on something that wasn't the immovable line in front of me. The Jumping Java Bean was my favorite coffee shop in all the land. It smelled like espresso beans, cinnamon rolls, and happiness.

I loved it here, despite the interior looking like a Smurf and a French aristocrat had a baby who then threw up everywhere. The walls were—no joke—Smurf blue. Giving the blue a run for its money were white curtains, jam-packed with a gold fleur-de-lis pattern, which was repeated on the tile countertops and a few of the throw pillows for good measure.

To top off the delightfully gaudy decor, gold leaf crowns topped stuffed animals randomly placed around the shop.

The original owner of the coffee shop, Verna Kowalski, was not French. Or a Smurf, although occasionally she dyed her hair bright blue. Kole Fitzpatrick had bought the shop from her five years ago but hadn't bothered to change the look of the place.

Thankfully for everyone in Harmony Springs, he more than made up for the overdose of blue and gold by making the best cup of joe that I had ever tasted. High praise, considering I used to call Seattle home.

Seattle. Where I'd met my blindingly hot neighbor ten years ago.

*Not going there, Molly.*

The line finally budged again, leaving only three people between me and nirvana.

"Yes," I breathed in relief as my ass buzzed. I dug my phone out of my back pocket and struggled to keep the smile off my face.

> Jase: I hope your sign doesn't suck. I'd hate for you to have sign envy.

Despite my better judgment, I'd texted Jase last night after I'd gotten the landlord's email. To thank him. Not because he'd been raking his backyard yesterday afternoon without his shirt on. His heavily muscled shoulders and back had clenched with each movement. Like my vagina.

> Me: my sign is so good it will make your sign cry

> Jase: Signs don't cry.

> Me: signs dont but you will when you see how awesome my sign is <crying face emoji>

> Jase: Lol we'll see.

I looked up from my phone and saw Tyson staring at me. Along with everyone in line.

"What?" I could feel my forehead scrunch as I scowled at the people nearest me. They had the good sense to look away, but Tyson tilted his head and studied me.

"You were giggling," Tyson said, a few people in line nodding in agreement.

I scowled. "Uh, I do not giggle."

"Until thirty seconds ago, I would have agreed. But—and

I realize I'm saying this at great physical risk—you literally just giggled."

"I. Don't. Giggle."

I had totally giggled. Fucking vagina and its fucking low standards. Like it was so impressive that a man I'd sworn to hate forever had helped me with our landlord and then had the audacity to be hot *and* have a wicked sense of humor. Yesterday, I'd caught myself thinking it wouldn't be the most awful thing ever having him as a neighbor.

If I wasn't careful, he was going to weasel his way back into my life. And my pants.

*Nope. No. Not going to happen*, I thought, shoving my phone back into my pocket. No matter how much my pants might be willing to drop to the ground in submission whenever he sauntered half naked around his backyard. Or how perfect his stupid pecs looked shimmering when the sun hit the beads of sweat sliding down cut abs that I itched to drag my fingernails over.

*Ugh.*

Tyson said nothing. He didn't have to after a lifetime of friendship. His raised eyebrows and a ghost of a grin practically shouted at me.

"Shut up," I said, feeling my cheeks warm.

"It's okay to like him," Tyson said with a knowing smile.

"No, it isn't," I countered.

"Molly—"

"No, Tyson. No second chances."

Was he hot as sin? Yes. Was that enough to make me forget how he'd fucked me and forgot me? Not even a little.

"Okay." That was his whole reply. No judgment. Just kindness. If I could get out of my own way, I could maybe learn a few things from him.

The line shifted forward as another coffee-worshipping senior citizen got their caffeine fix.

Only two people left between me and salvation.

"Thank the Vulcan gods," I murmured.

"Don't celebrate just yet," Tyson whispered, his chin pointed down. "Incoming."

I turned to see what he was talking about and immediately regretted it.

"Molly Sanders!"

Candice fucking Shoowater came barreling towards me, blond hair piled on her head, cleavage pushed high and proud. The scowl she aimed at me made her look madder than a rabid skunk and caused the people standing around us to shrink into the background like they'd just been sprayed.

She pointed a hot pink bejeweled fingernail at me. "Your dog is a threat to humanity and floriculture, and if I have anything to say about it, I will see him put down like the monster he is."

*Oh, goodie.*

6

# MOLLY

*A*s an entrance, it was a tad overdramatic, but given Atlas had likely done whatever Candice was accusing him of doing, it was also not entirely unwarranted.

Candice was glaring so hard her eyes were bulging. Any minute now, they'd pop right out of her head, ruining the perfectly contoured makeup adorning her face. What a scene that would make.

"Ow," I said, rubbing my side as Tyson nudged me with his elbow.

"You were giggling again," he said under his breath, not taking his eyes off Candice. That would be like showing weakness to a hyena, and we'd both learned in grade school what a bad idea that was.

I cleared my throat of any lingering giggles and met Candice's glare. "I don't know what you're talking about," I lied. I knew *exactly* what this was about, but if Candice expected me to shrink under her wrath, I was going to make her work for it.

Candice pointed her bony finger towards my nose, the

jewels on the end of her nail catching the light like a suncatcher. Her ring finger had a giant yellow flower painted on it, contrasting with the bright pink base polish. It matched the yellow of her deep V-neck tank top and the pink flowers on her white miniskirt. The entire outfit was planned to highlight Candice's many physical assets—natural and augmented.

She was perfection in four-inch wedge sandals. If I didn't know the festering personality underneath, I might have been jealous.

"You know exactly what I'm talking about," Candice countered. "I swear I've had it with you and your dog. If you can't keep him on a leash, I'll call animal control."

Sure, she could do that. But they'd just drop him off at my shelter because it was the only place in Morris County that housed animals. My eyes started to roll, but I knew if I couldn't stop the motion, Candice would rain hellfire down on me, and the poor unsuspecting patrons of the Bean would catch the shrapnel.

*Must. Not. Roll. Eyes.*

"I'll probably regret this, but what do you think my dog did?" I asked.

"He destroyed my entire peony garden yesterday!"

I swallowed my sigh. After I moved back to Harmony Springs, Atlas channeled his inner flower child and began napping in the neighborhood flower beds. Unfortunately for Candice, hers were the biggest and best and, therefore, Atlas's favorites.

Had my dog slept in Candice's prized peonies? Probably. Would I admit that to Candice? Fuck no.

"I'm sure whatev—"

"Save it," Candice snapped. "Those were blue ribbon blooms, and I was planning to enter them at the state fair this year. They are ruined. *Ruined!*"

Those precious fucking flowers were the only thing Candice prided herself on more than her appearance—and she gave high regard to the way she looked.

"I don't know what to tell you, Candice. Atlas was with me at the shelter all day yesterday." Except for the forty-five minutes when he mysteriously disappeared.

"I don't care what you say. I know it was your dog."

"Prove it."

I thanked the tech gods for minor miracles because Candice's home was one of the few in the neighborhood that hadn't upgraded to a camera doorbell. Her neighbors might have seen Atlas strolling down the street late yesterday afternoon on their cameras. But it was unlikely anyone tracked him after he moseyed around the side of Candice's house.

Or if they had, they weren't saying anything.

"There is only one thing in this town that leaves prints that size, Molly."

"Please," I snorted. "We live in the mountains. There are lots of things with giant paws around these parts."

"Such as?"

"Bears."

Candice crossed her arms and tilted her chin up. "Try again."

"Bigfoot."

Candice rolled her eyes. "Seriously?"

"What? You're not a believer?"

Candice tapped her foot.

"Fine. Cougars." Like the one standing in front of me, tapping her foot.

"Nope."

"I've heard they're suckers for a good floral arrangement," Tyson said, my hero. There was a better than fair chance he knew Atlas had rolled in Candice's flower beds. He lived three houses down from Candice and had installed a camera doorbell last summer. There wasn't anything on that block that he didn't see.

Someone in line snickered. Candice snapped her head towards the sound, but whoever made the noise was smart enough to go silent.

She turned back to me. "I should have known you'd deny it."

"I'm not—"

"It doesn't matter." A grin formed on Candice's lips.

*Uh oh.*

"I'm here to deliver some good news," she finished.

Tyson cleared his throat next to me and raised his eyebrows. My stomach churned.

Candice batted her eyes at me before continuing. "The Sunshine Festival committee met Monday night and voted to raise the entry fee for booths this year."

"And that's good news, how?"

"Your entry submission is short one hundred and fifty dollars," she cackled. "Doesn't look like you'll be getting a booth this year."

Candice's Cheshire Cat smile grew in direct proportion to the rate my stomach dropped. No booth meant a serious drop in adoptions *and* donations for the year. Both of which I desperately needed if I was going to grow the rescue.

"I already have a booth," I said slowly, frowning. "I got confirmation from the committee."

Tyson stepped forward. "And Molly's a nonprofit. You know we give them a break on fees."

"We?" Candice said, staring at both of us like we were third graders trying to explain advanced quantum theory to a physics professor. "I know that's how it worked when *you* were on the committee, Tyson."

She paused and picked an imaginary piece of lint off her skintight tank before clasping her hands in front of her.

"But under my chairwomanship this year, we decided all entrants should be treated equally. It simply isn't fair to ask the hardworking business owners of this fine community to fund the activities of others."

"That's literally the definition of a nonprofit, you useless twatwaf—"

Tyson put a hand on my shoulder and shook his head. "Not helping," he sang under his breath.

I took a deep breath in and held it, closing my eyes. I didn't trust myself to react rationally right now.

One hundred and fifty dollars was a lot of money to my barely surviving business. With some budget cuts and extra donations, I might swing it.

I exhaled and opened my eyes. Candice was still grinning. *Fuck*.

"Is there something else?" I asked through clenched teeth.

Tyson squeezed my shoulder in solidarity. Neither of us wanted to know what was lurking behind Candice's shit-eating grin. But not knowing would be worse.

"The committee also decided any booth featuring animals would need to pay an extra two hundred and fifty dollars to cover the costs of cleaning up the park. You know, because of the issues we encountered with last year's cleanup efforts."

My jaw dropped. "That wasn't my mess, and you know it."

This was utter bullshit, and the way Candice's chin jutted out and her arms crossed said she knew that, too.

I struggled to breathe as spots formed in front of my eyes.

The town had hired a company to set up a petting zoo last year, but they'd failed to secure the fencing after the festival's last night. The town awoke to animals raiding the park and businesses up and down Main Street. It took me, the two petting zoo workers, and several of the braver sheriff's deputies, the better part of the day to round them all up.

"You have until Monday to turn in the additional money, or I give your booth to someone else."

"Today is Saturday," I said, swallowing the panic rising in my throat.

"I know," Candice cackled. "I would have told you sooner, but I was too busy cleaning up my garden after, well, you know."

She spun on her wedges and strutted to the front of the line. "My usual, please, Kole."

*Un-fucking-believable.*

I tried to ignore the stares I felt from everyone around me as Tyson kept me grounded with the hand that hadn't strayed from my shoulder.

"What are you going to do?" he whispered.

With the entire festival committee backing Candice, what *could* I do? I couldn't stop her. No one could. Which meant I had two days to find four hundred dollars.

"How much are kidneys going for these days?"

Tyson patted my shoulder as the line moved forward. Kole nodded at me before reaching behind him and handing me and Tyson our drinks.

Kole was easily six and a half feet tall and looked like he had just walked off a prison movie set. Tattooed sleeves covered both arms and crawled up his neck. He had dark hair, darker eyes, and more muscles than biology suggested could be packed onto the human frame.

I met him my first weekend back in Harmony Springs, when I'd gone into caffeine withdrawal tending to my mom for a week straight with no breaks. In all that time, I'd never heard him string together more than four words. Emojis, on the other hand, he could weave together like a well-written essay.

Definitely not your stereotypical barista. But he knew coffee.

"Wait a minute," Candice screeched, making her way over from the pickup counter. "Why do they get their drinks before *me*?"

Kole took two more orders from the customers behind me and filled three more cups full of his magical potion before he answered in his deep baritone voice.

"Because your iced grande vanilla matcha with two pumps, brown sugar, oat milk, sweet cream, cold foam takes a little longer to make than a medium mocha latte extra hot and an Earl Grey tea."

*Huh.* Guess he could string together more than four words. Doing it at Candice's expense, well, that was just the whipped topping on the mocha latte of my life.

I grinned as I watched Candice's lips disappear and eyes bug out.

Kole looked up at me. "Next time, just grab your drinks."

"I don't want to jump the line when you're this busy." My eyes cut to Candice in time to see her neck and cleavage blotch red. *Hah.*

"Monday, Molly," Candice quipped. "Then your booth goes bye-bye."

Maybe the universe would take pity on me and send a meteorite crashing down on Candice's cherished Mercedes tomorrow. Preferably while Candice was in it.

Until then, I had to figure out how to make money grow from the aspen trees in my backyard. Maybe Google would have some ideas.

"Come on, Tyson, we've got work to do," I said as I turned to leave. And ran smack into a wall instead.

*Who the hell put that there?*

"Son of a bitch, that's hot!" shouted the wall. Which, judging from its ability to talk, was not, in fact, a wall.

I looked up into piercing blue eyes that I had tried—and failed—to forget.

Jase Tugwater.

The universe clearly hated me.

Before I could apologize to Jase for the mocha latte bath, the Bean erupted into raucous applause.

I squeezed my eyes shut.

"I hate everyone," I muttered to absolutely no one.

7

JASE

*J* looked down at the angry, coffee drenched woman standing before me, trying to see who was responsible for my wet shorts and the hellfire threatening my dick.

Molly.

Her eyes went from wide to pinched tight as the sizable crowd continued their applause.

"Fancy meeting you here," I said as I thought about icebergs and igloos and looked around for a napkin. Or a beach towel.

"Of course," she muttered through clenched teeth.

"Um…" I said, my brain unable to form words thanks to the coffee, which had soaked both my shorts and her shirt. Her *white* shirt. Making it very easy for me to see the outline of her lace bra. *Head out of the gutter, Tugwater.*

"Hey," Molly replied. "Eyes up here, Pervy McOgleface."

My eyes snapped to hers, which were molten gold and fiery. A grin formed on my face, which I quickly shut down based on the frown forming on hers.

The clapping continued, and Molly's face mottled red.

She stared at the ground and muttered something about Klingons.

I looked around at the looky-loos. "How about we save the applause and go find some napkins?"

The applause slowed, and someone handed me a tissue. *What am I supposed to do with this?* I thought, handing the tissue to Molly. "Hey. Ignore them."

She took the tissue and dabbed it against her chest, which only made her shirt cling more tightly to her breasts. *Snow drifts. Cold showers. Icy Hot on my testicles.*

A man who'd been standing quietly next to her reached towards a table and grabbed a handful of napkins. Exchanging them for her now empty cup, he pulled the bag off her shoulder in a move that seemed familiar. Intimate. Instant hate registered like a kick to my gut.

The dude was good-looking—if you liked the golf pro type, right down to the green striped polo shirt and khaki shorts. Since when was Molly into polo shirts?

One hundred percent not my business.

Keeping myself out of their business, I stretched a long arm to the counter and grabbed more napkins. Blotting the coffee off my shorts, I avoided actively touching my crotch, which was sporting a stiffy at Molly's still see-through shirt. One brush from my hand would take me from half-staff to loud and proud, and this crowd did not need to see that.

"Great," Molly said, looking at the bag now draped over Golf Pro's shoulders as she continued to dry her shirt. "My tote is ruined."

"We'll get you another one," Golf Pro said.

*We?*

She shook her head. "It's fine..."

The urge to hug her and make all her problems go away was strong. "I'm happy to replace it," I offered.

"It's... it's fine," she said.

"We'll figure something out," Golf Pro said as he placed a hand at her elbow and I struggled to keep my inner caveman locked up. One weekend a decade ago didn't give me any right to claim her.

I needed to pull myself together. No matter how much I still wanted Molly, I had a business to tend to. Business partners like Sam to keep happy. And I didn't move in on someone else's woman. Ever. No matter how much I wanted to.

*Head in the game, Tug.*

"Oh em gee. You're a bigger disaster than your dog," sneered a petite blond woman in sky-high wedges holding her phone up. The sound of a camera shutter snapped.

The red in Molly's cheeks spread down her neck, and I clocked the blond as the woman who'd been arguing with Molly when I walked in.

I turned towards Molly to offer my support against the grating woman, but she was holding Golf Pro's hand. My hands closed into fists as jealousy I had no right to feel swirled through me.

"You're pathetic," Blondie said to Molly. She crossed both arms and hefted ample breasts dangerously close to chin territory. Despite all the fakery, the woman was beautiful, if a little too made up. Even in heels, she barely reached my chin. Loose waves fell over her shoulders, heavy makeup done to enhance her features. All suggesting she spent hours in front of a mirror each morning.

She didn't hold a candle to Molly's natural beauty. Long chestnut hair plaited down her back. Simple and—thanks to me—stained tee and cutoff shorts. Full lips that I remembered being soft yet firm. Same with the rest of her, if memory served. But those eyes, normally shiny amber jewels, were dulled.

Why wasn't she fighting back? She'd taken me to task

over a building sign yesterday. I knew she could bite if she wanted.

"Hey, I'm the pathetic one," I said to draw the blond's attention away from Molly. "I can't even see where I'm walking. Now I look like I pissed myself."

Why wasn't Golf Pro stepping in to help her?

Blondie turned a discerning gaze on me. It was an impressive look. But I'd faced worse.

"It's fine, Tug," Molly gritted out through clenched teeth.

"You keep saying that," I answered. But she didn't seem fine.

"Because it is," she replied. "Come on, Tyson. Let's go."

And with that, they dismissed me.

Tyson led her towards the door with a hand on her back. She looked defeated. My hands opened and closed as I fought the urge to go to her. My feet made my decision for me and I took a step towards Molly.

"Mr. Tugwater," the blond troublemaker said, blocking my path. A set of bright white teeth smiled at me, her smile looking as fake as the rest of her. "Candice Shoowater." She extended a hand towards me expectantly. "Harmony Springs's favorite real-estate agent and Sunshine Festival committee chairwoman."

"Quite the title," I joked, instant regret setting in as I took her hand. The act was as automatic as breathing after years of meeting fans and schmoozing sponsors. But her wrist was limp, almost like she expected me to bend at the waist and kiss her hand. Yuck.

Molly glanced back at us, her morose face turning to a scowl as she looked at our hands. She quickly turned and kept walking.

"As Harmony Springs' newest business owner, I just couldn't believe it when your name wasn't on the list for the Sunshine Festival," Candice said.

"What's a Sunshine Festival?" I asked, not really caring about the answer as I tracked Molly and Tyson. The bell at the top of the door tinkled. I watched, helpless, and trapped by the wrong woman, as the right woman and her boyfriend walked out.

"It's the first festival of the summer festival season."

"There's a festival season?" *Stop asking questions, dummy.* I needed to get my coffee and get out of here.

"Of course."

Of course?

"The Sunshine Festival is followed by the Celebration of Our Nation Festival in July," she confirmed, like it was an actual thing to have a festival season. "Then the Summer Blues Festival, right before school starts up."

"Don't forget the Batten the Hatches Quilting Days, Color Me Fall Fest, the Holiday Kick Off, Harmony Spring Days," said a woman sitting at a table to my right. She ticked off each festival on bony fingers capped with pointy nails all painted different colors of the rainbow.

"Yes, yes, Hillary," Candice interrupted.

"And the May Day Fest," Hillary finished quietly.

Jesus, I needed coffee for this nonsense. The giant barista, with the best RBF I'd ever seen, took my order as I tried to process everything. The urge to follow Molly kept pushing me towards the door. I needed to know she was okay and—what? Offer to walk her home since her boyfriend, who hadn't bothered to defend her when she was being verbally abused by Candice, clearly wasn't cut out for the job?

A redhead next to Hillary shook her head. "They renamed that one the Fergus Festival two years ago, remember?"

Candice silenced the women with a look. "The point is," she said, turning her attention back to me, "there are ten festivals throughout the year that bring in tens of thousands of tourists each season. I don't have to tell you how that translates for our local businesses."

*Cha-ching!*

Sam was right. Head in the game. And the best way to do that was to focus on my business.

"Only finding out about it right now," I said, turning my entire attention to Candice. "So, how about you sign me up?"

I hit her with my biggest, schmooziest smile. The one I used when trying to land a new endorsement or convince someone with too much money to part with it for a good cause.

The Catcher's Box Brewing Co. seemed as good a cause as any.

But instead of falling at my feet like she was supposed to, Candice gave me a sad smile that was as fake as her baseball-bunny smile. "Sorry, but I can't do that."

"I thought you said you were the chair?"

"I am."

"Great. Then you can just add my name to the list."

"No."

"No?" That was not the response I usually got.

"No."

*Huh.*

"Okay, I guess there's always next year," I said with a shrug. No way was I begging for help from this woman.

Now that I knew about their weird obsession with festivals, this town just found its new number one festival fan. The Catcher's Box Brewing Co. would have the biggest booth at every event.

The barista handed me a paper coffee cup the color of a radioactive blueberry. It looked like everything else in here. Very blue. I took a small sip. Damned delicious. The online reviews I'd read—*crazy-ass decor but coffee so good it will make your meemaw weep from the grave*—were spot on.

"Well, ladies," I said, bolstered by the power of the magic coffee. "It was a pleasure to meet you all." *Not even a little.* "Candice, please put me down for a booth at the next festival."

She sucked in a breath. "Ooo, sorry, Jase. Best I can do is the waiting list."

"Waiting list?"

"Waiting list," she said, as if that explained anything.

I rearranged my face into something I hoped looked sincere. The one that said, *you can trust me, I'm a professional athlete.* The one every commercial director for product endorsements had taught me to make.

"You sure there isn't anything you can do?"

"Sorry, Jase. Rules are rules. I'm sure a man of your professional background understands." She shrugged a shoulder. "Best I can do is the waiting list. But rumor has it we might have a recent opening, so you won't have to wait long."

Sauntering out of the coffee shop, she gave a little finger wave over her shoulder.

I understood alright. Understood I was royally screwed if I couldn't get my business into one of those booths for the summer festival season.

Time to get creative.

8

# JASE

ome on, you sweet thing. You know you want to move. Show me the goods."

I wriggled the small metal rake hook up and down in the lock, willing the driver pins to slide into place. Was I expecting to be a master thief after buying a lock pick set from eBay and watching a couple of YouTube videos? No. Had I hoped it would be enough to break a stupid house lock? Yes.

After thirty seconds of jiggling and cursing, I sat back on my heels, the mystery room still very much a mystery. "Fine, you stingy, stuck-up piece of metal. I don't want to see what's behind your door, anyway."

Was it too early for a beer?

I stomped down the hall to the bar, checking my phone for the time. Eleven thirty. Close enough. *Beer o'clock, here I come.*

It seemed like everything was vexing me this week. The lock. The Sunshine Festival committee. Molly.

Whom I hadn't talked to since the coffee disaster. Even Larry had been uncharacteristically MIA.

Two days ago, I'd nearly texted Molly when I noticed Larry pacing the fence line, looking like she was about to start something. But when Molly appeared and dragged Larry, bleating miserably, back to her pen, I'd ducked behind a post holding up my patio roof and watched her like a lovesick stalker.

I'd distracted myself from further stalking by attempting to schmooze my way into a Sunshine Festival booth. Unfortunately, no one seemed able, or willing, to help.

Pouring a pint of the chocolaty stout I'd tentatively named the Seventh Inning Stretch, I sat at my bar. Pine resin from the hops hit my nose as I let the beer settle and swiped open my phone to check my email.

I'd finally tapped Junior last night while sending emails that got more and more desperate as the night went on. When all attempts to reason with the other members of the festival committee had failed, I shot off an email to the mayor, an older woman named Frances Cobb, all but promising her season tickets to the Vistas home games if she could find me a booth.

Not my proudest moment, skirting the line between desperation and bribery. But it was far from my worst.

I swallowed a couple of swigs of the stout to fortify myself. Roasted coffee, milk chocolate, and a hint of dark caramel. Perfection.

Rubbing a hand over my face, I opened my email app. The mayor's reply sat there, unopened. My thumb hovered over the subject line, trying to sense whether the email contained good or bad news.

"Screw it." I tapped the email and scanned the first few lines before chucking my phone against a bag of hops and yelling.

"*BLLLEEEEET!*"

Wait. What?

That wasn't me. Was it? I was pretty sure I'd yelled *shit*, not *blet*.

Larry, the Princess of Darkness herself, peered at me around the corner, her freaky, rectangle eyes unblinking. She was wearing a sparkly pink collar around her neck with a matching leash hanging from it. That was new.

How had she gotten in? I'd added a second lock to my back door after the first break-in. Which meant she'd bested two high-end locks just to scare the shit out of me.

Maybe I should let Larry take a shot at the mystery room.

As if reading my mind, Larry trotted down the hall, her leash dragging along the floor.

She stopped in front of the locked door, reared up, and charged.

*Bam!*

"What the actual fuck, Larry?"

She backed up to take another run at the door, which was holding strong despite a good first crack from Larry's skull.

"Good grief," I muttered as I swiped her leash off the floor before she could do any actual damage. Sure, I wanted to see what was in the room, but I doubted my insurance would cover this.

She bleated, unhappy with my goat blocking.

"Knock it off, Princess McHeadbutty."

While I was happy to have a legitimate excuse to talk to Molly, explaining why her goat was concussed wasn't exactly the opportunity I wanted.

Juggling the goat in one hand and my beer in the other, I completed my circus act by kicking open the patio door with one foot, warm summer air pressing up against the air-conditioned interior. The door swung back on me, but I deftly swerved around it, leash still in one hand and an unspilled beer in the other. *Go me.*

If only I could solve all my problems with that level of

awesomeness. Like how to get a booth at the Sunshine Festival.

The mayor's email had said the same thing everyone else had. She couldn't do anything once all the booth spaces were taken. At least she'd gone the extra step and offered to put me in contact with other businesses that might be willing to share booth space. Something I hadn't considered until now.

Maybe I could talk the extra large barista into a beer and coffee partnership for the festival.

I reached the gate between our yards when I heard Molly's voice coming from somewhere inside.

"I know that skank is behind this."

I looked around for a skank, but all I saw was Atlas, sunbathing on the cement slab, clearly enjoying the warm afternoon sunshine. Molly must have turned away from the window because the next few sentences were muffled. All I heard were the words *uberskank*, *trouble* and *Sunshine Festival*.

As much as I wondered who the uberskank was and if he or she was the cause of said trouble, her reference to the Sunshine Festival piqued my curiosity. Hating myself just a little, I clicked open the latch on the gate to sneak closer to the window.

The giant dog raised his head at the sound of metal on metal, considered me and Larry for a beat, yawned loudly, then rolled over with what looked like an incredible amount of effort to sun his other side.

I placed my beer on top of a fence post and inched the gate slowly forward to minimize the noise. I couldn't afford to get busted before getting the lowdown on the festival.

Did it make me a creeper? Only if your definition included tiptoeing next to the open window while I quietly put Larry back in her pen so I could listen in on Molly's conversation before scurrying back to my brewery, all without her knowing I was there.

"I don't know," Molly said with a sigh, bringing me to a halt. She sounded… defeated. The urge to rush to her aid warred with my need to stay put and find out what she knew about the festival.

"I could barely scrape together enough cash for the original booth price. How am I going to afford the increase?"

There was a pause before, "Candice and her overpriced boob job can burn in hell."

*That was interesting.* Molly had a booth but needed money. I had money but needed a booth.

The mayor's email swirled around my brain as my business degree kicked in and a plan formed. It might work…

The gate slammed shut behind me. *Shit.*

Atlas picked up his head. The dog looked at the leash and then at the goat. He unfolded those long-ass legs and shook his head, thick ears clapping loudly against his head.

The goat, who'd been oddly silent this whole time, realized her error and jumped up in the air, letting loose a bleat that sounded like a call to arms.

I stepped back, distancing myself from the sound, and knocked over an empty terracotta planter onto the stone paver walkway. The bang caused the goat to yell louder and Atlas to bark.

*Double shit.*

"Hang on, Jeff," Molly said. "I've got a snooper outside."

Busted.

My face flushed with embarrassment.

"What? No post to hide behind this time?" Molly said as she opened the slider and stepped outside, eyes narrowed.

Of course she'd seen me lurking behind the post.

Even irritated, she was beautiful. She'd pulled her hair back into another ponytail. Her trademark Star Trek tee shirt sported a smear of something I didn't want to think about over the face of a character I didn't know. Cutoff shorts did their best to contain long, lean, tanned legs, which were covered in scratches and bruises from whatever furry monsters she was battling behind those doors.

She was a fucking mess. I'd never wanted anyone more in my life.

I was so screwed.

Larry frolicked over to Molly, rearing up to head butt her like the furry instigator she was.

Molly outstretched her hand in front of the goat. "Stop."

And just like that, the goat stopped.

*So. Hot.*

The thought of Molly using that tone while she straddled me, demanding my full attention while I drove up into her, sent a lightning bolt of desire straight to Tug Junior. I shifted my weight, pleading to the universe that I wasn't about to pitch a tent in my pants while having to have a business conversation with her.

Because that was all we could have—a business relationship.

"Candice giving you trouble?" I asked.

Her lips pursed, making them look soft and full, and now I was imagining them wrapped around my cock, making my pants grow more and more uncomfortable. *Head in the game, Tug.*

"You two looked pretty cozy the other day. Shouldn't you know?"

"Wait… are you jealous?"

"As if," she replied, picking at the spot on her shirt.

She *was* jealous.

*Suck it, Golf Pro!*

I should put her out of her misery, but this felt too good.

"What would Tyson think about that?"

Her head snapped up, eyebrows squished together. "Tyson? What does he have to do with anything?"

If Tyson had any idea how Molly had played a starring role in my fantasies lately, or the number of times I'd jerked off thinking about her, he'd care. He'd care a lot.

"Guys usually care when their girlfriends are jealous over another guy."

She snorted. "Girlfriend?"

"Yeah… girlfriend." I was missing something.

"His spouse, *Jeff*, might have an opinion about that."

"His…"

"Spouse." She drew out the syllable like I was a toddler learning an unfamiliar word.

"Spouse."

She nodded. "Spouse."

"So he's…"

"Gay." She nodded sagely. "Yes."

"So he's not…"

"My boyfriend? Not since the fifth grade. And even then, it was just hand holding."

*Huh.*

"And you're not with anyone now?" I asked. Not that it was any of my business. But the places my mind was begging to go were almost overwhelming.

"Not that it's any of your business," she said, echoing my thoughts as she crossed her arms. Which, unlike Candice, made her tits look tantalizing and tempting, not like a weapon of mass destruction. "But no."

*Interesting.*

"There's nothing between me and Candice," I said, needing for her to understand that there would never, *ever* be anything with Candice.

Her chest rose and fell as a giant breath left her. "Okay."

One word. *Okay.* But I knew in my soul it was more than just a word. It was… a truce. A chance. A next step.

"I think you and I should talk."

"About?"

"Possibilities."

"Tug," she warned.

"Festival possibilities," I clarified. It was a half lie, but baby steps. I could go slow. For Molly.

She gnawed at her lower lip, making my brain explode with ideas of what I could do to those lips. "What do you have in mind?"

I looked at the beer I was still holding in my hand.

"How about we start with a beer?"

9

MOLLY

here was something seriously wrong with me.

I'd left the rescue in the hands of Mitzy and Fergus McFallon, two of my longtime volunteers, as Atlas and I followed Jase to the Catcher's Box on the promise of a beer and a solution to all my problems.

Vague, and unlikely, given the sheer magnitude of all my problems. But here we were. Atlas, sprawled at my feet on the wood floor, snoring gently—well, as gently as a Great Dane could snore—and I, unable to take my eyes off the man pouring us a second round of beer.

Jase's forearms, dusted with coarse blond hair, flexed as he pulled on the tap handle and poured the beer like he'd been doing it his whole life. He turned towards me, offering me the dark-colored beer as a small smile teased his lips. Lips I remembered as being extremely talented.

My thighs clenched involuntarily at the memories.

I took a sip.

I didn't even like beer, especially not the glass of stout perfection Jase handed me. It tasted like a chocolate-covered espresso bean, which would be delicious if I liked beer.

*Which I don't,* I thought as I took another sip and tried to keep the groan of appreciation from escaping my mouth.

*Why was I here again?*

Maybe because I was so fucking relieved Jase hadn't hooked up with my blond nemesis that all willpower to resist whatever proposal he was dangling in front of me had fled my body in the aftermath.

*Or,* my brain reasoned, *I liked beer more than I let on.*

*Screw the beer,* my vagina weighed in. *Look at that ass.*

Perfectly round ass muscles clenched as his weight shifted from leg to leg as he poured his own beer.

*Yum,* my vagina said.

Jase sat down next to me at the maple-colored high-top table and twisted his full glass between long, strong fingers. His hands were huge, which gave him an advantage on the field—and, as I recalled, in the bedroom.

The table was one of about a half dozen that littered the open room. There were matching chairs stacked up along one wall. Wooden seats with iron backs, matching the iron legs on the tables. The lights were balls of thin wire hanging from the ceiling, making it look like the sky was raining metal baseballs.

The opposite wall housed a half-finished bar top that looked like it would also be maple. The entire space was going to be beautiful. Locals and tourists alike were going to love it. I loved it.

He picked up his beer and turned it, examining it as though it were a piece of art. While he was distracted, I allowed myself a long glance, soaking him in. Age had sharpened his features. The jaw I remembered as full and strong was now chiseled. Lines creeped in around eyes bluer than the Colorado sky. He'd been good-looking before.

Now? He was stunning.

Parts of me that had given up on ever having sex again were dusting themselves off and doing warm-up stretches.

*Easy, girls.*

"I know you only like wine, but what do you think?" he finally said, raising his eyes.

"Passable. For beer," I said with a shrug, before taking another drink. It was good. Really good. This place was exactly what the town needed to support the rise in tourism.

"If you don't like it, I'll pour it out."

Jase reached for my glass and smirked as I pulled it out of his reach. "Thought so."

Smug bastard. "I wouldn't want it to go to waste."

He set his glass back on the table between us, Larry's mournful bleating next door reminding me I was here for a reason.

"So what was it you wanted to talk to me about?"

"I have a proposition for you," Jase said, twirling his glass.

"No."

I took a big, fortifying sip. This beer was excellent. I needed to be careful, or I was going to stumble back to the shelter. Or worse, into Jase's strong, muscled arms.

"You haven't even heard what I was going to say."

"Correct."

He leaned in, one giant hand wrapping around my glass, making it look like a sippy cup. He slid it to the side and leaned across the table, closing the space between us. I could smell the leathery scent of his aftershave mixed with hops that probably clung to him night and day. It was more intoxicating than the alcohol swirling through my brain.

His eyes dipped to my mouth, and I gravitated towards him, unable to resist the force of attraction tugging at me.

Would it be so bad to kiss him again? It's not like it would mean anything. It definitely wouldn't lead to anything.

Just one small kiss.

All I'd have to do is tilt my head up a fraction of an inch, and—

*Snnzzz!* snorted the dog at my feet. Atlas raised his head, eyes blinking as he looked around. Deciding that whatever danger had woken him had passed, he settled back on the ground and closed his eyes again.

I sat back in my chair. Holy Klingons, that was close. What was I thinking?

That it had been so long since I'd felt the touch of anything but my own fingers or Mr. Buzzypants, my trusty vibrator, I'd forgotten what it felt like.

A look that I couldn't decipher flashed across his face and was gone just as quickly as he cleared his throat.

"I think we should partner up," he said.

*Okay!* my vagina said.

"What?" I said.

"For business," he clarified, a little too quickly. "We should partner up for business."

I swallowed my disappointment. Of course, we wouldn't *partner up*. I wasn't partnering-up material. He'd made that clear ten years ago.

*Boo,* cried my vagina, which could just simmer right the hell down.

"And what, exactly, does that mean?" I looked around. "In case you hadn't noticed, I don't have a liquor license, and you aren't licensed to care for animals."

"No, I just return them." A smirk lifted one side of his mouth before being overtaken by the full megawatt smile that had helped crown him the King of Baseball.

I wanted to kiss that stupid grin right off his stupid face, feel the scratch of his short scruff as he claimed my mouth.

Wait, what? *Slap.* I meant *slap* that grin off his face.

"Touché," I said, scrunching my eyes shut. *Focus, Molly.* "So, what's your proposal?"

He folded his hands on top of the table, looking every bit a businessman and shone those baby blues at me. Vulcans help me, he was beautiful.

"The way I see it, you need money, and I have it."

I froze, feeling like I'd just been slapped. Was I really hearing this?

Larry let loose a battle cry, loud enough it could have come from inside the brewery. *Please let her still be in her pen,* I prayed to the image of Jean-Luc Picard on my shirt as I looked around the space. No Larry. Good. So my only problem right now was the man sitting in front of me, insulting me to my face.

"I'm making a mess of this."

"That's an understatement," I muttered.

He shook his head, lowering his arms and softening his body language. "Let me start over."

"Please do," I said, unable to keep some of the snark out of my voice.

"We both know you need money."

*What the ever-loving fuck?*

Silently congratulating myself for swallowing my beer instead of spraying it across the table at his stupid handsome face—because I was mature that way—I took a moment, the beer all but boiling in my belly.

"Excuse me?"

"Your rescue," he continued, not noticing the death stare I was shooting him. "I overheard you talking this afternoon about needing money for the Sunshine Festival. I can pay for the booth."

I sat back, feeling like he'd punched me in the stomach.

"You're frowning," he said. "Why are you frowning?"

Without that booth, kitten season would kill me. The rescue would never recover financially without the donations and adoptions the booth always brought in.

"You can't have my booth, Tug. I need it."

He held his hands out in front of him. "No, no. I don't want your booth. I mean, I do."

I closed my eyes and took a breath. "You're not making sense. Do everyone a favor and stop sniffing the hops."

He smirked and then blew out a breath of his own. "I want to share your booth. With you. Team up. We can call it Brews and Mews," he said, swiping his hand widely across the space between us like a salesman.

Share the booth. That actually wasn't the worst idea in the history of ideas. The name Brews and Mews might be.

This would certainly solve my immediate problems. And I'd get the added benefit of rubbing it in Candice's over-makeup'd face.

"I'm confused," he said. "Why the hesitation? Isn't this what you want?"

I stood, sliding my unfinished beer towards him. Taking a step back, I bumped into Atlas, who continued his nap, blissfully unaware of his owner's distress.

"I don't need you to solve my problems."

I mean, I sort of did, but I was too pissed off to acknowledge he might be right. The only thing people loved more than kittens was alcohol. Putting those two things together would be festival gold.

One of Jase's perfectly blond eyebrows cocked up as he just stared at me, waiting.

If he thought he could swoop in and fix my money problems, he could think again. I unclenched my jaw and faced him, calm and collected businesswoman to rich business asshole.

"Regardless of what you may or may not have overheard from a conversation that was and continues to be none of your fucking business, whether my rescue needs money is also *none of your fucking business.*"

My tennis shoes squeaked as I stepped over Atlas and headed towards the back door.

*"Bleeeat!"*

Larry, all fur and fury, was charging down the hall, head down, screaming, running right at me. At the last minute, the goat veered, angling a shoulder into me and bodychecking me right into Atlas like a pro hockey player.

My arms flailed as I fought to keep my balance and avoid hurting myself and my dog.

"Shit!" I said as I lost the fight against gravity.

Jase's giant hand snapped out, grabbed me by Jean-Luc Picard's face, and pulled me upright.

Straight into his rock-hard chest.

His arms wrapped around me, keeping me tucked in tight against him. He was solid and warm and irresistible and I didn't hate it.

"You okay?" He looked down at me, not letting go.

"Yeah," I whispered, not wanting him to let go.

All my girly bits swooned and fanned themselves.

We were so close. Close enough that all I needed to do to taste his lips was push up on my toes.

So close.

*It was just a kiss, right?*

A thank you for saving me and Atlas from certain goat-instigated doom.

*Just a kiss.*

Before I could overthink it, I raised up on my tiptoes and pressed my lips against his. Unlike his chest, which felt like it was molded from marble, his lips were soft. Strong.

Memories flooded in, threatening to overwhelm me. Two glorious nights, those beautiful lips that slowly made their way up and down my body, branding me, making me feel like I belonged, like I mattered.

Seconds ticked by before I realized he hadn't moved.

Why wasn't he moving?

*Oh. Oh, shit.*

He didn't want this. He didn't want me.

*Stupid, stupid, stupid.*

I started to lower myself when he tightened his grip, stopping me. He slid a hand down my back and angled his head as he took over the kiss.

*Halle-fucking-lujah!* my vagina cheered.

*It's just a kiss,* I reminded it.

His tongue skimmed my lips, pressing me to open for him. I threaded my arms around his neck, scraping my nails softly through his hair and gave him the access he asked for, matching him stroke for stroke with my tongue.

*Just a kiss.*

One hand kneaded my ass, pulling me in, while the other cupped my head, holding me there, diving into the kiss and claiming me. He tasted like chocolate and hops, the muscles in his shoulders flexing under my hands as I held tight, fighting against the heady combination of memories and heat. Holy Spock, this kiss was… amazing. New and familiar all at once.

*Just a kiss.*

I needed to end this. Before it became more than just a kiss. Every part of me that had just awakened fought me for control because it felt too good. Too much like dreams of what could have been.

*Just a kiss.*

That's all this was. All it could be. I slowed my movements, pulling back slowly, achingly.

He placed several soft kisses against my lips, which felt hot and swollen, and moved both hands in soft strokes across my back.

"That was…" he started.

Incredible. Toe curling. Un-fucking-believable.

And so wrong.

"Yeah," I finished, unable to make eye contact. What had I been thinking?

*Just a kiss, my ass,* my vagina chided.

*Shut your pie hole,* I told it.

"So… Does this mean we can be partners?" He smiled down at me, placing a soft kiss on the tip of my nose.

Partners?

I'd been wrapped up in the implications of this kiss, and he was still thinking about the festival.

Of course he was. Because it was just a kiss.

I was an idiot.

"No, Tug," I said, easing away from him, the room between us feeling like an icy expanse in contrast to the heat we'd just generated. "We can't be partners."

Did I need money to pay for the booth at the Sunshine Festival? Yes. But I didn't need some misguided knight in dented armor to ride to my rescue. I'd figure it out the same way I did everything else in my life.

By myself.

1 0

JASE

*J*checked the temperature gauges on both fermentation tanks. Junior's was spot on for the hazy IPA that it currently housed. Rosita, however, was running high for her amber ale. I tweaked the dial to keep it from overheating and spoiling the burgeoning beer and rubbed the back of my neck.

The process of brewing my beer was something that normally soothed me. I should have been obsessively checking the yeast in both tanks, ensuring they were doing their job, turning the sweet wort into something I would be proud to serve.

Instead, I'd been unsettled all day, thanks to the Kiss.

It had been pure instinct to reach down and pull Molly's flailing body up by her shirt. But once she was upright and pressed against me, her soft angles matching my broad lines, I couldn't let go.

I'd almost talked my arms into releasing her when she lifted her head and kissed me. Pure shock had stilled me for all of two seconds before instinct once again kicked in and need took over as I captured her mouth the way I'd fantasized far too many times since I'd moved to Harmony Springs.

I tried to caution myself to go slow, to allow Molly to set the tone and pace, to make sure she knew she was in control. But when her nails scraped through my hair, my restraint had snapped. My hands took over, pulling her flush. My mouth demanded more from her, plunging deeper. My dick celebrating when she responded.

When she finally pulled back, I remembered she was supposed to be running this show, not me. Which is why I'd stopped instead of thrusting my hand down those sexy cutoffs she always wore and making her come on my hand, right there in my bar.

Tossing my work gloves at the fermentation tanks with a growl, I glared at them like they were the source of my frustration. They just sat there, happily ignoring me, while they created magic in a pint glass.

Both tanks were stainless steel. But where Rosita was six feet tall and gleaming, Junior was shorter and stouter and all hammered steel.

My oldest niece, Chloe, was a budding graphic artist. For Christmas last year, she'd drawn me a curvy red-headed woman dressed as a baseball player. I'd loved it so much I promptly turned it into a life-sized stencil, named her Rosita, and had a local Denver artist paint it on the tank. When I'd sent Chloe a picture of my new tank, she emailed me her newest creation—a gap-toothed chubby-faced blond boy with a bowl cut—which was now proudly displayed on Junior.

"I'm sorry, Rosita." I placed a loving hand on the tank. "You're still the sexiest beast west of Chicago."

Talking to my equipment like a lover probably qualified me for the looney bin, but I was desperate. Rosita was lovingly cooking my flagship beer, a deep red amber ale that was just the right balance of hops and caramel, tentatively named Grand Slam Ambeer. If she quit on me now, it would ruin my grand opening during the Fourth of July weekend—less than five weeks from now.

Especially if I couldn't get a damned booth for the festival.

The major letdown Molly handed me yesterday afternoon after kissing all thought and reason from me had been a sharp rap of reality to the head. Not that I blamed her. This failure was all mine.

*We both know you need money.* Jesus, had I really said that?

Of course she'd told me to take a hike.

Embarrassment, mixed with a heavy dose of regret, blanketed me. I owed her an apology, but I hadn't been able to bring myself to walk the sixty feet from my back door to hers to do it.

Tomorrow. I'd suck it up and apologize tomorrow, after I'd figured out what the hell was wrong with Rosita's heating unit.

I closed my eyes, hand still on Rosita to reassure her—and me—and took a deep breath. In through my nose… one, two, three… out through my mouth… one, two—*blet.*

Fucking Larry.

She was probably chewing her way through the fence. I'd considered hiring someone to lay a brick wall between the properties—*let's see you eat through brick, you mischief-making menace.*

Then Fozzy texted me a meme of goats in trees.

Fucking goats. In fucking trees.

A shudder rolled through me at the thought of goats falling on my head as they screamed their way to the ground.

No. Just no.

I should make sure Larry wasn't eating the fence. Or my patio furniture.

And apologize to Molly.

Hopefully, I'd figure out what to say to Molly before I got there. And swallowed my foot a second time.

I picked up my gloves, gave Rosita another soothing caress, and saluted Junior for his hard work. Before I reached the back door, my phone rang.

Taking my phone out of my pocket, I checked the screen. Mom.

This day just kept getting better.

Hesitating another second, weighing a cringy apology and a fence-eating goat against my mother, who stacked up surprisingly strong against those contenders, I hit the answer button.

"Mom. Hey."

"Sweetie, I let Eliza know you were going to call her this week," she said, launching right into the middle of a conversation she'd likely been having with herself since the last time we'd spoken.

I bit back a sigh of frustration. "I told you last time that I'd call her when I had time."

Like never.

Not that I didn't like my oldest sister. I did. How could I not? She was a mother of three, had built a small ad agency empire in my hometown of Chicago, sat on the boards of several large charities and flew around the world speaking at conferences. I wouldn't be surprised if she had a side hustle helping Santa deliver presents every Christmas Eve.

If you looked up the definition of perfect, Eliza would pop out of the dictionary, hand you a homemade sugar cookie and a five-year business plan, and compliment your tie.

A close second would be my other older sister, Evie, who hosted a successful house-flipping television show with her husband, Lucas.

I knew why my mom wanted me to talk to Eliza. For the same reasons I knew I should call her. She probably had a dozen ideas I hadn't thought of. Did it make me stubborn to want to do this on my own? Prove to myself—and my family —that I was more than just an athlete?

Yep.

Would it take me longer to achieve that level of success as a result?

Also yep.

But I was going to do it my way, damn it, and my mom and sisters could just deal with it.

"You know I'm only looking out for you. Eliza owns her own company."

"I also own my own company."

"Of course you do."

She was placating me, treating me like a surly little boy.

"But honey, you make beer. Eliza knows how to run a proper business." And there it was.

I rubbed my forehead as the headache that usually followed our conversations took root.

"I'll call her." Next month. Maybe.

"Okay, sweetie. Your dad is waiting for me. We have a two o'clock tee time at the club, and your dad wants to get there early to show off his new putter."

*Thank you, Dad.* "Give him my love."

"I always do. Talk to you next week."

Exhaustion settled in my bones as I hung up. Hand on heart, I loved my mother, but it seemed like every time we talked, she bit off another little chunk of my soul. Subtle digs, like pointing out that I "just made beer," had been making their way into her conversations every week since I announced my post-retirement plans to start up a micro-brewery.

Molly and Larry would have to wait.

I needed to prove to my family that I could do more than just catch baseballs. Which would not happen if I couldn't figure out how to get into the festival booth rotation.

If Eliza could conquer Chicago, and Evie could conquer network television, I could conquer Harmony Springs.

# MOLLY

I glared at the broken fence post. Specifically, I was glaring at the crack that split the post nearly in two thanks to the efforts of a hard-headed demon goat while I pondered my options. It didn't take long. There weren't many options. I couldn't afford to fix it, but if I didn't, Larry's world domination plans would be that much closer to fruition.

"I think it's broken," Jeff said unhelpfully from my desk chair which they'd dragged outside.

They were wearing pale blue Bermuda-style shorts, a tie-dyed Grateful Dead tank top, and their trademark flip-flops. In matching blue, of course.

"What gave it away?" I asked. "The giant crack down the middle? Or that it's leaning like your Uncle Frank after his fourth pre-dinner scotch at Thanksgiving?"

Jeff tilted their chin down and looked at me over the top of their aviator sunglasses that were more fashionable than my entire wardrobe.

"Bitchy, but accurate."

When Jeff had shown up this morning, I'd assumed they

were going to walk my shelter dogs like they did every day. As a shelter owner, it was handy to have a best friend who owned the local dog-walking business. Usually.

"Don't you have dogs to walk?"

"Too warm for little Stella," they answered, referring to the senior dog who'd been in my shelter for the last four months. "Weatherman says clouds are supposed to roll in this afternoon. I'll take them then."

"You going home, then?"

Jeff waved me off with one hand and pushed their sunglasses back up their perfectly straight nose. "Tyson went to Haven Falls for a teacher's conference. And I'd rather watch you try to fix a fence pole than hang out at the house by myself."

"You mean watch for Jase."

"Amen, sister."

Larry tugged at the end of her leash, which was currently tethered to the neighboring post.

*Blet!*

"Shut your pie hole, Larry."

I wiped the sweat from my forehead. Jeff was right. It wasn't even noon, but the day was already a scorcher. The Colorado mountain climate was usually warm during the days, but not hot. Today was an exception, with the temps expected to climb into the nineties. Based on the swamp-like conditions forming in my bra, it was well on its way.

Jeff continued watching me from their chair, pursing their lips like they were working on a solution to my many, many problems. There wasn't a drop of perspiration anywhere in their vicinity, like they'd forbidden their body from dampening their clothes. In the meantime, I was sweating my lady balls off, looking like a wet dog. Unfair.

I jostled the fence post back and forth, testing its sturdiness. The part of the post buried in the ground didn't move.

The part above the crack wiggled and creaked, threatening to fall off and take the wire fencing with it.

Larry jumped up and tried to karate kick the leash in protest.

"Larry's in a mood today," Jeff said from their shaded throne.

"Larry's always in a mood."

I never really understood why my mom had brought home the tiny little creature that grew into a Grade A Troublemaker. But at least the goat wasn't one of those colossal asshat goats that head-butted everything.

Until today.

Today, Larry decided the fence needed destroying. So she went at it with all the enthusiasm normally reserved for mangling my last nerve, and cracked the damn thing.

Maybe if I wished hard enough, the crack would turn into a magical portal to the Mystical Land of Money and start shooting out hundred-dollar bills. At least then I could afford the repair bill, along with everything else I needed to pay for. Like a festival booth.

*Jase could afford it,* a sneaky little voice in my head reminded me.

I snuck a peek at my neighbor's yard.

"Twenty-six," Jeff said.

"What?"

"Nothing."

I shook my head. Today was not the day to wonder what my neighbor was up to, or whether he was thinking about our kiss, too.

What the hell had gotten into me? I'd kissed him. On the lips. With an open fucking mouth. And I... hadn't hated it. It had been deep and warm and slow. Sensual, with a promise of more than a simple kiss, done on a whim to satisfy my curiosity.

It had been an incredible kiss, even better than I remembered. Not that I delved into those memories. Much.

No, yesterday's kiss was one time only. One kiss to get it out of my system so I could move on.

As much as was possible with the King of Baseball next door.

Did I regret turning down his offer to pay for my festival booth? Hell no. He'd been a total ass about it and deserved the figurative kick to the balls. But after my second glass of wine last night, I conceded maybe he had been trying to help me. In a really shitty way, which irritated me. If he'd done a better job, I might not be trying to figure out how to squeeze money from a fence post.

With another glance at Jase's empty building, I untied Larry from the fence. She let out a long *bleaaat* before bouncing her way to the chicken coop.

"Twenty-seven."

I looked over my shoulder at Jeff, who had stretched out like a cat sunning itself. The jerk still wasn't sweating. Meanwhile, a river slid down my back and pooled in my underwear.

"Twenty-seven what? What the hell are you counting?" I walked back to the patio and sat on the plastic chair next to Jeff. They handed me a water bottle.

"Drink," they said. "And not what. Who."

"Who what?"

My brain had spent most of the night unhelpfully lobbing fantasies of Jase at me. The sleep deprivation made following Jeff's cryptic attempts at conversation more difficult than usual.

"Jase," they answered. "It's the number of times you've looked over at his place since I got here two hours ago."

"That… uh, what?"

"You like him," Jeff sung.

"I'm annoyed by him," I corrected.

"Those two things aren't mutually exclusive," they said, sipping their fruit-infused water bottle.

"He tried to take my festival booth yesterday."

Right before I assaulted him with my lips. And he reciprocated. Like a fucking champion.

I still wasn't sure how I walked home last night with wobbly legs and a vagina spinning in happy circles. My face heated. Was it getting warmer outside?

"How'd he do that?" Jeff asked.

"He offered to pay for it."

I pulled a weed out of a crack in the cement patio and waited for Jeff's response. Expecting "what a jerk!" or "the gall of some people!", they instead met me with silence.

I checked to see if they'd fallen off their chair. But they were staring at me, sunglasses slid low on their nose, like I'd said aliens were taking a bubble bath in my tub.

"That sneaky, sexy scumbag," they deadpanned.

Atlas meandered out the dog door and walked up to me, giving my hand a quick lick and leaning in for the Great Dane version of a hug. Atlas and Larry were polar opposites. Where Larry was all unhinged mayhem, Atlas was a gentle love of an animal. I gave my faithful companion a good scratch on his chest and belly. At least he loved me unconditionally.

Unlike my bestie, who was skating close to friendship treason if they thought Jase was in the right. Even if he was. Jeff was supposed to have my back, not Jase's.

"I don't need Jase's help."

Jeff pushed their sunglasses up their nose. "Never said you did."

"I don't," I insisted.

I patted Atlas on his flank then watched as he lumbered to the shady spot under the oak tree and flopped down with a groan. I made a mental note to fill the kiddie pool for the dogs' outdoor time this afternoon.

"So what's the plan?" Jeff asked. "Besides glowering at the world and hoping to spot your hunky neighbor in the wild?"

"Says his stalker," I replied as Jase's back patio door opened. I glimpsed a white tee and black shorts doing their level best to cover a body that made my core tighten. He moved patio furniture around, broad shoulders threatening to tear through his shirt Hulk-style as he lifted metal and wood chairs like they were made of plastic.

A bright pink scar nearly the length of my forearm ran along the side of his knee, marring the perfection of his muscular legs. A career-ending injury, according to every Denver news station and sports channel. An injury that had thrust him back into my orbit.

"Holy sex on a cracker, I want to take him home and do unspeakable things to his body in the name of research," Jeff said from behind me.

Same.

Jase waved at me, a small smile hinting at his perfect, kissable mouth.

My hand raised itself without my permission and waved back to the man. Jase's smile turned full wattage, and my mouth, also acting of its own accord, smiled back.

Betrayed by my body.

"Oh. Em. Gee," Jeff stage whispered.

I fought the urge to stare at my sex magnet of a neighbor, who was keeping my body at full attention, and turned towards Jeff. But they weren't ogling Jase. They were looking at me.

"What? It's nothing," I said, hoping to preempt an inevitable interrogation. If I told Jeff about the kiss, they'd make it into a Thing.

"Oh, it's definitely something."

The theme song to *Star Trek* saved me from further interrogation. *Thank Vulcans for minor miracles.*

I read my phone screen, not recognizing the number.

"Sorry, I need to take this," I said, not even a little sorry, unable to keep myself from watching Jase. He'd moved on to pulling weeds, glancing up as if sensing my attention. He smiled at me again, and my stomach cartwheeled. *Gah.*

"Twenty-nine," Jeff said. "And we're definitely revisiting this."

"Happy Tails Animal Rescue," I said into the phone, flipping Jeff off as I walked into the air-conditioned building, relieved to be out of the heat.

"Yes, is this Molly Sanders?" a woman asked.

"It is," I replied, closing the slider behind me.

"This is Nora Walker from Chester County Municipal Shelter, in Haven Falls."

Oh.

*Oh no.*

"Nora, of course, how are you?" I replied, trying to keep the panic out of my voice as I hightailed it to my desk. The sticky note with Nora's name and number was buried under a pile of Sunshine Festival flyers in danger of becoming litter box liners if I couldn't raise enough money.

*Shit. Shit, shit, shit.* I'd completely forgotten to call Nora back last week. Too many things competed for my attention. The shelter's finances, the Sunshine Festival, Jase Tugwater and his stupidly distracting mouth.

"Good, good," Nora said. "I hope now is an okay time to talk?"

*No, Nora, it is not. Could you maybe call back in six years when I finally have my life together?*

"Yes, sure. Now works."

I put the call on speaker and dropped my head against the

wall, praying for a Romulan to walk through the front door and blast me out of my misery.

"Is everything okay?"

"Yes," I replied, shaking my head against the wall. "Why?"

"I heard a thump. It sounded like you dropped something."

I picked my head up and rubbed my forehead. Oops.

"Nope, all good. What's up?"

*Please don't ask me to take any animals.*

"I was calling to see if you had any capacity to take a few animals."

I glanced over at the dog room. I had a couple of empty kennels. My food supply was getting low. Kitten season was eating through my financial and emotional resources like a starving tapeworm.

"Um, well. I'm not sure."

"I'm sorry to call you out of the blue like this. I know we'd talked about doing something later this summer."

"Yeah, it's just…"

"I realize you're probably as busy as the rest of us, but I wouldn't have called if I had any other options."

I rubbed my heels against my eyes.

"What's going on?"

I really didn't want to know, but I also really needed to know.

"The sheriff's office raided a home yesterday and rescued about a dozen dogs and other animals from a hoarding situation. They brought them here, but, well…"

Yeah, I knew. They did their best, but the Chester County shelter could only keep animals for a couple of weeks. Any not lucky enough to find homes in that time would be euthanized.

If I didn't take these animals…

I clicked a couple of keys on my laptop and pulled up my budget. I was still in the black, but barely.

"How many animals?"

"Six dogs, mostly small and medium-sized, two adult cats, a rabbit and a chicken."

I heard the slider open, and Atlas padded over to me. Jeff must have let him in. He rested his giant head against my hip, somehow sensing I needed a little encouragement. I rubbed one of his thick, velvety ears and considered the kennel area again.

The chicken could go in the empty coop outside, if I could keep Larry away from it. If I converted a cat kennel into a rabbit habitat and housed a few of the smaller dogs together, I could probably swing it. Maybe I could convince someone to foster a couple of the easier dogs.

I looked at the budget again. It was impossible. I needed a miracle. I needed money. I needed help.

Jeff's head appeared in my doorway with my desk chair. "Everything okay?" they mouthed.

I nodded, a pang of guilt plucking at my chest as I lied to one of my best friends.

"Molly?" Nora asked.

"I'll do it."

"Wonderful!" Nora cried. "I've got a volunteer who's agreed to handle transport and can be there next week."

Cue the Romulans.

1 2

## JASE

*J* stared at the 137 unopened emails in my inbox, almost wishing Rosita was still acting up—it had taken a grand total of fifteen minutes after a quick YouTube tutorial to fix her heating unit. Now I was left with this mess.

Among the requests for appearances, promises to grow my penis size by three times—*I had no complaints in that department, thank you*—and my accountant's weekly updates, only two really needed my attention.

The first was a reply to an email I had sent two days ago to Suzi-Q's Scratch 'N Sniff, Handyperson Services and Scent Design. Their bright pink website stated Suzi-Q could not only handle most DIY projects and repairs but also sold hand-poured soy candles of varying scents. At the bottom of an impressive number of five-star testimonials was the tagline.

*We fix what ails your house—and your nose!*

Despite my better judgment, I'd sent Suzi-Q an email to confirm if their handyperson services included locksmithing, since the mystery room had so far thwarted my efforts to break in.

The second was from Candice Shoowater, responding to my email asking for a list of businesses who had booths for the Sunshine Festival. If I was going to convince one of them to share their space with me, I needed to know who I was dealing with.

The thought of working with Candice made my head hurt and my skin crawl. But unless the mystery room held a dusty lamp with a resident genie who could grant my wish of a Sunshine Festival booth, I needed to rip off that Band-Aid.

Clicking on Candice's email, I ground my teeth as I read her reply.

Jase,

In my capacity as Harmony Springs Festivals Committee Chairperson, I regret to inform you I cannot accommodate your request. The HSFC takes privacy seriously. We do not produce a list of booth sponsors prior to the release of marketing materials, which go out one week before each festival.

However, if you'd like to discuss your potential involvement with next year's festival, here's my number.

-C

Damn.

The Sunshine Festival was proving as hard to get into as my mystery room.

I looked at the locked door.

"Open sesame."

The door remained closed.

"Abracadabra?"

Nothing.

"Come on, talk to me."

"You miserable excuse for a goat. *Leave the fucking kittens alone*," said the door.

No, wait. Not the door. Molly. Her voice carried through the common wall between our spaces, followed by an indignant sounding *bleehhht*. What I hoped was a screaming kitten and not an infant demon from whatever circle of hell Larry hailed from sounded off next.

"Ow! Stop that. I'm trying to save you, you ungrateful little fur ball."

*Scratch, scratch.*

"Now what?" I muttered.

Unlike the argument happening on the other side of my mystery room, the scratching noise came from the backdoor. I put my laptop in sleep mode, my knees popping and cracking as I stood, and went in search of whatever—or whoever—was scratching.

Molly's Great Dane stood at my back door, nose smashed up against the glass, tail swooshing gently back and forth.

"Hey big dude," I said to the dog, sliding the door open. "What's up?"

*Woof,* the dog answered, the bark sounding more like a faint cough.

*"I swear to every Star Trek god from here to Vulcan that I will only feed you leafy green vegetables until your dying day. Put. The broom. Down."*

"Came to get away from the chaos, eh?"

*Woof.*

"Come on in."

I opened the door wide enough to allow Atlas entry, but the dog just stood there, looking at me.

"It's okay. You can come in." I could use a little company to take my mind off things. Plus, unlike Larry, Atlas wouldn't try to eat my profits.

The dog looked over his shoulder towards Happy Tails and gave a small whine.

*Wait, was he...?*

*Huh.*

Atlas wasn't here for peace and quiet. He was here for help.

The dog's front paws marched in place. He was getting more and more agitated with each bellow from human and goat.

I looked back at my laptop and the 136 unread emails.

Atlas made a faint chuffing noise and nudged my leg with his snout. Almost like he was saying please.

I was a sucker for good manners. Besides, I still owed her that apology.

"Fine," I said, stepping outside and closing the door behind me. "But for the record, I'm only doing this because you asked nicely."

Atlas trotted towards the gate, which was open despite my having locked it after my run this morning. *Larry.*

The dog and I had just made it to the shelter's cement patio when Molly bellowed. *"Gaaaah! Out!"*

I stepped aside as Larry leaped and kicked her way through the open back door, screaming bloody murder. Atlas lay down on his raised bed under the shade of the small awning, his head settling across his paws as he looked up at me.

"Chicken."

The dog snorted.

Knowing I was probably going to regret it, I knocked at the open back door and stepped inside. Molly stood in the middle of the open room, pointing a broom at Larry, who was still kicking and screaming. Her other hand held three of the dirtiest, scruffiest looking kittens I'd ever seen.

An equally scruffy black kitten ran across my foot, spinning out on the tile as it tried to take the corner.

"Stop that kitten!" Molly yelled while eyeballing the goat.

"And for Spock's sake, close the fucking door before Larry comes back in."

I slid the door shut behind me as the kitten skidded into a wall. It stopped moving for a split second, stunned, before righting itself and shaking its head. I bent and palmed the mobile dust bunny, who had the audacity to mew pathetically at me before curling up in my hand and purring.

Molly blew a strand of hair out of her eye and glared at me.

"Where do you want me to put it?" I asked, ignoring her glare and looking around the space.

Metal and plastic crates were stacked in misshapen piles all over the room and as far down the hallway as I could see. Empty cardboard boxes were stacked on top of some crates, others were tipped over on their sides.

"Hold this." She handed me the broom and scooped the kitten out of my hand, bundling it in her arms with the other three. "Could you open that orange crate over there?" She nodded towards a pile of medium-sized crates.

I obliged, holding it up so she didn't have to bend down. She was a bigger mess than the room. More hair was out of her ponytail than in. Her shirt was so wrinkled I could barely make out the word "Engage" across the bottom. She had a streak of what I hoped for her sake was dirt and not kitten shit across one cheek, and there were dark circles under her eyes.

She looked exhausted.

I could help. I *wanted* to help. If only she'd let me.

But she'd made it very clear she wasn't interested in my help. I was determined to respect that. Respect her.

So instead of asking if she wanted help, I went with, "You okay?"

She ignored me as she gently put the crate down by her

feet and sat next to it. Tears welled in her eyes, threatening to spill down her beautiful face.

And just like that, my resolve disappeared.

I leaned the broom against a wall and sat down next to her, unable to keep myself from sitting close enough for our shoulders to touch. Close enough for her to know she wasn't alone.

"What's going on?"

A tear slid down her cheek. She swiped it and used the bottom of her tee shirt to wipe at her nose. The motion bared the skin above her waistband, smooth and silky. I itched to slide my fingers across it.

Now was not the time for Tug Junior to make his presence known. I needed to buckle down and show her I could be here for her.

Her head thumped quietly against the wall as she lay it back. "You should go, Tug."

I didn't want to go. I wanted to give her the apology that she deserved—for the kiss and everything else. But if she didn't want me here…

She wearily got to her feet, knocking dust and maybe kitten poop off her jean shorts. I followed her lead and stood, not touching but close enough that I could.

"Molly—"

"I don't need help."

The sadness dripping from her voice was killing me. Whatever else she needed, she could use a shoulder to cry on, a strong port in the storm. I could do that for her.

"Bullshit," I said. Or I could do that, instead.

"Excuse me?"

Her arms crossed in front of her, covering all but the bald head on her shirt. Her face turned tight, amber eyes flickering like fire, all danger and beauty.

That was better. I was all for letting Molly set her own course—she'd done just fine so far as I could tell, whether or not she knew it. But damned if I was going to let her wallow in pity.

Pity was for the weak. And Molly wasn't weak.

"You look like you haven't slept in days. You're arguing with a goat and look like you've been bathing in litter boxes. You. Need. Help," I challenged, gesturing to the beautiful hot mess in front of me.

Her eyes narrowed. She looked like she wanted to punch me.

"You want to help? Find me some more fucking space so I can save those poor fucking animals."

"What animals? The kittens?"

"Never mind," she said, picking up the kitten crate. "It's my mess. I'll fix it. Somehow."

"Molly, if I had extra space, I'd give it to you."

I would. God help me, I would. But I didn't. Not unless I wanted to tear down walls, reroute wiring and petition the town planning council for a major amendment to the plans I'd already submitted. Which was doable, but took time. And money. Only one of which I had.

*Blet!*

We both looked over at the sliding door. Larry stood there, *on the inside of the very much still closed door.*

"H-how?" I stuttered.

Molly muttered a string of curse words and marched towards the goat, who was now pawing at the floor, looking like a bull winding up to take on a matador.

This would not end well.

"Wait—" I said as I took a step forward.

Larry turned on her toes—*hooves?*—like a ballerina and spun gracefully around us both, head down, baring full tilt towards the wall dividing our two spaces.

"Larry Petunia Sanders, don't you dare touch that wall!"

The goat stopped and turned her head towards Molly.

*Bleehht!*

The tension lit the air with electricity. Two of the most stubborn creatures I'd ever known were in a stand-off, battling for the upper hand.

"Don't. You. Dare," Molly threatened.

Larry dropped her head, let out one more short *blet* and rammed the wall, putting a dent in the drywall.

"Larry!" Molly yelled.

"Holy shit!" I yelled, hopping out of the danger zone.

The goat took three steps back. She wasn't really going to ram her way through the wall. Was she?

I could practically smell the smoke coming out of Molly's ears as she reached for Larry's collar.

Two steps too late.

Larry reared up and rammed the wall, this time knocking a hole clean through to the other side.

Dust spilled out of the opening, coating the floor. Hoof-prints followed Larry as she trotted to the back door, bleating.

Molly looked through the opening in the wall, her face reddening. "Oh, holy mother of Spock. I'm so sorry," she whispered. "I don't—"

"Just some drywall," I said, joining her to inspect the damage.

What I saw through the hole brought me upright. It couldn't be… I was looking at a large room, nearly empty except for a couple of boxes that probably just held old receipts and paperwork I didn't want.

I was looking at my mystery room. And it looked like it might be big enough for Molly's animals.

"I'll be damned."

13

# MOLLY

"I can't believe it," Jase said, his face scrunched.

"What is this?" I peered over his broad shoulders and ignored the urge to run my hands over them. "It looks like an empty room."

It looked like an answer to my prayers.

Jase stood, hands on hips. "I'll be damned."

"So you've said."

"I wonder if Suzi-Q does renos?" he asked, looking around the space.

How did he know Suzi?

"She does," I answered.

Did he intend to just patch up the hole? I stuck my head further into the room, drywall dust graying my hair.

It was perfect. There was room for at least a six-bank of double-decker kennels along the long wall, and plenty of space for larger single kennels on the opposite side.

I could house all of Nora's animals plus some. The possibilities...

Larry was still screaming to go outside like she was being

murdered. Spock only knew why Larry could let herself in but not out.

The short walk to let the menace loose in the backyard gave me time to work out how I could ask Jase to ask the landlord for that space. And how to pay for it.

For a half second, I contemplated seducing him to seal the deal. It was tempting—for my business *and* my vagina, but I dismissed it almost as quickly.

"My vagina can just shut her pie hole," I mumbled as Atlas sauntered inside, swapping places with the four-legged horror movie soundtrack.

"You say something?" Jase asked, his head now poking through the hole.

*Yes! Let's have sex!* my vagina shouted.

"Nope."

Atlas walked over and sniffed the wall, sticking his head through the opening next to Jase. When he pulled it back out, he brought a few more chunks of drywall with him, enlarging the opening.

I let out a big breath. This was ridiculous. I needed to pull my big girl panties up and ask for what I wanted.

"I was thinking—" I said.

"I have an idea," he said at the same time.

"Oh, um, you go first," I said, chickening out.

He looked at me with a grin I didn't quite trust. Partly because it made me want to kiss it off his gloriously sexy face, but also because he looked like he'd just hit the jackpot.

Except it was *my* jackpot. Assuming Jase agreed. And the landlord didn't act like a dick. And Suzi agreed to do the renovation for free.

Easy peasy.

"Stop grinning like a dork and spit it out already," I said.

"That room is empty." He gestured towards the hole. "I've been trying to unlock the door since I moved in."

"And?"

"And, how about I offer you a trade?" he asked. His intensity made my stomach tumble and other parts of me shiver.

"I'm listening," I said, even though it was hard to hear over the sound of my ovaries doing cartwheels.

"I give you this space, and in return, you let me share your booth at the Sunshine Festival."

*Holy shit.*

He was giving me the room. I wouldn't even have to sleep with him.

*Boo!* heckled my lady bits.

"And before you say anything," he said quickly, "I'll pay."

He stepped towards me, invading my space. He smelled like warm leather, cinnamon, and regrets.

"For what? The booth? Or the construction?"

"Both."

"No."

The answer came out of my mouth before I could stop it. I was happy to accept the space, but I couldn't take his money. No matter how much I needed it.

Jase ran his hands through his hair and turned in a circle. "Why the hell not?"

Good question. I was drowning, and the man was throwing me a lifeline.

"Because."

*Brilliant response, Molls.*

A pair of perfect lips pursed as he stared at me, nonplussed.

"You'll have to do better than that."

I blew out a sigh and stared at my feet. My legs were filthy and two days past needing a shave. My tennis shoes were worse, covered in mud and probably dog shit. At least my linoleum floor was clean. Or was before Larry coated it in drywall dust.

I may neglect myself sometimes, but the animals always had clean cages, fresh food and water, and a sanitized space.

"What about our landlord?" I asked.

Was I hiding behind excuses? Maybe. Shut your pie hole.

Jase's eyes shifted to the hole and back to me.

"Don't worry about him."

"You keep saying that." I was starting to wonder if he knew something about our landlord that I didn't.

Even if I trusted him to handle our landlord, that would still mean I'd be indebted to him for the money.

"What's the catch?" I finally asked, facing blue eyes so bright they were almost silver. In contrast to my hot mess, he was perfection. Dark blue tee, bits of drywall clinging to it like I wanted to. His brewery logo stretched across broad shoulders and pecs that made my insides go swoony. Jeans hung on narrow hips and hugged his thighs. I remembered how much fun it had been to get naked with him and wanted to do it again.

*Gah. Get it together, girl.*

"I need a booth at the festival if I want to drum up business for my opening over the Fourth of July weekend," he said, a grin tugging at the corner of his mouth. "And I just want to help."

"Why?" My voice came out almost as a whisper.

Jase's grin became a full megawatt smile.

"Come on, Molly. Take a chance."

His look was so earnest, his eyes wide and bright, his hand raised towards me, asking me to take that leap with him.

*Just jump.*

Nerves fluttered in my belly, telling me something would probably go wrong. I was better off on my own, where I could control everything.

Fuck it.

I held out my hand.

"Deal."

The surprise on his face disappeared as quickly as it appeared. He took my hand in his, but instead of shaking it, he held it. Held my gaze.

"Deal," he whispered, dropping his gaze to my lips.

I should pull away, but it was so easy to lean into his warmth, his strength. To let go for just a moment and pretend that everything would be okay. I slid my other hand up his chest, slowly savoring the softness of his shirt, the power of his chest as my hand cascaded up and around his shoulder. *Dear Picard, did the man have muscles everywhere?*

Dragging my hand down, I skirted it over the waistband of his jeans. How would it feel to push my hand down his jeans, grab hold of that fantastic ass? Maybe move to the front, grasp his erection and enjoy the way he grew harder as I gripped him?

This was probably a bad idea.

*Are you kidding? This is the best idea we've ever had!* cheered my vagina.

For once, I wouldn't argue.

Jase had been statue-like, holding my hand and watching as I explored. Only his eyes, which had gone dark and stormy, like a thunderstorm over the mountains, had changed.

I moved closer, pressing against him, and felt his hardening length against my stomach. Emboldened by the effect I had on him, I rose on tiptoes and stroked his bottom lip with my tongue. His breathing deepened, and his hand that had been holding mine moved to my neck and cupped me, a rough thumb stroking gently across my cheek.

I should stop. Before this went too far. Before Julie showed up for her shift. Before Jeff showed up to walk the dogs.

I didn't want to stop. Reaching behind him, I threaded my fingers through his short hair, and pulled him towards me, for once, taking what I wanted, consequences be damned. Responsibilities sat heavily on my chest every morning when I awoke and tucked me into bed every night. It was exhausting. Just once, I wanted to do something for myself that expectations or obligations didn't dictate.

So I did what I swore I would not do again, no matter what, and kissed him.

This time, Jase didn't hesitate before jumping in. His lips parted and his tongue took over, meeting mine thrust for thrust, his cock hard against my stomach as he clutched my ass.

Lifting me, he set me on the counter. Festival flyers spilled over the edge as I adjusted, spreading my legs, needing him closer. My eyes closed when he complied, grinding his hardness against my clit. A few more moves like that and I'd be coming like a fucking freight train off the rails.

Vulcan gods, he was huge. How could I have forgotten that?

His hands cupped my face, tilting my head to deepen the kiss as he continued the assault with his talented tongue. My nipples strained against my soft cotton bra as goosebumps erupted across my skin and my fingers flexed against his shoulders. Mounds of hard, tight muscles flexed with each movement he made, his fingers tracing over my clavicle. He tugged at the collar of my shirt and slipped a finger under my bra strap.

He changed the tempo of the kiss, slowing the urgency I felt as I climbed higher towards that release I so desperately needed.

Impatience had me grabbing his hand and moving it to my breast. Thankfully, he took the hint, cupping my breast, which felt heavy as he kneaded and flicked a thumb over one sensitive nub.

I rolled my hips, rubbing against him, chasing my release. I was so fucking close. It didn't even matter that I was fully clothed, spread wide before him and about to come all over a bunch of paperwork I wouldn't be able to look at without thinking about this. About how Jase felt as he worked every inch of me.

Strong, warm lips caressed my jaw, moving down my neck. His tongue darted out, licking the hollow at the base of my neck, while his fingers pulled on the taut bud he'd been playing with.

"Oh, fuck, that feels so good," I gasped, rolling my hips to increase the pressure on my clit. "More."

"For you," he said, his breath tickling my neck, "anything." His voice was thick with the arousal I could feel in his pants. He bent his head and sucked my nipple through my shirt, teasing it between his teeth.

"Yes, yes, yes, like that," I whispered, my hips grinding against his rock-hard dick like they had a mind of their own. My core tightened. I could feel myself spiraling up, up, up. I was so close. *So fucking close.*

"That's right, baby. Come for me," he said before biting down on my nipple.

On command, my body exploded into a thousand shiny stars as I cried out. My core clenched and throbbed in time with my clit. My hips rolled against him, prolonging my release.

*Whoopie!* cartwheeled my ovaries. *We're back in business!*

*Hell yes!* shouted my vagina.

My chest rose and fell as my heartbeat pounded against my chest. Holy Klingons, that was…

*Amazing,* my vagina squealed.

*I second that,* my clit responded with a satisfied sigh.

Jase held me, hands gripping my hips, his forehead pressed against mine, watching me. A knowing smile gracing his sexy face.

"Not usually the way I seal a deal, but I have to say, I'm a fan," he said with a chuckle.

I laughed softly as I registered what we'd just done. What *I* had just done. I was going to have to toss the flyers under my ass into the garbage. No way they made it unscathed.

He was still rock hard against me, but didn't seem in any hurry to change his situation.

*Bleeht!*

Larry stared at us through the glass door, eyes wide as if she'd just seen something she couldn't unsee. A wad of grass fell out of her open mouth.

"Serves you right, you furry little Peeping Tom," I said, unable to keep a smile off my face.

Thankfully, Atlas was smart enough to stay out of the room.

"Well, on that disturbing note," Jase said before placing a soft kiss against my mouth and standing, adjusting his crotch. "I assume you'll want to give Candice the good news about the booth?"

I grinned, pleased to notice his smile matching mine.

"Hell yes!"

14

# JASE

 stared at the hole in my wall. The hole that now created an unobstructed entryway into my business for a she-goat hell bent on destroying the hopes and dreams of humanity. And my brewery.

When I'd offered Molly the room, I hadn't thought about the fact that it would create an opening between our businesses that might allow Larry unfettered access to my hops. I'd been more concerned with making Molly come, something I was desperate to do again, this time seated deep inside her.

I hadn't gotten a stitch of work done since then. As happy as I was to get this space ready for Molly, spending my days chasing Larry the Wonder Beast around the Catcher's Box all day wasn't the most productive use of my time.

Suzi Quackenbush, the Suzi of Suzi-Q's Scratch 'N Sniff, rounded the corner, Larry bleating mournfully behind her. I'd gotten lucky. Suzi had a last minute cancellation and was able to start on the job the day after Molly and I sealed the deal, as it were.

"Dude, you gotta do something about your goat," she said, her raspy voice suggesting a lifelong smoking habit.

Suzi looked nothing like I'd imagined. Honestly, I wasn't sure what I expected from a general contractor-slash-candle maker, but it wasn't this.

She was on the taller side, five-eight or five-nine. Her white skin was tanned to a fine leather consistency, making her somewhere between the ages of thirty-five and sixty. A bright pink baseball cap with her logo on it—a three-wick candle with a screwdriver as the middle wick, obviously— covered her long, blond locks.

Crow's lines surrounded impossibly green eyes, suggesting her normal constitution was one of joy. Her olive green cargo shorts sagged on her bony frame. And despite the ninety-degree weather outside, a fluorescent pink and yellow long-sleeved flannel shirt covered sharply pointed shoulders.

"She's not my goat," I said, frustration and exhaustion straining my words.

"She's in your space, makes her your goat," Suzi replied, unaffected by my tone or the fact that Larry was trying to pull the hanky out of her back pocket. "If she keeps stealing tools out of my crew's belts, I'm gonna have to charge you overtime." She took back her handkerchief from Larry and walked away.

Super.

"I'll take care of it."

I turned down the hallway to my office. Larry's leash had to be in here somewhere. Unless she hid it with the tools that she kept pilfering from my construction crew.

A stack of papers that should have been filed or tossed three months ago threatened to topple as I rooted through my disorganized office. Would I rather have been fantasizing about Molly kissing me—again—and using my cock to make herself come? Absolutely. That was hot as hell to watch.

But Suzi had to finish her work. Which meant Larry had to go, which meant I needed to find her leash.

My cell phone buzzed in my back pocket.

"Not really the best time, Sam," I said, placing the call on speaker and setting it on my desk. I slid a precariously balanced pile of file folders sideways, causing an avalanche of papers to spill onto the floor.

"Fine. Let me know when would be a better time for us to talk about what you did?"

Well, that was vague and unhelpful.

"Care to enlighten me on what I supposedly did?" I said, digging through the mess on the floor.

"You sent me an email that says you're giving over a hundred square feet of space to your hot neighbor."

Ah, that.

"Her name is Molly."

"Good for her. Why are you giving her space in our brewery?"

"Because she asked for it," I grunted, reaching under my desk and pulling out a dust bunny the size of a baseball, but no leash.

"If she asked you to sign over your fortune, you gonna give her that, too? How about your soul?"

"She wouldn't ask for those," I replied without hesitation. Because she wouldn't. She wouldn't even ask for a couple hundred dollars that I knew she needed.

"What happened to our plan to release small seasonal batches to correspond with baseball season?"

"Our what—oh." *Oh.*

The next phase of our business plan included building out a seasonal menu of beers to cater to visitors and locals year round. In my haste to get Molly to agree to sharing her booth, and then… *after*… I'd forgotten.

Sam was right. That room would be perfect. It was just the right size for a small batch set up and maybe a couple of tables for special tastings.

"Yeah," Sam said. "*Oh.*"

"I'll find another space," I said.

"Space for what?" asked a voice from behind me.

I looked over my shoulder at Molly, who had snuck up behind me.

She was a vision. Her hair was down today, shiny and flat across her back. Her tee was one from her rescue, teal with the white logo in the corner, the V-neck a bit too high to see any of the good stuff I knew was there.

And she was smiling at me.

I wanted to throw her over my shoulder, carry her down the hall to my bedroom, and show her how my mouth and fingers and cock could make her come.

"Hey you," I said instead as the tool thief peeked out from behind Molly, weird eyes unblinking.

"Hey who?" Sam's voice boomed from my phone.

I was still on speaker.

"Uh, Molly's here," I answered, watching her as she tilted her head and raised her eyebrows.

"Molly? The hot girl next door?"

Molly's eyes narrowed as her hands went to her hips.

"Better a hot girl than a douchey guy," Molly retorted.

I smiled at her. I could have used a lot more of her sass when I was working my way through the majors. If only I hadn't been so stupid, maybe I could have.

"Sticks and stones, Hot Girl," Sam said. "You gonna tell her, Tugwater, or should I?" he asked me.

"I've got this," I said, trying to unlock my phone so I could take it off speaker.

Larry pranced down the hallway, probably off to steal a power saw.

"I can come back later if you're busy," Molly said, watching the goat disappear in the direction that definitely wasn't towards my back door. I needed to find that leash.

"No, no," I said, pausing my phone fumbling to give her my complete attention.

Those amber eyes watched me with a hint of humor creasing the edges. All I'd done in the last two days was think about the next time I'd be able to make her come. I still couldn't believe we hadn't shed a stitch of clothing. Something I intended to remedy the next time.

Assuming there would be a next time.

*God, please let there be a next time.*

"Um, what did you need?" I asked, phone still in my hand.

"I was just wondering if you'd gotten permission from the landlord to start the work yet, but since the work has started, I guess that's a yes."

"You haven't told her?" Sam asked, his voice raising at the end.

*Shit.*

With the monstrous pile of other priorities and a goat with anger issues running around my place of business, I had conveniently forgotten to mention I was her landlord.

"Tell me what?"

A better man would just spit it out. What was the harm, anyway? So what if I was her landlord? It's not like it would change anything. Right?

I was being ridiculous. I was just going to tell her.

"Tell you the landlord is…" My voice caught on the next word.

"An uncommunicative jackass?" Molly finished.

Or maybe not.

"Yep, that. And he signed the confirmation yesterday."

"Oh, for fuck's sake," Sam quipped.

I was a coward.

"Don't suppose I can get a copy?" Molly asked. "Since the jerk has been ignoring my emails again?"

"Sam," I said, finally unlocking the phone and taking him off speaker. "Can you make sure he sends Molly the letter?"

"Dude—"

"Take care of it," I barked, ending the call.

A text message flashed on my screen before I could pocket my phone.

Sammy: TELL HER.

Sammy: Chicken shit.

Me: Bock, bock.

"Everything okay?" Molly asked. She was leaning against the table, long legs stretched out in front of her. I wanted to run my hands and tongue up that smooth, bare skin.

*Focus, Tug.* Now wasn't the time for fantasies. I was knee deep in building supplies, behind on my opening-day work plan, and hadn't even thought about the festival booth yet.

"'Scuse me, comin' through."

Suzi shuffled down the hall carrying a ladder over one shoulder, interrupting my dirty thoughts.

"Oh, hey, Molly," Suzi said, setting the ladder down. "I have those 'better than wet dog' scented candles you asked for. Stop by this week and I'll get them for you."

"Awesome. How much do I owe you?"

"You helped fast track the permit for my new workshop. Call it even."

Molly shook her head. "I didn't do anything. Just asked Oscar to look into it."

"And Oscar told Brant, who reminded his mother, the mayor, to sign the damned paperwork."

"Poor Frances. I'm glad she's finally retiring."

"She was a great mayor. But it's time for fresh blood," Suzi replied. "Stop by sometime with a bottle of wine and say hello to sweet Lou-Lou. Been two years this month since we adopted her."

"Consider it done," Molly replied. "Looks good around here," she said.

"Be better if someone would keep the goat from eating my tools," Suzi replied, hefting the ladder back up to her shoulder before continuing down the hallway.

"What's Larry doing now?" Molly asked me.

"Being Larry," I replied, running my hand through my hair.

Molly wandered down the hall towards the gaping hole between our spaces.

"How long before it's finished?" she asked.

I pulled a file off a stack of papers and handed it to her. "Suzi said two weeks, maybe longer, depending on their supply shipment."

"Two weeks?" She looked over the paperwork, a crease worrying her brow.

"What's wrong?"

I'd signed the paperwork without consulting Molly. Maybe I should have talked to her first. But then she'd know I was the landlord. Which I seriously needed to tell her. Eventually.

"I was hoping for something a little sooner, that's all."

She shook her head and pulled out her phone, swiping through what looked like emails.

"Why? What's going on?"

"I've got animals coming next week."

"Next week? Why so soon?"

She sighed. "They were going to be euthanized. How do you say no when lives are on the line?"

And just like that, all my petty worries about seasonal beers washed away with a giant dose of reality.

"Okay. I'll talk to Suzi, see what I can do."

I was rewarded with a small smile. She pulled a leash out of her back pocket and shook it, the chain at the end rattling softly. Larry came bleating and hopping down the hallway towards the sound.

With the goat finally leashed—*thank the goat gods*—Molly led her to the back door. She paused, turning towards me.

"I'm getting together with some friends tomorrow night to drink wine and work out the booth logistics for the festival. You should come."

I couldn't have prevented the grin that appeared on my face if I had wanted to.

"Text me the details. I'll be there."

She considered me for a moment before finally nodding. "Don't make me regret trusting you, Tug," she said, pointing a finger at my face.

"Wouldn't dream of it," I replied, unable to stop the grin from becoming a full-blown smile. And I wouldn't. I'd get Molly her space. Whatever the cost.

"Suzi!" I hollered, heading off in search of my contractor. "How'd you like to make a little extra cash?"

15

# MOLLY

*I* can't believe Jase Tugwater is coming to our house!" Jeff exclaimed for the forty-seventh time since I had arrived an hour ago.

They were currently tidying the house in a flurry of activity that would make Mr. Clean's bald head spin.

"I can't. Believe. Jase Tugwater. Is coming. To. Our. House!"

Make that forty-eight.

They were making me regret asking them to help with the Sunshine Festival planning. Mostly, I'd done it so I wouldn't be alone with Jase any longer than necessary.

I hadn't seen him since yesterday, when he dropped the bomb that the space would take two weeks to finish. That was too late to house the new animals coming in next week, but I'd figure something out. I always did. Maybe I could talk Jeff and Tyson into fostering a dog or two. It's not like they'd notice another wagging tail with the size of their pack.

I'd barely made it out of the brewery yesterday without throwing myself at Jase and begging for another mind-blowing orgasm. Swear to Jean-Luc Picard, I'd never experienced a climax that intense. Not even with Mr. Buzzypants.

And I wanted to do it again. Despite my better judgment, every time the man walked into my periphery, I wanted to strip down to my plain cotton undies and throw myself at him.

Which would not happen. No matter how badly the thought made my vagina throb.

General lifted his giant head and snorted in my direction, like he didn't believe me. Atlas probably would have, too, but he was currently occupying the role of pillow and cuddle partner for the two smallest dogs in the Fishers' pack.

The doorbell rang and Jeff made a sound like one of Atlas's squeaky toys as their eyes bulged and the smaller dogs started barking.

"Deep breath," I said, patting them on the back while Tyson greeted their guest, dogs racing around his legs. "Remember, he puts his pants on one leg at a time, just like the rest of us."

"Oh *god!* Why did you say that? Now I'm thinking of Jase Tugwater pantsless. I wonder if he goes commando?"

Great, now we were both thinking of Jase Tugwater going commando.

"Um, am I interrupting?" Jase's baritone voice filled the room, and Jeff squeaked again.

Long strides carried Jase into the room. He wore his standard cargo shorts, today paired with a checkered button up. He looked freshly showered and shaved. A hint of leather wafted past my nose, like he'd been oiling his glove. It smelled earthy and sexy and made me want to rub against him.

"Jeff," I said slowly, willing my vagina to stop its throbbing. "Meet Jase."

"Hey," Jase said, extending one hand in Jeff's direction, a

kind smile crinkling his eyes. In Jase's other hand was a brown glass jug. "Good to meet you."

"Jase. Tugwater. Is. In. My. House," Jeff stage whispered as they did their best to shake Jase's hand right off his arm.

"They're a fan," Tyson said as he gently removed his spouse from Jase's personal space.

Jase's face was scrunched in a losing struggle to not laugh as he lifted the jug. "I thought you guys might like some beer. Fresh out of my tank."

"How thoughtful," Tyson replied while Jeff did some deep-breathing exercises beside him. "Jeff, sweetie, can you grab some pint glasses for us?"

Jeff nodded, their cheeks still sucking and blowing like a puffer fish as they dashed to the kitchen.

Beers poured, we made our way to the table. Jeff made a move like they were going to sit on Jase's lap, but Tyson steered him to a different chair. Away from Jase.

"So, the Sunshine Festival," I prompted.

"We haven't done a shared booth before," Tyson said. "This should be fun."

"I know the Sunshine Festival is a Harmony Springs institution," Jase said. "But help a new guy out. What have I gotten myself into?"

"You ever go to a county fair growing up?" Jeff asked.

"They speak," Jase replied.

"Eek!" Jeff squeaked, nearly falling out of their chair.

I laughed.

Jase apologized, which only sent Jeff spinning themselves into the kitchen mumbling something about channeling their inner Ina Garten and pulling themself together.

"Don't mind Jeff, they're just… easily excitable," I said.

"I'd say it would take a bigger person than Jeff to scare me off, but I'm not sure that's true," Jase half whispered, giving me a chance to lean in close enough to sniff him without looking like a creeper.

"Oh, I'm low-key terrified of what will come out of their mouth at any moment," I agreed.

His baritone laugh vibrated through me, giving Mr. Buzzypants a run for his money.

*We want more!* chanted my vagina.

I squeezed my thighs together to relieve some of the pressure and tried to focus on something other than the memory of how hard he'd felt against me as I rubbed myself over—

"Shall we get to it, kids?" Jeff came sweeping into the room, jitters apparently forgotten in their quest to be the hostess with the mostest, as they balanced platters of food in each hand.

"*E'voila!*" they said, placing the platters on the table with a flourish.

Jase looked at the trays and then looked at me, eyebrows raised in question.

"Pigs in a blanket?" he said.

I had to be seeing things. Jeff loved hosting. They always put out a crazy array of amazing food. Never anything so... *mundane.*

Until this moment, I wasn't sure the word was even in their vocabulary.

"Jase Tugwater visits and you decide to serve him finger food from the third grade?" I asked.

Jeff made a shushing motion with their fingers. "This is *une petite saucisse enveloppée dans de la pâte,*" they said in the worst French accent I'd ever heard.

"What does that mean?" I asked, dreading the answer.

"A tiny sausage wrapped in dough," Jase laughed, surprising me.

"You speak French?"

What other interesting things did I not know about him?

No, not interesting. Humdrum. This was a humdrum fact that did not turn me on at all.

*Oo-la-la!* crooned my vagina.

Jase just shrugged and popped *une petite saucisse enveloppée dans de la pâte* into his mouth. My lady parts were suddenly very interested in watching him swallow. *Down girls.*

"Oo-la-la!" Jeff said, echoing my vagina and fanning their face with a paper napkin. "The language of love." They blew a kiss to Tyson, who caught it and placed his hand against his chest.

Ugh. They were totally going to have hot jungle sex tonight. I, on the other hand, was going home to Mr. Buzzy-pants to imagine Jase whispering to me in French while we made love.

*Where the fuckity fuck had that come from?*

"You okay?" Jase was watching me intently.

"Huh? Yes. Why wouldn't I be?"

It was suddenly very warm in here. Who switched off the AC?

"You looked like you were having a hot flash," Jeff answered.

"Or an orgasm," Tyson added.

"No. *Another* orgasm," Jeff said, tiny-clapping their hands in front of them.

Jase coughed, pounding his chest with a fist.

I ignored the flames of heat searing my face as I wished for a Klingon ship to sweep by and flatten the Fishers' house —with me in it.

"We gonna chatter like a bunch of hens in a chicken coop? Or are we going to actually work?" I asked, willing my body temperature down to a less stroke-inducing level.

"Clunky segue," Tyson replied with a cheeky grin. "But seeing as you may be recovering from a long-overdue orgasm, I'll let it slide."

"I won't," Jeff said. "I want to talk about the orgasms."

*Sweet baby Spock on a starship. Please save me from this hell.*

"There are no orgasms," I insisted before swallowing the rest of my beer and wishing Jase had brought the whole keg.

"Someone's pants are on fire," Jeff said.

"I'm not lying," I lied.

"That is definitely your lying face," Jeff said, waving a finger around my face.

"I don't have a lying face."

I *totally* had a lying face.

"What have you got to say for yourself, Muscles?" Jeff asked, swinging their finger towards Jase.

A tinge of pink colored Jase's cheeks.

*Aww*, crooned my ovaries.

"Who'd like a refill?" Jase asked, standing so quickly he nearly toppled his chair.

"The growler is empty," Tyson said, his eyes darting back and forth between Jase and me, smiling. The smug, knowing bastard.

"Great," Jase replied. "I'll run to my place and get us another one."

"Oh. Em. Gee," Jeff exclaimed. "*You two had sex!*"

That declaration froze Jase in place. "I… uh… we…"

"We did nothing of the sort," I said.

"Huh," Jeff said, disappointment tugging their eyebrows together. "No lies detected."

I wasn't lying. Thank the Vulcan gods Tyson and I had clarified in the tenth grade that sex only counted if there was actual peen penetration.

"Don't need to have sex to have an orgasm," Tyson muttered, reading my mind. Some days, I really hated how well he knew me.

I needed to get everyone back on track and off the orgasm train.

"Jase, please sit," I said, coloring my voice with my best Tyson the School Teacher impression.

I turned to my nosy best friends. "Tyson, since we're out of beer, could you open a bottle of wine? Jeff, plate up your, um, tiny sausages."

Jase snickered beside me. I bit the inside of my cheek to keep from joining him.

"We're clearly not going to get to everything tonight, but let's at least figure out how to divide the booth so we can both use it," I continued as everyone—shockingly—did what they were told.

"I just want to give out samples of my beer," Jase said, accepting a glass of white wine from Tyson. "The permits were emailed to me yesterday. As long as I have a spot where I can hook up a couple of mini-kegs, I'm good to go."

"Easy enough," Tyson said.

"I want to use the booth to showcase animals up for adoption, but I don't know how many I'll have by then."

"Why not?" Jase asked.

"I can't really bring in new animals until the new space is done, which won't be until the festival is over."

That was a phone call I'd hated to make, but luckily Nora had been understanding and agreed to keep the animals another week. It had taken a promise that I'd take the animals by that time no matter what, and a not small donation to cover the animals' food and care for that time—along with a few other things that the Chester County shelter needed. But at least I could afford it, since Jase was funding the booth.

A thought that filled me with both hope and dread.

"Space will be ready by the weekend," Jase said casually.

"Which weekend?" I asked.

"This weekend."

16

JASE

"I thought you said you'd be done yesterday?" I looked at the surrounding chaos. Bits of board and drywall were scattered over my floors, creating tripping hazards where there was once order throughout my beloved brewery.

"It would have been done two days ago," griped Suzi, knocking dust and dirt off her neon pink baseball cap. "But that damned goat of yours keeps eating through the drywall, so we have to keep patching over it."

"I've already told you she's not my goat."

"She's in your building."

"Still not my goat."

"Just be happy I'm not charging you hazard pay," Suzi said as she stuffed the hat back on her head.

As if on cue, Larry poked her nose around the corner, blinking at us. She was chewing a piece of paper, her jaw moving sideways as she destroyed something I was sure would piss me off if I knew what it was.

But what really caught my attention was the hammer hanging from her collar.

"Is that—"

"My fucking hammer," Suzi said, stalking towards the four-legged thief. "I thought it dropped out of the back of my pickup last week, so I bought a new one yesterday."

Larry jumped up and spun 180 degrees, playing keep-away from the contractor.

"Add it to my bill," I told Suzi as I angled around Larry, hoping to corner her before she could take off.

"Already did," Suzi said right before she lunged. Larry let out a scream, dropping the piece of paper she'd been mauling. Suzi grabbed hold of Larry and untangled the hammer from her collar before she squirmed away.

How it had gotten there in the first place was a mystery I didn't feel like solving.

Suzi returned to the mystery room, hammer in tow, cussing the goat out with each stomp of her pink work boot.

*Stomp.*

"Stupid."

*Stomp.*

"Asshole."

*Stomp.*

"Leave my tools alone."

"I told you to keep the door locked," I said, unable to help myself. I had. Not that it would have stopped Larry from breaking and entering. But it might have slowed her down a bit.

Larry let loose one more short scream before she disappeared down the hallway. I picked up the paper she'd been chewing and tried to decipher the part that had taken on less damage than the rest. "Morris County Health Inspector."

Damn it.

She had chewed up my copy of the health inspector's notice. This was the list that told me everything I was going to need to have ready for my inspection. Which I needed to pass if I was going to open on time.

At least I still had time to get ready.

I smoothed out the paper, hoping to decipher a few of the items on the list.

Oh no.

No, no, no.

At the bottom of the page, in the inspector's heavily slanted writing, right next to the words "revised inspection date" was today's date.

Oh hell.

The inspection was this afternoon. How had I forgotten?

She'd called last week to reschedule, saying something about a surprise Alaskan cruise from her husband to celebrate their twentieth anniversary. I'd been happy to accommodate since the timing worked with the bonus I'd promised Suzi for finishing the mystery room project early.

But thanks to all the work on the Sunshine Festival, not to mention my near constant daydreams starring my sexy neighbor, I'd forgotten all about it.

"Suzi! I need this stuff moved out yesterday."

"You and me both, buddy," Suzi replied from the mystery room. "Goddamn it! Jase, come get your fucking goat."

"Not my goat," I muttered as I headed towards Larry's happy bleating. Before I could do anything useful, she raced and kicked her way past me, dragging an electric drill behind her.

*What the hell?*

This madness had to end. I unlocked my phone and texted Molly. This stupid room was hers. The least she could do was take care of her goat.

> Me: Can you please come get your goat?
> She just stole an electric drill from Suzi.

I watched while three bubbles appeared and disappeared twice, nope, three times.

Molly: why does larry need an electric drill I have one here she can use

Me: Ffs. I'm serious.

Molly: so am I

Me: I'm begging you, please come use whatever voodoo magic you use to banish the demon goat from these premises.

Molly: lol you sound like a character from game of thrones

"Anyone seen a Phillips head screwdriver? Or any screwdriver?" asked Carlos, one of Suzi's crew, as he wandered past me, muttering something in Spanish. I caught the words *el diablo* and *maldita*.

I pointed in the direction Larry had headed—towards my dining area that was being inspected in mere hours—as my head throbbed.

Me: Jesus H. Christ, she's also absconded with all the screwdrivers. PLEASE TAKE MERCY ON US AND RETRIEVE YOUR GOAT.

A scream I hoped was the goat and not Carlos echoed down the hallway as I waited for a reply.

"Fucking goat," I muttered.

"I thought this was supposed to be finished yesterday?" Molly said from behind me, startling me.

She was half smiling, but worry creased the corners of her deep honeyed eyes. Today's nerdy tee was bright purple with a spaceship flashing across the front, the words, *"To boldly go..."* in retro seventies font under it. But instead of her trademark cutoff shorts, she was wearing olive green linen cargo pants, which hugged the curve of her ass. Surprisingly, the entire outfit was stain-free.

The sight of her instantly eased some of the throbbing on my forehead. I wanted to hold her and breathe in that lavender and outdoorsy scent that encircled her.

*Bleht!*

But as Larry reminded me, I didn't have time for that. I had an inspection to get through, which would not happen if someone didn't make this goat disappear.

"It was," I said, sighing.

"What happened?" Molly asked, placing a hand on my arm, anchoring me to her.

"Larry," I said. "Larry happened."

"Didn't you tell Suzi to keep the doors locked?"

She was trying to look past me into the room.

"I did, but do you really think a measly lock was going to stop the Princess of Darkness from wreaking havoc across her domain?"

"No. But it might have slowed her down," she said.

"That's what I said."

She checked her phone. "The new animals will be here in a few hours," she said, her voice tight with worry. "I've got to get stuff moved in."

"Trust me, no one wants this mess cleaned up more than I do."

I looked at my phone. The clock was ticking down and every second I spent explaining my problems, or chasing a goat, or calming down a contractor, was a second closer to losing my business.

The sun through the back window sparkled off Molly's

eyes, making them seem like jewels. She was watching me, waiting. Not pushing me, just waiting.

I could tell her. Tell her I'd messed everything up and I was going to lose my business and her animals would be homeless and I should never have come to this town and bought this building and ruined both our lives.

I could tell her.

"The health inspector is coming in less than four hours," I admitted in a rushed breath, hating myself a little for not being able to tell her the truth.

"Can you call her and reschedule?"

I shook my head. "Alaskan cruise," I said.

"Oh, that's right. Arlene's been annoying everyone about that cruise for weeks." Molly looked up at me and shook my arm gently. "Hey. We'll fix this."

Suzi stomped down the hall towards us, her hat off-kilter, the back of her flannel untucked. She was breathing deeply, but I couldn't tell if she was out of breath or channeling her inner peace.

"Sorry, boss, but your goat just parkoured itself off Carlos's back."

"Oh, for the love of Spock," Molly muttered. "Suzi, can you finish this up in the next..." She checked the clock on her phone. "Two hours?"

"As long as the goat stays out of our way, I don't see why not."

Molly nodded and turned on her heels, silent as death itself, and marched down the hall towards Larry's last known location.

Suzi and I followed along like little lambs. I didn't know about Suzi, but Tug Junior was awake and interested. Take Charge Molly was sexy as hell.

I wondered what Take Charge Molly would be like in the bedroom and how she felt about props.

*Bleeaaaaat!* yelled Larry.

*Poof*, went my fantasy.

Larry, destroyer of wet dreams, was standing over a pile of screwdrivers, the drill still hooked to her back hoof, staring at Carlos. She dug a front hoof into the tile floor, challenging, then screamed like an Amazon princess.

"LARRY."

Molly's voice cut through the murderous noise, startling everyone, including Larry, who mercifully stopped her shrieking. Molly faced the goat head on, hands down at her side, looking every bit like she was about to draw down.

*Oh, hell yes!*

Take Charge Molly had nothing on Wild West Molly. I made a mental note to price out chaps the next time I was near the hardware store.

"OUT," Molly shouted, pointing at the back door. Larry bleated once more and trotted outside.

"Huh," I said.

"Huh," Suzi said.

Molly looked back at us both.

"You have two hours," she said to Suzi.

"Yes, ma'am."

Smart woman, that Suzi.

Molly faced me, indecision coloring her beautiful face.

"Thank—"

A hug—big and warm, hinting at what could be—interrupted my words.

"Larry is a flaming pile of moose shit," she whispered. "You've got this." She let me go and disappeared down the hallway.

"Impressive," Suzi said, a smirk on her lips as she sauntered back towards the mystery room.

"Yes," I replied. "Yes, she is."

17

# MOLLY

arks and meows reverberated off the walls as I stood up from my desk and rubbed the back of my neck. Onboarding new animals always came with an adjustment period as they learned what their new normal looked like. But this? Hours of nonstop noise and I'd finally had it. No amount of aspirin and caffeine could quell this.

I turned down the dimmer on the overhead light, glad I'd had it installed. It allowed me to create a calmer environment in the new kennel space. Hopefully that would relax the half dozen dogs, ranging from a yellow lab mix to what was probably a Yorkie mix once the little dude got a bath and a haircut.

Glancing at the dog-shaped clock on the wall outside the kennel space, I willed my headache to hold off for a few more hours. Just a few more hours, then I could go home.

It was half past eight. I'd changed into shorts two hours ago, after one of the dogs had an accident as I was lifting her out of the crate she'd come in. She'd peed all down the front of my pants. Such was the glamorous life of a rescue advocate. It was why I kept extra clothes at the shelter.

My last volunteer had finally left at seven to go home and feed her family. How had my mom done this every day? By this time, Belinda Sanders would have had the dogs bathed, the cats brushed until she could work out which ones would tolerate a bath, and the bunny and chicken, well, whatever one did to them. She also would have pulled off a welcome party for the animals, complete with homemade treats and party hats.

All I had managed was the basics.

Despite Suzi's best efforts, she'd delivered the space to me two hours late, which put me very behind where I needed to be. And I had hours left before I could call it a day.

So no baths, no homemade treats, and no party hats for my animals. Just the bare minimum.

I was drowning in mediocrity and failure.

A knock came from the back door. Atlas was asleep in his bed in my office, and Larry never knocked before barreling into my space, or any space, for that matter. Which left one possibility: my sexy neighbor who made me feel things I had no time or inclination to feel—like wanted. And desired.

I ignored the second set of knocks, hoping maybe he'd get the hint and go away. I had a giant mound of paperwork calling my name. Besides, I didn't need a reason to relive that hug.

It was supposed to mean nothing. Just a way to say, "I'm sorry my goat causes chaos and destruction wherever she goes. She sucks."

Instead, it had felt like… more. So much freaking more.

No. I didn't need Jase here, in my space, reminding me of that hug. Or our first kiss. Or that other kiss. And let's not forget the earth-shattering orgasm he'd given me without even laying a hand on me.

No. Nope. Not going there.

*We should totally go there!* shouted my vagina.

*Sorry, not gonna happen.*

*Boo,* my nipples answered.

Where was I going with this?

"Atlas is staring at me, Molly, so I know you're in there," Jase called from beyond the glass door.

"Fine," I mumbled, walking to the back door, steeling myself as I went. I was a strong, independent woman. Just because I dry humped the man and then hugged him in a way that was supposed to say "hey friend" but felt more like "I want to have your babies" didn't mean I couldn't face him.

"Come on, Molly. Will you open up? Larry looks like she's about to head butt me through the glass."

I walked over to the door and stood next to Atlas, who leaned his body against mine. Jase's face was pasted against the glass, looking terrified of a hundred-pound troublemaker.

I should probably let him in. Larry was standing a few yards behind him, eyeballing his very fine ass. Not that I could blame the goat for her taste in rear ends. Jase's was as fine as it got. Even if it was attached to a man I spent too many waking hours daydreaming about.

He rested his forehead against the glass, looking almost as worn down as I felt.

Damn it.

Larry jumped up and down in place, bleating, warming up for her big approach. I sighed. As much as I would like to keep a door between me and Jase—literally and figuratively —I didn't have the budget to replace a sliding door. And any damage done to that juicy ass would be a travesty.

I unlocked the door, and Jase slipped in, closing it quickly behind him. Larry let out a baleful yell over the loss of her target and trotted over to her shed, likely plotting her next act of chaos and commotion.

"What the hell is her problem?"

*She's got great taste in asses.* "She hates late-night callers."

Jase ran a hand through blond waves, causing his hair to stick up even more than it already was.

*Hello, sailor!* crooned my ovaries, which could pipe right down.

He clearly hadn't showered since Suzi had left, so there were bits of dust and drywall in his hair and covering his broad shoulders. It even stuck to his arm hairs, making him look like he was graying.

*Older men are sooo hot,* squealed my neglected vagina.

Oh, for fuck's sake.

Turning, I walked into the kitchen area and filled up a giant water bowl for Atlas, setting it down in front of him. He lapped it loudly, water splashing every which way. Raising his head, rivers of slimy water fell down both sides of his mouth, pooling on the floor. I took the towel I always kept near his water dish and wiped off his mouth before he could wipe it against my leg. A lesson I'd learned the hard way. Dropping the towel, I toed it around to dry the lake Atlas had created on the tile.

"There a reason you're here?" I asked, knowing he was behind me because I could feel the heat coming off him.

*Sex, sex, sex!* chanted my ovaries.

"I wanted to say thanks," he said, the timbre of his voice low and sensual, and my ovaries swooned.

I really needed to get laid. For real.

*Yes!* they cried.

By someone who wasn't Jase Tugwater.

*No!* they sobbed.

"For what?" I asked, picking the towel up and hanging it on the hook. I made a mental note to throw it in the next load of washing as I dug my fingernail into a small hole in the wall where a dog had clawed.

Was I avoiding eye contact with the man whose very

presence in my tiny kitchen was making my pussy throb? Yes. Yes, I was. So sue me.

"For being you," he said.

Surprise caused my eyes to pop up and look at him. Hooded eyes looked back at me. Like he saw me. Every doubt. Every flaw. Every insecurity. And he still wanted me.

*Yippee!* shouted my vagina.

"Being me?" I asked, ignoring my overly enthusiastic lady parts.

"Suzi was minutes away from walking out and taking every chance I had of opening on time with her. If it hadn't been for you, taking charge of Larry…"

His eyes darkened like a Colorado rainstorm as he said it, making him look every bit a predator. My vagina very much wanted to be his prey.

*Down, girl.*

"I didn't do anything," I said, my voice faltering under the weight of his attention.

He shook his head. "Only you could have gotten Larry to trot out of my brewery like it was her idea." He swallowed, and my eyes tracked every movement of his throat. "It was… hot."

Was it me, or had he inched closer to me? And who the fuck had turned on the heater?

His hand moved to my cheek, gently tucking a strand of hair behind my ear, lingering before running his thumb softly across my cheek.

"Molly."

My skin erupted in goosebumps that traveled down my body. So much for being too warm. My body was a fucking walking contradiction around him.

"I take it you passed your inspection?" I asked, too chicken to say what I was really thinking. Which was decidedly not PG-rated and likely to lead to more orgasms.

*Yay!* shouted my vagina.

*No.* I did not need more orgasms. I needed to finish up with the animals so I could go home and give Mr. Buzzy-pants a proper workout and put this whole confusing day behind me.

"Yes. Thanks to you."

"And Suzi," I said, my voice nearly inaudible.

Jase dipped his head, his breath warm against my cheek, and slid his hand behind my neck. He smelled like chalk and cedar and orange peel. A combination that shouldn't work but did.

"Why do you keep changing the subject?" he murmured against my neck. The goosebumps returned, multiplying. My nipples stood at attention, making it very hard to concentrate.

"Am I?" My voice sounded distant and uncertain.

He nodded, his nose brushing my neck as he breathed in. "I want to thank you properly."

*Hell to the yes!* shouted my entire fucking body, which had been reduced to a shivering puddle of lust and longing.

I swallowed the ball of desire forming in my core, willing myself to stay still.

*Distance, Molly.*

My body didn't want distance. My body very much wanted to be naked and climbing this perfect male specimen while I begged for release.

My heart, on the other hand… It still remembered the sting of his rejection from that weekend, no matter how long ago it had been.

Needing to get control of myself before I did something I would regret, I stepped back, cold air replacing his warmth against my body. I smoothed back my hair, giving myself another few seconds to regain control over my sanity.

"I, uh," I stuttered. *Get it together, girl.* I cleared my throat.

"I need to make sure the new animals are okay, and I have a ton of paperwork to finish."

The disappointment on his face was undeniable. It looked like my vagina felt. Sad and lonely.

Well, that's what it got for lusting after something it couldn't have. Because no matter how much my body wanted to ignore what had happened, it had. And it had hurt more than I would admit.

He and I could be business partners, neighbors, maybe even friends someday. But we couldn't be this. Whatever *this* was.

Unable to face him, I did the only thing I could. I turned my back and got to work.

18

JASE

She did *not* just walk away," I said to Atlas, who was the only one left in the room with me.

Atlas licked my hand gently before following his owner into the bowels of the shelter, dismissing me, but at least he was nicer about it than Molly.

Barks and meows echoed off the bare walls that could use a fresh coat of paint. The black-and-white linoleum floor looked like it had seen better days but was clean. The place looked worn, a little tired, but spotless. It was clear Molly took a lot of pride in this place and put in the work to show it.

Her work ethic was impressive, but her stubborn streak was more so.

I found the wilful woman in a room full of cages filled with all manner of cats and kittens, dragging a purple plastic tote across the floor. I crossed the room, bent down, and picked it up.

"I'm busy, Tug. Go home," she said, narrowing her eyes at me, glare fully on point. Her hands were on her hips, but all I noticed was her long, toned legs stretching out from. Her cutoff shorts.

*Head in the game, Tug.* I wasn't here to convince her to change her mind and sleep with me, no matter how much I wanted to. She'd made it clear she wasn't interested, and I would respect that.

*So stop gawking at her legs, perv.*

"Where would you like this?" I asked, ignoring her command. She looked like she wanted to kick me in the shins. Or some place further north.

Well, tough shit. I was tired of her claiming to be busy and exhausted but refusing any help.

I was here. I was able-bodied, and despite the fact that my cock was knocking at the zipper of my cargo shorts to come out and play, I would do whatever she needed doing if it meant she'd go home before midnight.

"I have a few ideas where you can put it," she said, her brows pressing together in a scowl. It was cute. I kept eye contact, but kept my face and posture neutral. She'd for sure kick me in the balls for thinking her mean muggin' look was as cute as that orange kitten staring at us from between the bars of its cage.

The tote probably weighed fifty pounds, but you didn't get to my level of professional sports without being able to muscle your way through a problem. Even with my bad knee, I could hold it for however long it took her to work through whatever was going on in that big, beautiful brain of hers.

She blew a long strand of hair out of her face and pointed towards the corner of the room. "Stack it there, you stubborn jackass."

"Pot, meet kettle," I replied, hefting the tote into place.

She swung a smaller green tote onto a hip. I took it from her and tilted my head towards the corner. "This one, too?"

"I didn't ask for your help. In fact, I'm pretty sure I told you to go home."

Ignoring her, I placed it on top of the purple tote. "I want to help."

"I don't need help."

"Everyone needs help," I said, grabbing a broom and sweeping the dirt and debris from where the totes had been.

"Damn it, Tug." She reached for the broom, but I held on tight, waiting for her to look at me.

It was like the bright Colorado sun broke through the clouds when she finally met my stare, her chin tilted up, challenging.

*Challenge accepted.*

"Let me help, Molly," I said, keeping my voice soft. It wasn't a demand. It was a request. One I sincerely hoped she would accept. Because I was going to help her, whether or not she wanted it.

"Do you even know how to clean a cat cage?" she asked, her golden eyes softening around the corners.

"No, but I've got two hands and according to my last general manager, I'm pretty coachable when I wanna be."

A grin ghosted across her full lips. "That a direct quote?"

"I think his exact words were, 'Tugwater, pull your head out of your ass and figure it out!' But I'm pretty sure that's what he meant."

She lost the battle with her mouth and grinned, shaking her head and letting go of the broom.

"See?" I said, turning back to the dirt on the floor. "Was that so hard?"

"Stubborn," she mumbled, pulling a small plastic bucket of cleaning supplies out of a cupboard.

"Pot." *Sweep, sweep.*

"I thought I was the kettle?" she said, still failing to keep the grin off her face as she opened the first cage.

Smiling, I shook my head, sweeping the small pile of dust into the dustpan. Falling into an easy rapport with Molly was something I definitely could get used to.

"Now what?" I asked, emptying the dustpan.

"Here," she said, as I put the broom back where I found it. "Hold this."

She handed me a tiny white kitten. It had black ears, a black tail, and one black leg. It didn't even fill the palm of my hand.

"What am I supposed to do with this?" I asked.

"Keep her out of trouble while I finish cleaning the mess she made."

I peeked over her shoulder and nearly threw up. There was cat shit everywhere. It ran over one side of the litter box and up the side wall of the cage. How? A SpongeBob-themed blanket had been dragged into the middle of this nightmare and dropped unceremoniously into the litter pan. Poor SpongeBob.

"This little thing did all *that?*" It looked like a horror-movie set, but with piles of runny cat poop instead of blood and gore.

"Kittens are cute for a reason," Molly said, as she got to work, scrubbing the cage spotless in less time than it took me to stop gagging. The kitten curled up in the crook of my arm and started purring, her little eyelids shut, looking adorable and not like she was a giant shit machine.

"Got room for more?" Molly asked, her voice gentle enough to make me forget about my nausea.

She was holding out two more kittens, a genuine smile gracing her beautiful face and making it glow. How in the hell was I supposed to say no? I'd adopt every animal in this place if she smiled at me like that every day. I looked at the litter pan in the empty cage and shuddered. Maybe.

I nodded, not trusting my voice, and she placed a kitten in

my outstretched hand. The orange kitten was bigger than the others, but seemed happy to be held as it started licking its paw and cleaning off its face.

The smaller tabby with wide yellow eyes army crawled its way up my arm and rested in the crook of my neck, massaging my shoulder with the knives.

"Ow! Why are they so stabby?"

I extracted the tiny wannabe murderer off my neck. It wailed, sucker punching me with a giant dose of guilt.

"Goddamn it," I muttered as I ignored my survival instinct and put the kitten back. It immediately quieted down and went back to its murder massage.

Molly laughed, and just like that, my looming death was forgotten as heat wrapped around my chest and my cock took notice. Fuck, I wanted her. More than that, I wanted her to want me.

"You look like a kitten tree," she said.

"I feel like I'm being assassinated by a tiny butcher."

"Being the biscuit factory is a thankless job, but he wouldn't be turning your neck into baked goods if he didn't feel safe up there."

I only understood about ten percent of those words, but it didn't matter because she was looking at me like I was doing something very heroic. Which I probably was, because the urge to pluck the kitten auditioning for the part of Freddy Krueger off my neck was very, very strong.

Who knew kittens made such good wingmen?

"Jase Tugwater, reporting for biscuit duty," I said, grinning like the fool I was.

"Weirdo," she said, gently taking the white kitten from my arm and placing her back in her freshly cleaned cage. The kitten turned two circles on a fresh blanket, blinked her eyes, and fell back to sleep, her little paws extending and contracting.

Making biscuits.

"That's too fucking cute," I said as the murderer on my neck started purring, its massaging easing up as the purrs got louder. The orange cat had stopped its facial, so I shifted it into the crook of my elbow, where it immediately started purring.

"Dammit," Molly said, her hand on her forehead.

"What? I thought I was doing good? Is the purring not good?" I asked.

She took a breath as I held mine, not understanding what I'd done wrong.

"You're fucking perfect, you giant ass," she said, blowing out her breath as she took the two kittens and placed them in with the white kitten. Swinging around, she grabbed me by the shirt and pulled me towards her.

"I don't underst—"

"Just shut up and kiss me, Tug."

I HADN'T BEEN JOKING WHEN I SAID MY GENERAL MANAGER thought I was highly coachable. It had been a running theme since T-ball in the second grade. I could take direction better than nearly anyone, and if Molly wanted me to kiss her, I was going to kiss the ever-loving hell out of her.

A faint whiff of litter and cleaning supplies mixed with Molly's scent—lavender and cedar chips—as I tilted her head and teased her mouth with my tongue. She opened for me and I dove right in, accepting her invitation. I wasn't sure which one of us groaned, probably me, but my dick was hard, making my shorts uncomfortably tight.

*Easy, boy.* She had invited me for a kiss, not a fuck. I willed myself to slow down and focus on the task at hand— Molly's very kissable lips.

I shifted my hands to cup her neck, running a thumb down each side. Goosebumps grew under my fingers as her nipples hardened against my midsection.

Would playing with her tits be off limits for a kiss? I slid one hand down to test the waters, flicking her bud and then rolling it gently between my thumb and fingers.

"Fuck yes," she panted, pressing her breast into my hand. "More."

I could do more.

I ran my hand up and under the spaceship on her shirt, palming a breast over the soft cotton of her bra as I massaged her nipple with my thumb.

"Harder," she said on a breath, so I pinched.

"Fuck. Yes, that," she said, pushing on my shoulders, urging me down.

Tug Junior *loved* Take Charge Molly.

She lifted her shirt up and off, rewarding me with two perfectly shaped buds, begging for attention underneath her pale blue cotton bra. Far be it from me to disappoint.

I sucked one nipple into my mouth over the fabric, pulling and tugging between my teeth as I rolled the other between my fingers. My cock was growing painfully hard as I listened to the whimpers and other little noises coming from her mouth.

Which made me think about filling that sweet sounding mouth with my incredibly hard cock and seeing how much of me she could take. *One step at a time, Tug.*

I switched sides, giving her other nipple equal attention with my tongue and teeth. Between gasps, Molly pushed down on my shoulders.

Her wish was my command.

My free hand ran up one smooth leg, my thumb grazing her inner thigh, and Molly widened her stance. I looked around, desperate to find a place to lay her down so I could devour her pussy properly. Without the distraction of my bad knee screaming at me for kneeling on a hard floor.

"Meet-and-greet room, next door," Molly said, as if reading my mind, her hands running through my hair. "There's a bench."

"On it," I said, helping her up by her perfect ass. She wrapped her legs tightly around my core and barked out one word directions as she sucked and nipped my neck. I was going to have marks tomorrow, but fuck if I could care right now.

Entering the room, I placed her gently on the bench and she eased back, her knees falling apart as she opened for me. The room was basic. One window overlooking another room, two plastic purple chairs against one wall, and the bench where Molly was splayed out, her hands playing with her nipples.

"Fucking gorgeous," I said, thumbing open the button of her shorts and unzipping them.

"Please, Tug," she said, tugging at her nipples as she arched her back.

I crouched at the end of the bench, sliding her shorts down, and noticed movement in the window.

There, staring at us in what might have been horror, or possibly just curiosity, was a brown-and-black cat. It was standing in a cage, which gave it a perfect view into the room where I was about to strip Molly naked and make her scream my name. The cat's green eyes dropped to the bulge in my crotch and then back up at me. *Was it judging me?*

"Um, Molly?"

"If the next words out of your mouth aren't 'get naked' or 'you taste delicious' I don't want to hear them."

I looked at the cat, then back at Molly, her legs spread for me, a damp spot on her pink cotton panties. She smelled like fucking heaven. I looked back at the window. The cat meowed and pawed at the window.

*Fuuuck.*

"We have an audience."

"What?"

"We have an audience," I repeated, nodding at the window.

Molly tilted her head back. "Fucking judgmental cats," she muttered. "Please tell me you don't have stage fright."

"I… no, I just…" Holy blue balls. Could I really have sex with Molly while being judged by a ten-pound cat with better resting bitch face than my older sister?

No, no I could not.

I stood up.

"Come on, Tug, it's just a cat," Molly said, not moving.

I held out a hand. "I have a better idea."

She looked at my hand, then back at me, her brows furrowing.

"Trust me," I said.

"This better be worth it," she muttered, accepting my hand.

I gave her just enough time to tug her shorts back up before I bent at the waist and hefted her over my shoulder, marching us next door. Towards my bed in my tiny bedroom in the brewery. Without windows or curious cats.

It was going to be a tight squeeze to fit us both, but at least we wouldn't have a feline audience.

"I promise," I said, smacking her playfully on the ass and making quick work of the walk to the Catcher's Box.

19

MOLLY

*I* was hot and bothered. And wet.

So. Fucking. Wet.

I hadn't planned to end my evening hanging upside down and staring at Jase Tugwater's very fine ass because he promised me sex on something that wasn't a hard wooden bench. But I was going with it because the man definitely knew what he was doing in that department.

At least he had the last time we'd had sex. And as long as baseball wasn't the only thing he'd gotten better at in the last ten years, I was in for the ride of my life.

*Halle-fucking-lujah!* my vagina cheered.

Larry let out a bleat from behind us. I lifted my head and saw the wannabe cockblocker poke her head around the corner of the house.

"Shut your pie hole, Larry. Mama needs to get laid."

"What's that?" Jase asked as he stopped to unlock the gate.

"You should hurry. Larry looks like she wants to fuck around and find out."

"Ah, hell," he said, squatting so he could set me down. He

138

quickly shut and locked the gate, much to Larry's disappointment, as she bleated at us.

"Let's go," he said, grabbing my hand and dragging me into his brewery like a cave dweller. It was hot as fuck and I defied any feminist to disagree.

"We're trading a perfectly serviceable bench with… a bag of hops?" I asked, not really caring what the answer was as long as it ended with me riding the hell out of Jase's dick.

"What? No." He opened the back door and led me down a hallway towards the far end of the building. Flicking on a light, I saw a small bedroom, barely large enough for the double bed and a makeshift cardboard side table. "I wanted a place where I could do this properly."

He captured my face in his giant hands, his fingers nearly wrapping around my entire head. Those were going to feel *so* good inside me. If I could get him to stop talking long enough to get naked.

"I want to worship you, Molly."

I shimmied out of my shorts and stood before him in nothing but my cotton bra and panties, the former wet with Jase's saliva, the latter wet from how badly I wanted to come on this man's cock.

Grabbing him by the shirt, I shoved him towards the bed. "I don't want to be worshipped, Tug. I want to be fucked."

The blue in his eyes all but disappeared into a dark storm of lust. That was better.

"Condom?" I asked as I stripped the rest of the way and pulled Jase's shorts down to his knees. A very impressive dick greeted me, laying heavily on his torso, and my pussy throbbed with need.

*Patience, you needy little vixen.*

"Shorts," he all but grunted.

I dug around in his pockets until I found his wallet and tossed it on his chest. "Suit up."

A cocky grin lifted one side of his mouth as he followed instructions and rolled the condom on, stroking himself.

I licked my lips, wondering how much of him I could take in my mouth.

*Me first!* shouted my vagina.

I crawled on top of him and grabbed his dick with both hands, mimicking the way he'd stroked himself.

"Jesus, Molly," he cried out as he bucked into my hands.

Perfect.

I lifted myself and notched him right at the entrance of my pussy before slowly sliding down his length. My eyes rolled as I took him all in.

"Holy fuck," I whispered.

Stilling, he grabbed my hips, digging his fingers deep into my skin. Would it leave bruises? The idea thrilled a not-small part of me.

"Fuck, you're tight," he gritted out. "You... good?"

Was I good? Judging from the way my pussy kept spasming, I was about to have the orgasm of a lifetime with a man I'd spent years trying to forget.

I was... confused.

*I'm not!* sang my pussy as it clenched his dick and he grunted.

"So good," I answered, grinding my clit against him. "I need you to fuck me, Jase. Now."

Growling, he lifted me up and brought me down, fast and hard, as he rose to meet me.

"*Fuuuck...*" My eyes rolled into the back of my head. He was so deep, stretching parts of me that could have used a proper warm up before tonight's activities.

"Too much?" he asked as he slid one hand across my belly, circling my clit with his thumb.

"No," I said, barely getting the words out before he slammed into me again.

Spock help me.

I had picked this position, thinking Jase was going to hold back on me and I'd have control.

Oh, how wrong I was.

Jase was in full control. Of the pace. The intensity. My body. Everything. All I could do was hang on and wait for the oncoming train that was my orgasm.

"Don't stop," I gritted out between gasps.

"Wasn't gonna," he answered, his voice tight with concentration as he pounded into me. Lordy, this man could take directions. I met him thrust for thrust as my core tightened around him. Holy Klingons. If he got any deeper I'd be able to taste him.

This felt so fucking good. I missed this. I missed *him*.

Wait, what? No, I missed sex. Not Jase. He was just a penis. A large, gloriously talented penis that was about to make me come harder than I'd ever come in my life.

He swirled his thumb around my clit again and that was all it took to launch me into the stratosphere. A voice I assumed was mine screamed as tremors rocked me.

Jase sat up, still hard inside my very happy pussy, and kissed me. Softly.

*Oh, hell no.*

This was not soft-and-gentle, let-me-worship-you sex. This was supposed to be hard-and-fast, fuck-your-brains-out sex.

Instead of kissing him back, I grabbed his nipple and pinched, causing him to buck up inside of me and set off another round of spasms.

"*Fuuuck* that feels good," I moaned.

He kissed my neck.

Twist.

"Dammit, Molly," he said, standing up with me still impaled on his large member—*holy fuck, how hot is that*—

and I scrambled to wrap my legs around him before I slid off.

He spun us around and laid me on my back while he kneeled in front of me, grimacing for a split second. No way kneeling on the hardwood floor felt good on his knee. I moved to sit up to make room for him on the bed—*how in the hell did he sleep in something this small?*—but he grabbed both my wrists and pinned them above me.

"You want to be fucked?" he asked.

I had about a second to catch my breath and nod before he drove into me.

*Slam.*

"Gods, yes," I gasped, the sweet pain of Jase filling me.

"Then you'd better hold on."

That was all the warning I got before he started pumping. In and out, in and out, like a piston. My vagina was singing songs of worship at the punishment this man was doling out, and all I could do was grab his shoulders and enjoy the ride.

Jase slowed down just long enough to grab one leg and prop it up on his shoulder while he hooked my other leg with his arm, spreading me wide.

If someone had told me he could drive any deeper into me, I would have told them to fuck off. And I would have been very, very wrong.

"I know you're about to come again, Molly," he said, not slowing his pace even a little. "I can feel your pussy grabbing my dick, begging to come."

"Yes," I gasped.

"Then come," he commanded, his dick continuing its glorious assault, and my pussy obeyed.

"Fuck!" I cried out, stars bursting from behind my eyes, my entire body convulsing around him.

"Molly," Jase said as he grunted his own release.

I'd wanted to be fucked, and wow had this man delivered.

My limbs were overcooked noodles and my brain was a foggy mess of post-orgasm bliss. The weight of Jase's body as he draped over me, his breath still coming in bursts, felt nicer than I'd admit.

"Holy shit," he said, lifting himself off me and kissing my forehead. "Sorry if I was smothering you." He peppered my cheek and jaw with soft kisses as he made his way down my neck. Goosebumps followed the trail his mouth was leaving.

I should have felt smothered, if not by his weight, then by the tenderness of his movements. But I felt... fine. Happy even.

*What the hell was that all about?*

My heart pounded, but not from the exertion of multiple orgasms.

I pushed his shoulder. "Off." I needed to get out of here before I caught feelings. This was just supposed to be sex.

Jase moved, his eyes searching my face for an answer to a question I didn't want him to ask.

"Please," I said as I struggled to sit up.

"Did I do something wrong?"

"No, I just need to breathe," I answered in the most truthful way I could.

Jase stood and took a step back. "Ow! Shit!"

"What's wrong—?"

His knee buckled, and he fell, straight towards me.

I scrambled to move, but the blankets tangled around my feet. Kicking, I sat upright just as Jase lost his battle with gravity. Our heads collided and stars blinded me.

"Ow, fuck!"

"Shit," Jase swore as he rolled off me, landing on the floor with a loud thump. He held a hand to his head. "Are you okay?"

I touched my nose, gently, checking for blood. It throbbed like it was in a competition with my vagina but wasn't bleeding. I could, however, taste blood in my mouth. At least nothing felt broken.

"I dink tho," I said. Shit, maybe my nose *was* broken.

"Let me see your face," he said as he sat up, keeping his bad leg straightened in front of him. Rough hands brushed the hair out of my eyes and gently, more gently than I imagined someone with hands that size could be, he felt around my nose.

"Does this hurt?"

"A little," I said, pushing myself to a sitting position. "But I don't think it's broken."

I ran my tongue around the inside of my mouth to find the source of the blood. My tooth had cut the inside of my bottom lip. Great. I was probably going to wake up tomorrow morning with two black eyes and a fat lip. The rumor mill would have a heyday with this.

"How's your knee?" I asked as I looked around for my clothes. My panties were hiding under my left ass cheek and my shorts had somehow ended up across the floor. I tiptoed to my shorts, stopping on the way to swipe my bra.

Jase was rubbing the nasty scar that ran along the inside of his kneecap. "I'll live."

I finished getting dressed and handed Jase's shorts to him. Accepting them, he stood up carefully and dressed before limping over to me. He pressed a small kiss to my lips, and then my forehead.

"Promise you're not hurt?" he asked.

I rubbed my hands up and down his chest, coarse hair tickling my fingers, considering his question. It should be me asking him that. I wasn't the one who'd had a career-ending knee injury that I may have just made worse.

"Yep, all good. You?"

He kissed me again, lingering, and I let him. My heartbeat increased, reminding me of what was at stake.

"I'm fantastic," he whispered against my lips.

"I was talking about your knee," I said.

Jase bent his knee, wincing as it crackled. "This ol' war wound? A little ice and some Advil and I'll be ready for round two in no time."

Round two. As in, more sex. More time together without our clothes on.

*Count us in!* shouted every part of my body that had been worked over by the sex god limping around his bedroom looking for his shirt.

"Sorry if I didn't make this clear, Tug, but this was a one-time thing."

The look of disappointment that flashed across his face was hard to miss, even if it was only there for a brief second before being replaced by a smile that didn't quite reach his eyes.

"If that's what you want."

"It's what I want," I said, even as my ovaries threatened a coup. The words felt like a bad pair of dentures that didn't fit in my mouth.

Jase nodded, kissed me on the cheek, and walked out of the room, naked and limping, with that fine ass on display, making me instantly want to shout "just kidding!" and jump his bones again.

But that's not what this was. This was one and done. To get it out of my system.

So I let him go.

*Waaah!* cried my vagina.

*Same, girlfriend. Same.*

## 20

## MOLLY

$\mathcal{A}$wkward.

That was the only word that described my current predicament: standing shoulder to shoulder with Jase fucking Tugwater in a Sunshine Festival booth stuffed full of kegs and kittens while I tried to act like we hadn't had mind-blowing sex last night.

I adjusted my sunglasses which were necessary in the harsh Colorado sunshine that was gracing its namesake festival with its very best effort. They were also necessary to cover up the two black eyes I sported. Unfortunately for my nose, they rested on the exact spot Jase had nailed with his forehead in the broom closet he called a bedroom.

My bedroom wasn't large by any stretch, but there was room for sex without risking injury.

Not that I'd be doing that again anytime soon. *Once was enough*, I lied to myself as I bumped my arm against Jase. He was setting a stack of red plastic cups on the plywood table we were using to serve his beer and fill out paperwork for anyone willing to adopt a kitten today.

"Sorry," he said, limping to the supplies to grab a handful of pens decorated with his Catcher's Box Brewing Co. logo. As he arranged them in one of the plastic cups, his arm kept brushing against mine, sending shock waves straight down to my vagina, who was positively reveling in how small our booth was.

I took a half step to my left. To give him more room to work, not because I was two arm brushes and a sideways glance away from jumping him.

That was not the sort of booth aesthetic we were aiming for.

Jase looked at me, eyebrows raised in question, before turning back to the pens, turning them each so the logo faced outward.

"It's a festival booth, not an art show," I said, feeling grumpy now that we weren't touching anymore.

*I can fix that*, my vagina whispered.

"It's product placement," he replied.

"It's product placement," I mumbled in Jase's voice. Holy Klingons, I was annoying this morning.

For a brief moment, I had actually thought we could be friends. But *nooo*. I'd gone and fucked that up by sleeping with him, and now we were... awkward. *Good one, Molls. Hope the orgasms were worth it.*

I turned, forcing my face to relax , and watched the crowd navigate the aisles between the booths in the large field hosting the Sunshine Festival. Most were locals, but there were a fair number of tourists, too.

All the festivals used to be held in the small park in the middle of town. But the Sunshine Festival had grown too large for the park, so four years ago, I convinced the mayor to move it to the empty field on the edge of town. Right next to my shelter. It was the perfect space. Okay, yes. It was also convenient for me—less so after Larry realized she could get more attention, and therefore food, by screaming at all the festival goers walking by. But Jeff had snapped last year after listening to her scream all afternoon, so they dragged a chair next to the fence and offered five bucks to anyone walking by who could out scream the goat. Larry had been so offended by all the screaming, she didn't show her face for the rest of the festival.

This year, Jeff had set an empty metal folding chair out by the fence. It seemed the threat was enough to keep Larry under wraps. For now.

"There you are!" Jeff yelled at me, huffing and puffing down the dirt path in front of the line of booths.

Speak of the devil.

"Why are you all the way back here?" Tyson asked.

"Why are you scowling?" Jeff asked. "Did we miss the beer?"

They dug into the belt purse attached to their waist and pulled out a tulip-shaped beer glass with a flourish. It had a silhouette of their face etched on the front of the glass, complete with bun and beard.

"You brought your own glass?" I asked. My nose throbbed uncomfortably. I wanted to shift my sunglasses, but didn't need the nosy twins to ask questions I didn't feel like answering.

"You didn't?" they asked, holding out their glass to Jase, who looked like he was going to give himself a hernia holding in a laugh.

"Keg is ready to rock and roll as soon as the cannons fire at two," he finally spit out, placing a soft hand on my waist as he reached behind me for something I couldn't see without turning around and creating more contact between us. *Gah!* Why was he always so fucking close?

Was he doing this on purpose? Just to torture me? He didn't seem to notice that he was touching me. Meanwhile, my ovaries were overheating, and my vagina was threatening a meltdown.

*Sweet baby Spock, somebody help me.*

"Two o'clock? Why so late?" Jeff asked, waving their beer glass around as Tyson gently redirected their arm down.

"Uh," I replied intelligently, thanks to all my lady parts hijacking the higher functions of my brain to concentrate on Jase's hand, which was still very much on my waist. For the love of Picard, why was he still touching me?

Jase eased back and removed his hand, giving my body a bit of breathing room and my brain access to my words again. *Finally!*

"Candice fucking Shoowater," I finally answered.

My nemesis had surprised all the booth sponsors selling alcohol—ours included—with an email yesterday afternoon, notifying them that serving alcoholic beverages before 2 p.m. was now prohibited at the festival.

I had been counting on Jase's beer sales to keep a steady stream of interest in my adoptables throughout the day, especially since Candice had relegated us to a space in a back corner that got little foot traffic.

Jase showed up this morning with a two-story kitten funhouse to help draw attention to our booth. Thanks to the blue tarp we put over it to create much needed shade, it looked like a double-decker circus tent filled with twelve tiny demons who were currently busy chasing bugs and each other in between battling blades of grass that dared to move in the soft summer breeze.

It was also a very large reason there was exactly zero room to move around one another without touching. The thing was enormous. Good for the kittens. Bad for my libido.

"Well, Candy can eat my armpit hair," Jeff said.

"You don't have armpit hair," I replied. "You shave it during the summer."

"Well, then she can eat my shaved armpit hair," Jeff replied, shoving their glass under Jase's nose. "Fill 'er up, Baseball King."

"I really don't think—" Jase said.

"Pish," Jeff said. "If Dandy Candi wants to try to police when I get to consume alcohol, then she's going to have a hell of a time finding a stylist in this town who will fix up that god awful root situation she has going on." They waved their glass back and forth before Jase took it, eyebrows raised at me.

"It's ten o'clock in the morning," I pointed out to my friend before turning to their husband. "Do something with them," I said to Tyson.

Tyson just shrugged. "It's not like anyone can prove where they got it, since it's their glass."

"Ha," Jeff said triumphantly.

Jase limped his way back to the keg.

"What happened to your knee?" Tyson asked as Jase hobbled back and handed Jeff their glass, half full of an amber beer that I knew tasted like heaven.

Then he did something completely inexcusable and stood behind me. He was close enough for me to lean back into him. Into the strength I knew he carried, even with a bad knee. An injured knee I may have caused when I didn't insist he join me on the tiny bed last night because I wanted him to finish fucking me senseless.

"Spent too much time kneeling on it yesterday," he said, his breath warm across my cheek as I did my best impersonation of someone whose pussy he didn't punish like the dirty, dirty girl I was less than twenty-four hours ago.

Jeff took a sip of the beer, their pinkie lifted, and they

smacked their lips. "Delicious," they said. "I approve this for sale."

"Gee, thanks," Jase deadpanned.

I couldn't take the throbbing any longer—my nose, not my vagina, not that it was any less insistent right now—and adjusted my sunglasses, which slipped from my nose and off my face. Shit.

"Mike Tyson on a popsicle stick. What happened to your face?" Jeff asked.

Tyson looked at me, concern etching across his eyes. Then he did the worst thing he could have done. He looked at Jase's knee. Then back to me. His lips spread slowly into a grin.

Damn it. He knew. I don't know how, but he knew.

"I, uh, got hit in the face by, um… Larry," I said lamely, bending to pick up my sunglasses, hoping they weren't too scratched to keep wearing.

"Larry, huh?" Tyson asked, the smirk on his face all but shouting that he knew it was a big fat lie.

Jase turned to the side, favoring his bad knee, which made him lean into me. My eyes closed briefly at the contact, remembering what his weight felt like against me last night.

"Oh. Em. Gee!" Jeff squealed.

I opened my eyes. Jeff was staring at me, mouth open.

"You guys had sex," they said, pointing a finger at me, sloshing beer down the side of their glass. "You had sex!"

"Shhh!" I replied, looking around but not seeing anyone. Seems like Candice did me a favor after all, sticking me in no-man's-land.

Not quite ready to face my friends with the truth, I turned and grabbed a black kitten who, in all the excitement, had climbed up the cage wall.

Jase, bizarrely unaffected by our nearness, reached around me, his chest rubbing against my back in a move that should not have been as erotic as it felt, and took the little orange kitten who was trying to mount an escape. It closed its eyes in bliss as Jase gave it a chin scratch.

I'd never been more jealous of a cat in my life.

*Purr*, my vagina said.

*Stop that.*

"We did not have sex," I whispered, readjusting the black kitten in my hands as it tried to wriggle free. Jase looked at me, a flash of disappointment darkening his stupidly handsome face, and I swallowed a wad of guilt that clung to the back of my throat.

"You not only had sex," Jeff said, putting their nearly empty glass down on the plywood table with a thud. "But you had kinky sex."

"What?"

"You both have sex injuries. Ergo, kinky sex."

"Or a small-ass bedroom," I muttered.

"I knew it!" Jeff shouted.

Jase was cuddling the orange kitten, a giant smile lighting up his face like he couldn't think of anywhere else he'd rather be.

I was silently praying for the Enterprise to beam me the hell out of here. Unfortunately, the crew of the Enterprise had better things to do than worry about my mortification.

A family of tourists made their way down the path and Tyson took pity on us and took his spouse by the arm. "Let's go see who else is giving out free samples, love."

Jeff hesitated, looking back and forth between me and Jase, before finally narrowing their eyes at me.

"Fine, but I expect details." They snuggled into Tyson's side. "P.S. I'm happy for you," they stage whispered before they both headed off to their next victims.

"Didn't have sex, huh?" Jase asked, the sound low and deep, as he deposited the orange kitten back into the circus tent, where a tabby with way too many whiskers for its tiny face tackled it. They went rolling along the grass, a tumble of raucous innocence, as I stood, unsure of how to respond.

Why was I denying it? As my friends proved, they supported my right to an orgasm. So what was stopping me from owning up to my actions? It was just sex. Amazing, ruin me for all other partners, sex, but still just sex. I had nothing to be ashamed of. Especially since it would not happen again.

*Boo-hoo-hoo!* cried my vagina.

*We'll have sex again.*

Someday. Maybe.

I turned to Jase. "Look, I'm sorry—"

"Kitties!" interrupted a small, screaming child.

Jase eyed me, eyebrows slightly raised, like I'd surprised him. *Join the party, friend.*

"Looks like we have our first official customers," he said, nodding towards the family that was now in front of our booth.

"Right," I said. I had kittens to re-home, and a shelter to keep in the black. I didn't have time to rehash a one-time lapse in judgment that led to two black eyes and a whole lot of confusion.

Except I really, really didn't want to spend the next two days shoulder-to-shoulder with a man whose very presence turned my insides into a burning bowl of lust, pretending nothing had happened when something very much had happened.

*Big girl panties, Molly.*

"No, not right," I said, squaring my shoulders to the man as best I could with a squirming kitten in my arms. "We should talk about last night," I said, rushing to get all my words out before another interruption.

"Okay." He crossed his impressive arms in front of his more impressive chest.

"Mom! Look!" said the previously screaming kid, tugging on the sleeve of the white woman next to her. "Can we pet?"

"You bet," I said, opening the cage and grabbing the first kitten within reach.

So much for my big girl panties.

21

JASE

*I* folded my arms and leaned against the makeshift counter as Molly walked the family through the adoption paperwork for the kitten. According to the young girl who couldn't stop jumping up and down with excitement, she was going to name it Black Cat. Or Squiggles. Or Cotton Candy.

The poor kitten was going to suffer an identity crisis before it hit adulthood.

Molly placed the kitten in a collapsible cardboard carrier and handed it to the family. "Congratulations," she said.

Waving at them as they left, I turned back to Molly, my knee twinging at the slight movement. I regretted not listening to my knee last night when it was screaming at me to move to the bed. But I did not regret a single other thing about the evening. Except maybe how it ended. And Molly's black eyes.

When I'd turned up this morning and saw the damage, it took everything I had not to reach for her, take her home and take care of her.

But then I remembered how she'd ended one of the best damned nights of my life. I had wanted to plead with Molly to change her mind. To give us another chance. Instead, I'd walked away because that's what she wanted.

Even if it killed me to admit it, something told me my best chance with Molly was to give her the time and space she needed to work through everything. Well, time I could definitely give her. But thanks to the size of our booth, there was no way I could give her space.

Not that I was complaining.

I studied her as she bent down to put the adoption paperwork in the tote stowed next to the cat castle, which I had to say was a stroke of genius. I'd been to a lot of places in this big world, but I'd never seen a double-decker fun house for cats, built entirely from scraps from my own construction projects. Even Suzi-Q would be proud.

Molly straightened up, and I jerked my head away, looking at anything but that perfectly shaped ass. Not that it mattered. She was ignoring me. Again. This woman's ability to ignore what was right in front of her was maddening. But she'd breached the silence. She'd said she wanted to talk.

So we were going to talk.

"I'm waiting," I said, taking small pleasure in the way she stiffened, but impressed when she turned and met my gaze.

"I don't want what happened last night to make things… weird. Between us, I mean."

"Neither do I."

We were on the same page. This was good. I could work with this.

She let out a breath and a small smile appeared on her beautiful face before she adjusted her sunglasses. "Good," she said. "Then we're agreed. It can't happen again."

The fuck?

"No," I said.

"No, it can't happen again?" Her eyebrows lifted.

"No, we're not agreed."

Her eyebrows changed course and scrunched her forehead together.

"Tug, we can't do that again."

"Agree to disagree."

"I'm serious."

"Same."

She crossed her arms, causing her perfect tits to lift. I could still feel and taste them, the memory of it burned into me, and I shifted my stance.

"Damn it, Tug."

"Damn it, Molly." I mimicked her stance, ignoring the protest from my knee as I put weight on it.

She opened her mouth but was interrupted when two tiny women tottered up to us, one light skinned, one dark skinned, both shrink-wrapped by time. The duo was dressed like they were on their way to the senior buffet at a Vegas casino. The white woman had bright blue hair permed within an inch of her life and wore a satin tracksuit that matched the tint of her hair perfectly. Her counterpart also wore a tracksuit, this one a jade green color. It made the silver hair that framed her face like a soft cloud look almost ethereal.

"Yoo-hoo! Hey girly!" the blue-haired woman yodeled as she waved in their direction.

"Mrs. Kowalski," Molly said, pushing her sunglasses all the way up her face, completely hiding her black eyes. She turned to the other woman. "Mrs. Benson."

"Aren't you going to introduce us to your boy toy?" Mrs. Kowalski asked, giving me a waggle of her thinly lined eyebrows as Mrs. Benson nodded up and down like a bobble head, sizing me up like an all-you-can-eat buffet. I'd been the object of more than my fair share of "cougars" during my time in the majors. These two miniature women put every one of them to shame.

"He's not my boy toy," Molly said.

I held out a hand to Mrs. Kowalski. "Jase Tugwater." Her bony hand was stronger than I would have guessed, as she shook my hand with enthusiasm. I turned to Mrs. Benson and offered my hand. She didn't have quite the grip her friend had, but what she lacked in strength she more than made up for in enthusiasm.

"You can be my boy toy," Mrs. Benson said, smiling.

A sharp pain radiated from my backside. "What the hell?" I squeaked, looking over my shoulder and rubbing my ass. Something—*or someone*—had pinched me. Please let it be a kitten and not one of the wrinkle twins.

Mrs. Benson was looking at me like I was a Denny's special.

*Help!* I mouthed to Molly over her head.

Molly's lips twisted as she stifled a laugh. Easy for her to laugh. She wasn't the one being felt up by an octogenarian.

"Let's try to get through the festival without another harassment claim, shall we, ladies?" Molly said, taking pity on me and gently extracting Mrs. Benson's knobby hand from my backside.

"Spoil sport," Mrs. Benson said.

"Come on, Bennie," Mrs. Kowalski said. "Let's go tell everyone about your new boy toy!"

She hooked arms with Grabby Hands Benson as they shuffled down the path, probably off to molest some other poor unsuspecting soul.

"Thanks for the save," I said, still rubbing my ass. "I mean, I'm sure they're harmless, but—"

"Oh, they're the opposite of harmless," Molly replied.

I shuddered at the thought of those two shuffling their way through the festival, pinching asses.

"I'm sure they're nothing you can't handle," she said, giggling.

"I'd rather not find out," I said as I turned my attention to all the animals we'd brought this morning, grabbing two kittens who had been playing in the water dish. One kitten immediately crawled onto my shoulder while the other began licking the stubble on my face.

Molly's lips pursed together as she scowled at me.

"What did I do now?" I palmed the kitten on my shoulder, and bent to place it back into the funhouse, swallowing the grunt as my knee buckled with the motion.

The kitten jumped on a fuzzy yellow ball that jingled when it moved. The noise caught the attention of the kitten licking my face, who launched itself off my chest towards the ball. It missed spectacularly and rolled a few times before righting itself and pouncing on a sleeping black kitten.

"Stop looking so…"

"Hot?" I supplied, straightening. "Tasty? Fuckable?"

I lowered my voice to a soft growl for that last one and watched her mouth open in surprise, right before her scowl grew more scowl-y. It was fucking adorable.

"Knock it off, Tug." She grabbed the towel we'd placed on the ground as a makeshift bed for the kitties and shook the grass and dirt off it.

"Look, Molly," I said, doing the same with another towel, as a black-and-white kitten tried to swing from it. "I get you want space, and I'm happy to give it to you." I extracted the ninja kitten from the towel and placed them both back in the cage before securing the door. "But I don't see why we can't, you know."

She turned towards me, hands on her hips. That stubborn tilt to her chin signaling she was about to give me some excuse that she'd concocted to avoid the feelings we were both feeling, but only I had the courage to acknowledge.

"Because we barely know each other, Tug," she said, her voice cracking, knocking the wind out of my waiting rebuttal.

"Molly," I said. A scream from the bowels of hell disrupted the rest of my thought.

"Oh, no," Molly said, turning towards her fence. "Please, not this year."

*Bleeeeht!* replied the goat.

"Jeff!" Molly hollered.

"Was that Jeff screaming?"

"No, you idiot. That was Larry. Jeff!"

"On it!" Jeff yelled from two rows behind us and a cheer rang out.

"Fuck me," muttered Molly.

Jeff breezed by, their skinny legs churning up the ground as they unzipped their fanny pack and whipped out a stack of bills.

"Not today, Satan's moll," they said, plopping themself onto the metal chair that had been sitting next to the fence all morning.

Larry yelled at Jeff, who looked completely unfazed as they peeled a bill off the stack and waved it in front of the first person in a line that had quickly formed in front of them. It was currently a dozen people deep, but I watched as more people walked over and joined the line.

A woman faced Larry, who was jumping and kicking her back feet out behind her. Larry stilled as the woman took a deep breath, her back bending, face up to the sky, and she let out a scream that would have made Xena, Warrior Princess, turn tail and run.

Larry flicked her tail and screamed back.

"Maybe next year, Doreen," Jeff said before turning to the man behind Doreen.

"What the actual fuck?" I turned to Molly. "What's going on?"

"What?" Molly asked as the dude yelled out his best Bigfoot impersonation. Not to be outdone, Larry hollered back.

"What is happening?" I asked, louder this time.

"Every year—" Molly spoke a few more words, drowned out by the goat. "—and they scream—" followed by more unheard words.

Another scream sounded from the fence line. Whether from human or goat was anybody's guess.

It was impossible to have a conversation. How in the hell were we supposed to adopt out any animals? Or sell beer? How was I supposed to convince Molly we were worth another shot before she convinced herself otherwise?

*Bleeeaht!*

*"Ahhhhhhh!"*

Christ. Despite every survival instinct in my body telling me to keep my distance, I walked into Molly's space, favoring my knee, which was threatening to lock up on me, and leaned in close.

She tried to pull back, but the two-story cat castle blocked her retreat. *Good.*

"We're not done with this conversation, Molly," I said, my mouth so close to her ear I could reach out my tongue and lick her neck. Nibble on that soft spot behind her lobe that I found out last night made her whimper.

"Yes, we are," she answered, but the waver in her voice suggested she wasn't as confident.

"No, we're not," I said. The scent of lavender and cedar

that was all Molly nearly overwhelmed my self-control. "And do you know why?"

I watched as she swallowed and shook her head, her slender neck all but begging for my attention. She wasn't ready. Not yet. But when she was, I'd be here. Ready. And more than fucking willing.

"Because when you change your mind—"

"If," she argued, her voice soft, as if even she didn't believe it.

"I'm going to spread you out on my bed and feast on you."

I couldn't hear much over the caterwauling from the field, but I could see the rise in her chest as she gasped at my declaration.

"I'm going to go slow, tasting every fucking inch of you, so you have plenty of time to realize how good we are together, Molly."

Easing back, her breath came in short bursts, the cool breeze filling in the space between us. "But only when you're ready."

I hobbled a step back, my knee definitely protesting the hours of standing I'd already done and the hours more that were yet to come. Molly tracked my movements, her pupils dilated, as she licked her bottom lip.

*Don't touch, don't touch, don't touch.*

"I'll be waiting," I said, turning around, feeling pretty damned pleased with myself.

*Bleeeaht!*

"Fucking Larry," I said.

"Fucking Larry," Molly said.

"What the fuck, Molly?" said a voice that didn't belong in this conversation.

I turned towards the front of the booth.

Candice Shoowater stood, hand on one hip, leg jutted out, glaring at Molly.

"Candice," I said, drawing her attention away from a glaring Molly. "Here to adopt a kitten?"

"A beer to cut the clown!" she yelled over the scream of a large woman.

"What?" I shouted before Larry could rebut.

"I'm here to shut you down," she repeated in the silence.

*Ah. Damn.*

# MOLLY

*I* didn't have time for this. Not when Jase's confession left my mind, and lady parts, reeling over all the ways and places he would fuck me senseless.

Except he hadn't said that. He said he was going to take his time. Feast on me.

*Lay us out and dive right in,* my vagina moaned, overcome by happiness and making it very hard to focus on anything else. What was I doing again?

"Did you hear me, Molly?" Candice screeched over the top of Larry. "You need to shut this booth down now!"

Oh, right. Candice fucking Shoowater was here. Threatening to ruin me. Again.

"Over my dead body," I muttered as I adjusted my sunglasses and glanced over at Jeff, making sure there was no evidence of the beer they'd talked us into an hour ago. All I could see was Jeff, their stack of five dollar bills, and a line of people much longer than last year's.

No beer. No beer glass.

Good.

"What's your problem this time?" I asked, knowing Candice wouldn't leave without having her say.

A portly tourist screamed at Larry while someone, probably his wife, filmed the contest on her phone. Larry screamed back, but not as loudly. She was clearly losing some of her steam. Thank Spock. Jeff handed five bucks to the guy, who turned and waved it at the camera, grinning from ear to ear.

Despite all the screaming, I wasn't that annoyed because while Jeff was busy handing out money, they were also talking up the rescue. Last year's contest netted me a cool thousand dollars in extra donations. Judging by the size of this year's line, I'd easily clear that.

"Are you really going to let that continue?" Candice asked, glaring at Jeff and Larry.

"It's either that, or let Larry scream at everyone for the next two days. Pick your poison," I responded.

"That goat is a menace to society," Candice snapped. "And Jeff's no better. I don't know what Tyson sees in them."

I looked over at Jeff. They were handing money to one of the high school baseball players, but watching me. *You okay?* they mouthed.

I nodded once.

"I do," I replied. And I did. Jeff was good people. Jeff was *my* people.

Candice rolled her eyes but stayed silent, showing more self-preservation than I would have guessed.

No one messed with Jeff and Tyson and got away with it. I'd take a fucking bullet for them. Not anywhere vital, but definitely in a fleshy part.

Jase had slid behind me during the exchange. I hadn't seen him or heard him, impressive given the hitch in his gait. But I knew he was there, all the same. Something about his presence made the air around me hum and my vagina vibrate.

Peeking over my shoulder, I congratulated my senses for being right. His legs were wide, his arms crossed, staring down Candice like I had seen him stare down batters. Not that I'd admit to watching his games.

"Can we help you?" Jase asked, stepping around me and using his size to block most of my view of the blond menace. His shoulders looked like boulders across a wide expanse of back muscles as he stared down my nemesis.

*Picard save me.* Why did he have to look so good all the time?

I glanced down at myself. I had what I hoped was just kitten poop on my sleeve. Dirt and scabs from old kitten scratches dotted my legs—legs which had a few days' worth of hair growth on them. I'd meant to shave this morning but forgot. Hair blew around my face, tangling in my sunglasses. The braid I'd attempted this morning was already falling to pieces.

I was a big, fat mess.

While Candice had a perfect top knot, white shorts without a spot on them—*how in the hell did people manage that?* —and a bright green satin tank that barely contained the girls. She probably even remembered to shave her legs last night, the put-together bitch.

"You can pack up all your stuff and head out," Candice replied.

"On what basis?" I asked as I leaned around Jase's broad shoulders. Candice's arms were also crossed, her cleavage standing tall and proud.

"I heard you were selling beer before two o'clock." Candice's lips pursed and her eyebrows raised. She looked every inch the woman who was used to getting her way about everything.

"You heard? From who?" I asked, keeping my eyes on Candice and not Jeff.

"Bob Mulhoney told me he heard Nikki Jones talking to her boyfriend about someone walking around with a glass full of beer."

I looked at her, praying Jase would do the same and not blow this. "That's it?"

"That's enough."

"That's bullshit," Jase said. I cracked a grin, unable to stop myself.

"Excuse me?" Candice said, her hand flying to her chest.

"You can come look at the keg. It's untapped." Jase was pointing to the keg which I very much had seen him tap earlier. At some point this morning, he'd removed the hose from the keg, which I didn't realize could be done. Score one for the beer man.

"And as you can see from the payment jar," he continued, gesturing to the empty plastic pickle jug on the counter, "there are no beer tokens. So no sales."

"Well," Candice said, tapping a foot. "Bob is very reliable." Some of her vibrato had gone from her voice.

"Bob is as reliable as a wet paper sack," I countered. "The only reason he has a shot at winning the election for mayor is because he's running unopposed."

Candice narrowed her eyes at me. Candice might be pissed, but she knew I was right. Bob Mulhoney owned the grocery store, but his wife was the reason they kept the lights on. Bob couldn't manage his own bowel movements without help.

"Plus, we're using plastic cups," Jase said, pointing to the stack he'd meticulously lined up earlier. "Not glasses. Didn't you say someone was drinking from a glass?"

*Thank you, Jeff, you little diva!*

"That's right. No glasses here." I shrugged. "Against the

festival rules. Wouldn't want it breaking and hurting someone."

Candice looked like a bull ready to charge at a waving red cape, but she couldn't figure out which one of us was holding it. I could practically see steam coming out of her ears.

"You two think you're clever," she said, pointing a finger at me, then Jase. "But I will figure out what's going on. And when I do—"

*BLEAAAT!*

"Jesus, Molly. Do something about that intolerable pain in the ass!" Candice turned on her heels and marched back towards the rest of the festival.

"Hey!" I shouted. "She might be an intolerable pain in the ass, but she's *my* intolerable pain in the ass!"

"Nicely played," Jase said, leaning on his good leg but standing shoulder to shoulder with me as we watched the actual intolerable pain in the ass yell at someone standing in her path.

Shoulder to shoulder. Like he had not only my back, but Jeff's too.

*He's perfect!* cooed her ovaries.

The fuck he was. But there was something about the way he stood there, with me—not in front, not behind, *next* to me. I could almost believe he'd follow me into a fire.

"Thanks," I said, a small smile peeking from my lips.

Jase turned and greeted the couple who'd walked up to our booth. Kenny Rogers and his fiancé, Ginger Mulhoney, Bob's youngest daughter, who thankfully took after her mother. They were a few years younger than me, but Kenny had been a mechanic at my dad's garage since high school, and he had finally bought it last year. He was practically a brother.

Jase held up an orange kitten. "You guys looking for a

new family member?" he asked, turning on the Tugwater charm that had crowned him the King of Baseball.

I pulled my phone out of my back pocket and texted Jeff.

Me: need me to call tyse to relieve you

Jeff: I got this. You survive Hurricane Candy?

Me: barely

Me: she heard a rumor about someone drinking beer

Jeff: <eye roll emoji> some people think rules don't apply to them

I grinned

Me: you would follow me into a fire right

Jeff: absolutely

Jeff: As long as it's one of those streaming fire videos on YouTube and not an actual fire. My hair wilts in extreme heat

I chuckled. I could live with that. They loved their hair almost as much as they loved Tyson. It was a high bar.

Jase looked over his shoulder at me, a grin on his own face, and my vagina started blowing kisses at him. Stupid, handsome jerk who defended Jeff.

"How's it going?" I asked Kenny and Ginger, ignoring Jase's attention and the heat building in my lower regions.

Ginger was holding the fluffy orange kitten I had nicknamed Brutus because he was nearly twice the size of the other kittens his age. Kenny had a tabby in his arms. By the white points on its ears, it was probably Arwen.

"Hey, Molly," Kenny said. "Nice sunglasses."

I pushed the glasses up my nose, which didn't appreciate the pressure, but it could just deal with it. I didn't need more people knowing about my black eyes.

"They're trying to decide which kitten they want," Jase said, leaning a hip against the cage. "I told them they should get both."

"That seems like a lot of… well, kittens," Ginger said.

"It does," I agreed as Jase's brows furrowed. "But actually, adopting two kittens together isn't much more work than adopting one. They're social creatures by nature, so adopting two means they always have a playmate or someone to cuddle with, even if you're not there."

"Maybe," said Kenny.

"Think about how convenient that will be, say, on mornings when you want to sleep in," Jase said.

"Or on your honeymoon," I added, keeping the attention on the couple.

"Hey! Congratulations," Jase said, his perfect, annoying smile growing.

"Plus, you can always foster," I said to Ginger. That's right. Focus on the couple. Not on Jase and his mouth and what he promised me he would do with it. "That way, you can have some time to decide before you commit."

I had plenty of space at Happy Tails, thanks to the new room that was now an official part of my lease. But one of the easiest ways to convince someone that an animal—or animals in this case—was right for them was to let them foster. No strings attached.

"Oh," said Ginger. "We hadn't considered that."

"Fosters get first shot at adoption," Jase added. I looked at him, my eyebrows raised. He shrugged his shoulders. "I read the handouts while we were setting up," he whispered, nodding towards the stack of paperwork I'd prepared for potential adopters.

*Hot* and *attentive*, my vagina said.

*Mmm, the total package,* my ovaries agreed.

"Yeah," said Kenny, a grin forming on his face as Ginger nodded at him. "We can do that."

"Great," I said. "Let me get a foster application for you to complete."

Ten minutes later, Kenny and Ginger left with two happy kittens safe in a cardboard crate, headed to their forever home, even if Kenny and Ginger didn't know it yet.

"We make a pretty good team," Jase said, nudging my shoulder with his elbow.

I scratched my nose, wincing at the sharp pain as I considered my reply.

We had made a great team. Between thwarting Candice's scheme to shut us down, and convincing Kenny and Ginger to take two kittens, we'd played off one another pretty damn well.

I looked up at him. He looked pleased with himself.

Bumping him back, I let a smile loose. "Yeah, we did."

He bent down and kissed my forehead. As much as I wanted to hate the gesture, I didn't.

I wanted more.

"Come on," I said, as more and more people made their way down our aisle. "We've got kittens to adopt."

The sound of a cannon came across loudspeakers set up throughout the site, signaling the time was two o'clock. A cheer rang out throughout the festival.

"And beer to sell," I added.

"Yes, ma'am," he said, saluting and hobbling his way over to the front of the booth, toothy grin on full display.

Spock help anyone who tried to resist it. I sure as hell couldn't.

## 23

## MOLLY

I waved. "Thanks for stopping by, Mrs. Chen," I said. A large black cat walked next to her, wearing a harness attached to a leash attached to the older woman's paisley fanny pack.

"People always walk their cats in this town?" Jase asked, drawing another beer for the person next in line.

"Just Mrs. Chen. She adopted Teddy from me three years ago, after her husband died. They go everywhere together."

I loved being able to arrange an adoption in town. It meant I'd get to see the animal again. Usually because I was passing by their house on my way somewhere, but occasionally, like today, they stopped by to let me know how great their new family member was doing.

Jase handed the beer to Heath Hennigar, the high school gym teacher who'd been patiently standing in line while Mrs. Chen had been regaling us with Teddy's newest obsession, DIY channels. Jase made a funny face when she'd mentioned the name of the show, *Everything Evie*, but stayed silent.

"Thanks for stopping by," he said as Heath dropped a drink token in the plastic pickle jug. The cannon had only rung out an hour ago, but there was a good number of tokens at the bottom. By the time the festival had ended last night, the jug had been nearly full. And all my kittens had found homes. I only hoped today was as successful.

"That's my line," I muttered, staring at him from behind my sunglasses that were still hiding bruises that, thankfully, were more purple than black today. At least the swelling and pain in my nose had gone away overnight.

"It's a good line. I decided to steal it," Jase said, nudging me with his shoulder. He'd been doing a lot of that lately. Touching. A gentle nudge to my shoulder. A soft hand at my waist. It was maddening how badly I wanted to strip down and let him touch me everywhere.

*Do it!* cheered my vagina.

I was considering the merits of that suggestion when Kole walked up to the booth.

"Hey, Molly," he said in his deep, gruff, baritone voice.

"Hey, Kole."

"Jase," he said, offering a hand to Jase.

"Kole," Jase replied, shaking his hand. "You here for a beer or a puppy?" he joked.

"I'll take a beer," he said. "Allergic to dogs."

"How about bunnies?" I asked as Jase pulled a beer for Kole.

"You have a bunny?" Kole asked.

Jase's eyebrows shot up in surprise as I turned towards the cage to hide my smile. Kole may look like a prison escapee, but behind the tattoos and perpetual scowl on his face was a soul as kind and soft and sweet as the gray bunny I gently lifted from the cage.

"Meet Tofu," I said, turning to Kole.

Tofu kicked her back feet and wriggled like she wanted down.

Kole smiled at the furry little ball and ran a sausage roll finger lightly down the bunny's back, instantly calming Tofu.

"Hey little thing," he cooed in his deep baritone voice.

Tofu stretched out towards the giant. Kole obliged and took her from me as he continued to stroke her fur.

Love at first sight.

"I had one almost this color as a kid," he said. He continued to stroke Tofu, making me think that confession was for the bunny, not for me or Jase.

Jase looked over at me, his mouth falling open in surprise. I shrugged. If the dude liked bunnies, who was I to judge? Especially if I could convince him to adopt this one.

Larry bleated softly from behind my shed. She'd been hiding most of the day, only peeking out once early this morning when I carried dog food to my car. A skinny kid barely into his teens had won yesterday's yelling contest. Chasing Larry away had earned him twenty bucks from Jeff and a free milkshake from the Shack Attack Grill, who'd gotten in on the fun yesterday and promoted the contest from their booth. They promised me a big donation at the end of the festival and told Jeff they'd sponsor next year's contest. I almost felt sorry for Larry.

*Bleaaaat!*

Almost.

Jase handed Kole a beer, who adjusted the bunny so he could hold her in one arm.

"Aww," said a teenager as she walked past the booth with a group of friends. "Look at the sweet bunny!"

Kole ignored the group and took a drink of the beer. "Good balance," he said, nodding at Jase. "Don't suppose you'd be interested in letting me sell this at my café?"

Jase's face lit up like the Fourth of July. "I think we could come to an arrangement."

"Come to an arrangement?" I teased, shaking my head.

"I've got some paperwork here, if you're interested in keeping Tofu," I said to Kole, pulling the adoption packet from the stack next to the kitten castle and setting it on the countertop. "No pressure."

"Oh, honey, look at that sweet dog!" Two men walked past, hand-in-hand. They rubber-necked past the booth but didn't stop.

After miraculously adopting out all the kittens yesterday, I decided to showcase some of my other animals today. Besides Tofu, I'd brought four small- to medium-sized dogs and two large breed dogs. All of whom had been there all day. I'd had lots of people stop by, saying they were interested only to leave with a "Let me think about it."

Was it really too much to ask of the universe for a single fucking adoption today?

"Shit," Kole said, setting down the beer, the sudden movement causing Tofu to wriggle. "What time is it?"

"Just after three o'clock," Jase replied.

"Can I come back later?" Kole asked, handing the bunny back to me.

"Let me guess," I said, mimicking the words said to me a hundred times today. "You need to think about it."

One more disappointment today. I wasn't surprised, given how the day was going, but it still stung coming from my favorite barista.

"Tell you what," Jase said. "You adopt Tofu today and your first beer at the Catcher's Box is free on opening day."

"I don't need your help," I grumbled at him.

"Maybe not, but Kole might," he whispered back.

Sexy and insightful. The man was infuriatingly competent.

*Infuriatingly hot*, my vagina corrected.

On that, we could agree.

"What? No," Kole said. "I am coming back for this sweet

girl. I left Conner Leftee in charge of my booth so I could come over and see if this beer was as good as everyone said it was."

I watched as Jase puffed his chest ever so slightly at the compliment. I wanted to run my hands over the rock-hard planes and—no. *No.*

*Spoilsport*, grumbled my lady parts.

"I need to get back before he breaks Lucile," Kole finished.

"Lucile?" Jase asked.

"My espresso maker," Kole replied.

Jase grinned like he'd just made a new friend. "Named my beer tanks Rosita and Junior."

The men nodded at each other like that made any kind of sense.

"Men are weird," I said to Tofu, placing her back in the cage, squealing on the inside at the fact that at least one of my animals was going to a good home today. Even if it meant Jase had helped by pulling out the *I'm a big-time baseball star* thing to do it.

I handed Kole the folder. "Just fill this out and bring it back with you after the festival is over."

Kole smiled, a look that seemed strange on the otherwise stoic man, and walked back the way he came.

"He left his beer," Jase said.

"He wasn't here for the beer. At least not *just* the beer," I replied, smiling. "He was here for the bunny."

"How did you know?"

"About every third person you've served today has mentioned the bunny. There's no way Kole didn't hear about it."

Score one for the Harmony Springs busybodies, using their power for good for once.

"Did I hear that if you adopt an animal today, you get a free beer?"

I looked at the man who'd asked the question. A tourist wearing a gray Garden of the Gods tee and khaki cargo shorts. The thinning black hair on top of his head made me want to hand him a tube of sunscreen to fend off the Colorado sun.

I looked at Jase, eyebrows raised. There was no way he'd agree to give away his precious beer, just so I could send home a few animals.

"Sorry—" I started.

"Absolutely," Jase said. "You in the market for a dog?"

"What?" I blurted out before I could stop myself.

"Really?" the man asked, smiling. "I noticed the big lab earlier, but didn't want to commit to anything too early in the day."

The man was pointing to Jolly, a yellow lab mix who was as round as she was happy.

Wait a minute. I wasn't sending dogs home with some random stranger just because they wanted a free beer. These people needed to be serious adopters.

A pleasantly round woman and a little boy walked up to the man. "Dad! Which dog is it? Which one?"

The man pointed at Jolly.

"She's just what I wanted," sobbed the boy as the mom picked him up and rubbed his back in circles.

"He's been upset ever since we had to say goodbye to Patches, our labradoodle," she explained.

"We weren't planning to get a dog this weekend, but..." said the man.

"Free beer," Jase finished.

"And a happy son," the mom said, a laugh lifting her voice.

"And the perfect dog," finished the man.

How was I supposed to say no to all that?

"Well then, let's get Jolly out so she can meet you guys," I said, not believing Jase's ploy actually worked. I leashed the dog, whose tail wagged so hard it caused her entire body to wiggle. Almost like she knew she was going home today.

"Hey, I heard you guys were giving out beer if you adopted an animal today."

It was the woman who had spent the morning playing with Basil, a fifteen pound pile of massive orange fluff. She looked like a fuzzy potato. The dog, not the woman. She'd left me and Basil with a noncommittal, "Let me think about it." *Really, lady?*

Basil stood up, wagging her tail at the lady. She clearly remembered the woman.

Hell. Who was I to deny a dog its destiny? I grabbed another leash to let Basil out of the castle.

Jase busied himself scribbling on the back of a stack of business cards, handing one to Jolly's new dad. "Just present this when you come back."

"Oh, man. A dog, free beer *and* Jase Tugwater's autograph? This is the best weekend ever!"

I handed Basil to her new mom, along with the adoption paperwork, and glanced at Jase. He was positively beaming, which did things to my southern hemisphere that were definitely not suitable for young children's eyes.

*Get a grip, Molly.*

*Yeah, a grip on Jase's massive cock!* giggled my vagina.

"Oh, for fuck's sake," I mumbled.

"Everything okay?" Jase asked, looking at me over his shoulder. He had three cups lined up and was pouring beer into a fourth. The line behind the counter had grown, and I noticed more people pointing at the animals.

"You really going to give out a free beer for every adoption today?" I asked quietly, so the crowd couldn't hear. I didn't think he was serious when he said it to Kole. But even if he was, that was one beer. I had seven animals here today.

He shrugged. "Why not? It's for a good cause, isn't it?"

"What about your business?"

"What about it?"

I turned and faced him, crossing my arms. "Aren't you worried about giving away your profits?"

He faced me, mimicking my crossed arms and looking much more intimidating—*and hot*—doing it.

"It's just a few beers," he said. "That's nothing compared to the word of mouth I'm getting."

*Ah ha!* I knew there had to be a catch. This wasn't about my animals. He was marketing the Catcher's Box.

*And helping your animals get adopted,* my ovaries chimed in.

*Stay out of this,* I replied.

"Well," I said, turning back to the line of potential adopters. "As long as you're okay with it."

"Molly."

I looked at him over my shoulder.

"*Are* you okay with it?"

The furrow of his brow and the way his mouth went all soft when he said it made my insides squishy. Like he really wanted to know the answer, and he really wanted me to be okay with it.

Was I? Was I okay with him using his beer as a mechanism to draw attention to the booth and my animals? I looked at the line of people forming at our booth. People who weren't just waiting for a beer.

"Yes," I said, a smile forming on my face despite my best efforts to remain irritated with the sexy jerk. "I'm okay with it."

He smiled at me.

*We love when he does that,* my lady parts sighed.

*Same.*

"So let's get these people what they came for," I said.

"A beer and a dog!" Jase answered.

# 24

# MOLLY

I closed the sliding glass door of my rescue. The sun was setting, casting the backyard in oranges and purples. It was beautiful. Or it would be, if Larry wasn't pressing her face against the glass, her warm breath fogging it up as she puffed out her disappointment at not being let in.

Atlas stood next to the goat, his tail wagging slowly at me before he turned to go do his business. Good boy.

*Bleht!*

Mouthy goat.

Every bone in my body felt like it had been wrung dry and left to rot in the sun. The festival ended last night, but cleanup was this morning. Jase and I had spent the last four hours hauling totes and kegs of our own, and pitching in to help neighboring booth-owners with their tear-down activities. I was spent.

"I just don't understand," Jase said as he placed a crate on the floor next to a row of dog kennels and stuck his fingers through the bars, petting the single animal we hadn't been able to adopt today.

A few people had considered adopting Stella, a sweet

senior terrier mix, but none had taken the plunge. Which was a damned shame, because this dog was the sweetest little thing I'd ever encountered, even if she was getting on in years.

"Don't understand what?" I said, yawning, rubbing the side of my neck with one hand. I needed a shower and a gallon of wine to recover from this weekend. And maybe an ice pack for my nose, which was throbbing again. How long did it take for a bruised nose and two black eyes to heal, anyway?

Jase grimaced as he stood. Probably less time than a bum knee, I thought, guilt tickling my chest.

*Worth it*, said my vagina.

*Second that*, said my ovaries.

"I did everything I could," Jase said. "I talked to everyone who stopped by, cajoled people into coming over who looked like they might skip us. Everything. But no one wanted her."

"Her family is out there. We just need to be patient."

I opened the crate and let the dog out. Stella immediately went to Jase and sat at his feet, beaming at the man. She practically had hearts dancing in her eyes. Jase gently lifted her up, and she licked his face.

*Jealous!* cried my vagina.

He looked as sweaty as I felt, but he made it look sexy. Unlike me, who looked like the aftermath of a tornado.

His green tee shirt with the Catcher's Box logo clung to him. I forced my attention away from the cut of his back, which tapered down to a narrow waist. I was absolutely not staring at his perfectly perfect ass and thinking about sinking my teeth into it.

*Holy shit, Molly. Get a grip.*

I probably smelled like a wet dog. I definitely should not be fantasizing about dropping to my knees and sucking his cock while I dug my fingers into that fine ass.

"Ahem." Jase stood in front of me grinning, his biceps flexing as he continued holding a very happy Stella.

"What?"

"See anything you liked?"

*Definitely.* "No, just… making sure you didn't have any dog shit on your shorts."

He frowned and twisted, trying to look at his ass. "Do I?"

*Hah.*

"Nope," I said, taking Stella from him and putting her in her kennel. "All clear."

"You were totally checking out my ass, weren't you?"

It wasn't so much a question as a dare.

"I'd hardly be the first woman this weekend to do that," I said, not denying it.

"Maybe," he replied, shoving his hands in his pockets and immediately drawing my attention to his crotch. "But you'd be the only one who mattered."

*Hooray!* my vagina cheered.

I swallowed and tried to remember why this was a bad idea, as his gaze dropped to my lips and his breathing intensified. He stepped into my personal space and dipped his head.

"This is a bad idea," I said.

"You trying to convince me? Or you?" he replied, his lips brushing my cheek.

"Yes," I said before grabbing his face and shoving my tongue into his mouth.

He chuckled as he walked us back to the same bench we'd almost had sex on three days ago. Had it really only been three days?

This time, instead of laying me back, he lifted me up and sat down on the bench with my legs wrapped around his waist. I ground my clit against his hard length.

"Mmm, I love this angle," I muttered, kissing my way down his neck.

"Easier on the knees."

"And the nose," I agreed.

He shoved his hands up my shirt and teased my nipples through my bra.

I tilted back to give him better access. "Harder."

He pinched my nipple, making me gasp, before releasing it and drawing my shirt over my head.

He tugged the cup of my bra down and sucked on my very sensitive bud. "I thought we weren't doing this again," he said against my breast.

"We're not." I grabbed his hair and held him in place.

The heat from his chuckle shot through to my core as he moved to the other nipple. "If you say so."

Okay, fine, we were totally doing this again. But it was just once more. We'd found homes for nearly all my animals, and sold a lot of beer. That was worth celebrating, wasn't it?

"Shut up and fuck me." I lifted off him just enough to unbutton his shorts. He leaned to one side, almost tipping me off his lap.

"What are you—?" I asked as he reached into his back pocket, pulling out his wallet and handing it to me.

"Condom. Inside slot." He sat back down and unhooked my bra, sliding it down my arms far enough to continue his glorious assault on my breasts.

I complied, taking the condom out and tearing open the package. Jase stopped just long enough to unzip and slide his cock out for me.

Standing, I shimmied my shorts and underwear down my legs before rolling the condom down his shaft. I squeezed lightly and grinned as he bucked into my hand.

"Jesus, that feels good," he said.

I crawled back into his lap and seated myself at the tip of

his cock, pausing before I slid, slowly, down his length, giving myself enough time to adjust to his size. He felt even bigger than the last time, which didn't seem possible.

"But that," he said, tilting his hips up and taking me even deeper. "That feels even better."

"That feels fucking incredible."

I rose up and slid back down, enjoying his hot, hard length, filling me completely.

So. Fucking. Incredible.

He grabbed me by the hips and thrust into me as I rode him like the dirty, sweaty cowgirl I was.

*Yee-haw!* crowed my lady bits.

"More," I said.

"Your wish is—"

"Hey you two beautiful creatures!"

Jeff's voice cracked through the sexual haze as they walked around the corner into the kennel room, holding Tyson's hand.

I shot off Jase's lap like he was on fire. Jase, not ready for the intrusion on our sexy time or my sudden absence, jolted back, banging his head against the cabinet door.

"Ow. Fuck!" he shouted, his talented dick hanging heavily against his leg, practically begging me to jump back on and finish the ride.

"Jase Tugwater naked! Christmas has come early," Jeff crowed as Jase used his hands to cover his cock, which was sadly deflating as Jeff continued to ogle him.

Smiling, Jeff turned to me. "I saw—ohmygod! Lady bits! Lady bits! *My eyes!*" They put a hand over Tyson's eyes. "Don't look! We didn't see anything!"

"Says you," Tyson replied before Jeff grabbed his face and pulled him back down the hall.

"Oh, for fuck's sake," I said, all too aware of my naked-ness. Looking around for something, anything, to cover up, I grabbed Atlas's blanket from his bed and wrapped it around me. Dog hair went flying.

Jase rubbed the knot on his head with one hand and shoved himself back into his shorts with the other.

"You okay?" I asked Jase as I plucked my shorts and panties off the floor.

"Yeah." Jase dangled my bra from a finger as he held it out for me. "Just a little banged up."

I accepted the bra and let the blanket drop, throwing my clothes back on as quickly as I could manage. My shirt was on inside out, but as long as it covered the important parts, who cared?

"So, pretty average for us," I joked.

"Nothing about our time together is average, Molly."

The intensity in his eyes made my vagina clench in anticipation.

Jeff poked their head back into the room, eyes still firmly shut. "Not looking! But Candice was looking for you, yelling something about a goat named Mercedes? Or maybe it was a goat *and* a Mercedes? Doesn't matter. Just steer clear. She looked pissed."

"Super," I said, blowing out a sigh. Just what I needed to go with my unhappy vagina. A pissed-off nemesis.

"I saw nothing!" Jeff repeated. "But let me know if you need an ice pack for Little Miss Muffet after riding that humongous tuffet!" they shouted, disappearing around the corner.

Jeff's head popped back into the doorway.

"Jesus, Jeff. Out!"

"I'm going! But I just wanted to say… I totally knew you two were having freaky shelter sex!"

"We're not having freaky shelter sex!" I yelled as Jeff vanished, for good this time if the front door opening and closing were to be trusted.

Good riddance. I freaking loved Jeff, but their timing sucked.

"I mean," Jase said, tucking his shirt back into his shorts. "Maybe not the freaky part, but we were having sex in a shelter."

"How do you know it wouldn't have been freaky?" I challenged, an eyebrow raised. What the hell was I doing? I shouldn't be having sex with him at all, let alone challenging him to freaky sex.

*We should totally have freaky sex with the sex god*, my vagina corrected.

*We'd be down for some more action*, my nipples added.

*Not gonna happen*, I replied.

*Boo*, my ovaries chided.

"Is that a challenge?" Jase asked, the corner of his mouth tilted up.

*Yes!* my lady parts replied.

"I don't have time for challenges. I need to figure out what Candice's problem is, and then I have a date with a bath and a bottle of wine."

"Anything I can do to help?"

"I don't need help bathing."

A long, slow smile grew on his stupid, sexy face. "I was talking about Candice, but I'm happy to scrub your back if you need it."

*Yes, please!* my lady bits cheered.

"Thanks, but I have a loofah for that."

He shrugged, still grinning. "You know my number if you change your mind."

I took in his long limbs, dusted with coarse blond hair, broken up by the red scar down one leg. Even with the scar, every bit of him looked strong and confident. The exact opposite of how I usually felt.

How could one man look that good after working in a

dirty booth, sweating in the summer heat all day? I wanted to lick him like a salt block and let him finish what we'd started.

Would that be so bad?

*The only thing more relaxing than a hot bath is multiple orgasms*, my vagina helpfully pointed out.

"Maybe—" That was all I got out before the door to the rescue slammed open, banging against the wall.

I peeked around the corner. Candice Shoowater stood in the doorway, her eyes wide and wild, her lips puckered like she'd just sucked on a lemon.

"You're in so much trouble, Molly Sanders," she said, pointing a bony finger at my chest.

*Oh, goodie.*

2 5

JASE

What else is new?" Molly said, her hands fisted on her hips like Wonder Woman in tattered shorts and a poop-stained tee, as she faced down Candice like a goddess of war.

I wanted to worship at her feet, but kept my position just behind her. She may not want my help, but I could at least have her back.

Candice pointed a bony finger at Molly's chest. "You're a menace to this town and to society. I should have tried harder to shut this place down after your mom died."

I couldn't see her face, but I felt her breath hitch before she squared her shoulders.

"Sorry to be the bearer of bad news," Molly replied, chin raised in defiance. "But I'm fresh out of fucks for today, so unless you're here to leave a donation, you can remove yourself from my property."

"Your property?" Candice replied, looking right at me.

*Uh oh.*

"Hey Candice," I said, hoping to interrupt whatever she

was about to say that probably wouldn't be good for me. "What brings you in?"

"Her goat trampled my Mercedes," Candice said, turning her attention back to Molly.

"That's impossible," Molly countered.

Was it though?

After Saturday's weird yelling contest, the goat was unusually subdued yesterday. And except for a few bellows during the morning, which seemed like they were coming from the far side of Happy Tails, she'd been completely quiet the rest of the day. Who was to say she hadn't gone on a walkabout?

Candice dug around in her designer leather handbag and pulled out her phone, thrusting the screen at Molly's face.

I peered over Molly's shoulder at a video. The quality wasn't great. The camera person kept adjusting the camera in jerky motions, making it hard to focus on what was happening, but suddenly the camera stilled and a silver car came into focus. I could see a Mercedes emblem on the hood.

And right there, standing tall and proud on the roof, was Larry, bleating the song of her people.

It was hard to hear Larry over the voice that was probably Candice's screaming things like, "Get off my car, you monster!" and "I'm going to fucking kill you, Molly Sanders!"

Molly watched the video, her face impassive, but I could feel the heat coming off her in waves. I put a hand on her shoulder. I probably imagined it when she leaned into me, ever so slightly.

"What do you want?" she asked, defeat softening her words.

I felt it like a punch to the gut. Where was her fight? Where was my goddess?

"A new Mercedes," Candice answered.

Molly snorted. "Fat fucking chance."

*Ah, there she was.* I felt a stirring in Tug Junior as I watched her face down the angry blond.

"Then you can pay my deductible so I can get it fixed."

Molly's jaw clenched. "How much?"

"One thousand dollars," Candice replied, crossing her arms, almost daring Molly to challenge her.

Molly's breath escaped her in a sharp puff of air.

There was no way she had that kind of cash, and based on past experience, she wouldn't accept my help to pay for it. That didn't mean I couldn't help in other ways. I just needed to figure out how.

"I don't have that kind of money lying around, and you know it," Molly finally answered.

"Then I suggest you find it," Candice said.

"I think we can find a compromise here," I said, my voice low but my meaning clear.

"This is none of your concern, Jase," she said to me even though she hadn't taken her eyes off Molly.

"Don't tell him his business," Molly said, surprising me. "He's a guest here. You're not."

There was that take charge attitude of hers again, turning me on and making my shorts uncomfortably snug. That we *still* hadn't finished what we started—*twice*—in the room with the bench wasn't helping. I positioned myself almost directly behind her. No sense in letting Candice know see turned on I was.

"He's hardly a guest," Candice said, cutting a look at me, as if daring me to contradict her.

"What the hell is that supposed to mean?" Molly asked, crossing her arms in return.

Candice ran her eyes over me. A grin spread slowly across her face like a predator ready to pounce.

*Oh. No. No, no.*

"I'm sure as your landlord, he has the right to be here, invited or not."

*Shit. Shit, shit, shit.*

"Molly."

I tried to get her attention, but she looked down at her feet for a split second before lifting her head and taking a deep breath.

"Not that it's any of your business, but my lease specifically states that my landlord has to give me five business days' notice before setting foot on my property for anything except an emergency. Since the only emergency here is what's happening with your roots, and Jase hasn't given me any sort of notice that he'll be on my property today, I think we can all safely assume he's here as a guest, and not my landlord."

*Huh.*

Candice ran a hand over her hair self-consciously as I watched the color of hell itself blanch up her neck and across her face.

"You'll be hearing from my lawyer," she said.

"If you're talking about Wallace Doomey," Molly replied, "his mom still packs his lunch and he moves across the street to avoid Atlas on our walks. I think I'll take my chances."

Molly's wide stance, arms crossed, said she was ready to take on the fucking world, even if it was mostly empty bravado. But damn, it was sexy.

Candice let out a single huff before turning and marching out the front door.

Molly stood still, watching the door as it closed.

"Molly—"

"What the actual fuck, Tug?" She spun on her heels and jabbed a finger into my chest.

"Ow."

Her chest rose and fell as her face reddened, and her eyes

narrowed to slits. The angrier she got, the harder my dick got. Hopefully, she'd keep her eyes on my face and not my crotch, which was growing uncomfortably tight.

"Don't you fucking 'ow' me. I repeat. What." *Stab.* "The actual." *Stab, stab.* "Fuck." *Stab.*

"I... um... well..." I started, rubbing at the sore spot on my chest as I tried to think of something—anything—that wasn't how much I wanted to fuck her. "How'd you know?"

"That you're my landlord? *I didn't!*"

"But you just—"

"There was no fucking way I was letting that twatwaffle think for a second I had no fucking idea what she was talking about."

She paced down the length of the hall and let Atlas inside. The gentle giant sniffed Molly's shoes before nudging her hand with his snout.

"Look, it's not like I lied... exactly."

Molly's eyes rolled as her face lifted to the ceiling. "Baby Spock, help me."

She reversed back towards the front door and locked it before turning and hitting me with the full intensity of her amber eyes. Eyes so angry they looked like she could light me on fire.

"A lie of omission is still a fucking lie, Tug."

She was right. Of course she was.

I should have told her when she caught me dancing in front of the building at my sign. Or any of the other times I had the chance. Instead, I chickened out. Just like Sam accused me of.

"Okay, maybe I should have told you."

"Maybe?" She snorted. Which was adorable and one more thing I couldn't get enough of. Like her legs wrapped around me as I drove into her. I really wanted to finish what we started in the bench room. But I owed Molly an explanation. Maybe even an apology. So Tug Junior could just wait.

"No maybe about it, Tug."

"You're right."

"So why didn't you?"

I sat with the question for half a second before answering. I may have been less than truthful with her before, but that stopped now. She deserved that much from me.

"I guess I liked the thought of being the nice guy helping you out." I looked right at her as I said it, making sure she heard the honesty in every word.

She broke eye contact and looked down at Atlas, who'd been watching our exchange.

"Who's S. R. Duncan?" she finally said.

"Duncan?" I repeated, the subject change catching me off guard.

"The person who keeps sending me emails and signing documents. You know, like a landlord." She enunciated those last words like she was speaking to a toddler.

"That's Sam. My business partner. And agent. And friend."

"Douchey guy from the phone?"

"Yeah, look. I'm sorry. After I bought the building, I had a lot going on. Sam told me he'd take care of everything. I didn't realize he wasn't responding to emails until you told me."

Which was mostly true. The fact that Sam had asked me about responding to emails and I had told him I'd take care of it and then didn't seemed like an inconsequential detail at the moment.

"Sam seems like a douchecanoe," she responded. "You need new friends."

What I needed was something I couldn't have. The urge to close the space between us was so strong I could feel it in my bones. Instead of backing her into the wall and letting her feel how much she was turning me on, I inched into her space, enough to reach down and pat Atlas, who was now sitting on her feet. Not at her feet. *On* them. Molly was either used to the intrusion or had lost all feeling in her feet and couldn't move.

She watched my hand as I continued to stroke the dog's head.

"I'm sorry, Molly. Can we talk about this over a beer? We can go to the Catcher's Box and open the new keg." And jump back into my bed where I could show her all night long just how well I could apologize.

"This isn't a conversation for beer."

"I don't have anything stronger." I'd been meaning to add a few bottles of harder stuff for those days when I needed something stronger than beer—like now—but I'd put it off. Just like I'd put off telling Molly about being her landlord.

I was a giant, procrastinating prick. I deserved for Molly to reject me.

"I do."

"I understand—Wait, what?"

She rubbed her forehead and squinted her eyes shut. "I'm probably going to regret this, but…"

"But…"

*Please, Molly. Give us a chance.*

"Give me thirty minutes. I need to feed Atlas and shower." She tilted her head as she looked at me. "You should probably do the same."

*Yes! Yes, yes, yes!*

"Thirty minutes," I confirmed with a nod. "Need me to bring anything?"

Leashing Atlas, she looked over her shoulder at me. "Condoms."

# 26

# MOLLY

*I* dug through my underwear drawer for something that didn't scream *my grandma lives here*. After feeding Atlas and loading the dishwasher with all the dirty dishes I hadn't bothered with this weekend, I'd left myself exactly five minutes to shower before Jase would arrive. Not enough time to wash and condition my hair, but enough time to run a razor over all the important bits.

Yanking a pair of cute cotton panties with yellow polka dots and a little lace trim out of the drawer, I considered my bra options. Maybe I'd forgo a bra. I had never considered myself small, but wasn't so big it would be obvious if I went without. The Goldilocks of boob sizes.

Pulling the damp towel from around my chest, I tossed it on the bed with a pair of teal-colored sweatpants and a black cropped tee with a blue silhouette of the Enterprise space-ship on my bed. They were uninspired, but they were clean. The sweats made my ass look great, and, most importantly, they were easy to remove.

"What was I thinking, inviting him over?" I asked Atlas as he lay curled up on his bed in the corner of my room.

Spoiler: I knew exactly what I was thinking—multiple orgasms.

Thanks to the showdown with Candice fucking Shoowater, I was riled up, and the way Jase had had my back... well, my insides had been doing cartwheels and backflips over his brief but effective protective streak.

The acrobatics came to a screeching halt when Candice had revealed Jase as my landlord.

Why did he have to be such an idiot?

He said he liked being the nice guy helping me out.

I'd liked it too. So much so I ignored the obvious signs that should have clued me in. Signs like complaining to him about the landlord not doing something and it magically getting done the next day.

He'd basically spent the last few weeks lying to me. So what had I done? I'd invited him over for drinks and sex.

Who was the real idiot here?

Atlas picked up his head as the doorbell rang. "Just a second!" I shouted, throwing on my clothes and tossing the wet towel in the hamper on my way to the front door.

Pausing before I opened it, I checked in mentally. "Am I really going to do this?"

*Hell yes, we are!* shouted my ovaries.

*All night long, baby!* sang my nipples.

*Gimme that dick!* answered my vagina.

"Unanimous vote, then."

I tugged open the door and Jase stood there, in all his male glory. Why did he have to be so good-looking all the time? How was any regular woman supposed to resist six-feet-three inches of solid muscle topped off by a face that should grace the cover of every magazine on the planet?

His hair was damp, darkening it, which only made his blue-gray eyes that much brighter. Light brown scruff dusted a jaw that looked carved from marble.

He was perfection in shorts and a Denver Vistas tee shirt that was wet in spots where his muscles pressed against the fabric as he stared at me from my front porch, holding a bouquet of wildflowers I knew came from Mulhoney's Market.

He'd shown up at my house with flowers, and was waiting for me to invite him in.

Like a fucking gentleman.

I'd issued a clear invitation for sex, but there he was, giving me an out.

I was so screwed.

*Don't you dare wuss out,* my ovaries warned.

*Strip him down and fuck him!* my vagina encouraged.

I could just see the edge of his truck parked in my driveway. My neighbors were probably already texting everyone in town that Jase had shown up at my house with flowers.

"Come in," I said, tamping down every urge to listen to my baser parts. If he could play the gentleman, I could at least offer him a drink first before throwing myself at him. "Whiskey?"

He nodded and then offered the flowers to me. "For you."

"This isn't a date," I said, taking the flowers anyway and walking into the kitchen to find a vase, hiding a smile. Just because it wasn't a date didn't mean I couldn't appreciate the gesture.

Jase followed close behind me, his scent wrapping itself around me like a soft blanket. Warm leather and spice and something that was uniquely him.

It made me want to wrap myself around him and never let go.

Swallowing that thought, I poured a couple fingers of whiskey into two glasses and handed one to him.

"Cute place," he said, taking the bourbon but holding on to it, keeping my gaze.

"The coat closet you call a bedroom has its charms, too," I answered before taking a nice fortifying sip of my own whiskey.

"Sure, if you like the feeling of having sex in the back of a compact car."

I snorted. "My bedroom's a bit bigger. I think you'll like it."

Shit. Why'd I say that? Because right now, Jase Tugwater was sipping his bourbon but looking at me like he wanted to pour it over my naked body and spend all night licking it off me.

*Okay!* said my nipples.

"So if this isn't a date, what is this, then?" he asked.

Shivering under his scrutiny, I considered his question. "Just two friends, sharing a drink."

*Liar*, said my vagina.

*Shut your pie hole*, I replied.

"We're friends?"

I shrugged. "Aren't we?"

He continued to stare, his gaze unwavering.

Was it getting hot in here suddenly?

I took a drink of whiskey and tried not to notice the way he watched my lips on the glass, or my neck as I swallowed. The sweetness of the bourbon warred with the spice as it burned my throat on the way down, distracting my mind from Jase's intense focus. My insides, however, were not so easily sidetracked. Every time Jase breathed out, my pussy clenched. Every time his eyes moved over my face, my core heated.

I was primed and ready, and he hadn't laid a hand on me yet.

*Help me, Jean-Luc Picard.*

*Help nothing*, my vagina responded. *Let's get naked!*

He reached for the bottle. "Another?"

Words failed me, so I nodded, pushing my empty glass towards him. He poured me another finger and handed it to me, his had brushing against mine as I reached for it.

A jolt of electricity shot up my arm and straight to my core, which felt like molten lava. Hot and ready to explode.

*Ladies, start your engines!* revved my vagina.

"We made a pretty good team this weekend," he said, fingers trailing back down my arm, a trail of goosebumps following in their wake.

He was wrong. We'd made a *great* team this weekend. I'd never had so much success during a festival. And it wasn't because he went out and pimped himself for adoptions. He'd given away a few free beers, but that wasn't the reason we'd been so successful. It was because we worked together, making sure that the animals we sent home were going to good homes.

"We did," I said, my voice catching on a breath as he stroked back up my arm.

"We're good together, Molly."

We were. If only he would stop giving me reasons to not trust him.

And that, right there, was the catch.

I couldn't trust him. Not with my heart. Maybe not even with my business if he was okay lying to me about owning the whole fucking building.

But I didn't have to trust him to sleep with him. That didn't require trust. Just a healthy libido, two willing participants, and some condoms. Which hopefully he remembered to bring.

"We were good together," I finally said, putting my glass down and facing him straight on. "This weekend. But you still didn't trust me with the truth, Tug. And that hurts."

*Boo!* jeered my lady bits.

*Oh, shut up.* This was the right decision. I deserved to set those boundaries, and he deserved to know where we stood.

He nodded as he put his glass on the counter and closed the distance between us. His hand wrapped gently around the back of my neck as a thumb strummed softly against my jaw.

"You're right." He dipped his face towards mine and brushed his lips against mine. "I'm sorry," he said against my mouth, right before he claimed it.

Lips that were strong and soft, demanding and comforting, caressed mine. I placed my glass on the counter, fumbling and nearly breaking it, so I could rise on both feet and meet him. Tilting my head, I invited him in deeper, stroking my tongue to meet his.

He moved across my jaw, leaving open-mouth kisses down my neck.

"Never again."

It would be so easy to believe him.

He kissed lower. "I won't lie to you again."

Could I really believe him?

He licked the soft spot between my neck and clavicle, and my clothes nearly jumped right off my body and lay themselves at his feet in worship. Goosebumps erupted on my skin.

"Can you forgive me?"

"This is just sex, Tug."

His teeth nipped my skin as his hands slowly made their way up my ribs. "Then let me earn your forgiveness."

"There's nothing to earn—"

Words failed me as Jase dropped to his knees and pulled down my sweats, running his hands around the back of my legs and up my hamstrings, cupping my ass.

"Polka dots. I like polka dots."

*Yay for polka dots!* my vagina sang as he moved my panties to the side and stroked one finger between my folds.

"Holy yes," I said on a groan as he worked the finger inside me.

"So wet," he said, kissing my stomach. His other hand worked my clit. I would never look at polka dots the same way again.

He grunted as he shifted position and stretched out one leg to the side.

"Are you ok—*Ah!*" His mouth replaced the hand working my clit as a second finger entered me. I was seconds away from coming.

"Bedroom, Tug."

He swirled his tongue around my sensitive button, causing my knees to buckle. A strong arm wrapped around my waist. "I've got you," he murmured against me, nearly setting me off. But he grunted as he shifted again. He was clearly uncomfortable kneeling on my hard kitchen floor.

"Bedroom. Now."

There was no way I was going to allow him to hurt his knee again. Jeff would never let me hear the end of it.

Jase stood, lifting me into his arms. "Point the way."

I navigated us down the hall to my room, barely able to think. Atlas stood to greet us, stretched his long limbs, then lumbered his way down the hallway we'd just come from. Good boy.

"Smart dog," Jase said as he settled us both down on my bed and stripped me of the sweatpants around my ankles, following it with my panties. I shrugged out of my shirt, leaving me stripped bare in front of him.

"Beautiful." He kneeled in front of me, wrapping an arm under my leg and laying soft kisses on the inside of my thigh.

"Holy fuck, that feels good," I whispered. Or shouted. It

was hard to tell with the pending orgasm pounding in my ears in time with the throbbing in my pussy.

He licked up my core, causing me to buck under him.

"Again," I panted.

*Lick.*

"Fuck yes. Again."

*Lick. Lick.*

He sucked on my clit, and I launched into the stratosphere. Stars exploded, blinding me, the roaring of the sea deafened me. I was pretty sure I screamed.

Jase continued to stroke me with his tongue as I rode out the waves of my orgasm and tried to clear my head. Holy shit, that was amazing. Even Mr. Buzzypants couldn't get me off that fast.

My breathing slowed as he kissed his way up my torso, giving extra attention to my breasts, before finally reaching my lips.

I returned his kisses, tasting myself on him.

"Forgive me yet?" he asked.

"No. But it's my turn," I said, rolling him over and straddling him.

His hands smoothed up my stomach, squeezing my breasts gently as he rubbed his thumbs across my nipples. "I can work with that."

*Yee haw!* my boobs shouted.

# 27
## JASE

*T*hank you, whatever god is in charge of perfect breasts. I sucked one taut, plum-colored bud into my mouth and bit back a groan as Molly bucked against me.

Tug Junior was ready to Hulk his way out of these shorts. But every time I tried to pull away, Molly grabbed me by the hair and held me to her chest as she ground against my dick. Not the worst thing I'd been forced to do, but there was no fucking way I was going to come in my shorts. I was going to do it right, losing myself inside her as she screamed my name.

Switching breasts, I rolled the nipple I'd been sucking on between my thumb and forefinger as my teeth slid over the other, the double assault making Molly gasp.

I sat up and rolled her over so she was under me, shoving my free hand into my pocket and pulled out a string of condoms.

"Well, you came prepared," she panted, unbuttoning my shorts and fisting my cock.

*"Fuuuck."*

I slowed her hand and gently pulled it away, sliding it

above her head and wrapping her wrist with my hand as I kissed her. Letting Molly continue to squeeze me was a sure-fire way to end the night early. Gripping my tee shirt by the back of my neck, I stripped it off before removing my shorts and boxers and tossing them on the floor.

Molly had opened a condom packet while I undressed, so I took it and sheathed myself.

She spread her legs, giving me a perfect view of that sweet pussy. Unable to stop myself, I bent and licked her, tasting her sweet juices. She cried out as her hips thrust off the bed.

"What are you doing?" she asked, her breath coming in heavy pants.

"Anything you want me to," I answered, moving up her body before pinning both of her arms above her head.

"I want you to fuck me," she answered.

"What's your rush?" I locked her wrists in one hand and slid the other to her slick crease, pressing one finger, then two, inside her and stroking in and out.

"Oh," she gasped. "No… no rush."

"Good," I said. "Now tell me what you want."

She groaned, arching. "More."

"More what?" I swirled my thumb over her sensitive nub as I continued to plunge my fingers in and out of her pussy.

"That."

I felt her tighten. She was close, so I increased the tempo.

"Jean-Luc Picard, more of that!"

I let go of her arms and dipped my head down, replacing my thumb with my mouth as I sucked and swirled my tongue around her clit.

Her voice broke as she cried out, shudders racking her body, her pussy clenching my fingers.

"Ready for more?" I asked, lining my cock up at her entrance. Should I have given her a little more time to recover from her second orgasm? Probably. But I wanted to feel her wrapped around my cock so badly I could barely see through the haze of my hard-on. Guess she wasn't the only one in a rush.

Lids half-closed, she nodded as her knees dropped open, a willing invitation. "I need you to say it, Molly."

She moaned as I slid my cock through her wet folds.

"Come on, baby, tell me what you want."

"I want you."

I knew she meant my dick, but a not so small part of my ego wanted to believe that she meant *me*.

"I've got you," I said, plunging into her. She cried out as I sank into her. She was soft and hot and slick and it took every ounce of self-control I had not to spill into her with that first thrust. "Fuck, you feel amazing."

"So full," she said, tilting her hips towards me to take me deeper. "So hard."

I pulled out and paused before driving back into her. The last ten years of my life had been one incredible opportunity after another. Playing professional baseball for my favorite team, getting voted into the all-star game the last three years of my career, being named MVP twice. It was everything I thought I'd wanted.

Until now. Until Molly. Hearing the little noises she made every time I bottomed out, feeling her hands grab my ass and pull me into her, watching her head drop to the side as I climbed higher and higher with her.

This was what I wanted. The pennants and titles and bank account were great. But Molly... she was utter perfection. And I'd do anything to make sure she knew it.

Her eyes closed, she bit her bottom lip. I stopped, waiting for her to look up at me.

"What are you doing?" she asked.

"I want to know you're here with me. You and me."

"I am." She reached up and softly brushed her fingers through my scruff. "You and me, Tug."

I lowered myself and kissed her, slow, intentional. I needed her to know I was here with her, too.

Sighing, she smiled up at me. "Now, can we get back to business?"

I drove into her. "Yes, ma'am."

She moaned. "Harder."

I lifted her legs, propping them over my shoulders to deepen the angle.

"Again."

Gripping her shins, I thrust again.

"Faster."

I could do faster. Lowering one leg, I changed up the angle again and began to move.

"Fuck yes," Molly panted. "Whatever you just did, please, Spock, do more of that." She met me thrust for thrust as I drove into her, her head knocking back into the padded headboard.

A few more and I'd be finished. I needed her to come, now. Reaching out, I rolled her nipple between my thumb and forefinger and tugged.

Molly shrieked as her whole body shook, and she arched into me. I could feel her squeezing me in waves that sent me over the edge. Growling, I buried my head in her neck as I emptied into her.

"Holy fucking Klingons," she whispered.

I lifted myself just far enough to keep the bulk of my weight off her and dropped a kiss onto her forehead. Rolling over, I pulled her with me, tucking her against my chest.

I fully expected her to resist, but when she ran a hand over my chest, trailing her fingers through my chest hair, and snuggled against me, I had to temper my heart, which was trying to beat its way out of my chest with happiness.

We lay in silence, our breaths slowing and synchronizing. The silky smooth feel of her arm as I brushed my hand up and down felt like heaven under my fingertips. I allowed myself a moment to believe that she was as happy as I was. That it was right. It was real. And she wanted this as much as I did.

I allowed myself to believe that she could forgive me for every stupid thing I'd ever done and we could move on. Together.

"You can't stay the night," she said, yawning, breaking the silence, and my fantasy.

"I know."

I did know, but that didn't mean I didn't want to.

"I need to take care of the condom," I said, getting up and padding to the bathroom. Closing the door behind me, I looked at my image in the silver oval mirror hanging above the white vanity. I knew I needed to earn her trust. And that started with giving her as much space as she needed, for as long as she needed it. I wasn't going anywhere. Not this time. And each day I'd prove that to her. Prove that I could go the distance.

For her. For us.

I disposed of the condom and turned on the cold water in the sink, my hands gripping the sides of the vanity as I leaned towards the mirror.

"You can do this, Tugwater," I said before splashing cold water over my face.

I wiped the water off on the soft hand towel next to the vanity and headed back into the bedroom. I grabbed my boxer shorts and shirt off the floor.

"What are you doing?" Molly asked, long limbs stretching gracefully like a cat.

"Getting dressed."

"What's your hurry?" She turned to her side and propped

her head on her hand, her long hair spilling down her arm, her body on full display without an ounce of insecurity. Long and lean and beautiful. And not mine.

Not yet.

"You said I couldn't stay." I pulled my shirt on.

"I said you couldn't stay the night."

"It's okay, Molly," I said, stepping into my boxers.

"What if I want to bask in the afterglow of three life-altering orgasms? I can't do that if you're not here."

I looked at her. Sleepy eyes met me with a challenge.

"Life altering, huh?"

She snorted. "Like you didn't already know that. Get undressed and get back in bed."

My clothes hit the floor in record time and I slid next to Molly, pulling her in tight. "Anything you want."

She let out another yawn. "So you keep saying."

I pressed a series of kisses along her neck and jaw and was rewarded with a sigh as she settled into me. Tracing lazy circles along her back with one hand, my other ran softly up and down the arm she had draped over my torso.

"Feels nice," she murmured against my chest.

"Mmm," I agreed.

Her breathing slowed and evened out.

Was she asleep? Or was she just super relaxed?

A small snore answered my question. Freaking adorable.

Picking up on my cue to leave, I lifted Molly's arm so I could scoot softly out from under her. But her arm reached around me and pulled me back in.

"Molly?" I whispered.

"Zzz…"

Well, this was a bit of a pickle.

On the one hand, I wasn't about to defy Molly's request.

On the other hand , she looked so comfy and after the weekend we'd had, she needed the sleep.

She'd roll off of me eventually, right?

I'd leave after she moved. Until then, I would let her sleep. It was the least I could do after giving Molly three life-altering orgasms.

*High-five, Tug Junior.*

*I* snuggled deep into my covers. There was nothing better than great sex followed by an amazing night's sleep to make the morning a little more palatable. Maybe I could reconsider this whole this-is-the-last-time mindset. I could do with a few more orgasms in my life, especially ones that contained magical sleeping potions.

The arm wrapped around my midsection was heavy and warm and felt like heaven. I snuggled closer, pulling the arm around me like a blanket. Yes, this was the way I wanted to wake up every morning.

*Poke.*

*What was that*, I thought hazily as I snuggled deeper into my fluffy duvet.

*Poke, poke.*

I cracked an eyeball. Wait. Why was there an arm wrapped around me? A big hairy man arm.

And what the hell kept poking me in the back?

Turning my head slowly, I peeked over my shoulder.

Jase pressed a kiss against my neck, his eyes still closed.

"Morning, sunshine," he said, his voice low and gravelly in the early morning.

*Swoon*, said my ovaries.

*Swoon? You don't say swoon. You just swoon.*

*Swoon*, echoed my vagina.

My heart, which had been steadfastly ignoring any conversation about Jase to date, was poking her head around the corner to see what all the fuss was about. Apparently, everybody had a thing for raspy morning voices.

"Why are you here?" I croaked. Great. Jase had a sexy morning voice. Mine sounded like a dying frog.

Jase startled and looked around, panic making his blue eyes twinkle.

*Adorable*, my vagina said.

*Totally*, my ovaries agreed.

*For fuck's sake, you guys.*

"Jase."

"What? Where? What?" Jase was scrubbing his eyes with one hand as he looked around the room. "Molly?"

I pulled the duvet around my shoulders and narrowed my eyes at him.

"What time is it?" he asked, sitting up and running one hand through his hair. It stood on end, making him look lickable.

No, not lickable. He looked like a mad scientist. A mad scientist who took advantage of my post-orgasmic state and invited himself to stay in my fucking bed.

"Time for you and Mr. Stiffy to leave," I said, getting up and pulling the duvet with me.

Jase looked at the sheet covering his lower half, which was tented thanks to the raging erection he was sporting. "Tug Junior," he mumbled, gathering the sheet up around his crotch.

"Tug Junior?"

"That's his name," he shrugged.

"You named your dick Tug Junior?"

Standing, he wrapped the sheet around his waist and walked towards me. "Better than Mr. Stiffy."

He yawned and stretched the hand not holding the sheet over his head. The muscles in his abs flexed and pulled taut with the motion.

*Yum*, said my vagina.

"Don't suppose you have any coffee?" he asked.

Was he being serious right now? "People who overstay their welcome don't get coffee."

"I tried to leave. Three times. But you told me to stay."

"*Pfsh*," I said majestically. I absolutely did not.

His eyebrows rose, a smirk growing at the corner of his mouth—a mouth that did unspeakable things to me last night. "You did."

"Didn't."

Except… *Anything you want.*

I didn't ask him to come back to bed.

Did I?

Jase bent down and picked up his tee shirt before looking around. "Where are my boxers?"

He scratched his head with the hand that had been holding the sheet up, leaving it defenseless against gravity.

*Oh my*, my vagina crooned.

I licked my lips as the sheet slowly slid down his hips.

What had I been saying?

*We're ready for round two!* cheered my ovaries.

*Give me the dick!* agreed my sore but happy vagina.

Looking down at the sheet, Jase realized gravity was about to win the battle and hitched it up.

*Boo*, said my vagina.

*Hiss*, said my ovaries.

"I could have sworn they were in a pile with the rest of

my clothes…" he said, reaching up to scratch his head again before remembering the sheet.

I did not have time for this. I had shit to do today, and it wasn't getting done by me standing around waiting for Jase's sheet to drop so I could, what? Drool? Jump him again?

*Hell to the yes!* hollered my vagina.

"Sounds like a you problem," I said, grabbing my own clothes off the floor and tiptoeing to the bathroom, the duvet wrapped tightly around me like he hadn't worshipped every inch of my naked body last night. "But I'm sure you've got this. I've got my own problems right now."

I closed the door behind me and took a breath.

*Get undressed and get back in bed.*

Oh, hell. I'd said that to him. Right before I fell asleep. In his arms. Feeling satisfied and safe and… happy.

*Fuuuck.* I did not need Big Feelings today. They needed to go somewhere and hide for the next twenty-seven years until I was ready to deal with them.

I tugged on my clothes—yes, they were yesterday's clothes, but my clean clothes were on the other side of the door. Where Jase was. Naked. Unless he'd found his boxers.

*We hope he didn't,* said my ovaries.

A thud sounded from the bedroom.

"I hope that sound means you're dressed and leaving," I hollered, tying my hair back.

"I'm trying, but your dog isn't cooperating," he shouted back.

My dog?

I poked my head out of the bathroom door.

Atlas was standing on my bed, wagging his tail, Jase's boxers in his mouth. Jase was at the end of my bed, arms spread wide, the sheet pooled at his feet.

*Yum!* my vagina reiterated as I stared at Jase's bare ass.

*Agree to agree.* It was a fine ass. *Also, stop saying that.*

"Come on, buddy. Give me the boxers and I'll buy you a steak dinner." Jase tugged at the boxers, which Atlas mistook as an opportunity to play tug-of-war.

"No, don't," I started, but didn't finish because Atlas launched himself off the bed and took off down the hall, boxers waving out the side of his mouth.

Great Dane zoomies before my first cup of coffee. Today was going to be a great day.

"What the hell?" Jase said, still standing there, very naked.

Before I could respond, Atlas barreled back down the hall towards the bedroom. He was coming in hot. Too hot.

The motion of his gallop caused the underwear to flip up onto his face, covering his eyes. Instead of swerving at the last minute to avoid a collision, he plowed right into me, knocking me sideways.

I twisted to catch myself and caught Jase across the mouth with my elbow before my tailbone hit the floor.

"Ow, fuck," I said.

"Mmpf," Jase said, offering me a hand. I grabbed it, but Atlas shook the boxers like he was killing a rabbit, and knocked me into Jase.

Straight into his dick.

My face. Was on. His dick. Which seemed very happy with our new predicament.

I sat back. Heat radiated up my chest and neck and I was pretty sure my face was going to spontaneously combust from the combination of mortification and pure lust.

Because it was a *fine* dick.

Jase grabbed me under the armpits and pulled me upright.

"Thanks," I muttered, trying to ignore the way Tug Junior kept pointing at my vagina.

*We are open for business!* my vagina confirmed.

I forced myself to look at him. Jase. Not Tug Junior.

*Although…* my vagina said.

*Not the time!*

Jase's lip was bleeding. "Are you okay?" I asked as my own ass throbbed in answer.

"Mmpf," he repeated.

Limping to the bathroom, I grabbed a couple of over-the-counter pain pills for me, and a washcloth that I wet with cold water for Jase. I limped back to Jase, handed the washcloth to him and downed the pills.

"Thanks," he said. At least that's what I thought he said. It sounded more like "thanths."

"Sorry my dog's a doofus," I replied.

The doofus in question was lying on my bed, happily chewing on the underwear like they were his new prized possession.

"He can keep those," Jase said as he donned his shorts.

A burst of laughter escaped. "Probably a good idea." Although I made a mental note to throw them in the garbage the next time he took a nap.

We hobbled our way down the hall towards the front door—two injured humans and a blissfully unaware Great Dane wagging his tail in front of us, still carrying the boxers.

"Um, I guess I'll see you?" Jase asked as he pocketed his keys from the kitchen counter.

*Ugh.* This is why I hadn't wanted him to stay. The awkward morning-after nonsense. Should I kiss him good-bye? Hug him? Shake hands?

I had no fucking clue because it had been so damned long since I'd been in a relationship with anyone but my animals, that I had zero romantic skills.

"Yup."

*Can anyone say awkward?*

*We can,* sulked my lady bits.

*You're doing good, kid,* said my heart.

*All of you can shut your pie holes.*

I followed Jase out the door, locking it behind us.

"Howdy, neighbors!"

Fuck me dead.

I turned around. Jeff and Tyson were standing at the end of my sidewalk, four of their dogs on leashes and their ancient Chihuahua mix, Spicy, laying regally in a red wagon stuffed with fluffy blankets.

Jeff and Tyson were grinning, Jeff's eyes ping-ponging between me and Jase as they bounced on their toes, positively giddy at catching me doing a walk of shame from my own damned house.

"Hey!" Jase waved back.

"Don't encourage them," I whispered as I nodded at my best friends. "Sorry, can't stay to chat. Gotta get to the shelter. Animals to feed, etcetera."

Unfortunately, Atlas had different plans. He bounded down the sidewalk to greet his besties, still carrying those fucking boxers. Tails wagged, noses sniffed, the dogs all circled each other as Tyson tried to keep the leashes from getting tangled.

"Are those… underwear?" Tyson asked.

"Oh, for fuck's sake," I mumbled.

"I knew you were a boxer guy!" Jeff squealed. "Wait. What happened to your mouth?"

Jase raised a hand to his lip, like he'd forgotten I'd clocked him not ten minutes ago, right before I face-planted on his dick. "Um, I fell?" Jase responded.

Jeff looked at me. "And are you limping? Why are you limping?" they asked me, their voice increasing in volume.

"I also fell."

Tyson's face split into a giant grin. "I'm glad you finally made it to a house."

The dogs continued to sniff and hop around Atlas, still very interested in his new toy.

"Although we're still okay with the kinky shelter sex," Jeff added.

Jase made a sound somewhere between a laugh and a cough.

"It wasn't kinky… oh, never mind," I said before calling Atlas over. He sniffed his buddies one more time and trotted to me.

"Not kink shaming, sweetums. I am one hundred percent here for this," they said, emphasizing each word in that sentence as they grabbed the handle to the red wagon. "Bee-tee-dubs, you still owe me the tea from the last time. Wine it out at our place tonight. Unless you have plans to sprain an ankle later with Mr. Tall, Blond, and Fabulous?"

Jase, who'd been wisely walking to his truck while all this was going down, stopped and smiled at me. "I promise to be gentle next time," he said, winking at me before getting into the truck and driving away.

"*All* the details, Ms. Sanders," Jeff said before they and Tyson walked back the way they came.

I loaded Atlas into my SUV and closed the door, leaning my forehead against the cool metal. Klingons give me the strength to make it through that conversation.

No more sleepovers, I promised myself.

*As long as we still get orgasms, we can support that,* my lady parts answered.

Super.

29

# MOLLY

I stood on Jeff and Tyson's front porch, a bottle of white wine in one hand, my other hand poised to knock, Atlas at my side.

*If I just ran now...*

"They wouldn't even know I was here," I said to Atlas, who was standing next to me, waiting for me to open the front door so he could visit his besties. He leaned his shoulder against my leg, tail swishing gently behind him.

"We can see you through the doorbell camera, Sanders." Jeff's voice sounded tinny through the doorbell speaker, causing me to jump.

"Sweet baby Spock."

"Stop stalling and get your sweet little ass inside so I can live vicariously through your sexual exploits," they finished.

So much for leaving.

"Here goes nothing," I said to Atlas as I opened the door.

The Fishers' dogs were standing at the entrance, tails wagging, happy feet clicking on the wood floor. General, their blue-gray pit bull mix, towered over the smaller pack members and *woofed* a greeting at Atlas before spinning around and marching them all back to the living room. The little dogs would use Atlas as a jungle gym while he and General play-wrestled until everyone tired and spread out for the Nap to End All Naps.

It was the same routine every time I visited. Usually, that normalcy gave me a sense of peace.

Today, I wanted to be part of the pack so I, too, could play and nap my day away. Instead, I was headed towards the Interrogation to End All Interrogations.

Slowly making my way to the kitchen, I briefly considered whether I could still make a run for it. With my luck, I'd drop the wine.

"We don't waste wine," I muttered in Tyson's voice.

"What was that, sweetie?" Tyson asked as he set out glasses on the kitchen island.

"I brought wine," I said louder, setting the bottle on the counter next to the glasses.

Jeff peeked over Tyson's shoulder from their position at the stove. "Ooo! That will go great with dessert." They were stirring something that smelled like a cinnamon roll and a creamsicle had a baby that they wrapped in a chocolate blanket.

My stomach growled.

After the chaotic start to my day, I'd done everything possible to keep from thinking that the man who'd given me orgasms so powerful I'd practically levitated off the bed was just a wall away, doing whatever he was doing and probably looking like a wet fucking dream doing it.

You could officially eat off my kennel floors—and walls and ceilings—by the time I was done with all my busy work.

But all that work actively ignoring Jase had come with a price. A price my stomach was now demanding to be paid.

Jeff pointed at the charcuterie board in the center of the

island. "Help yourself. Babe, can you top me up?" They held up an empty glass towards Tyson and wiggled it.

Tyson complied while I skipped the meats and crackers and made myself a plate of cheese. It was the only food group that mattered, and my stomach deserved the best after being neglected all day.

"You need more than cheese for this conversation, sunshine," Jeff said, eyes still focused on their mystery dessert, but knowing me well enough to know I'd filled up my plate with cheese. "Plate up."

Rolling my eyes, I added a multigrain cracker and a slice of what was probably *Dave and Busty's* elk salami, a local favorite.

"Better," they replied.

Tyson grinned while he handed Jeff's wine back to them and poured two more glasses.

"So," he said, sitting on a bar stool and handing me a glass. "How was your day?"

I felt the heat roll across my face. Tyson's grin morphed into a full-toothed smile.

"That good, huh?"

"Ooh, don't get to the good stuff until I'm done!" Jeff said, pouring their magical concoction into a greased baking dish and sliding it into the oven.

"Okay," they said, untying their apron and plonking themselves down on the stool next to Tyson. "Tell us *everything*."

What was there to tell? I'd had earth-shattering sex with a man so talented my vagina was still quivering.

Big deal.

*Very, very big deal*, my vagina reminded me.

*So big*, my ovaries agreed.

*Mmm, hmm*, chimed my boobs.

"Well? We're waiting," Jeff prompted.

"Fine, we had sex," I admitted before gulping half my wine down.

Tyson refilled my glass without breaking eye contact or losing track of his annoying smile. "And?" he asked.

"And what?"

"And how was it?" Jeff asked. "How many times was it? Did he go down on you? Or the other way around? Or both? How about his gigantic penis? Does it come with a manual or did he know what he was doing? Where? When? *I need details, Molly Jean Sanders!*"

Jeff's hands were gesturing wildly around them by the time they'd run out of breath.

Tyson moved their wine glass out of the way, still grinning.

"Feel better?" Tyson asked, cupping Jeff's cheek as they huffed and puffed. He turned to me. "They've been holding that in all day."

"I can tell," I said, sipping my wine, trying to decide where to start.

"How about you start at the beginning?" Tyson suggested, reading my mind like he'd been doing since forever.

This was a safe space, no matter how uncomfortable Jeff's rapid-fire questioning tactics might seem. I knew I could trust these two people with my life. And that included my sex life.

Taking a deep breath, I shrugged. "It just… happened."

"When?" Jeff asked, fanning their face.

"Since the night before the Sunshine Festival."

"Oh em gee, and you're just telling us this now?" Jeff gulped down their wine and waved at Tyson for another refill.

"It was only supposed to be that one time. I didn't think there was anything to tell." Which was the Vulcan's honest truth.

"Except…" Tyson prompted, popping a piece of Brie into his mouth and handing Jeff an olive from his plate.

Jeff swatted his hand away. "I don't have time for food, love. This is focus time."

I sighed. No way out of this except through. I charged forward. "Except, then it happened again, which you know because, well…"

Because they'd walked in on me, about to have an orgasm.

"Right, the kinky shelter sex," Jeff answered.

"It wasn't kinky, oh, never mind." Not the battle to pick today.

My friends stared at me, clearly waiting for the rest of the story.

"And then it happened again."

Jeff bounced on their stool and clapped their hands. "How many 'agains'?"

I stuffed a piece of sharp cheddar in my mouth and chewed.

"Stop stalling, legs," Jeff said.

"Um, does it count if your clothes don't come off?"

Jeff bent their head down towards their lap and hyperventilated.

"Do you want it to count?" Tyson asked as he rubbed circles on their back.

Maybe. Yes. No.

Because it didn't matter. Because it was just sex, and even if it happened again—

*Oh, it's happening again or we go on strike,* harrumphed my vagina.

Even if it happened again—*I side-eyed my vagina*—it was still just sex.

*The most impossibly amazing sex to ever happen in the entire universe of great sex,* corrected my vagina.

Fine. It was really good sex.

"It was just sex," I said out loud for the benefit of my friends, who would probably institutionalize me if they knew I was arguing with my lady parts.

Jeff took a big gulp of air and sat up. Their eyes were bugging out of their head and their face had turned a fun shade of not-red-but-also-not-purple. "I'm sorry, sweetie, but there's no way that sex with that fine specimen of a man —no offense, Tyse—is 'just' anything."

"None taken," Tyson said, still rubbing their back in a display of love and devotion that made the cheese in my stomach curdle.

Because I wanted that. I wanted someone to be so devoted to me that even if I lusted over the hottest man on the planet, he'd be okay with it because he loved me. Weird parts and all.

"It was pretty good sex," I admitted, my voice coming out small. Which, fuck that. It was terrific sex, and I fucking loved it, and I was going to own it. "It was fucking terrific sex," I corrected, loud and proud.

"Yeah, it was!" Jeff said as the timer on the oven went off. They squeezed my shoulder as they moved past me.

"Happy for you," Tyson said.

"That I had sex?"

"That you had amazing sex," he clarified.

"Me too," Jeff said, placing the dish on a hotplate in the middle of the counter. "I was worried your virginity was growing back."

"I don't think that's how it works." Probably. It had been a very long time.

Jeff shrugged. "So, when are you two lovebirds going to paint the town purple?"

Love birds?

"Oh no. No, no, no. No love. No birds. No dating. Just sex," I said. No matter how much fun I had when I hung out with Jase, no matter how great I slept last night wrapped in his arms. It was just sex.

My heart peeked around the corner. *Promise?*

*Yes, sweet thing. We're just giving the girls a good time.*

*So good*, agreed my vagina.

*See?*

"If you say so," Tyson said, walking to the fridge and pulling out the white wine I'd brought.

"I say so."

Jeff snorted as they drizzled caramel over their concoction.

"Smells delicious," Tyson said, looking over Jeff's shoulder.

"Orange chocolate bread pudding with bourbon caramel," they replied.

"Holy Klingons, that looks good," I said. My stomach shoved the cheese to the side to make room.

"Almost as good as that lie you're telling yourself," they said, dishing out three servings.

"What lie?" I asked as my phone dinged. Pulling it out of my back pocket, I tamped down the smile that immediately threatened to explode on my face.

> Jase: In case I forgot to tell you this morning, I had an incredible time last night.

> Jase: Let me know if you're free tonight. I could bring pizza.

"That lie," Jeff said, pointing a spatula at my face, which felt warm and was probably the same color as Jeff's hyperventilation face.

I shoved my phone back into my pocket and schooled my features. *Poker face, poker face, poker face.*

*We want to be poked again!* shouted all my lady bits at once.

*That's not what poker face means, you guys.*

"No lies here," I said, picking up a fork and stabbing a bite of pudding, shoveling the thought that Jase was asking me on a date—the exact thing I just told Jeff and Tyson I wasn't doing—into my mouth with the bread pudding. Along with how badly I wanted to say yes.

Dear Spock, the bread pudding tasted like angels were singing in my mouth.

Eating my feelings with yummy dessert was a sure-fire way to give me heartburn. But the alternative was far, far worse.

"We're here if you want to talk," Tyson said.

"Nothing to talk about." The lie made the sweet goodness in my mouth taste bitter. "It's just sex."

"If it were just sex, then why did you look at your phone like that?"

*If it were just sex,* my heart said softly, *you wouldn't be so worried.*

"It's just sex," I repeated, resolving to make that statement the absolute truth by doing the only thing that made sense.

I would fuck the worry right out of me.

*Whoopie!* cried my vagina.

I sure hoped Jase was up for the challenge.

3 0

# MOLLY

*P*laying hide and seek with a goat was not on my bingo card for today. Neither was running late because I was too busy trying to fuck Jase out of my system.

But here I was. Doing both.

"Larry Penelope Sanders, where the hell are you?" I shouted into the backyard.

The goat hadn't been in her pen when I'd opened the shelter this morning. Maybe if I used Larry's government name, the goat would know I meant business.

"If you're back there, show yourself right now!"

A silence that put me on edge followed.

Fine. Time to try a new tactic.

Four gnomes, gifted to me by Mrs. Kowalski after I took over the shelter following my mom's death, stared at me from beyond the patio. They looked like deranged serial killer leprechauns. I put them out there to appease Mrs. Kowalski, but hadn't been brave enough to put them closer to the back door.

Just in case.

"If you let me know where you are, I'll let you eat the lawn gnomes!"

Nothing.

Fuck a goat. If that didn't entice the spawn of Satan to show herself, then Larry was well and truly not here. Spock only knew what trouble she was getting into, with the entire county at her disposal.

I snatched my phone off the table and fired off a text message to Jeff and Tyson.

> Me: mayday mayday lps is mia again please tell me youve got eyes on her

> Tyson: Nooo we just planted new mini rose bushes in the front.

> Jeff: Lock up your prized possessions. Our favorite furry felon is on the prowl and she's hungry!

> Me: JEFF NOT HELPING

> Me: we need to find her stat

> Tyson: Should we activate HHL?

*Jean-Luc Picard help me.*

The Harmony Help Line was the town's version of an emergency phone tree, but far less efficient. Think kid's string telephone toy, but run by the town's most gossipy residents.

It was helpful if your teenager was out past curfew and you were worried about them having sex in the back of your neighbor's SUV. Which had only happened once, but once was enough when you found two teenagers humping like furless hamsters in the back of your car because you forgot to lock it.

It was far less helpful for goats with a penchant for troublemaking. Especially if Candice found out Larry was loose. There was no way I could argue my way out of paying her deductible then.

Me: not yet but scour the neighborhood

Me: covertly

Me: looking at you j <eyeball emoji>

Jeff: Roger-dodger. Activating stealth mode

Tyson: Will do. Let us know if you change your mind.

I blew a strand of loose hair from my face and looked around the shelter, marveling at how quiet it was this morning. At least the shelter animals were giving me some peace, even if my goat wasn't.

I had agreed to take another group of animals from the Chester County Municipal Shelter last night. Besides the senior dog, orange kitten and the chicken I had left after the Sunshine Festival, I now had three dogs, five cats, three kittens and two guinea pigs.

When I'd closed up last night before dragging Jase to my house for another round of "fuck him 'til I'm over him," the animals had been too tired to put up much of a fuss about getting back in their kennels.

They must still be tired if no one was barking or meowing or squeaking for attention and food. Thank Spock for that minor miracle. Because they were going to have to wait until "Operation Find Larry Before She Burns Down the Town" was resolved.

I placed my phone on the wireless charger on my desk and ran through my mental checklist for the day. After feeding my animals, I was supposed to sanitize the empty kennels, order next month's food and litter supplies, call foster applicants, and do the dozen other chores I normally did on a random Tuesday. Even if I had any volunteers scheduled today, which I didn't, there was no way I was going to catch up. At least not before I turned forty.

All thanks to Larry.

There was a weird sort of comfort in knowing that when I got to the shelter each morning Larry would stare at me through the sliding door, even if it was a bit unnerving. I jumped out of my skin more mornings than not when I threw back the curtains to let the light in, those beady little eyes glowing golden through the glare of the glass.

The absence of the freaky little fur ball was so much worse.

I picked up my phone again. Maybe Jase had spotted her.

Sometime between fucking me with his mouth and his dick during our shower this morning, I thought he mentioned something about needing to run into town. Or was it go for a run? It was hard to focus when you were busy orgasming.

Before I could press send, a voice designed to make Satan himself curl up in the fetal position and weep broke through the silence.

"Molly Sanders!"

Candice fucking Shoowater stood in my lobby, one hand on a hip, the other clutching a file folder. As usual, she was done up to the nines. Bubblegum pink lipstick, matching claws, er, nails, and a tennis outfit so white it was like looking into the sun.

"We're not open yet," I said. "You'll have to come back and ruin my day later."

Candice ignored me and slapped the folder onto the reception desk.

"I am shutting you down," she said, jutting her pointy chin out towards me.

I stared at the folder. "I hate to burst your happy little bubble, but you can't shut me down. Despite what you think, you don't run this town."

Candice flipped the folder open and tapped a sharp pink nail against the papers inside. Phrases like "dereliction of duty" and "health hazard" jumped off the page. "This is a petition to close Happy Tails Animal Shelter."

I picked up the folder and flipped through the pages, noting a fair number of signatures on the last page, most of them members of Candice's self-proclaimed Harmony Springs Beautification Committee or their spouses. Beautification Committee was code for cookie-cutter, as far as I was concerned.

"Why would you want to close my shelter?" I performed an important service for the town, the county even, by taking in strays and unwanted animals and finding them new homes. Why would anyone want to shut me down?

"Because you are unfit to keep animals."

"What proof do you have of that?"

My records were impeccable and beyond reproach. The Department of Agriculture always gave me glowing reviews during my inspections. My adoption rate was one of the best in our little corner of the state. I did good work, damn it.

"This." Candice thrust her phone in my face.

The shaky video of Larry climbing Candice's car like a mountain was playing.

*Oh, Larry. Why couldn't you be a Volkswagen lover?*

"You can't close Happy Tails, Candice." Probably.

"Watch me," she replied. She pointed her bony finger

towards the folder in my hand. "This petition is on its way to the town council as we speak."

*Oh, come on.* This was not what I needed this morning. What I needed was four more hours of sleep, Larry to magically appear in the backyard having spread nothing more nefarious than sunshine and rainbows while she was MIA, and an extra large mocha latte from the Bean.

Instead, I had… Candice.

This had to be payback for all the great sex I'd been having recently.

*Touché, universe.*

"If you're so hell bent on shutting me down, why tell me about it first?" I asked, placing the folder back on the desk.

"To give you time to move your animals," she replied, self-importance dripping from her lips. "I'm not a complete monster."

All evidence to the contrary.

"How generous of you," I said, failing to keep the sarcasm out of my voice but stopping the eye roll that was threatening to knock me backwards. Score one for me.

"I'm insisting the council puts this on their next agenda. You have until then to figure out what to do with all your misfit creatures."

"When is that?"

"Two weeks from today." Candice practically cackled.

*Two weeks?* How was I going to convince the city not to shut me down before then?

Candice picked up the folder and looked around. "Why is it so quiet in here?"

"Probably because I'm good at my job." One missing goat notwithstanding.

"Not for much longer, thank god," Candice quipped, and my stomach dropped to my feet.

A flash of red caught my eye out the front window over

Candice's shoulder. Jase's truck, cutting off any response I might have had. Which was good, because I was about to start begging.

Why was Jase parking in front? He usually parked in the lot across the street like the rest of the businesses on this block. Trying not to take my eyes off my nemesis for too long, I watched Jase exit his truck and walk to the bed, where —HOLY FUCKING KLINGONS.

"Larry!"

"What? Where?" Candice shouted, moving behind a chair. Why, I didn't know. Larry could be an asshole, but she'd never attacked people. Cars and fences? Yes. People? No.

The front door opened and Jase walked in, followed by Larry, a rope looped loosely around her neck. *Spock, help me.*

Jase beamed at me, and my insides did a little happy dance. Loose running shorts covered thighs that belonged on a Greek statue. His tee shirt was soaked in sweat that somehow unfairly made him look delicious and not gross and sweaty. Blond hair sprouted out from under his ball cap.

He looked like he'd been on a run. *Ah ha!*

"Molly! Look what I—"

"Jase!" I interrupted, nodding towards the chair Candice was cowering behind. "Thank you so much for taking Larry with you on your run. She really needed to burn off some energy this morning."

His eyebrows lifted as he looked at a crouching Candice before looking back at me. "My run. Right. It was absolutely no trouble," he drawled.

*Bleht!* yelled Larry.

"Get that creature away from me!" Candice yelled, digging her claws into the pleather chair back.

*Bleeht!* yelled Larry again, this time with a stomp of her feet, looking very much like she wanted to use Candice for head butting target practice.

"My car! Where's my car?" Candice shoved open the front door, then stopped and turned towards Jase. "As her landlord, this is also your problem," she said, before racing outside.

Candice's head swiveled back and forth, scanning the street for her precious Mercedes before she took off running.

Jase handed the rope to me. "What's my problem?"

I sighed, walking Larry to the back door and letting her out. Jase stood behind me, the nearness of his body heating my outsides. And my insides.

"I am."

"You're a lot of things to me, Molly Sanders, but a problem definitely isn't one of them."

*That was a nice thing for him to say*, I thought as my eyes got a little blurry. Stupid allergies.

"Candice is trying to shut me down." My voice sounded tiny, like I was down a dark tunnel. Which I may as well have been.

Saying the statement out loud plunked a large dose of reality into the pit of my stomach like a large, unwelcome boulder. Would the council really side with that primped up windbag? I didn't think so, but there were a lot of signatures on that petition, many of whom I knew.

"She can't do that," Jase replied, rubbing circles on my back. "Can she?"

The continuous motion of his hand felt nice. Intimate. Like he cared. Like we were something more than fuck buddies.

If only…

Needing to put space between us before I did something I'd regret later, like start relying on him, I stepped away from him towards the kennels. The dogs needed to go outside.

"I don't think so, but knowing Candice, she'll bulldoze the council into getting her way."

"Screw Candice."

I snort-laughed as I pushed open the door to the dog kennels. "She'd probably like that."

Jase shuddered, looking like he'd swallowed a lemon slice. "No thank you. Need help?" Jase asked, following me but giving me a little distance.

*We don't want distance. We want him,* my ovaries complained.

*Correction. We want him inside us,* my vagina added.

*I don't hate the closeness,* my heart whispered.

*Oh, no you don't,* I warned my heart. *You stay out of this.*

"Sure," I said.

Asking him to stay and help wasn't relying on him. I just didn't want to be alone. Alone would just allow my brain to hijack my feelings and spiral me into a hole of self-pity and despair. The animals deserved better from me.

*I* deserved better from me.

"We just need to let the dogs out and…"

I stopped at the doorway to the kennels.

"Where are all the animals?" Jase asked.

*Oh no.*

"Larry, what did you do?" I whispered into an empty room.

3 1

JASE

*I* wasn't sure how many dogs were supposed to be here, but that number was currently zero. Molly paced the empty room, muttering to herself. Words like *how* and *where did they go* and *fucking Larry* drifted past my ears as she strode past me, helpless to do anything but stand there.

The sex bench was visible through the window of the room we were in, and an image of Molly splayed out in front of me like a Thanksgiving buffet hit me right in the groin. I fucking loved that bench. I'd have it bronzed for posterity if we could finish what we started on that bench.

Not that I or Tug Junior were ready for another round. We'd gone two rounds last night. It was almost three rounds. TJ had totally been up for that challenge—heh—but Molly had rushed us out of the house before I could make it happen. Which was a shame, because all her mumbling about my superstar penis making her late again made me want to haul her back in the house and prove just how super my dick was.

What? I'm an overachiever.

Something had gotten into Molly this past week. I didn't

know what, but hell if I was going to stop it. I would, however, restrain from taking her on the bench this morning —even superstar penises needed rest. And Molly needed help.

So here I was. Returning a runaway goat, lying about taking her for a jog—*who the hell in their right mind goes running with a goat?*—and trying to piece together a puzzle I couldn't see all the pieces to. Yet.

Every kennel door was wide open. Toys and blankets littered the floor. It looked like whoever was here had thrown a heck of a party before they left.

Molly plopped onto a plastic chair sitting near the door and hung her head in her hands, her ponytail flopping forward and hiding her face.

"Want to tell me what's happening here?" I asked, squatting down and moving her hair so I could see her.

When she didn't respond, I nudged her shoulder with mine. "Maybe I can help."

"How in the hell did she pull this off?" Molly asked.

"She who? Candice?"

"Fucking Larry," she answered.

"What—?"

"Fucking hell… they're really gone." She stood and turned in a circle, hands on top of her head.

More hair was out of her hair tie than in it by this point. It was sexy, in a messed-up, I-love-how-passionate-she-is kind of way. And probably in an I-love-her kind of way.

Nope. Not going there. Not yet.

"What can I—"

"Catch," Molly said, darting out of the room.

"Catch?" I said, following her down the hall into a large corner room, my brain desperately trying to fill in the blanks. *Catch what? Catch me? Catch my drift? Catch a cold?*

Kitten mews hit my ears as she pushed open the door.

Oh. *Cats.*

"Thank fuck," she muttered, following it up with a "No, no, no, no."

Two rows of kennels, one on top of the other, lined the two longest walls. Plexiglass doors dotted with air holes showcased little condo-like living spaces. They looked like giant dollhouses. Some had blankets piled up in corners. Others had small, cushy-looking beds. All had a plethora of toys.

In the top right corner condo, a scruffy gray kitten with white ears was scratching at the door while its equally small roommates tumbled around, oblivious to everything but each other.

The rest of the upstairs cat condos were empty, the doors closed tight.

The downstairs condos were also empty, but unlike their upstairs neighbors, every single downstairs condo was open.

She turned to me, her eyes watery, which tugged on every instinct I had to pull her into a tight hug and fix all her problems. Which right now looked like her animals were missing.

"Oh, Larry," she mumbled.

The lightbulb went on over my head.

"Did Larry let your animals out?"

She nodded, a single tear spilling down her cheek and cutting me to the core.

"Hey." I swiped a thumb softly across her cheek. "I'm sure they're in here somewhere."

I didn't sound nearly as confident as I'd like to be. If Molly's animals were here, wouldn't we hear them? They'd be scratching at a door, or whining, or doing whatever dogs and cats did when they were loose in a shelter.

Which were all thoughts I kept to myself because I had more self-preservation skills than you might suspect, thanks to growing up with two older sisters.

"Were all your doors and windows closed when you got here?"

She nodded. "I'm sure of it."

*Squeak.*

"Did you hear that?" I asked, looking over my shoulder. It sounded like a squeaky toy that my sister's Weiner dog liked to play with.

Molly spun in place, looking around the room. She ducked, looking under the kennels, putting her very fine ass on display. An ass that I'd spent an inordinate amount of time kneading this morning with her legs wrapped around my head.

*Not now, Tug!*

She stood, hands on hips, before darting towards a closet at the back of the room and throwing it open. A giant brown-and-black cat that looked almost as ragged as Molly ran out, leaping into the air.

I shoved off my bad knee to snatch the cat out of the air like a fly ball. Unfortunately for my knee, it wasn't at one hundred percent—might never be—which meant instead of the graceful landing I'd pictured in my head, I stumbled, cat in my arms, knocking up against a utility closet. The handle dug into my side as my knee buckled.

"Holy Spock," Molly said, coming quickly to my side. She scooped the cat from my arms, which allowed me to push myself off the floor. "Are you okay?"

A shockingly delicate and high-pitched squeak answered Molly.

"I think that means we're both okay," I said, not quite sure I believed it. The cat definitely seemed to come out of this with fewer battle wounds.

"Oh, Clarence," Molly said, and the cat burst into a purr that sounded more lawn mower than cat.

"What happened, sweet boy?" she asked, rubbing her face

against his fur and then placing Clarence gently in an upstairs cat condo.

*Mew.*

"I know, buddy. I'll get you some food in a second," she said, latching the door and checking that it was closed.

"Are you sure you're okay?" she asked me, placing a hand on my shoulder as I rubbed my side and tried to ignore the throbbing in my knee. I'd have to ice that later.

"Yeah," I said. Because as much as I hurt right now, Molly was hurting more. Maybe not physically, but the frown across her face, the way the hand on her shoulder had a death grip on my arm, the way her other hand was clenching and unclenching. Yeah, she was hurting.

A helpless feeling in my gut all but paralyzed me. I was used to taking charge. When a pitcher needed a minute to collect themselves, I called a timeout. When the shortstop missed a snag on a hard-hit ball, I made sure he knew the team had his back. I made things happen on the field.

But I didn't know what to do here.

*So ask, dummy.*

The voice wasn't mine. Or Tug Junior's. It was my sister's, and it was clear as day to me.

I still remembered the day she'd said those words to me. I'd been at the hospital visiting my newest nephew when Eliza had burst into tears after her husband had left to check on their older daughter.

*Tears.*

My oldest sister was crying.

I had no idea how to process what I was seeing. I'd grown up watching her obliterate any challenge in her way. Debate opponents, professors who thought they had something to prove, a board of directors who didn't think it was appropriate for a CEO to take a maternity leave.

None of those even made a sweat mark or a pit stain. It

was who I'd channel when I first got to the majors. Would Eliza back down to the all-star hitter standing at my home plate? Fuck no.

But there she was, sobbing, and I couldn't move. After approximately eighteen hours that was probably thirty seconds of watching my oldest sister fall apart, I finally made my mouth work.

"I don't know what you need," I finally admitted, feeling like a failure. What kind of brother didn't know how to help his big sister?

She smacked me on the arm. "So ask, dummy," she said on a hiccup.

*So ask, dummy.*

"Molly," I said, getting her attention and waiting until she looked at me. "What do you need? How can I help?"

The pause seemed an eternity. I was about to ask again when she answered.

"We need to find them."

It came out as a whisper, but at least it was a plan. Not a highly detailed plan, but I could work with it.

"Okay. Then let's find them. How many are gone?"

"Four dogs and five cats," Molly said a little more loudly. "And, oh shit, maybe a chicken? I didn't hear Barbie when I came in this morning, but I was so preoccupied with Larry missing that—Oh, gods. What if they're hurt? What if they got hit—"

"Nope," I said, cupping her shoulders and facing her head-on. "We're not going down that path. We're going to find every one of these animals and bring them back here, safe and sound. And then I'm going to scour the internet for a Larry-proof lock, so she stays where she's supposed to."

Molly looked up at me, those bourbon-colored eyes pleading for me to be right. I was right, damn it. I had to be. There was no room for failure.

"How can you be so sure?"

"I just am." I so wasn't.

Molly blew out a breath. "If Candice finds out…"

"She won't," I said with way more certainty than I felt. Fake it 'til you make it, right?

She shook her head. "This is a small town. People talk."

"Not all people."

"Enough people."

"We just need a little sleight of hand. Something that makes them think they're looking at something else."

Like calling for a changeup as I squatted behind home plate. A pitch designed to look like a fastball or a curveball or any other pitch than what it was. An off-speed pitch designed to make the batter swing too soon, striking them out.

A small grin formed on her perfectly kissable lips. I'd take it.

"What do you have in mind?" she asked.

I steeled my face so she could see my determination. "Honestly? I'm not sure. But I am sure we will think of something."

And I would. I'd come through for those lost animals. For Molly.

Whatever it took.

I TURNED ON THE RECIRCULATING HOT WATER PUMP FOR THE mash tank and groaned as I stood. Working my bum knee back and forth, I stretched my neck. When had I become so old?

I checked my phone. I'd been crouched over, fiddling with the composition of my mash tank for over an hour. No wonder my body was unhappy with the current working conditions.

*Ding.*

Swiping my thumb up, I unlocked my phone to check my texts, unable to keep the smile off my face when I saw Molly's name pop up.

> Molly: feeling flirty meet me at the bean and bring your wallet... ill be the one in a fur coat and a feather in her cap

Molly and I had come up with a sort of code to use whenever someone spotted one of her animals, to keep Candice from finding out what we were doing. The code was probably overkill, but it was fun sharing a secret with Molly.

Any message starting with a reference to flirting meant she was on her way to pick up an animal. Bring your wallet: she needed my truck. Fur coat meant a dog. Feather in her cap was… something. I wasn't sure, but knowing Molly, it would be an adventure.

Underpinning the entire plan was a ruse to make it seem like we were dating. That way, no one would bat an eye at seeing us together. Tyson and Jeff were also in on the plan, so double dates had also become a thing.

And I didn't hate it because so far, I'd helped rescue a dog and a cat, spent more time with Molly, and had the support of an entire town that believed we were dating.

We'd also extended the code for when one of us was horny. Molly had used the phrase *I've got a kink in my hose* yesterday. Turned out she was home showering and wanted to get, ahem, creative with getting clean.

But it wasn't just the sex that had made these past few days some of the best of my life. It was the time I got to spend with Molly. Conspiring. Laughing. Hanging out. All of it.

We *were* dating. Molly just didn't know it yet.

Me: Be there in 5. I'm buying.

I stuck my phone in my back pocket, slapping a cap on my head and grabbing my keys off the bar top, feeling good. Another animal rescue. Another shot at showing Molly I was here for her, no matter what.

"What the actual fuck?"

I turned around at the familiar voice, which should not be here. It should be far, far from here.

"Sam?"

My business partner, agent and best friend stood in the doorway.

"What are you doing here?" The plan was for Sam to come out right before opening, but that was still three weeks away.

"Hello to you, too, dickhead," Sam said, running a hand back and forth through thick black hair, causing it to stick up in places. A tote was slung diagonally across his shoulder. His tie was loosened, his shirt wrinkled.

He looked like he'd been left in the dryer too long.

My phone dinged before I could respond.

"Why, in god's name, is it so fucking hard to get to this town?" Sam groused. "I almost threw up three times. Fucking driver and those fucking switchbacks. Jesus fucking Christ on a cracker."

He dropped his bag and slung off his tie.

"Get me a fucking beer." Pausing, he narrowed his eyes at me. "Unless you've given it all away?"

Oh. *That's* why he was here.

I had emailed him after the Sunshine Festival to let him know we should double our estimates on the first weekend opening. My social media was buzzing with all the hype about my new opening thanks to the word of mouth we'd achieved from our booth. Who knew that handing out free beer cards and autographs with a few adoptions would be so fruitful?

I hadn't heard from Sam, but I'd been pretty busy with other endeavors. Like licking Molly's pussy in the shower yesterday.

But instead of looking excited about me all but guaranteeing a successful opening weekend, Sam looked like he was trying to unalive me using the Force. I could practically hear the "Imperial March" playing in the background as he strode into the room.

I walked calmly around the bar and poured a Grand Slam Ambeer into a pint glass.

"I take it you got my email?" I asked, holding the beer out to Sam.

Sam grabbed it and swallowed half of it in three large gulps. Wiping the foam off his mouth with the back of his arm, he took two full breaths before answering.

"We haven't even opened yet, and you're already giving away beer."

*Ding,* went my back pocket. *Ding. Ding.*

Shit. I needed to let Molly know I was delayed.

"You need to answer that?" Sam sneered.

Yes.

"Nope," I said, wiping down the bar that didn't need cleaning. Molly could handle a dog and whatever else without me, right? I just hoped she didn't view this as a betrayal and freeze me out again. We had a really good thing going.

"Good. Then what the actual fuck, Tug?" Sam repeated, pulling out a folder from the tote he'd dragged into the room like a dead corpse and slapping it on the wet counter.

It was our business plan. The same one I fiddled with on

my tablet every morning over my coffee. And every lunch spent eating at my desk. I knew that business plan better than my own face by this point.

"I don't know exactly what your concern is—" I started before Sam jumped in.

"My *concern* is you're giving away profits we haven't even made yet."

*Ding.*

Fuck.

"It was for a good cause." The best cause. The look on people's faces as they walked away with their new family member and an autograph from the King of Baseball was priceless. And being able to help Molly hit her goals that weekend was just the topper.

"Yeah? What cause is that?" Sam asked, finishing his beer and putting the empty glass down a little harder than necessary. "Your dick?"

"No," I replied, keeping my voice steady as I refilled Sam's glass and set it—gently—in front of him. "The animals."

"Hmph. I stand by my original statement."

Sam took another, smaller drink this time. "Fuckin' A, this is good beer."

"I know," I said. "Which is why I doubled the opening weekend estimates."

"People should *pay* for this beer." Sam eyed me.

"And they will," I answered, keeping my tone light. "They may come for a free beer, but I'm confident they'll stay for a second. And come back for more. This is the only brewery for miles."

"If you build it, they will come… really, Tug? How cliché." Sam cocked an eyebrow.

What could I say? My beer made people happy.

Oh, that was good. I should put that on a hat.

"Exactly!" I answered, grinning at my best friend.

"It's too fucking early in the morning for baseball movie quotes," Sam replied, taking another drink.

It was almost noon.

*Ding.*

"For Christ's sake, answer your fucking phone so we can get to work."

I pulled out my phone. There was a long string of messages from Molly, starting with *cant wait to see you sugar pants* and ending in a frantic *where the fuck are you there are chicken feathers in my fucking bra this is not code for sex i need your wallet stat.*

"I, uh…" I looked at Sam, who was flicking through his phone like it, too, had pissed him off.

"There a problem, lover boy?" Sam asked without lifting his eyes off the screen.

"No. No problem." Just chicken feathers in undergarments. "I just need to make a quick call."

Sam waved a hand at me, dismissing me. I walked quickly to my office and shut the door. Calling Molly was probably a non-starter. She sounded like she had her hands full—her newest text message was *youre dead to me tugwater.*

So I did the next best thing. I called Jeff.

"*The* Jase Tugwater is actually calling me? I might actually die," Jeff answered.

"Jeff. I need help."

"Finally! You tell me where and when, hot stuff. Don't worry, Tyson is totally on board. You're on my approved list of celebs I can do if I can convince them to sleep with me."

"Um…" I liked Jeff better when they were starstruck. This newer, friendlier Jeff was a little… *too* friendly. "Molly's at the Bean trying to rescue a dog and maybe a chicken?"

"A chicken?"

"I honestly don't know. All I know is that it sounds like all hell is breaking loose and I'm, uh, tied up here."

"Say no more, Savior of the Stolen Bases. I've got your back."

"I owe you," I said, regretting it immediately but also meaning it. I was glad Molly had friends like Jeff and Tyson she could rely on.

Unlike me.

I needed to get Sam sorted and get down there. Molly should be able to rely on me, too.

> Me: Sorry, Cupcake. Beer emergency. Sending backup.

Molly: WHAT WHO WHY CHICKENS

Sorting through the important parts of that hot mess of a text, I shot off a quick reply.

> Me: Jeff is on their way. I might owe them a favor now lol.

Three dots appeared and disappeared twice before Molly's responses came through.

Molly: i hope they make you serve them breakfast in bed in your underwear while dancing the macarena

Molly: which is code for we are never having sex again

Molly: I FLOCKING HATE CHICKENS

I owed Jeff big time.

Molly might hate me after this, but I'd make this up to her somehow. I had to. There was no going back for me. Only forward.

Right after I got things sorted with Sam.

## 3 2

## JASE

*I* maneuvered a bright blue plastic cart down an aisle of the local Stuff and Stuff Hardware—named after the two brothers who owned it, Wallace and Bart Stuff, and not the mountains of crap stuffed into every nook and cranny in the store. Greeting cards next to cans of spray paint next to patio furniture. It was a place of orchestrated chaos I could only assume was a deliberate attempt to upsell the entire store by making someone walk up and down every single aisle to find something.

My cart had one wobbly wheel that squeaked in time with my steps.

Step, *squeak*. Step, *squeak*.

Thanks to the boxes of pool noodles standing next to an array of toolboxes, the aisle was barely wide enough to accommodate my large body, let alone a shopping cart.

I was here because Sam had taken over my office and was currently elbow deep in our business plan. Which suited me just fine. I knew the business plan by heart and was confident that the dozen or so free beer passes I'd given out wouldn't affect the success of the Catcher's Box. Sam would figure that out too, in time.

So that's what I was doing. Giving Sam time to catch up, while I braved the looming avalanche of stuff at Stuff and Stuff's, locating the list of emergency supplies Jeff had texted me. Repeatedly. In all caps. While they attempted to wrangle a dog and a chicken into a carrier.

Sam, however, thought I was picking up lunch. Which I would. Right after making sure Jeff and Molly didn't die of dysentery.

Jeff's words, not mine.

*Squeak, squeak,* went my shopping cart as I turned the corner. Locating the face masks on a shelf next to bags of potting soil, I tossed two packages into my cart as my phone rang.

My sister, Eliza.

"Balls," I muttered. There was enough going on in my life right now with Sam breathing down my neck and whatever the hell Jeff and Molly were doing. I didn't need family drama too.

My thumb hovered over the ignore button, blowing out a puff of breath to dispel my irritation, before I hit answer.

"Eliza. Hey."

"Call your fucking mother already."

Jesus fucking Christ on a cracker. "Good to hear your voice, sis!"

"Yeah, all the niceties, blah, blah. Why are you ignoring Mom's texts?"

Was I? I flipped to my text messages. No texts from my mom since last month. There were twelve new unread texts from Jeff in the last three minutes, and one from Sam reminding me to order his sandwich without mayo. But nothing from my mom.

"I haven't gotten any texts from Mom."

"Oh, for fuck's sakes, that woman. She's probably been texting some poor schmuck in Florida who's wondering why they're being guilt tripped into calling their mother. *Landon, put down your sister's markers right now!*"

I held the phone away from my ear. Landon was my newest nephew. Now three, he was born thirteen years after his older sister, Chloe, thanks to a vasectomy that didn't take. My youngest niece, Edith, followed a quick twelve months after that. Eliza threatened to sue the doctor's office and cut off her husband's balls if they had another kid. Both my brother-in-law and the doctor triple-checked the latest procedure to make sure it took.

"Sounds like you're busy, sis. I'll let you go," I said, tossing a canister of Febreze into the cart, which I finally found in the same aisle as a selection of kitschy homemade wooden Live Laugh Love signs. For good measure, I grabbed two more canisters.

I checked my list. Rubber gloves. The last item standing between me and freedom from this hoarding situation pretending to be a hardware store.

Against my better judgment, I put my sister on speaker-phone so I could shop with both hands. A new string of text messages from Jeff pinged on my phone.

Jeff: WHERE ARE YOU???

Jeff: WHY ARENT YOU HERE YET??

Jeff: OMG THE SMELL

Jeff: TELL TYSE I LUV HIM IF I DONT MAKE IT BACK

"Call your mother," Eliza barked. "Or I will show up at your doorstep. With Mom."

"You wouldn't."

She wouldn't. *Would she?*

Of course she would. It was Eliza. She didn't make empty threats. A lesson I learned the hard way in the third grade.

"I wouldn't like myself," she said. "But desperate times, little brother."

She disconnected and I raised my face to the ceiling, which was strung with twinkling Christmas lights. I blew out a calming breath and refocused.

*Ding.*

   Jeff: BRING BLEACH

*Ding.*

   Sammy: See if they'll do extra pickles.

Christ almighty, I needed a vacation from my life.

"Focus on Molly. She needs your help and you're going to show her she can count on you." I pushed my cart as the wobbly wheel continued its off-key melody.

Turning down an aisle filled with empty flowerpots and diapers, I stopped as I heard a familiar voice.

"I know, I could hardly believe my luck," the female voice said from the neighboring aisle.

I peeked through a gap in the shelf between a pile of Colorado-themed teddy bears and boxes of wood screws—*why, Stuff bros?*—and saw a heap of familiar blond hair.

Candice Shoowater stood next to a man with male pattern baldness that also looked vaguely familiar.

Bob something? Bill? Buck? It was the dude who kept papering my front door with election pamphlets.

What were those two doing at Stuff and Stuff's together?

"You know you have the council's support," Baldy said.

"I can always count on you, Bob," Candice replied.

*Bob!* That's right.

"Even more so once I'm elected mayor," Bob replied.

Council support. Mayor? What were they talking about?
*Ding.*

> Jeff: FOR THE LOVE OF ALL THATS HOLEY GET YOUR HOT ASS HERE STAT

> Jeff: WERE GOING DOWN I REPEAT WER DOING DOWN

Shit.

I shoved something that looked like it might be an industrial cleaner into the cart and rolled my cart down the aisle, but Bob's next sentence stopped me cold.

"All we need is a way to postpone the opening of the brewery, and shutting down the shelter should be a cinch. According to Andrea Abernacky, Molly's barely afloat."

*What the hell?*

"I can't wait to get rid of that damned shelter," Candice spat out, the venom in her voice palpable even through the decorative pillows that made up an entire wall of shelving. "And Molly along with it. I hope she ends up homeless with her goat. It would serve them both right after what they did to my Mercedes."

I crouched down, trying to stay out of sight.

"That was a real shame," Bob said.

Was that what this was about? Revenge for her car? Why bring in Bob?

"She'll get what she deserves," Candice replied. "As long as you stick to the plan. Once they're both shut down, I can buy the land for a steal, raze that ratty building and have my luxury condo complex up and running in six months. Plenty of time for the ski season."

*Buy my building?* The woman was delusional. I had no intention of selling it, and even if I did, Candice would be the last person I'd sell to.

And if she thought there was any way I'd let anything happen to Molly or those animals, even Larry, she had another thing coming. If Candice wanted to mess with Molly or Larry, she'd have to go through me first.

*Huh.* Unexpected, but the longer I sat with those emotions, squinting through the pillows, the more I realized the truth. Molly was my past, my present, and my future. And I'd do whatever it took to make sure she knew that.

"I've already talked to a few of my colleagues," Bob said. "We are ready to pass the ordinance as soon as you file your petition."

Ordinance? Petition?

"Just do your part, and I'll make sure your election goes off without a hitch," Candice said, as they began walking towards the front of the store.

"Thank god you finally convinced Frances to step down," Bob said.

"I can be very persuasive when I need to be."

Election? I needed to tell Molly about this.

*Squeak.*

*Ding.*

Jeff: YOURE DED TO ME TUGWTER

"What was that?" Candice asked, trying to peer through the pillow wall.

I crouched down and duck-walked my cart as fast as I could to the next aisle.

*Squeak, squeak, squeak.*

"Just a shopper in paint supplies," Bob said.

I was too far away to hear the end of their conversation, but I breathed a sigh of relief when I heard the chimes of the front entrance doors play Jingle Bells. Peeking around a display of tissue boxes and spray paint cans, I watched Candice and Bob head in different directions.

Pushing the cart down the aisle—*squeak, squeak*—my mind spun in a hundred directions. I needed to tell Molly what was going on.

Grabbing whatever I could see that even remotely looked like it might be helpful in an apocalypse, I finally headed to the checkout stand.

"Well, hey there, Mr. Tugwater," one of the Stuff brothers said.

According to the name printed on his striped apron, it was Bart. I'd lived in Harmony Springs for three months now, and visited for many more before that as I made plans to open the brewery. I'd made plenty of trips to the store, but I still couldn't tell the brothers apart. Everyone in town swore they weren't twins, but they may as well have been. "I see you're doing some tar removal," Bart said.

"Tar removal?" I looked at the can in Bart's hand. Goo-OFF.

*Ding.*

I didn't have time to return the product to the shelf. "Um, sure," I replied, pulling my credit card out of my pocket.

It took Bart almost thirty seconds to decide which item to pull out of the cart first. I watched, my patience waning, as Bart looked at a box of tissues he must have accidentally bumped into my cart.

"Always good to have tissues on hand. My brother has allergies something terrible. We have a box of tissues in every room." Bart scanned it and placed it in a paper shopping bag before repeating the process, this time with a package of sandpaper.

Where the hell had I gotten sandpaper?

Bart repeated the process—contemplate, remove, inspect, comment, and scan—for the remaining items in my cart. Only half of which were on Jeff's list. The other half, well, I wasn't sure what I'd do with a five-pack of tweezers, but if anyone had an eyebrow emergency, I had it covered.

Stuff poked a couple of buttons on the register and waited for the total.

Forty-two hours later, a dollar amount glowed on the screen. "That will be two hundred and sixty-six dollars and forty-two cents with tax," Stuff drawled.

Jesus. What had I bought?

Miracle of miracles, Stuff's had a chip reader. I tapped and waited while the register spit out a receipt. One leisurely line at a time.

It had only been a few minutes since Candice and Bob had left, but I could hear the ticking clock in my head. The more time I spent here, waiting on slo-mo Stuff, the less time I had to stop them.

*How* to stop it was another matter, but I'd cross that bridge when I got to it.

Twelve more hours later, Bart handed me the receipt. "You need anything else," he lumbered, "you just come on back. We're fixing to have a fire sale on American-themed items for the Celebration of Our Nation festival next month, in case you need any decor for that brewery of yours."

"I'll be sure to stop by," I said, not wanting to step foot in this labyrinth again if I could help it, and picked up the paper sacks, nodding a farewell to the waving Bart. I shifted both sacks to one arm and shot off a quick text to Jeff.

Me: On my way

Jeff: ABOUT DUCKING TIME

Bags loaded into the back of my truck, I started the ignition right as my phone rang. My mom.

"Bad timing, Mom," I muttered as I hit the ignore button and put the truck in drive. Molly needed me and I would not let her down again. Mom could wait one more day.

33
# MOLLY

The list of things I would enjoy less than attempting to capture two runaway shelter animals from behind a dumpster that smelled like something—or *someone*—died in it was small. So small, I couldn't come up with even a single thing to put on that list at the moment.

"What in Satan's ass is that smell?" Jeff said next to me, covering their nose with their tee shirt.

At least my misery had company, even if it was Jeff and their over-the-top drama. It should have been Jase, but he'd had some vague beer emergency and hadn't shown up.

"Beer emergency. Like that's even a thing," I mumbled, creeping closer to the dumpster from hell and wondering how a basset hound with the same circumference as a small elephant squeezed into such a small space.

"*Ba-woooo!*" bayed Biscuit.

"I didn't ask you," I replied.

"*Bah-kah!*" yelled Barbie the chicken from my left, who looked like she'd just gotten a blow-out at Jeri's Salon and Spa down the block. She was currently trying to hatch what looked like an old tennis shoe and not going anywhere.

Good. I'd collect her as soon as I had Biscuit safely locked in the kennel that Jeff had brought. Instead of Jase.

"What was the point of even having a code if he's never going to show?" I asked no one in particular.

"Who you talking to over there?" Jeff asked.

"*Ba-wooo!*" answered Biscuit.

"Apparently the dog," I muttered, tiptoeing through something I hoped was a melted candy bar. "I hate my life."

Kole had called me earlier to let me know two of my animals were in the alleyway behind the Bean, chasing away his customers. That was nearly thirty minutes ago. So far we'd had no luck convincing Biscuit to come out of the small opening where she'd lodged herself the minute she saw the kennel. The kennel that Jeff had brought with them. Not Jase. Who I'd asked.

Not even his gold-medal dick was going to get him out of this one.

"I think she's stuck," Jeff said, peering around the side.

"How can you tell?"

"Science. Her ass is larger than the space she's currently occupying."

Crap. I did not want to crawl behind a dumpster full of demon guts to eject an overweight dog. I pulled a chicken nugget out of the fast food bag I'd set on top of the kennel and waved it in front of the opening behind the dumpster. Along with showing up with a kennel, they'd had the foresight to stop by the Cluck 'n Moo to grab a ten-piece nugget on their way here. I'd French kiss Jeff if he wasn't married to my best friend.

Nuggies were Biscuit's favorite treat.

"Come on, Biscuit," I cooed. "Who wants a delicious nuggie?"

"If she ate a vegetable once in a while, maybe she

wouldn't have this problem," Jeff said, directing their voice at the dumpster.

"*Woooooo*," Biscuit replied mournfully.

"Ignore them, Biscuit. They're just cranky because they smell."

"We both smell like a fucking dumpster fire. Maybe we should just burn this one and smoke her out," Jeff said.

The dumpster shook.

Jeff jumped back. "Holy shit!"

The shaking got worse and I worried it was going to tip.

"If your golden-dicked superhero were here, he'd know what to do," Jeff said, moving behind me and using me as a shield.

"He doesn't have a golden dick." It was a magical dick. But he could probably help lift a hundred-pound dog from behind a dumpster.

"Coulda fooled me. Hey, you think if we get covered in dumpster goo, we'll develop superpowers?" Jeff asked.

*Bang. Bang. Bang.*

"What the…?" I started.

Jeff squealed and shoved me in front of them.

"Hey!"

The dumpster stopped moving. We stared at it.

"Do you think it's safe?" Jeff whispered.

I shrugged. "I don't think it's *not* safe."

"Go poke it."

"I'm not going to poke it. *You* poke it."

"If Jase were here, he'd probably poke it. Just like he pokes you." They grinned and raised their fist.

"I'm not fist bumping for that."

Jase should be here. But he wasn't. So it was up to me to figure this out. By myself. Well, me and Jeff. Except they were cowering behind the dog kennel they'd brought when Jase decided he had other priorities. So basically by myself.

Their fingers were flying furiously over their phone. They better not be live-streaming this.

I stretched my neck, hand gripping onto something exceptionally cold and slimy—*ugh, gross*—as I got a better look around the side of the dumpster without moving my feet any closer. Just in case.

Biscuit whined from behind the dumpster.

"Come on, girl," I said, crouching and smacking my legs to get the dog's attention. "You've got this."

"Yeah, Biscuit," Jeff chimed in. "Just think skinny thoughts!"

I was peering into the dark recess when a black-and-tan blur shot out of the crevice and nearly knocked me over.

"Good girl!" I shouted at the dog, who was now sprinting up and down the alley like Usain Bolt. If Usain Bolt were a dog and had six-inch legs and a belly that nearly dragged the ground. And wasn't that fast.

"*Bah-KAH!*"

I had almost forgotten about the chicken. Barbie shouted like a feathery warrior queen as she jumped off her unhatched shoe and chased after the dog.

"Should we go after them?" Jeff asked, tilting their head as we watched the most bizarre race I had ever witnessed.

I shook my head slowly and crossed my arms. "No need. Watch."

The sprinting dog had already slowed, her tongue lolling out of the side of her mouth, long and droopy. The trot slowed to a walk, and in less than thirty seconds, Biscuit lay down in the middle of the alley and started snoring.

Barbie raced up to the dog, clucked a few times, and then hopped on Biscuit's back, settling herself, her shoe-egg clearly forgotten.

"Chicken nuggets one, Biscuit zero," Jeff said, shaking their head.

I nodded, grabbing the kennel and walking towards the animals. "At least she tried."

More than I could say about some people.

I lifted Barbie off Biscuit's back and gently laid her next to the dog. Jeff let out a grunt as they lifted the burly basset off the ground. Between the two of us, we got both the dog and the chicken safely into the kennel.

"How many animals does that leave?" Jeff asked, wiping sweat off their brow with their arm and airing out their shirt with the other.

"Five."

I'd gotten calls about all of them except sweet little Stella and the orange kitten. It was killing me that no one had seen them. I'd been getting up early to walk up and down the highway next to my shelter, hoping maybe they were huddled in a bush somewhere close. I left food out every night, knowing I was probably feeding Larry and not my missing animals, but I didn't know what else to do. And until they were all accounted for and safely back at Happy Tails, I'd keep doing it.

Jeff rubbed my shoulder, sensing my distress. "Don't worry, Molls. We'll find them."

All I could manage was a nod as we each grabbed an end of the kennel.

"Holy heavy hangover," Jeff puffed as we shuffled our way to my SUV. "Does this dog eat her chicken nuggets with a side of boulders?"

"Less complaining, more moving," I wheezed out, making a mental note to buy some diet dog food.

"You guys need some help?" a deep, familiar voice asked from behind me.

Jase.

"Well, well, look who finally decided to show up," Jeff

huffed out, setting their end of the kennel down and putting their fists on their hips.

"Oof," I grunted as I set the kennel down as softly as I could manage.

"Sorry I'm late," Jase said.

The words may have been in response to Jeff, but he was looking at me. Those icy blue eyes cut straight to my core, which was currently clenched as I remembered the many, many orgasms and happy feelings he'd been responsible for lately.

Well, he could just fuck right off if he thought—

"*Bah-KAH!*" screamed Barbie from her kennel.

"Is that… a chicken?" Jase asked, peering through the slats in the kennel.

"*Bah-rooooo!*" mourned Biscuit, causing Jase to tumble back a few steps.

"And a dog in need of a vegetable," Jeff said.

"A… what?"

"Did you bring everything?" Jeff asked, their head tilted, eyebrows raised, foot tapping on the ground. They looked like a disappointed parent waiting for their kid to give the wrong response.

Jase hefted the brown bags from the ground at his feet. "And a few extras."

"I don't give extra credit," Jeff said, digging through the bags and bringing out an industrial sized bottle of hand sanitizer and slathering themself with it. "I'm going to bathe in this when I get home."

"What are you doing here?" I asked. "I thought you had better things to do?"

Jase took the sanitizer from Jeff and offered some to me. Part of me wanted to decline the offer on principle. But the part that had been knee deep in garbage goo shut that down real fast and heaped on the gel.

"I said I had an emergency at the brewery, not that I had something better to do. And I really am sorry." His voice was soft and soothing, and my heart, well, that unreliable little organ was beating a merry tune and clapping vigorously at the fact that he showed up. He actually showed up. Over an hour late.

But he was here.

All muscles and strength and remorse, looking at me like I was responsible for his every breath.

*Hug him*, my heart whispered.

*Fuck that*, said my vagina. *Let's take him behind the dumpster and do dirty things to him.*

I'd just about had enough with all the opinions around this place. There would be no hugging or dumpster humping, no matter how glad I was he was here.

*Boo*, they all said.

"Focus, Horny McBoner," Jeff said, reminding me we were in an alley with a dog and a chicken, all of us in dire need of a hazmat spray down.

"How can I help?" Jase asked, eyes crinkling but still very much on me. The intensity of his stare made my panties melt. Or maybe that was the nuclear waste I'd been wading through for the last half hour.

His gaze suddenly turned sour. "And what in the hell is that smell?" He looked around as if he had only just registered that we were in an alley.

"Us," Jeff replied. "We've been dumpster diving in the seventh circle of hell, and if I don't get a shower in the next fifteen minutes, Tyson is going to make me sleep in the garage tonight. So let's make this quick."

I cringed. I was going to have to burn these clothes and probably my SUV after this.

"Um, okay," Jase said, his eyes watering from the odor. *Welcome to the club.* "But we have a problem," he said to me, handing me a package of wet wipes that Jeff swiped out of my hands before I could even get them opened.

I had about a hundred problems and half of them were currently in this alley. "Could you be more specific?"

"Candice Shoowater."

Great.

"What mayhem is Dandy Candi trying to spread now?" Jeff asked from behind me, pulling out wipes like confetti at a parade and scrubbing their face.

"She's trying to put us out of business," Jase answered.

"Seriously?" I asked.

Jase nodded. "I overheard her talking with that guy who keeps announcing he's running for mayor, Bob somebody, at the hardware store. Seems they're hatching some sort of plan with the city council to close our businesses."

"*Buk-buk*," Barbie said from inside the kennel.

"I agree, Barbie," Jeff said. "We need to take that skank down."

I rubbed my forehead, needing a minute to process, but I couldn't, because—*ugh*—there was gunk on my shoes. I liked these shoes. I was going to miss these shoes.

"Fucking Candice," I muttered.

"Fucking Candice," Jase agreed.

I looked up at him. He looked like he wanted to strip me down right here in the alley.

*Awesome!* said my vagina.

*Not awesome. Weird*, I corrected. *We're disgusting.*

*Dirty sex is still sex*, it argued.

Klingons help me.

I took a deep breath to recenter myself and nearly passed out. Seriously, was it possible to do a chemical peel to the inside of my nostrils?

"What do you think?" Jase asked, taking a wipe from Jeff

and gently rubbing at a spot on my cheek. "You ready to show them what happens when you mess with us?"

*Us.*

Not him. Not me. Us. Together. As a team.

But could I trust him to have my back?

*We looove him,* my lady bits crooned.

*We absolutely do* not *love him,* I corrected.

*We'll see,* whispered my heart.

"Time's a tickin', Swoony," Jeff said, pulling me out of my thoughts.

It was hard to concentrate with all these voices confusing me. But Candice needed to be taken down a notch.

Squaring my shoulders, I faced Jase. "Yeah," I nodded. "Okay, let's do this."

Candice fucking Shoowater was going down.

Jase beamed as he stuck out his hand, only to wince as whatever was on my palm squished when we shook on it.

*So. Gross.*

"Squee!" squealed Jeff, clapping. "Go Team Tuggers!"

# 34

# MOLLY

*I*'m sorry," I said, praying to the Vulcan gods that I hadn't heard that correctly. "Did you say Team Tuggers?"

"You don't like? How about Team Sandwater? Team Jolly?" asked Jeff, as if this was a normal response to a normal question.

"No," I replied, my eyes watering from the stench wafting up from the kennel.

"No," Jase agreed.

"Harsh," Jeff groused.

"Why do we need a team anything?" I asked. The better question was, why were we wasting time on this? We had plans to make. Revenge being at the top of that list. Well, not the top. Biscuit needed an industrial doggy bath when I got her back to the shelter. So did I. But after that? Revenge.

"Because badass teams that take down skanky hoes with bad boob jobs need a badass name," Jeff said.

I swallowed my sigh. Debating further wouldn't help us uncover Candice's intentions.

"Fine. How about Team I'm Going to Murder Candice and Leave Her Body for the Bears to Find Next Spring?"

"I vote for that one," Jase said, a half-cocked grin on his face as he looked at me for approval. *Gah!* How could I resist that? This whole "us" thing he was going for was sexy. It made me want to see how fast I could bring us to simultaneous orgasm in the bed of his truck.

*We vote for that!* my lady parts chanted.

*No time, ladies. We have thwarting of evil plans to accomplish.* Right after a shower.

*We can multitask!* they answered.

Not the worst idea they've ever had.

"Team Murder Bears it is," Jeff said, holding their hand out, palm down, as they looked back and forth between me and Jase.

"That's not—"

"Team Murder Bears...?" Jase echoed. He smiled at me before shrugging his shoulder and putting his hand on top of Jeff's, causing my ridiculous best friend to squeal softly like the fanboy they were.

They both looked at me—one my friend and the other my... what? Lover? Accurate, but no. Partner? Maybe.

Jeff was bouncing on their toes like they were about to pee their pants. Jase had a ghost of a smile that was part amusement and part dare.

"Oh, for fuck's sake," I muttered, putting my hand on top of Jase's. "Fine. Team Murder Bears."

"So, what's our first TMB mission?" Jeff asked, way too excited.

Jase's phone dinged. Taking it out, he muttered something about a fucking sandwich and put it back in his pocket. "We need to figure out how they're planning to shut us down."

"And why," I added. "What exactly did they say?"

Jase filled us in on what he'd overheard at Stuff's until Candice almost spotted him thanks to the squeaky wheel and Jeff's incessant texting. Thank Spock they'd been texting and not live-streaming.

"So now what?" I asked.

"Normally I'd suggest you have sex with Candice to draw out information," Jeff said, their face scrunching into a look of concentration. "But in this case, you can't."

*What the hell?*

"Won't," Jase replied, nonplussed.

"What?" I asked.

"Won't. I *won't* have sex with Candice."

"You can have sex with whoever you want," I said. So long as they weren't Candice. Or anyone else alive.

"You're wrong," Jase said, the focus of those sky-blue eyes making me swallow as I tried to remember my name and what we were talking about.

"And why's that?" I asked on a breath, trying to ignore the big-ass smile on my friend's face as their head swiveled back and forth following the conversation.

"Because I'm taken."

Was it me, or did his eyes just darken like storm clouds rolling across the Colorado sky?

*Yay!* cheered my ovaries as they practically exploded.

*Not yay.* What was wrong with me?

*Isn't that what we want?* asked my heart, her voice too soft against the noise of the celebrations.

*No. Yes. Maybe.*

*Gah!*

I needed to get out of my head.

My thumbs flew over my screen, typing out a text message as I let what Jase had said sink in. He was taken. By me.

He wanted us to be an *us*.

I hit send and looked up. Jase gave me a ghost of a smile, part amusement, part challenge. He knew he'd flustered me.

"We interrupt this awkward silence to bring you… more awkward silence," Jeff stage whispered.

"Shut your pie hole," I groused, hitting send.

"Who were you texting?" Jase asked, the challenge on his face practically screaming that he knew I was avoiding him and the declaration he'd just made, but he'd wait for me to be ready.

"Kenny."

"Why are you texting Kenny *the love muffin?*" Jeff asked, singing the last words.

"Who's—wait. Love muffin?" Jase asked.

"He's asked you to stop calling him that," I said to Jeff. "And I'm texting him because his fiancé is Bob's daughter and she might have a lead for us."

"Ohhh…" Jeff said in a sing-song voice. "We're going to turn Ginger into a double agent!"

My phone chimed. It wasn't Kenny.

"Crap," I said, looking at the screen.

"Is Ginger not going to help us?" Jeff asked, their eyes narrowing. "I knew we couldn't trust her. Too smiley, that one."

"It's not that." Ginger did smile a lot, but she was good people. "I just got a lead on one of the tabby cats. Brooklyn thinks she spotted one of them in the big oak in front of the senior center."

My phone dinged again.

"Another cat?" Jase asked.

"This one is Kenny. He and Ginger are heading out of town later, but can meet us at his house in the next hour."

An hour. I looked at the kennel where Biscuit was snoring, Barbie clucking softly next to her, and calculated the odds of me being able to load the animals in my SUV, drop them at Happy Tails, burn my car to ashes to get rid of the smell, extract a cat out of a tree and still make it to Kenny's in the next hour.

*Don't forget the sex*, said my vagina helpfully.

*Not now.*

*Hmph*, it replied.

How the hell would I manage all that? Maybe Jeff—

"No," Jeff said, sneaking a sniff at their shirt and wincing.

"I didn't say anything."

"Your face did, and the answer is no."

"You don't even know what I was going to ask."

Jeff raised a meticulously manicured blond eyebrow at me. "So you *were* going to ask me something." It wasn't a question.

Damn it. "Maybe."

"Oh, well, in that case, the answer is… still no."

"But—"

"Sorry, Molls." They looked at Biscuit and Barbie in the back of Jase's truck. "As soon as we get Satan's petting zoo back to the shelter, I have a date with a scalding hot shower."

I looked at my watch. There was no way I could do this without a time machine.

"I can help," Jase said, his quiet voice laying over my thoughts and fears like a warm, soft blanket.

I felt the heat fill my cheeks as I realized he'd been watching me, waiting.

"I've never washed a dog before, but I'm game if you are."

The heat from my cheeks immediately dropped to my core at the thought of us both wet and soapy.

*We love bubbles!* said my nipples.

"Actually," I started, hating myself for destroying that little fantasy. "I was thinking after we dropped off the animals, you could go talk with Kenny and Ginger."

"Oh." He actually looked disappointed.

"Is that a problem?" I asked.

"Nope. No problem."

Just like that, the look disappeared.

"You sure?"

"Yeah, of course," he said, all confidence and sex appeal. "I can also check in on their foster kittens while I'm there."

Him thinking of the kittens before I did turned me on. And made me realize I needed to get my shit together. Kittens should have been my first thought. Not sex with the sex god.

A snore that sounded like a monster truck choking on its own exhaust rose from the kennel at my feet where Biscuit and Barbie were sleeping off their alleyway zoomies.

"I'll follow you and Jeff to Happy Tails," Jase said, picking up the kennel like it was filled with rose-scented dreams and wishes instead of an overweight dog with a sinus infection. He placed it softly into the back of his truck, saving my SUV from a fiery death. *Praise be to Spock.*

Closing the tailgate, he turned and leaned against the bumper. "And then I'll go talk to Kenny and Ginger. If one of you can point me towards their house?"

Jase may have asked the question to both of us, but once again, he was only looking at me. His eyes had gone a soft, baby blue and looked full of promises. Promises of lazy mornings spent alternating between making love and napping. Of not having to carry my burdens alone. Of someone having my back.

Vulcan gods, that would be nice.

But could I trust it? Could I trust *him*?

*We won't know unless we try,* my heart whispered.

"Thank you," I finally replied, leaning towards him and pressing a kiss on those very kissable lips.

His eyes widened briefly before he softened his lips and kissed me back.

"I'm all yours," he whispered in my ear before striding to the driver's side and getting in his truck.

*Yours.*

*Ours,* my heart said.

*I volunteer as tribute!* my vagina yelled.

Jeff bumped my hip with theirs. "Let's go, lover."

I blinked and laughed softly. "Shut your pie hole, stinky."

"You are not wrong," they said, getting into my SUV. "Come on. Let's go punch Candice in her lady balls so you can go get your man."

"Not my man," I said, starting the car and lowering all the windows.

"Not how I saw it."

Perceptive *and* annoying.

"Doesn't matter. We have work to do."

"Correct," they answered, sticking their head out the window. "And as soon as I peel off the top layer of my skin, I swear I'm all yours."

*All yours.*

Jase honked as he pulled out of the alley.

Could I really trust him?

*Only one way to find out,* I thought as I followed him.

# 35

# JASE

What do you mean you forgot my sandwich?" Sam yelled, immediately killing the high I floated in on.

"I forgot," I replied, stretching my imagination to come up with something, *anything*, to avoid telling Sam I'd been helping Molly. The person Sam blamed for my distraction from the business.

Not that I was distracted. I was expanding my field of interests. The Catcher's Box Brewing Co. was very much a top priority for me. I would do virtually anything to ensure its success.

Luckily for me, in this case, "virtually anything" included spending more time with Molly to stop our mutual enemy. Go Team Murder Bears.

"You were gone for less than two hours. How in the hell do you forget a sandwich in less than two hours?"

Sam was looking at me from over the top of a pair of round purple readers, eyes scrunched, scrutinizing.

I couldn't lie my way out of this. Sam knew me too well.

"I ran into… a problem at the hardware store."

"Was the problem that hardware stores don't sell sand-wiches?" Sam's voice was getting louder and raspier.

Stupid not to have stopped for a sandwich for my friend. I knew better. Hangry Sam was an asshole.

"No. Look, I'll call in an order. Just give me a sec."

Sam closed his laptop, dropped his readers on the desk, and crossed his arms. "You ran into Hot Girl from next door, didn't you?"

Ran into? No. Sought out? Yep.

Also, how the hell did Sam figure that out so quickly?

"This has nothing to do with Molly. Except, well, actually it does, but—"

"Stop. I don't want to hear it." Sam stood. "I'm fucking hungry and until someone feeds me, I'm deaf to all problems except the one causing my stomach to go unfed."

"I wouldn't mind a sandwich," Molly said from the door-way, where she appeared like a vision on a cloud. She'd changed shirts, but evidence of the dog bath she'd just administered was still obvious. The end of her ponytail was dripping, and there were big wet splotches mixed in with the mystery goo on her green cotton shorts.

When I'd left, the plan was for Molly to finish Biscuit's bath and head to the senior center. I wasn't expecting to see her until much later. Hopefully clean, naked, and in her bed. A grin formed on my face, despite knowing all hell was about to break loose.

"Well, well, well," Sam said, crossing his arms and signaling Hangry Sam was about to raise some hell. "Hot Girl, I presume?"

"Sam…" I said, issuing a warning to my friend. Being an asshole to me was one thing. But if Sam thought he could attack Molly…

"Well, well, well," Molly mimicked, right down to the arm cross. "You must be the douchey friend."

My grin morphed into a full-blown smile. Of course Molly could hold her own with Sam. And damned if that didn't make me half hard.

"I'm going to need you to stop distracting my boy here with your long legs and little animal hobby. We've got grown-up business things to do."

"Sam," I barked. "Not—"

"Last I checked, *Sam*," Molly said, not backing down an inch, "your boy here was a grown-ass man more than capable of making his own decisions on how—and with whom—he spends his time."

She sized Sam up, giving him a long, hard stare.

I shifted as I tried to make room in my pants, which were getting uncomfortably tight.

"Also, talk about my legs or my *little animal hobby* again," she continued, "and I'll let Larry loose on your ass." She looked him up and down. "She loves a good tasseled loafer."

Sam looked down at his shoes, which weren't tasseled but were loafers, and frowned. "Who the hell is Larry?"

"Pray you never find out," I muttered, walking over to Molly and placing my arm around her shoulder. Territorial? Hell yes. But Sam needed to understand that he'd crossed a line. "She's right. Leave her the fuck out of this."

Sam's eyebrows shot up.

"Ooh! Out of what?" Jeff asked, bouncing in as subtle as the stink bomb they smelled like, with Tyson right behind them.

"Jesus H. Christ! What is that smell?" Sam shouted, his nose scrunched and eyes watering.

"Ode d'Satan's ass," Jeff replied, waving their hand around and spreading the stench of death further into my office. I was going to have to paint my walls with bleach. Or tear down the building.

Which was exactly what Candice was attempting to do, I

realized as my stomach dropped. Looking at Molly, who was attempting to wring out her ponytail on my rug, I sighed through my nose. I reminded myself that this group of people—the very ones crammed into my office, yelling and making a mess—represented everything I loved about my new life.

I may have been forced to retire from baseball, but I wouldn't trade a single thing that happened following my surgery. Not for another year playing with my team. Not for endorsement contracts. Not for all the fame in the world.

These were my people. And Candice fucking Shoowater was going to find out what happened when you messed with my people.

"What are you two doing here?" I asked Jeff and Tyson. "I thought you were going home for the 'shower to end all showers'?"

"We were," Tyson started.

"But then we saw all the people here," Jeff continued. "And since I can't smell myself anymore—"

"We can," Molly, Tyson, Sam and I all said at once.

Jeff looked at Tyson. "Please note that I'm choosing to take the high road and not point out that real friends don't smell odors. They love with all their senses."

"Noted," Tyson said with a smile. I couldn't imagine the level of love it took to smile like that at someone who smelled like death rolled up in a shit burrito.

"Your friends must have had their scent organs removed," Sam replied through his designer tee, which was pulled over his nose.

"We haven't," Molly said, angling herself away from her friend.

"We just stopped by to tell you Candice just emailed the city council giving them a heads up she was going to present something at their meeting," Tyson said, gently trying to nudge his spouse out the door.

"Already?" I asked.

"How'd you get it?" asked Molly.

"She 'replied all' to the council's meeting notice," Tyson answered.

"You'd think with all that money she claims she has, she could pay someone to teach her how not to 'reply all' to something," Molly said.

"Who the fuck is Candice?" Sam barked. "And why is she delaying me getting a fucking sandwich?"

"How are you hungry after smelling… that?" Molly pointed vaguely at Jeff and shrugged. "No offense."

"I hope you all catch dumpster-cooties." Jeff sniffed their shirt. "Is it really that bad?" they asked Tyson, who nodded.

"You can use my shower," I offered.

Jeff's eyeballs rounded as their mouth gaped open. "I… you… Tyse?" they stuttered, their voice getting higher with each syllable.

"Now you've done it," Molly muttered next to me.

"Can I? Can I?" Jeff wheezed at Tyson.

"Sure, sweetie. I'll bring you some clothes."

Tyson mouthed a *thank you* to me as he left the brewery, and Jeff sprinted down the hallway.

"Do they know where they're going?" Molly asked.

"Don't worry, I'll find it!" Jeff yelled.

I heard doors opening and closing, followed by a high-pitched squeal.

"I think they just found your bedroom," Molly said, laughing.

"At least we can't smell them anymore," Sam said.

"Hey," Molly replied, scowling.

"No offense, Hot Girl," Sam replied. "I'm sure your friends

are real sweethearts when they don't smell like a dumpster fire."

"The douchey guy has a point," Molly conceded.

"Her name is Molly," I said, nearly growling, causing Sam's and Molly's eyebrows to raise.

"Sorry, dude." Sam turned to Molly. "Molly."

Molly tilted her head. "Sam."

Sam turned back to me. "Better?"

I nodded.

"Good," he said. "Now, where's my fucking sandwich and who the fuck is Candice?"

Molly pulled her phone from her pocket, her fingers flying. "ETA on the sandwich is fifteen minutes," she said before re-pocketing her phone.

"A woman who gets shit done," Sam said, nodding appraisingly. "No wonder you're in love with her, Tugwater."

Molly sucked in a breath and started choking.

I patted her gently on the back.

I may have been in love with her, but I knew I was a few chapters ahead of her in the book we were both reading. At least I hoped we were reading the same book.

"Candice is trying to shut us down," I said to Sam, trying to ignore the dread pooling in my gut.

The shower turned on, and Jeff started singing. Badly.

"Is that… Lady Gaga?" I asked Molly, my hand stilling.

"Unfortunately for Gaga, yes. Yes it is," Molly answered. She'd mostly stopped coughing, but her face was still pink, and she was refusing to look at either of us.

Fucking Sam and his terrible timing.

"Christ. That's terrible," Sam said.

"You're not wrong," Molly muttered.

Sam shook his head. "So, tell me everything."

So I did. Molly nodded here and there, but remained silent, arms crossed over her chest.

"And Larry is…?" Sam asked.

"My goat." Molly finally spoke, her voice soft but firm.

"I'm sorry. Did you just say your goat?"

As if roused from the bowels of hell, Larry let out a battle cry from next door that rattled the windows.

"Holy fucking shit!" Sam yelled, jumping up and tripping backwards.

"Speak of the devil herself," I muttered, trying and failing to stifle my laugh.

"A goat made that noise?" Sam asked.

"Her bleat is worse than her bite," Molly said, giggling.

"*She bites?*" Sam shrieked.

"Only if you don't share your sandwich," I said, causing Molly's giggling to erupt into full-blown laughter.

"Don't worry," she wheezed. "I ordered enough lunch for both of you."

Sam's face paled as it whipped back and forth, looking from me to Molly and back to me. "You better be fucking with me, Tugwater."

*Woof!* answered Atlas, as he came padding through the door, nuzzling Molly as he walked past her.

"What the fuck!" Sam said, getting the dog's attention.

Atlas walked up to him and stuffed his nose in Sam's crotch.

"Why is there a horse in our brewery?" Sam asked, splaying both hands in front of his jewels.

"It's a dog," I answered with a laugh as Sam tried to push Atlas's head away. Atlas, not deterred, pushed back.

"Does it bite too?" Sam asked, his voice going supersonic.

"Nah," Molly said, wiping tears from her eyes and tugging the dog's collar gently, moving him away from the terrified man. "He just has a nose for boxer shorts."

Atlas, having satisfied himself that Sam was a new friend, leaned against Molly, pinning her to the wall. She smiled fondly at her dog, rubbing his thick ears and eliciting a deep groan.

I commiserated with the dog. I'd made similar sounds at the mercy of Molly's hands.

Sam side-eyed the pair from behind my desk. "So, what are we going to do?"

"About Larry?" I asked.

"Candice," he said, fingers massaging his forehead. "But we're gonna circle back to the goat thing."

"I'm going to talk to Bob's daughter, see if she knows anything," I said, looking at the clock on my wall. Shit. We were running out of time.

"And you?" Sam looked at Molly. "Besides keeping your man-eating animals away from me, I mean."

Molly grinned at him. "Atlas likes you," she said. "Larry, well, she doesn't like anyone but Atlas."

"Lucky Atlas," Sam muttered.

"I have to rescue a kitten from a tree."

"Is that code for sex?"

Molly rolled her eyes. "No. This is a literal kitten in a literal tree. The code for sex is 'I've got a blown fuse. Bring your flashlight.'"

"I did not need to know that…"

"What about you? What are you going to do?" Molly asked my friend.

Sam looked at his laptop and ran a hand through his hair. This wasn't Sam's problem to fix. Not really. It was *my* business. And Molly's.

"Look, Sam," I started.

"I'll call Fozzy," Sam interrupted.

"Fozzy?" Molly asked.

"Fozzy," I said, nodding at my friend. "Yeah. Good idea."

Federico Antonio Bernardi, aka Fozzy Bear, was my former teammate. Best third baseman in the league. He and I had made the sports highlight reel more times than any other duo during our time together.

"What's a Fozzy?" Molly asked.

"A person who knows people," Sam answered, flipping open his laptop. "If anyone can find dirt on this Candice person, he can."

I grinned at my friend and my… Molly. *My* Molly.

Who was looking at me, golden eyes bright with hope.

Even Atlas wagged his tail.

*Thump, thump.* In time with my heart.

"Go Team Murder Bear?" I said with a shrug to Molly, who smiled her answer.

"What the fuck is a Murder Bear?" Sam asked. "Does it bite, too?"

I barked out a laugh. "We are."

"We are." Molly nodded.

*Woof*, Atlas agreed.

*BLEAAAAT!* Larry screamed from the bowels of hell.

"Holy fuck," Sam muttered. "Where's my fucking sandwich?"

I LOOKED AROUND AT THE COMPACT COURTYARD AS KOLE motioned me out the back door of the Bean. A door—and a courtyard—that until this moment I hadn't known existed.

"What is this place?" I asked. I felt like I'd transitioned from industrial chic at the Catcher's Box into a garden oasis in the middle of downtown Harmony Springs.

Birds tweeted atop the surrounding wooden fence that needed a fresh coat of paint but otherwise looked sturdy. The patio was full of potted plants of all shapes, sizes, and colors. Some I could identify by sight, like the tomatoes growing in an old tin bath. Others by their scent. Lavender rose tall in a blue ceramic pot while basil grew in a squat green plastic planter next to it, its leaves wide and bright. The rest of the plants covering the space were unfamiliar, but no less fragrant and welcoming.

"Private property," was all Kole said before he disappeared back into the café.

Modern-looking outdoor furniture edged a square patch of grass in the middle of the space. A cushioned sofa sat on one side, with two matching seats opposite it. A low-lying, glass-topped square table separated the set.

Sitting on the sofa were Kenny and Ginger. The reason for my mission here today. I'd left Sam back at the Catcher's Box, talking to Fozzy and googling furiously. Jeff was still showering and singing badly. I'd walked Molly to her car as we each left for our respective missions. Hers was to rescue a cat. Mine was to convince Ginger to help us.

A dog was lying at her feet. It looked like a chocolate lab who'd been fitted with the wrong legs. They were far too short for its barrel-like body, but the dog happily pranced its way over to me, stopping short to sniff my shoes.

"Don't mind Hopper," Kenny said, standing. "She's the welcoming committee."

I leaned down to pet the mismatched dog, who rolled over for a belly rub which I happily obliged.

Kenny held out a hand towards me. "Good to see you again."

"Same." I straightened and accepted the firm handshake. Kenny was a few inches shorter and probably a few years younger than me, and built like a brick shithouse with thick black hair. If I hadn't seen the guy swooning over kittens during the Sunshine Festival, I might have been a little intimidated.

"Man, I still can't believe we're getting a visit from Jase

Tugwater, King of Baseball," Kenny said, still shaking my hand.

"Friends just call me Jase," I answered, clapping the man on the shoulder with my free hand.

"Oh, sure, of course, sorry." Kenny let go of my hand. He might have been a little starstruck, but at least his version was much milder and less grabby than Jeff's.

Kenny's fiancé, with her honey gold hair and matching eyes, snuggled up to him and put a hand around his waist. She was wearing a light pink loose-fitting dress with a floral motif that matched the outdoor setting perfectly.

"You remember Ginger?"

"Sure. Good to see you," I said, nodding at her.

"I hope you don't mind," she replied with an easy smile. "But we stopped for some coffee on our way out of town and thought this would be easier than having you drive all the way out to our place."

Their place was about ten miles out of town and up a dirt road, at the base of Morris Hill, according to the instructions that Molly had given me before Kenny had texted with the new plan.

"Not at all," I said, truly not minding the shorter drive. Although the view from their house must be incredible. Even better than the one I would have from my land. If I ever got around to building my house. Once the brewery was up and running, I promised myself.

"Since we had the critters with us, Kole let us use his yard." Kenny nodded at the two fur balls I recognized immediately as they dashed in front of my feet.

"This is Kole's yard?"

"Sure is," Kenny answered. "He lives in the apartment above the coffee shop."

There was an apartment in this building? I looked up at the top of the painted brick building. Sure enough, there was a tiny metal landing connected to an even smaller metal staircase leading to the courtyard. Huh.

A kitten chased the tiny leash attached to its even tinier harness as it ran around and around a chair.

"Molly will be happy to hear the kittens are doing well," I replied, chuckling.

The furry speed demon met up with its sibling in a tumble of paws and tails. Righting themselves, the duo stilled as they stalked a dandelion swaying in the soft breeze that was keeping the summer heat at bay in the shaded yard.

Ginger laughed. "Growing like two weeds and keeping everyone, including Hopper, on their toes."

Hopper, seeing the attention the kittens were giving the dandelion, stood on her pint-sized legs, waddled over to the dandelion and lay on it. The kittens immediately pounced on the dog as a bunny hopped its way over to see what all the fuss was about.

"Is that Tofu?" I asked, marveling at three of Molly's animals here, playing together, like family. No wonder she took so much care in doing what she did. She was building families.

Something that might have been pride—or possibly heartburn from the sandwich I inhaled before rushing over—warmed my chest.

"It is," Ginger beamed.

The bunny had put on a few pounds, but looked healthy and happy as she bounced around the dog, playing keep-away from the kittens. Hopper's tail wagged in a circle, catching the attention of a kitten, who pounced on it.

"Molly said you wanted to ask us something?" Kenny said, sitting back on the couch and reaching for his coffee.

Right. I was here for a reason, not just to gawk and ogle adorable animals.

Opening my mouth to ask what I needed to ask, I hesitated. Could I really ask Ginger to spy on her dad? Back at the brewery, it seemed like such a simple thing: ask them if they knew what Bob and Candice were plotting. But here, now? With a couple that could have given a dentist a cavity with all their sweetness?

It felt… slimy. Like something Candice would do.

"Jase?" Kenny prompted.

I avoided eye contact as I watched Hopper, who was belly up on the grass as the kittens climbed her like a mountain and Tofu munched on a dandelion.

If I chickened out, decided that this was a step too far in my plans to keep my and Molly's businesses open, then what? Maybe Sam and Fozzy would find something to use against Candice. Or maybe not. We could still find another way to uncover her plans.

But would it be in time?

The alternative was worse: failing Molly.

I straightened and took a steadying breath. "Yes, sorry. We have a favor to ask and hoped you could help us."

"We?" Ginger asked, taking in my face with eyes that were far too observant for someone as young as she looked.

"Us?" Kenny asked, grinning. "So the rumors are true."

Shit. Were people already running around talking about our plans to take down Candice?

"Uh, what rumors?" I asked cautiously.

"That you and Molly are a thing," Kenny replied.

Oh. *That.* Relief loosened the knot in my stomach. "Oh, yeah, well… yeah."

Because we were a couple, even if she still thought we were only fuck buddies. It was more than sex for me. And I was sure it was more than sex to her, if she'd ever let herself admit it. Or at least it was before I fucked it all up.

I was going to do whatever it took to convince her to trust me again. To trust in *us* again. That's why I was here.

"Nice," Kenny said. "She's a good person. I can see why you two are together."

"So, what was the question?" Ginger asked before I could respond.

Right. The question. What the fuck were Bob and Candice up to? I could do this. Just take a breath… and ask.

"I… we… I mean, Molly and I. We're going to lose our businesses."

*Great job with the asking, Tugwater.*

Kenny's eyebrows raised as Ginger's eyes narrowed. She knew I wasn't finished. Knew I had something more to ask her.

"Candice is trying to shut us down, and…" I ran a nervous hand through my hair again. I needed to start wearing a hat to keep the nervous tic at bay.

"And?" Ginger prodded as Kenny rubbed a loving hand on her back, as if sensing she was going to need a little extra support and he was happy to give it to her.

Yearning punched me in the gut.

Molly and I could have that. I just needed to figure out how to fix this minor inconvenience first.

"We think your dad is working with her to do it and we're hoping you can help us figure out what they're planning," I finally spit out.

Ginger's face pinched in something that looked like irritation even as I hoped she, too, had heartburn.

*Smooth, Tugwater. Smooth*

"I'm sorry," I started, a hand going out to her to… what? Soften the blow that her dad was a giant douchebag?

"Babe?" Kenny whispered.

"No, it's fine," she finally said. "He's been acting weird ever since Frances announced her retirement and he decided to run for mayor. If he's teamed up with Candice… Just because she's got money and can afford fancy cars and trips to Vail, it's like she and that so-called beautification committee think they're all too good for us." Her face scrunched in disgust. "Like there's something wrong with this town."

She turned her head, her brows still scrunched, watching the animals playing in the grass. Kenny continued to rub her back, but looked back at me, eyes wide as he nodded for me to go on.

"I know this sucks to hear," I said quietly. "But Molly is going to lose everything, and I don't know how else to help her."

Kenny's attention turned back to Ginger, knowing, as I did, that it was her call.

She examined me for what felt like five minutes but was likely five seconds, scouring my face. Whatever she was looking for, she must have found it because she finally nodded.

"Kenny's right. Molly's good people. Let's figure out how to help her," Ginger said. "How to help both of you. And get my dad back on the right path."

*I* placed the cat carrier on the ground and looked up into the giant cottonwood tree in front of the Sunny Peaks Senior Community Center and Living Facility, glaring at the black-and-gray cat perched on a branch about fifteen feet up. For his part, Fancy looked like he didn't have a care in the world. He probably didn't.

I, on the other hand, had more cares than I could list. How to get this cat out of the tree before nightfall currently occupied a spot near the tippy-top.

Atlas stood beside me, also looking at the cat. But instead of irritation, his tail wagged slowly, as though he was happy to see his friend.

Irritation aside, I was happy to see Fancy, too. Especially since I'd been at this spot every day for the past three days. After the first call and failed attempt to find him, someone from the center had called me every day with another sighting. Which meant I'd drop everything and come running over, only to find out that the cat was gone.

Jase had offered to come with me this time, but I'd declined, figuring it would be a waste of his time. I'd left him with Sam at the brewery, arguing over opening weekend promotional strategies.

Atlas gave my hand a little lick and wandered over to a grassy spot where he sprawled out in the ample shade provided by the tree and let out a groan.

"You and me both, buddy."

I looked at the metal ladder I borrowed from Tyson and tried to gauge whether it was going to be tall enough to reach the limb where Fancy sat, feet tucked, looking like a loaf of bread. It was going to be close.

Why hadn't I taken Jase up on his offer?

Because Fancy was as elusive as a great white whale and I honestly didn't believe he'd be here this time.

But if I were being honest with myself, it was also because I'd needed a little thinking time. We'd hardly had sex in the days since Jase had dropped the Candice bomb on us. But the time we were spending together somehow felt more… intimate. Like we'd fallen into a familiar pattern of brief touches and gentle forehead kisses.

And I didn't hate it.

In fact, I liked it. A lot. Almost as much as sex with him.

*We don't love anything as much as we love that*, my vagina noted.

*Agreed*, said my ovaries. *Ten out of ten. Would fuck again.*

Fine. The sex was amazing. I did sort of wonder when we'd get back to that part of our life. But with Sam here, keeping Jase distracted with their opening, and Candice and Bob planning whatever they were planning, we'd mostly just fallen into bed exhausted at the end of each day, but still reaching for each other, like we needed that connection, even in sleep.

*Gah!* Relationships were hard.

Wait. We weren't in a relationship.

Were we?

*We're not* not *in a relationship*, my vagina answered.

For fuck's sake. *Focus, you guys.*

*Mew*, Fancy added to the conversation.

I tilted my head back. Yep, he was still there, watching me from his branch.

The cat blinked at me, then looked up the tree, like he was thinking of changing locations.

"Fancy, I swear to Vulcan, if you stay where you are, I will feed you sardines every day until you're adopted."

*Mew*, Fancy squeaked.

Taking that as acceptance of my terms, I adjusted the ladder, testing it a few times to make sure it was secure, and climbed.

*At least it's not a dumpster.*

Wind rippled the leaves gently as I slowly climbed, never letting go of the ladder. The last thing I needed was to fall and break something.

I really should have called the fire department, like Tyson told me. But, again. Fancy the disappearing cat.

Besides, this wasn't my first time climbing a tree. Sure, it was my first time climbing a tree in my thirties, when falling on my ass would hurt a hell of a lot more than it had at ten. Which, now that I thought about it, had been a lot.

I looked down.

*Ugh.*

No, nope. Not down.

*Up.* Keep looking up.

Praying for gravity to continue ignoring me, I focused on the top of my ladder and kept moving. Up, up, up.

Fancy kept his word and continued to crouch on the tree limb, watching me, but thankfully not moving any higher. Of course, he wasn't moving any lower, either.

"Come on, Fancy. Help a friend out and just climb down."

*Mew.*

Given Fancy's lack of movement, this mew probably meant *I rather enjoy the view from here, thank you very much.*

"Fine," I said as I took another step. I was two rungs from the top, but high enough maybe to shimmy myself up onto the branch. If I was very, very careful.

I looked behind me and my stomach flip-flopped as I wobbled. "Don't look down, dummy."

*Woof,* said Atlas.

*Mew,* said Fancy.

"Keep your opinions to yourself if you're not gonna help," I said to them both.

*Meow.*

*Woof.*

Arrogant animals.

I placed both hands on the branch, swallowed the bubble of terror caught in my throat, and lifted. My feet dangled as I adjusted my hands to hold my weight. It was difficult, but at least I wasn't falling.

"Okay, kitty cat, here we come."

Fancy's ears flattened as I looked at the limb above me.

"Don't you fucking dare," I threatened, my voice tight with exertion. I needed to get my ass up on this tree limb before my arms gave out. Or the cat bolted.

Momentum. I just needed a little momentum.

I kicked my legs behind me to swing up. It wasn't enough to launch me onto the branch, so I kicked out again, harder. My foot caught on the trunk, so I kicked one more time, as hard as I dared, finally lifting myself up onto the limb.

The bark scratched my belly as my shirt rode up, but I was totally up in this tree, sprawled unceremoniously across the branch, facing the cat. Not flattened on the ground, broken and bleeding. *Win!*

*Bam!*

*Nooo.*

I looked at Fancy, whose eyes were probably as round as mine, but were focused on something below us.

"For the love of Jean-Luc Picard… please tell me that the ladder is still propped up on the tree where it should be and not laying on the ground because I kicked it."

*Meow.*

*Woof.*

"Shit."

Willing myself to turn and see for myself—even though I totally knew what I would see—I adjusted my weight to keep from falling and peeked under my arm.

No ladder.

I stretched my neck a little further until I could see the grass below the tree.

*Yep.* There it was. On the ground. Next to the cat carrier. Atlas rose slowly and went to investigate while the trouble-making cat and I sat in the tree.

With no way down.

No worries. I'd just call for help. Shifting my weight to one side, I felt for the phone that was always in my back pocket.

No phone.

I checked my watch, which was always connected to my phone. The little red icon at the top of the screen mocked me. Disconnected.

Fancy blinked at me.

*Well, hell.*

"Hey buddy," I called down to Atlas, who looked up at me, tail wagging. "Don't suppose you can go find someone to help?"

He looked at the ladder and then back up at me.

*Woof,* he said before trotting off down the street.

"Please let him be going for help and not to Candice's fucking flower beds to take a nap."

*Mew.*

I scooted against the trunk so I had something to lean against as I waited for Atlas to work a miracle. Fancy, deciding my lap looked more comfortable than a tree, crawled into my lap and began purring.

Twenty minutes later, Atlas still hadn't come back.

"He's totally napping in Candice's garden."

I tried to adjust myself to give my back a little relief, but the cat's claws came out for purchase on my legs, halting all movement.

"You know what?" I said to the cat as I attempted to extract his claws from my skin. "I blame Candice fucking Shoowater. Her, and her stupid beautification committee, and her evil plans. It's no wonder I don't have a brain cell left for common sense and do stupid things like climbing a tree to rescue a cat without backup."

*Mew.*

"I knew you'd agree. She's the worst."

"I don't know who Candice fucking Shoowater is, but she sounds like the worst," an unfamiliar female voice said from below me.

37

MOLLY

*I* peeked over my knees and saw a woman, maybe a few years older than me. She looked tall, but that could have been the angle from being so high off the ground. Dirty blond hair cut in a long bob, looking both practical and stylish. Just like the ankle-length jeans and cute white tee shirt she wore.

She looked vaguely familiar.

The mystery woman adjusted the chubby baby she was holding in one arm while she placed two backpacks on the ground by her feet. Atlas was behind them, a toddler holding on to his leash.

*Woof*, Atlas said, and the kid squealed in delight.

"Atlas?" I said from my spot in the tree.

"Landon, honey, take the nice doggy over to the grass and sit. Mommy will be there in a sec."

Landon led Atlas to the grass. Atlas lay down and the young boy flopped against his giant tummy.

"I take it he's yours?" the woman asked, shading her eyes against the sun as she looked up at me. "The dog, not the kid. The kid's mine."

"Yeah," I replied. "Don't worry, he's super kid-friendly."

Atlas rolled over on his back, and the toddler drummed his belly. The dog's tail wagged as he wiggled on the ground, causing giggles to erupt from the boy.

"I can see that," she said, a smile lighting up her face as she watched the child play with Atlas.

The woman transferred the baby to her other hip. "So," she said, bouncing the baby gently. "Need some help?"

"Oh no. I was just up here, enjoying the view."

"Nice day for it."

"Yep."

Vulcan gods, my aptitude for avoiding the hard truths was astounding.

"So... the ladder laying on the ground here is just a lawn ornament?"

I swear to Spock I would marry this woman if she'd prop the ladder back up. But there was no way she could lift the ladder and hold a baby at the same time.

"Well," I replied. "I originally thought it should stand upright against the tree, but the ladder had other plans."

The familiar-yet-not face smiled. "Good to know you kept your sense of humor up there. Wouldn't do you much good down here on the ground. You know, with your ladder."

I laughed, surprising myself and Fancy, who tried to bolt up the tree. I reached out and snagged the cat before he got too far. My movement caused the branch to wobble. The woman below gasped as I clutched the cat with one hand and splayed the other against the trunk for balance.

"Fuck me," I gasped.

"Fuck me," mystery woman agreed.

"Tuck me!" shouted the boy.

"Shit, Penn's going to kill me," the woman muttered. "Can

I call someone for you?" She squatted and reached into a front pocket of one of the bags.

The smart thing would be to say yes. But the woman was clearly not from around here, otherwise she would have recognized Atlas. And without my phone, I shamefully couldn't list a single number outside of my dad's, who lived in Arizona. So unless I asked the woman to call my dad to ask him to call someone in Harmony Springs to help me—which I absolutely was not doing—I was stuck. At least until someone realized I was missing. Which could be hours.

*Mew*, Fancy said, as if feeling my distress.

"No, no, I think I'm okay," I replied, petting the cat to calm us both down.

"Does it physically hurt?" the woman asked, handing the toddler a bottle she'd pulled from a backpack.

"My back has felt better," I admitted.

"Not your back," she answered, her hand back over her forehead as she peered up at me. "Asking for help."

It hurt like a fire pit inside my abdomen, heating my brain to molten lava.

"I don't know what you mean," I lied.

She shook her head. "Stubborn. Just like my brother. You two would make a great couple."

Stubborn? No. Compelled to fix every problem myself? Maybe. Okay, fine. Yes.

But I'd sent Atlas to find help, hadn't I? It wasn't my fault that he'd brought back someone who physically couldn't help me.

"Look, I know you don't know me from Eve," the woman said, wiping something off the baby's face with her sleeve. "But take it from someone who knows. When someone offers a hand—or a phone, in this case—take it. We can't go through life doing everything on our own."

*Agree to disagree.*

*And look where that's gotten us*, my vagina said. *Fifteen feet up in a tree, sitting on a branch that's making me go numb.*

Point taken.

"My mom could." Why the hell had I just said that out loud? And to a total stranger.

"Mom's are overrated."

"You're a mom."

"Exactly. And look at me. I'm letting a stranger's dog babysit my three-year-old son, who, incidentally, has a mouth that will get him kicked out of preschool when he starts next year. All while I try to talk a woman and her cat down from a tree because I can't let go of this one," she hiked the baby up higher, "without risking her taking off down the road faster than a Formula 1 driver. Absolutely killing it down here."

I picked at a leaf while keeping a soft but firm grip on Fancy, who looked like he wanted to bolt. "I don't know what I'm doing," I finally admitted.

"Now that might be the first honest thing you've said so far."

*Harsh.* But true.

*Mew*, Fancy agreed.

The woman produced a pacifier out of thin air and gave it to the baby. "Look, do you want help or not? It's almost time for Edith's nap, and I still need to find my brother."

Could I really rely on others to help me when I needed it? I looked down at the woman, who was now looking over her shoulder, before turning to Fancy, considering my options. "What do you think, Fancy? You ready to get down?"

Fancy purred.

"Yeah, me too." I gave the cat another scratch. "Okay, random but super nice person. I give."

"Good timing," the woman said, looking back at me.

Whatever I had been about to say was drowned by a siren whooping its way down the street.

Spock help me.

~

"Who called the fucking fire department?" I said to no one in particular.

"Tucking fire part!" Landon said as he lay his head against Atlas's back. If Atlas seemed concerned that a fire truck was barreling down the road towards us, he didn't show it.

The woman shrugged her shoulders. "I hadn't thought of it, to be honest. Wasn't sure a town this small even had one."

We did, and thanks to the siren, the Harmony Springs rumor mill was up and running at top speed. This was going to be worse than the time I got stuck in a window at the shelter, trying to get back into the building after Larry broke in and locked me out. The fire department had shown up for that, too.

"I called the man candy brigade," came a squeaky, all too familiar voice. Mrs. Kowalski clapped her hands together, causing her arm skin to wave back and forth like a pageant queen in a parade as she shuffled her way down the walk from Sunny Peaks. Trailing behind her were nearly a dozen residents of the Sunny Peaks retirement center.

"Candy?" Landon stood up and jumped up and down. "I want candy from tucking fire!"

"Language, Landon," the woman called out to the still-jumping toddler as she untangled her baby's hand from her hair.

"Bennie!" Mrs. K called, looking back at the group. "Get your ancient ass up here! We've got some big burly men to ogle."

The helpful woman who'd tried to be my savior looked up at me, her eyes wide and mouth in a big grin.

"Seems like your help has arrived."

"Some help," I muttered, a sigh escaping my mouth.

Bennie waddled down the walk, just as a fire truck rounded the corner.

Two men and one woman jumped from the truck, wearing matching navy blue Morris County Fire Department tees and the bottoms of their turnout gear held up by bright red suspenders.

Mrs. K and Bennie immediately teetered their way over to the team and surrounded one of the men.

From my vantage point, it was hard to tell, but the poor man looked like my cousin Marshall Sanders. Marshall had been a few years behind me in school and was married to his high school sweetheart. They were expecting their first baby this fall.

Jealousy pinched my throat closed.

"Mrs. Kowalski, Miss Bennie," Marshall said, nodding to the women and suppressing a smile. "A pleasure as always."

He was keeping his arms as close to his torso as possible, minimizing the harassment the ladies could dole out. His coworkers looked busy fiddling with the side of the truck, wisely avoiding eye contact with either of the Sunny Peaks residents.

"The pleasure is all ours, Marshall," Bennie replied, patting the large man on the arm.

"Yeah," Bennie agreed, squeezing a bicep between her bony fingers. "You're our favorite."

"I don't know what's going on here," my not-quite-guardian angel said in a near-whisper. "But I can't stop watching."

Landon had disappeared behind his mom's legs and was peering out at the firefighters. The female firefighter pulled something out of the truck and walked towards them. Now that she was closer, I could see it was Petra Wolfe, a transplant from Haven Falls. She was nice enough, for a Havener.

Petra squatted down and held out a plastic red helmet to the boy. "How'd you like to help us out?" she asked Landon, a pretty smile on her face.

Landon nodded shyly before taking the helmet and placing it on his head. "I'm tucking fire part, Mama!" he shouted.

"Yes, baby," the woman said, her face cringing so hard I could see her discomfort from my tree limb.

"How's it going, Molly?" Petra said, looking up the tree while Marshall continued to be mauled by old ladies. Their third coworker was filming it all.

Super. Nothing this town loved more than video evidence.

"Oh, you know, just out for some fresh air. All good here."

Petra smiled and squatted down again so she was face-to-face with Landon. "As our newest firefighter, how about you take your mommy and baby sister over by Atlas, so they're in the safe zone?" She pointed towards the grass where Atlas was laying, completely asleep. At least one of us was having a nice afternoon.

"I can't believe you two called the fire department," I yelled down to Mrs. K and Bennie. I looked around at the growing crowd. "Is the whole town here?"

"You always know how to bring the town together, girly," Mrs. K replied, chuckling.

"Why didn't you just ask a nurse to come out and help if you saw I was in trouble?"

Mrs. K let go of Marshall's left bicep and gestured widely to Marshall, who was trying and failing to pluck Bennie's hands off his right arm.

"Those monthly calendars they sell on the Amazon don't

cut it, girlie," she replied. "We need the real thing. That's why Bennie called them last week when one of her curlers got stuck in her hair."

I peered down at Petra, who was climbing the now uprighted ladder. *Don't ask*, she mouthed.

My wannabe-rescuer burst out laughing from her spot in the shade, her baby sitting on the grass between her legs, petting Atlas, whose eyes were still closed but whose tail was wagging. Landon was watching Petra with wide eyes and a serious face. Looks like the fire department was going to get itself a new recruit in about fifteen years.

"Hey, Molly," Petra said as her head peeked over the branch.

"Hey, Petra."

Freckles dotted a pale face on the pretty blond woman. A kind smile greeted me.

"Not quite the same as getting stuck in a window, but a close second," Petra said, chuckling and reaching a hand up to scratch Fancy's head. "Hey there, sweet thing."

Fancy purred and rubbed his head against Petra's gloved hand.

"Need a little help?"

"Me or the cat?" I asked, honestly unsure.

Petra laughed. "Both of you, I suppose."

Biting back the *no* that came far too easily, I nodded my head as Fancy crawled into my rescuer's arms.

I wondered what that might be like, to trust someone so quickly and thoroughly. "That would be nice."

3 8

JASE

*I* spotted Molly climbing down a ladder while the crowd gathered on the lawn cheered and whistled.

"Why the fuck is everyone clapping?" Sam asked as we stood shoulder-to-shoulder at the back of the mob.

Why *were* they clapping? Did she get stuck in the tree? I swallowed a growl. If Molly had been in trouble and I wasn't here…

I shrugged a shoulder, hiding my emotions from Sam. He was getting along with Molly. No need to poke the sleeping dragon. "Dunno. Maybe they're cheering for the firefighters."

Whatever had happened, Molly looked like she wanted to crawl back up the tree and stay until dark. Instead, she took a cat from the firefighter and faced a familiar face.

"What the hell?" I asked, stalking off into the crowd. That was definitely Eliza, standing next to Molly, holding my youngest niece, Edith. "Oh, fuck me."

"What's wrong?" Sam asked.

I ignored him, pushing forward until I spotted the top of Landon's head. He was making grabby hands at the cat in Molly's arms.

302

"Mommy, Mommy! Have kitty!" Landon said, tugging on Eliza's arm.

"Sorry, bud. We already have three cats and a bearded dragon at home. This zoo is full," my sister replied. Landon erupted into tears.

"Kitteeeeee…" he wailed. Poor kid.

Edith, not to be outdone by her brother, started crying. Eliza's kids were approaching full meltdown.

"Hey, little dude," I said to my nephew, bending down and picking him up before placing a kiss on my niece's forehead. "How's my favorite nephew?"

Landon pointed at the cat still in Molly's arms and sobbed. "Kitty, kitty, kitty," before wiping his snotty nose on my shoulder.

"Ew," Sam whispered as he took in the surrounding scene.

"Better than cat poop," Molly said, causing Sam to bark out a laugh.

"Hey little brother," Eliza said. "And Sam, fancy seeing you here."

"Eliza, lovely as always," he replied.

My sister's mom-smile was firmly in place as she turned and looked at me. "Talked to Mom lately?"

"Yes."

She narrowed her eyes at me.

Hadn't I?

"Oh," I said.

"Yeah. Oh," my sister repeated.

I'd meant to call my mom back. But then I'd gotten distracted with Sam's sandwich meltdown, and the animal rescues.

And Molly. Whose eyes were as round as the cat's. They both looked like they were five seconds from bolting.

"Little brother?" Molly asked, petting the cat as though her life depended on it.

"Wait. You two know each other?" Eliza asked.

"Know each other, they're fu—*oof!*" Sam said, right before I elbowed him in the gut.

"Kids," I whispered.

"Mommy says we're not supposed to hit each other," Landon said softly as he placed his head on my shoulder.

"You're right, buddy, we're not. But Sam was about to say a bad word."

"Like tuck?"

"Like… what?"

Sam threw back his head and laughed. "Oh, that's classic. Tuck you, Tugwater."

"Funny, Sam," I said, holding Landon's head against my chest while trying to cover one ear. I turned to my sister. "Yes, Molly and I are—"

"Neighbors," Molly interrupted, not making eye contact with me. "Sort of. His brewery is next to my animal shelter."

Neighbors? We were more than tucking neighbors and the guilt on her face said she knew it.

Tucking—*heh*—my disappointment into a pocket until I could take it out and consider it more closely, I smiled at my sister. "Right. Neighbors."

"*Riiight.* Neighbors." She glanced at Molly, then at me. "I understand now why Mom's been the last thing on your mind."

"What are you doing here?" I rocked my nephew, who'd thankfully calmed down.

"Nice subject change," my sister said. "I got turned around looking for your place, so we stopped at the park for the kids to run off energy. Before I could call Mom to make sure she gave me the right address, that small horse over there found us and brought us here." She looked at Molly, who was holding onto the cat like a lifeline. "Where we found your, uh, *neighbor*, stuck in a tree."

I turned to Molly, who shrugged.

We were definitely circling back to that.

"No, I mean, what are you doing in Harmony Springs?"

Eliza shifted Edith to her other hip. The little girl had one finger stuck up her nose. She pulled a booger out and held it out to her mom.

"You, uh, need a napkin or something, Eliza?" Sam asked.

"Nah," she said, wiping Edith's finger on her shirt.

Sam made a vomit noise. "So gross."

My sister laid one of her classic glares on him, shutting him up instantly before turning that look on me. "I don't issue idle threats, little bro. I warned you what would happen if you didn't call Mom. You're lucky I brought my kids instead of her."

She turned back to Sam. "And don't call my kids gross."

Sam blanched. "Sorry," he said before adding with a shudder, "But boogers…"

Three people wearing matching Morris County Fire Department shirts walked towards us. Two older women that I recognized from the Sunshine Festival followed closely behind them.

The firefighter in the middle yelped and I saw Mrs. Kowalski remove her hand from the poor man's ass.

The female firefighter, who'd been the one I saw give Molly the cat, laughed.

"You need anything else before we go?" she asked Molly.

"No, I think I've got it from here," Molly answered. The firefighters walked back to their truck, keeping their backs wisely turned away from the seniors.

"Shoot," Mrs. K said. "Now we need something else to do this afternoon." She sized up Sam, who gulped and inched closer to me. "You're new."

"And hot," Bennie said.

"Help," Sam whispered, ducking behind me.

"Ladies," Molly said, still carrying the cat, who'd decided it didn't want to run away after all and had fallen asleep in her arms. Lucky cat. "Does Brooklyn know you're out here?"

"Brooklyn is a fuddy-duddy," Bennie answered.

"Brooklyn is right behind you," said a woman whose name tag identified her as, yep, Brooklyn. She was a few inches shorter than Molly, but roughly the same age. She had beautiful black hair pulled back into a bun and was wearing blue nursing scrubs with happy little suns printed all over them.

"Hey, Molly," Brooklyn said.

"I… you… yum…" Sam stuttered.

Brooklyn looked at my friend as if there might be something medically wrong with him before she continued. "Thanks again for helping Alyssa at my daycare get the paperwork she needed so she could hire help."

Molly scrunched her face, like it physically hurt to accept thanks from someone. "I just made a call."

Brooklyn nodded. "Maybe. But you always seem to know exactly who to call to get things done."

"Happy to help," Molly said, shrugging a shoulder.

"Glad you finally rescued your cat," Brooklyn said before turning to the mob of white-haired observers. "Sunny Peaks residents, back inside, please."

"Drill sergeant," Mrs. K said, glaring at Brooklyn and locking arms with her darker half.

"She can order me around anytime," Sam mumbled beneath his breath.

I elbowed him again.

"Come on, Bennie. Let's see if we can talk Rosie into letting us make Jell-O shots for the senior mixer tomorrow." The duo tottered their way back towards the senior center.

With the fire department and senior crowd gone, the mob thinned to just a couple of looky-loos.

"I wanna go play with doggie," Landon whispered. I looked at my sister, who nodded, so I let him down gently. Landon skipped to Atlas, who'd woken up briefly, licked the boogers off my nephew's face and lay back down, the boy snuggling next to him, softly petting his belly.

"That's the cutest fucking thing ever," Eliza said. "Makes me want a dog. Almost."

"I can hook you up," Molly said.

"Not a chance, neighbor girl."

Eliza shifted the baby again.

"Come here, kiddo." I plucked Edith from Eliza's arms. I'd missed my niece and nephew. A lot. They'd grown like weeds since I saw them over Christmas. I really needed to make a bigger effort to get home more often. Not that I had any spare time.

"Oh, no. No, no," Sam said as he jumped back.

I craned my neck and noticed Edith grabbing at Sam's shirt. "Uh, uh, uh," she grunted as she tried to launch herself at my best friend. Her chubby arms were wide out, asking to be held.

"You won't catch cooties," I said to my friend, who looked very much like he thought he would.

"Says you," he replied.

A smile ghosted across my sister's face. "She's been attached to me since conception. I keep waiting for her to find a new obsession." She glanced at Sam, who'd backed over to Molly and the cat. "Guess you're it, Sammy."

Sam shuddered, and Eliza cackled.

"Look," Sam said, putting as much space as he could between himself and Edith. "I'm sure your kids are perfect little angels. I just don't do kids."

"Neither did I," Eliza laughed. "Until I had them."

I tickled my niece's belly to distract her and was rewarded with a high-pitched giggle.

"I need to feed these two perfect little angels," Eliza said, turning to me.

"Where are you staying?" I asked her, handing over Edith. "I can give you directions."

"Since I'm only planning on staying for a night or two, I was thinking your place," she answered.

Molly snorted. "Good luck with that."

I could feel the heat on my cheeks as Eliza cocked an eyebrow. "Neighbors. Okay."

"Most places are full this time of year," Molly answered. "The Johansens have space at their inn, though. It's on the corner of Pine and Third."

"I think I passed that place on my way in," Eliza said. "Blue and white? Pretty flowers out front?"

Molly nodded. "That sounds right. It's clean, and Mary and Joe are super nice. Tell them I sent you. They'll sort you out."

Eliza reached for Edith, who went willingly, rubbing her little eyes. "Let me get these two sorted, then you and I can talk, little brother."

"Looking forward to it," I lied.

Eliza snorted as she collected Landon, promising they'd visit the giant puppy tomorrow. "His mama is neighbors with Uncle Jase," she said, eyes darting my way.

"Sam, can you show Eliza the way?" I asked, wanting some alone time with Molly to figure out this "neighbors" thing.

"But... kids...." He eyeballed Edith's nose and his face paled. "In my Jag."

"Relax, slick," Eliza replied. "I'll follow you in my rented mom van. Your Jag can remain kid free."

"Oh thank god," Sam replied on a gasp of air, following them —safely distanced from little grabby hands—to the parking lot.

I turned to Molly, who kept shifting the cat. I took it gently from her. It woke with a chirp, sprawled out in my arms, and quickly closed its eyes.

"So, neighbors, huh?" I asked, trying for light humor, but the flash of heat across Molly's cheeks told me I'd missed the mark.

Good. Her comment had hurt me. She should know it.

"I'm sorry," she said, her voice going quiet as she watched the cat. "I just… I don't know, panicked."

"Why?"

"Because your sister is so…"

"Bossy? Stubborn? A pain in my ass?" I supplied.

"Impressive," she finished.

"So are you."

Blush moved up her neck. "I'm a fucking mess."

"True."

"Hey!"

She was. And I loved every messy part. "You're perfect, Molly, messy parts and all." She lifted her eyes to me, the Colorado sunshine skimming off them like jewels.

"I wish I was more like her," she confessed, shaking her head.

"You don't want that."

"I don't?"

"Trust me. The world can't handle two Elizas. Please don't do that to us."

She laughed, the musical tone making me want to hold her instead of the cat.

"I need to get him back to Happy Tails." She nodded at the sleeping cat. "Wait. Why are you here?"

"Oh, right!" I pointed my backside in her direction. "You left your phone at my place."

Reaching for her phone, which I'd tucked into my back

pocket, she paused. "This better not be your way of initiating sex," she warned before grabbing her phone.

I chuckled. "I'm sure I can think of something better... unless it's working?"

She grinned as she woke up her phone and swore.

"What's wrong?" I asked.

"Ginger texted."

We hadn't heard from Ginger since the Bean, even though I'd met Kenny for a beer and the Vistas game last night. I hadn't wanted to bug my new friend when I was there. Now I wished I had.

"And?"

"She said her dad denied everything."

"But I literally heard him planning something with Candice."

"I know," she mumbled, still staring at the screen.

"So now what?"

She took a breath, pocketed her phone, and straightened her shoulders. Whatever was about to come out of her mouth would be as defiant as anything my sister could manage. Eliza was impressive, no doubt. What Molly didn't know yet is that she'd already surpassed her. Molly was a total badass, and Candice was a fool to underestimate her.

"We keep looking." She looked behind her at the senior center. "And I know just where to start."

# 39

# MOLLY

*W*hat have you got swirling around in that beautiful mind of yours?" Jase asked me, his eyes narrowing. He looked intrigued. Or maybe that was cat hair scrunching his eyes up, since he was still cuddling Fancy and making my ovaries do backflips.

I nodded at the senior center behind us. "This building may look like an ordinary brick building full of seemingly benign residents and nursing staff, but it's actually a central hub for everything that goes down in Harmony Springs."

Many of the staff were notorious busybodies. And the residents were tapped into the gossip lines tighter than the Poligrip holding their dentures in place. Between them, they knew pretty much everything that went on in Harmony Springs, sometimes before it happened.

"And you think someone might know something?" he asked.

"Candice is about as subtle as a rockslide. Someone is bound to have heard something," I continued.

"Oh, thank god! You weren't eaten by a mountain lion!" Jeff shouted from down the block.

They were running towards us at an alarming rate. Skidding to a stop, they flung their arms around me and lifted me in a hug, squeezing like it was their job.

"Can't. Breathe."

"Sorry," they said, putting me down. "Tyson said a mountain lion chased you up a tree. I thought I'd have to identify your body parts at the morgue, and I'd had a bean burrito for lunch that wasn't sitting well. I wasn't sure I could do blood and gore and body parts on top of an iffy burrito—"

"Dude. Breathe," I said, placing my hands on their shoulders.

Jeff nodded and closed their eyes. The breath they took in was so hard their nostrils collapsed in on themselves.

"Kenny texted me and told me he'd heard a call come in over his police scanner and thought you'd been in an accident," Tyson said, easing up behind his spouse and rubbing their back, which seemed to have a calming effect. "But... you're okay?"

"All good." As long as your definition of good included being stuck in a tree because you kicked the ladder to the ground and then got to meet the sister of the man you're sleeping with in the most awkward and humiliating way ever.

"I figured. Especially after Colin McDentry texted that you'd fallen into a well and Lassie had to rescue you," Tyson answered.

Why the dentist would know anything about my activities, or feel the need to share them with Tyson, was anybody's guess.

"Lassie?" Jase asked in that low, smooth, vagina-clenching voice of his, a hint of humor at the edges.

"It wasn't a well, it was an abandoned mine shaft," yelled Oscar Lewandowski, who was watering their lawn across the street while their partner, Bruce, pruned the hedge line.

"I heard it was a badger who chased her around town," Bruce said.

Spock, save me.

"By the way," Bruce continued. "Thanks for finally getting the trees on this block trimmed!"

"Let me guess," Jase said to me as I waived Bruce off. "You just made a call."

"Maybe."

"So, what *actually* happened?" Jeff interrupted.

"I, um, sort of got stuck in a tree?"

Tyson looked at Jase. "And you rescued her?"

"And her pussy," Jeff stage whispered.

Tyson cleared his throat and cut a glance at Jeff.

"What? He's been stroking her pussy since we got here."

"Jean-Luc Picard." I slapped a palm over my eyes, willing the heat in my cheeks to go away. "I can't with you today."

Jase chuckled, the deep timbre vibrating my lady bits.

*He can stroke me any time he wants*, purred my vagina.

"The fire department did all the rescuing," Jase explained, a smile on his lips. "I'm just here because Molly forgot her phone."

"And to stroke her pussy," Jeff added.

"Stop saying 'stroke her pussy'!" I said through clenched teeth.

"Not all heroes wear capes," Tyson said to Jase, patting him on the shoulder.

Atlas extracted himself from his prone position in the shade and walked over to us, leaning on Jeff.

"Well, pussy petting aside, I can't believe I missed all the drama," Jeff said, rubbing the dog's ears and eliciting a groan from him.

"You didn't miss much," I told them. Except Jase's sister. And Mrs. Kowalski and Miss Bennie sexually harassing the fire department. And Petra having to climb up the tree to get me and Fancy. Who Jase was still stroking.

"I got a text from Ginger," I added, changing the subject.

"Ooo! Did she dish the dirt on her dad?" Jeff asked.

"The exact opposite, actually," I replied, before catching them up. "So, I figured as long as we were here, someone could stop in and see what the nurses might have heard."

"Ooh," Jeff said. "And the residents. Everyone knows those crazy octogenarians have the inside scoop on all the tea."

"What about the Bean?" Tyson asked. "Kole's place is basically Grand Central Station for the town gossip train. Whatever the nurses and residents don't know, he will."

"That's a great idea," I replied. "We can divide and conquer."

"I'm not taking the senior center," Jeff said with a shudder. "The last time I was there, someone groped me."

"I think that's a bit of an exaggeration," I said.

"Verna Kowalski pinched my ass," Jeff hissed.

"It's a very pinchable ass," Tyson said, smiling at his spouse.

Jase's mouth twisted into a pucker. Spock bless him. He was trying his best to stop the laugh that was threatening to tumble out of his mouth. But if he held it in any longer, he'd give himself a hernia.

"It is, but that's not the point," Jeff said, crossing their arms in front of their chest. "I'm not doing the senior center. Verna over-sexualizes everything."

Jase had crossed his own arms in front of him, trying not to shake from the effort it was taking to keep his laughter silent. That just made me want to burst out laughing at my friend's hissy fit—which I absolutely would not do because that would only launch Jeff into a full-fledged melt down—so

I focused on Jeff's face, doing my level best to ignore the unignorable dimple forming in Jase's right cheek.

"To be fair," I said, placing a hand on Jeff's shoulder to keep them focused on me and not the fact that Jase was snorting. "She's like a hundred and forty-seven years old. If you hadn't had sex since the Nixon administration, you'd probably be horny, too."

Jase lost the battle and let out a roar that caused the giggle I had been holding back to escape. Oops.

Jeff huffed, and Tyson turned his head to the side to hide his own smile.

Jase's brilliant smile was on full display, his laughter booming. No wonder the Vistas schlepped him in front of the camera so often. He was fucking gorgeous.

*And lickable*, my vagina said.

*Very lickable*, my ovaries agreed.

"I'm glad you all think my pain is hilarious," Jeff said, sucking in their cheeks in a classic Jeff sulk.

"We don't," I finally got out between gulps of air.

"We really don't," Tyson agreed, morphing his smile into something more sympathetic. "It's not okay for anyone to pinch your ass but me."

"That's right," Jase said. "Want us to go kick her ass?"

"You all suck," Jeff said, scowling.

"We do," I agreed as Tyson nodded and Jase wiped his eyes. "To make up for it, we'll let you talk to Kole instead of the sexed-up seniors."

Jeff's eyes rounded at that suggestion. "But he's… scary."

*Oh, for the love of Spock.* "Scarier than Mrs. Kowalski's oversexed libido?"

Jeff shook their head. "Nothing's scarier than that."

"Then it's settled," I said, before Jeff could change their mind. "You and Tyson will go talk to Kole, and I'll take Atlas and scour the senior center for something we can use against our nemesis."

"I'll go with you," Jase said. His words were simple enough, but the tone made my insides go into heat. It was low, promising, and full of something I didn't dare put into words. At least not in front of my friends, who would start talking about him stroking my pussy again.

*Yes please*, said my vagina to absolutely no one.

"Actually," I replied, hating myself for what I was about to say, because for once I agreed with my vagina. Jase was one hundred percent lickable and the nights I'd spent doing exactly that were memories that would live in my brain rent free for life.

I didn't want to send him away. I wanted him standing next to me, just like he was.

*Stroking our pussy*, my vagina said.

*Purr purr*, my ovaries chimed in.

"Actually…?" Jase prompted.

*Gah. Focus, ladies!*

"I was thinking maybe you could talk to Kenny again?"

"Kenny?" Jase asked, his brows furrowed in confusion.

"Good idea," Tyson said.

"I'm lost," Jase said, shaking his head. "Someone clue me in?"

"Didn't you have beers with Kenny on Monday?" Tyson asked Jase.

"How did you—"

"Colin McDentry saw you."

Again with the dentist.

"I did," Jase said. "But I don't know what that has to do with anything."

He was squirming enough to jostle Fancy awake.

*Mew*, Fancy complained.

I scooped the cat from Jase's arms and placed him in the

crate. Standing up, I looked at Jase. Really looked at him. He'd been here for months now, but as far as I knew, the only people he hung out with were me and my two weirdo friends. Who were lovely people, but they were my people.

Sam was Jase's person, but he didn't live here. Jase didn't have any people in town. At least not until Kenny. When I heard he'd been invited for beers, I'd been knee deep in kitten baths. It hadn't registered at the time, but seeing it now, he'd been genuinely excited as he toted a couple of growlers of his beer out the door.

He finally had a friend in Harmony Springs. And I was about to ask him to convince his new friend to rat on his fiancé.

I officially sucked.

But he was our only direct connection to Bob and Candice. Without it, all we had was conjecture from the gossip mill, which was wrong as much as it was right about anything.

"I was thinking you could see if maybe he knows something Ginger isn't willing to say." I practically choked on the words.

"Oh." That was his only reply as he shoved his hands in his pockets and looked down at his feet. "Sure. *Neighbor.*"

He may as well have punched me in the stomach for how that word landed. *Neighbor.*

I was going to have to do some Grade A groveling tonight if I wanted to get back in his good graces. And his pants. I really wanted to get back in his pants.

*Orgasms!* cheered my vagina and ovaries.

*Easy, ladies. One step at a time.*

"I'm sorry," I nearly whispered, as Jeff and Tyson watched us. "I just..."

"No, I get it. We need to know what's going on. I just... He's my first real friend here. And I..."

"Hello, bestie," Jeff said, cocking their head to the side. "I'm literally standing right here."

"You don't want to ruin it," I said, putting my hand on his arm. I couldn't do it. I couldn't ask this of him. "I get it. We'll figure something else out."

"Come on, babe," Tyson said, his arm around Jeff. "Let's go interrogate a giant."

"Oh god, do we have to?" Jeff squeaked.

"Go Team Murder Bears!" I yelled to them as they walked arm-in-arm down the street.

"Not the time, Sanders!" Jeff yelled back, before placing their head on Tyson's shoulder, who asked Jeff, "What's a Murder Bear?"

I turned back to Jase.

"Why don't you go get your sister settled while I shake down the senior center for info? We can meet up later?"

Hopefully in my bed, wrapped tight in his arms.

He tucked a strand of hair behind my ear, a small smile on his face.

"Jase," I whispered. I needed to tell him. That we were more than neighbors. So much more. But the words stuck in my throat.

He pressed a soft kiss to my lips. "It's okay," he said, before turning and walking towards the Johansen's inn. Taking my heart with him.

I was so tucking screwed.

40
# JASE

Eliza sipped her coffee from a bright blue to-go cup from the Bean. We were sitting in the brewery's dining room. Her play pack, which we had thanks to Molly and a nurse at the senior center, was next to the soft brown suede couch I'd had delivered last week.

Edith was securely inside the pack, shaking a toy in each choppy hand, yelling triumphantly like the warrior she would grow up to be. Landon sat on the couch, headphones on, watching something on the iPad Eliza had pulled out of one of her many bags.

"This is good fucking coffee," she said, taking another drink.

"Is that why you put headphones on Landon? So he can't hear you swear?" I grinned at my sister over my own to-go cup, which held my favorite latte: rose cardamom with coconut milk.

Bougie? Yes.

Worth it? Also yes. Kole was a coffee god.

"That, and because if I have to hear the Bluey song one more time, I'm going to take a drill to my ear holes."

"Extreme."

"Trust me, it's not." She took another drink of coffee and sighed. "If I wasn't happily married to Penn, I'd marry that mountain man of a barista just to have him bring me a cup of this every morning."

I wasn't about to admit it to my sister, but so would I.

I played with the lid of my coffee. "So… when does the lecture start?" I asked, bracing for the impact of whatever words my sister was about to unleash.

"No lecture."

"Really?"

Since when had my big sister ever missed an opportunity to tell me all the things I was doing wrong? She'd drilled into me from the time we were little that, as the oldest, it was her god given right.

"Really," she said, cupping her coffee with both hands. "Just here to talk."

"Didn't really have to come all the way out here to do that," I answered. "They make these things called phones."

I recognized my mistake the minute the words came tumbling out of my mouth. Eliza, eyebrows raised, looked like a cat about to pounce on a mouse who'd forgotten to check who was on the other side of his mouse hole before venturing out.

"So I hear." Smiling, she took a sip. "God. This is like sex in a Smurf-colored cup."

Maybe I was going to get off easy.

"Now tell me, why have you been ignoring Mom's calls?" she asked.

So much for easy.

"Other than your neighbor, who we both know you're fucking," she continued, giving me a pointed look over the rim of her coffee.

I choked on my coffee. Blunt truths were Eliza's love language.

Guilt and regret punched me in the chest. I missed my family like an amputated limb. It was no wonder my sister was so frustrated with me. I'd barely talked to any of them since my injury. Where I used to spend my off seasons in Chicago, hanging out with my parents and sisters and their families, having backyard barbecues or playing on the beach, the move and the Catcher's Box Brewing Co. now consumed all my time that wasn't taken up by Molly. Some brother I turned out to be.

"I just… I don't know."

"Look, I know Mom can be a bit…"

"Much?"

Eliza grinned. "Maybe." She slid her coffee to one side and clasped both hands in front of her, leaning towards me. "But one thing I've learned from becoming a mom is that it usually comes from a place of love, no matter how it presents itself."

I sighed. "I know." And I did. I'd won the family lottery. My parents never missed one of my games all the way through high school. And after that, they accommodated the distance by getting the cable package with every sports channel on the planet, so they could watch me on TV.

They'd flown to Denver to watch my first professional baseball game. And had been at the hospital when I'd woken up from surgery, holding my hands while the doctor told me my career was over.

And how had I repaid them? By ignoring their calls because I was too busy.

"It's just… things here are… complicated."

"Then uncomplicate them," Eliza said. "And explain to me how that translates to not calling home?"

"Well, there's the brewery. I mean, you of all people know how much time it takes starting a business from scratch."

"Don't drag me into your delusions, little brother," she said, holding up a hand to stop the objection that was at the tip of my lips. "I'll give you starting a business is hard. But so are a lot of things. Calling your mom isn't one of them."

Again with the blunt truths.

"Then, well, seeing Molly again after all these years—"

"Wait. What do you mean, *again*?"

Why was I telling my sister all this? We'd never had the sort of relationship where we told each other our deepest, darkest secrets. But something about doing this today, with her, just felt… right. Freeing. Like taking off a heavy coat during a heat wave.

"Yeah, I, um, sort of had a fling with her the weekend I found out I was getting called up to the majors."

Eliza laughed. Not a *hahaha* happy laugh, or a snort of amusement. This was a deep belly laugh that sounded more like *my brother is an idiot and doesn't know it.*

"That explains so much," she wheezed when she'd finally caught her breath.

"I don't see how—"

"So how does this Candice person fit into all this?" she interrupted, clearly not interested in my continued attempts to justify my failures.

"Candice is planning to shut down my business. Mine and Molly's. And I… I can't let that happen, Lize."

She grasped my hand and squeezed. "So don't."

I stared at our hands, mine big and rough from all the years playing in the dirt, rubbing leather and pine tar. Hers, slender but still strong enough to take on the world. "It's not that simple. If I can't figure this out, my business is finished before it's even off the ground."

"So what?" she said before I could continue. "Most businesses fail within the first year. You were smart with your money from baseball, you'll land on your feet." She leaned back, and crossed her arms, daring me to contradict her.

"It's not just me who'd be impacted. Sam will be out his investment money. Molly will lose her business. The animals will be homeless. And what will Mom and Dad think?"

Eliza scoffed. "Screw Mom and Dad."

I picked my jaw up off the floor. In all our years as siblings, never once had I heard her say a single bad word about our parents.

She pointed a finger at me. "I love you, but I will murder your pretty camera-loving face if you tell them I said that."

"Lips are sealed." I raised both hands in surrender. "But seriously, sis. This is easy for you to say, with your perfect business and perfect kids and your perfect husband whose ass I don't regularly want to kick because he treats you like a queen."

"As he fucking should."

I tipped my head in agreement.

"Who cares what I've done?" she challenged. "Forge your own fucking path. Choose your own definition of success."

"I just want to prove to everyone I can do this. But I guess I can't. Not if I don't find a way to stop Candice."

"I have it on good authority that Candice is the worst."

"She is," I agreed. "But who'd you hear that from?" Knowing this town, it could be anyone. This town had never heard of stranger danger before. They loved everyone equally.

"Your sweet little neighbor with the big doe eyes and smackable ass."

"No. Just, no," I said as I took a drink of my coffee. No matter how very smackable Molly's ass was, I was not having a sex conversation with my big sister.

She grinned that annoying, knowing grin at me. "So… how's the sex?"

Coughing up coffee, I glared at her. "First, ew. Second, no."

"What is this?" she asked, tilting her head, her eyes searching for something as she watched me. "Do you like her?"

"Of course I like her."

"No," she said, tapping a finger on the table. "This is more than just sex."

"I never said we were having sex," I growled.

"*Ohh…* you *like her* like her." She smiled triumphantly. "I fucking knew it."

"Mama say tuck," said a little voice from the hallway.

We both whipped our heads towards the couch, where we'd left Landon. It was empty, save for a set of headphones and an iPad. Edith, for her part, was still happily engaged with her toys, safely inside her play pack.

Landon, however, was suspended midair, grinning at us. No, not suspended. Held there. By Sam. Whose arms seemed to have lengthened by several feet to hold the little dude so far away from his body. Like if any part of the kid touched Sam's designer polo shirt, it would slide off his body and crawl to a more deserving bachelor.

"Can someone please take him?" Sam asked, his voice hitching. I grinned as I stood to save my friend.

Landon sneezed. Sam froze.

"Please let that be a dry sneeze," he whispered.

Landon drew his arm across his upper lip, snot coating it with snot and spreading across his face. He swiped a hand over his nose before clapping, the mucus stringing between his hands.

"Guess you have your answer," Eliza said, glee sparkling in her blue eyes.

Sam heaved. "Someone better take this kid before I throw up."

"Unca Bam-Bam barf. Lanny barf too!"

"No, no, no, no, kid. No barfing. Uncle Bam-Bam won't barf if you don't barf."

Eliza giggled. "This is better than YouTube."

"Unca Bam-Bam funny!" Landon said, his high-pitched giggles piercing the space and bringing peace to my soul. I wanted this. All of it. Here. In my home. Even the boogers.

"You'd be kinda cute, kid, if you weren't a walking booger-making machine," Sam said as I reached out and took Landon, propping him on a hip.

"Let's get you cleaned up, little dude," I said to my boogery nephew.

"Love Unca Bam-Bam!" Landon said, raising his hands in the air like it was a cheer.

Sam's face softened for a second before he looked at his shoes and his eyes widened in horror. "He sneezed on my nine-hundred-dollar Loro Piana's."

"Get over it, Sparky," Eliza said, smiling. "They're just shoes."

"They're not just—"

*Bleeeet!*

"What the hell was that?" Eliza yelled, ready to throw herself in front of her kid.

"Fuck you, Larry!" Sam yelled as he moved behind my sister to use her as a shield.

"Unca Bam-Bam say tuck!"

Larry poked her little face around the corner and screamed again.

"Big titty!" Landon yelled, clapping and squealing in delight. He might be the only person in the history of the entire world who'd ever been excited to see the chaos demon.

"I'm starting to like this tucking kid," Sam said from behind my sister's shoulder.

I grinned. This scene just felt more and more right to me. The only thing missing was Molly. I resolved right then and there that if the universe came through on that, I'd do everything in my power to make it a permanent reality.

"There you are," Molly said as she walked in behind me.

Score one for the universe.

# 41
## MOLLY

*Y*ou talking to me or the goat?" Jase asked, holding his nephew, who kept chanting something about titties.

I checked to make sure I was wearing a bra. Yep, the girls were covered.

"How did Larry get out this time?" I asked at the same time my goat let out a bellow summoned from the seventh circle of hell and Jase's niece began wailing.

"Fucking Larry," Sam muttered as Larry eyeballed the crying infant.

"Larry, no!" I yelled.

Eliza, moving faster than an Olympic sprinter, swept her daughter out of the pack I had borrowed from Brooklyn, and turned to the goat.

"You," Eliza said, pointing to Larry and angling the little girl—*Edna? Edith?*—away from the goat in a protective gesture. "Outside if you're going to be that loud."

She was swaying her daughter back and forth, a hand softly circling her back. The baby was softly chanting "mama" over and over as she hiccuped her sobs.

Landon climbed down Jase's torso and ran to his mom, clinging to her shorts. "Bad titty," he chastised, pointing a finger at Larry.

I turned to Jase. *Titty?* I mouthed.

"He thinks Larry is a big kitty," Jase whispered, his mouth tight as he worked to keep a smile from breaking.

"Oh… *kitty*." That made so much more sense. "Yes. She is a bad kitty," I said, squatting down and meeting Landon at eye level. "You okay, little man?"

"Titty made sissy cwy," he answered, tears welling up in big blue eyes that looked just like his uncle's.

"I'm sorry, buddy," I said, mild panic settling in over the fact that I made Jase's nephew cry. "Bad kitty," I said, patting the little boy's back, trying to fix whatever I just broke.

"They're sympathetic criers," Eliza said, waving me off with one hand. "One cries, they both cry."

*Bleat!* Larry stomped a hoof.

"Is someone going to do something about this fu—uh, tucking goat before it eats one of us?" Sam asked, his eyes ping-ponging between Larry and Eliza.

Eliza handed Edith to Jase. The little girl curled up against Jase's neck as he rocked her back and forth, copying the back circling his sister had been doing.

And just like that, my ovaries exploded.

*We want his baby!* they shouted.

"I'm going to count to five," Eliza said, her voice calm and measured as she took a single step towards the goat. "You better be gone before I get there."

"Uh oh," Landon whispered. "Mommy's counting."

Larry stared at the woman, unmoving.

"One."

Larry licked the inside of one nostril and blinked.

"Two."

Eliza fisted her hands on her hips in a total Wonder Woman power pose. Larry stilled.

Wonder Woman versus goat.

Mom versus menace.

Spock help us all.

My stomach dropped. In my experience, the goat always won. Eventually. But the look on Eliza's face suggested she'd never lost a game of "I'm going to count to five." Ever.

"Three."

Larry pawed at the tile.

"Do not test me, kitty," Eliza said.

Holy Klingons. I was about to be responsible for the destruction of Jase's brewery and a life of therapy for two of the cutest kids I'd ever known, all because I couldn't keep my fucking goat in her pen.

I had to do something.

Before I could move, Larry let out a small *blet*, then trotted to the back door.

Which was closed.

Jase showed off his lightning-fast athletic reflexes and snatched out his free arm, sliding the door open.

Larry kicked her back feet in the goat version of *fuck you* as she walked onto the back patio and back to my side of the yard.

I looked back at Eliza, who was holding Landon's hand and watching the goat with a calm, disinterested gaze.

So. Fucking. Cool.

"You're wasting your talent on corporate schmucks," Sam said to Eliza. "With that kind of power, you should have been an agent."

"I already have three kids. I don't need any more," she quipped.

Sam barked a laugh. "Fair."

"Hey," said Jase. "I'm right here."

"Not you, obviously. You're a perfect client." The notes of sarcasm in his voice were subtle, but there.

Sam and Eliza both rolled their eyes at the back of Jase's head. I turned before Jase could see me laugh.

"Well, now that goatpocalypse is over, I think I'll get back to work." Sam squatted down until he was face-to-face with Landon. "Knock next time," he said with a wink, rubbing Landon's hair playfully.

Jase, still rocking his sleeping niece, nodded at his friend.

*Ooh la la! The strong silent type*, my nipples said, standing at attention.

*Make us scream!* cried my vagina while my ovaries went looking for a fainting couch to swoon over.

Jase cocked a grin at me, as if he could hear my thoughts, and my temperature rose to nuclear levels.

Needing a distraction before I mounted Jase and scarred Eliza's kids—and probably Eliza—for life, I looked at my new hero and wondered what it must be like to have that kind of confidence.

"I want to be you when I grow up."

Did I just say that out loud?

"Oh honey. Why? When you can be you."

Yes, yes I did.

How hot could a body get before spontaneous combustion happened? Because I was approaching that level.

"You're tucking fabulous," Jase added, his eyes bright as they stared right into my soul.

"I'm not fabulous," I whispered. I was a fucking mess whose goat nearly endangered the lives of people I cared about. Again.

Eliza looked at Jase, smiled, and then turned to me. "You own a lady goat named Larry. That's a badass boss move."

"Not sure if I *own* her. More like she eats everything in sight, and in exchange, I don't charge her rent."

Eliza barked out a laugh, which made Edith stir. But a few soft words and a couple of light bounces, and Jase had her back to sleep.

He turned that megawatt smile on me, the one that had dubbed him the King of Baseball. My breath hitched at the sight of this big, strong, insanely attractive man smiling at me while cradling a sleeping baby.

My ovaries were weeping with joy at the sight.

*Same girls. Same.*

*Take us!* My ovaries shouted as they tried to throw themselves at his feet. My vagina was lubing up to show him how much it appreciated seeing his softer side.

*Gah! Timing, ladies. There are children present.*

"Sissy otay?" Landon asked, tears dried now that no one else was crying.

"Sissy is great," Jase said, his voice soft and deep and safe. I wanted to curl up in it and let go. Just once.

"You were a trouper, little dude," I said instead. Landon rewarded me with a crooked grin.

"Come here, kiddo," Eliza said, taking his hand and walking him back to the couch. "No moving off the couch without asking Mommy."

Landon nodded with all the seriousness of a three-year-old as his mom unlocked the iPad and handed it to him. He snuggled back on the cushions and plopped a thumb in his mouth, content for now.

My phone dinged. Holy Klingons. In all the chaos, I'd forgotten why I was here.

"Crap," I said as I answered the text from Fritz Manly, a rancher out on the edge of town.

"What's up?" Jase asked as he placed Edith back in the pack, the little girl never stirring.

"I came over because someone texted me. They think they've found Stella."

"Really?"

"Yes," I said.

Relief had nearly knocked me to the floor when I realized my sweet little senior dog might be alive. I glanced at Eliza quickly before looking back at Jase. "I thought you might want to go with me, but if you've got things to do…"

Eliza waved a hand at me. "Go. Do your thing. Work doesn't stop for the boss just because she has to chase down her brother for proof of life."

Jase's cheeks tinged with pink before he kissed his sister on the temple. "I promise I'll do better."

Eliza nodded. "I know you will, little brother. Or I'll send Evie next time."

Jase's face paled, and Eliza cackled.

A tweak that might have been jealousy pinched my stomach as I watched the sibling exchange. Or it could have been Rusty Garcia's newest breakfast burrito flavor—the Rusty Bucket. Near as I could tell, it was all the leftovers from the week from his taco truck.

I knew Rusty hadn't given me food poisoning. You could eat off the floor of his truck. This was one hundred percent me.

My breath hitched as I realized I wanted this. Family. Friends. Chaos not always caused by a goat. Someone to care so much for me they'd fly halfway across the country with two young kids in tow to show it. Hell, I even wanted Sam, who was easily as jaded as me, but somehow still made it clear to his best friend how much he meant, in his own weird way.

Tyson and Jeff were my people. My ride or die. The ones who knew me better than I knew myself. Who forced Star

Trek marathons on me to help me through the dark days after my mom died.

But a not small part of me wouldn't be upset if my circle grew to include the people here.

More was better, wasn't it?

*What if they leave us?* my heart asked.

*Tyson and Jeff haven't left us*, I answered, surprising myself with how much I meant it. Neither had my dad, even if he was states away with his new lady friend. He deserved happiness.

So did I.

Was it possible my happiness looked like these people—big and small, soft and strong—standing in front of me?

"Let's go," Jase said, holding out a hand to me.

Fuck yes, it did. I grabbed it, my heart doing a soft swirl of happiness while my lady bits continued their trek through raunch land.

*Later, ladies, I promise.*

I nodded. "Let's go."

"Don't do anything I wouldn't do!" Eliza said as we walked to Jase's truck, hand-in-hand.

"Don't worry," Jase whispered, his breath warming my face. "My other sister Evie told me stories about Eliza's college days. We've got lots and lots of wiggle room."

*Jean-Luc Picard, give me strength.*

"So what's the plan?" Jase asked, hands in the pockets of his cargo shorts.

*I'd like to put my hands in his shorts*, my vagina said.

*Ew. You don't have hands*, I replied.

The wire-haired terrier mix barked at us from the small

island of dry land about two hundred yards from the stream that gave the town its name. This part of Harmony Creek was usually dry this time of year, but the last few wetter-than-normal winters had turned this section of the bank into a muddy bog. How Stella had made her way onto the island without getting stuck was a mystery. How Jase and I were going to make it out there to rescue her was an even bigger mystery.

"I guess we stick to the spots that look the driest and hope for the best." That was a plan, right?

Jase nodded. "Follow me."

"Hold up," I said, grabbing his arm. "Have you ever crossed a semi-dry riverbank before?"

Jase looked out at the expanse of dirt and puddles ahead of us. "Can't say that I have."

I cocked an eyebrow at him. "Try to keep up," I said, eyeballing the patch of grass in front of me. It would be a stretch. *Thank the Vulcan gods for my long legs.* I could do this. I *would* do this.

Crouching down, I pushed off the ground and leaped towards the grassy area.

"Be careful, Molly," Jase said from behind me.

"Easy peasy—*shit!*"

My feet hit the grass and slid out from under me, my ass making a splotch sound as I landed in a mud puddle.

"You okay?" Jase asked as he carefully stepped towards me, his shoes squishing in the damp ground.

Was I okay? I took inventory. Toes and knees, check. Elbows and fingers, check. My self-esteem had definitely taken a hit, but the rest of me seemed to be in one piece. "Yeah, I'm muddy, but good."

"Here," Jase said, holding out his hands. "Let me help."

"How are you not knee deep in this crap?" I grabbed his hands and winced. My ass sunk deeper every time I moved. I was going to be cleaning mud out of my crack.

"Professional athlete, remember?" He yanked, the movement creating a suction around my lower body as the mud fought to keep its new prized possession.

"Jesus," Jase said, pulling harder. "What's this stuff made of, cement?"

"Bad decisions and regrets," I huffed out. I tried thrusting my ass up and down to create an air pocket, hoping it would release me.

"You keep moving like that, we're gonna have a different problem," Jase said, his voice gravelly. Whether from exertion or being turned on, I didn't know.

"Bet your sister's never done it while being stuck in the mud," I said, grinning.

"Gonna need to bleach my brain later," he grunted as he dropped into a squat position and kept pulling.

I felt the mud giving way. "It's working!"

*Schlurp!* the mud belched as it finally released its grip on me and I flew up, up, up.

"Ow," I cried as I hit a rock-hard chest. And felt something else rock hard a few feet lower.

*Yum*, my vagina said.

"Uh oh," the rock-hard body said as it tilted backwards.

"No, no, no," I said, clawing at Jase's shirt, trying to keep us both upright.

"Molly..." he said as gravity won the battle and he plummeted backwards into the mud, with me right on top of him.

"Shit! Sorry," I said, my hands wrist-deep in mud on either side of that beautiful rock-hard chest that was heaving, causing me to ride up and down with him. Unable to stop myself, I ground on his dick, which was long and hard and ready.

"Mmm," Jase responded, squeezing my waist between his hands, eyes closing.

Maybe it would be worth it to get a little mud in my hoo-hah.

*Yee-haw!* my vagina crowed.

I rocked again, and my ovaries did a little cheer when Jase groaned.

"As much as I want you to do that again," he said, "if you don't want us both stuck in this mud, you should maybe… not."

*Spoil sport*, my ovaries said.

Jase was right. If he got stuck in the mud, there was no way I'd be able to pull him out. I'd have to call emergency services to bring a fucking crane to lift him out. Maybe two. This mud was equal parts dirt, water, and glue.

I needed to get off of him without pushing him further into a muddy coffin.

*You can do this. You're lighter than a leaf on the breeze. Fluffy clouds overhead. Delicate lace curtains.*

"Curtains?" Jase asked, a chuckle making his chest rumble beneath me.

*Yeah, baby,* my nipples said as they responded to the movement.

"Shhh…" I said to Jase. And my nipples. "I'm concentrating."

"And curtains help?"

"I'm trying to get us unstuck," I said, rolling to the side like air through a tree.

"Just stand up," he said, like I hadn't thought of that.

Of course I'd… Wait. I looked over my shoulder. My hands might be splayed in the mud, but my feet were on solid ground. I could just… stand up.

So I stood, the mud making a slurping noise as it let go of my arms. Wiping the mud on my jeans, I cringed inwardly. They'd never be the same after this.

Jase got himself unstuck with far less effort—*show off*—

and we kept moving towards the island. Jase led this time. I had to admit; it was a lot easier to just step where he stepped.

Before I knew it, we'd made it to the island. I congratulated myself for only mentally orgasming twice while my lady bits fanned themselves over the way his muscles bunched with each step he took.

Stella jumped up and down, continuing to bark at us even though we were now on her side of the mudhole.

"We're here now," I said to the dog. "You can turn the volume down."

I looked around, my heart sinking as I realized the orange kitten wasn't here. Damn it.

"Why's she still barking?" Jase asked.

I shrugged. "Because she's a dog?" I shouted over the dog, who was nearly howling now.

Jase shook his head. "I don't know. She seems distressed."

She did. That and the absence of the little orange kitten left a bad feeling in my gut.

"Come here, girl," I said softly, walking towards Stella until I was close enough to grab her collar. Before I could get my fingers around it, the dog ran behind a small willow bush that was the only shelter on the makeshift island.

"Come on, Stella. Now is not the time to play chase."

*Mommy needs to go home and get her vagina serviced by a professional athlete.*

Jase was rounding the other side of the bush so we could corral Stella when the dog popped out of the bush with something hanging from her mouth.

"What's that?" Jase asked.

*Please don't be a dead rabbit, please don't be a dead rabbit.*

Stella laid the pile of fur gently on the ground and sat. It looked like a wet, matted tribble. With my luck, the island would be full of tribbles who'd follow me home, and I'd never get a moment of peace again.

The fur ball moved and let out a squeak.

"Holy crap!" Jase shouted.

I grinned as the big, bad professional athlete with the rock-hard chest and other rock-hard parts that I very much wanted to play with later tonight took two giant steps away from the tribble.

"It's an animal," I said, peering at the blob. "In fact..." I said, moving closer.

Stella's tail wagged as I picked it up and rubbed off some mud with the bottom of my shirt.

"In fact, what?"

*Mew!*

Not a tribble. A kitten. Black and white and brown. Which on reflection might be dirt.

"Stella rescued a kitten," I said, turning and handing the little ball to Jase. Although not the kitten I'd hoped to find, I was happy to find it all the same.

"Ooh, Stella is a mom," Jase cooed as he engulfed the small creature in his humongous hands and my ovaries exploded for the second time today.

Before my imagination could carry me away to a land full of big dicks and orgasms, Stella jumped up and grabbed the bottom hem of my shirt in her mouth, tugging me towards a willow tree.

"Stella, knock it off," I said, trying to pull the shirt out of her mouth. I needed to leash the dog and get us all home before the sun went down and we all froze to death.

Stella let go and turned, burying her nose in the willow, her back end wagging.

"What the...?"

She scooted backwards out of the bush, another, slightly larger kitten in her mouth.

"Holy shit." The missing orange kitten!

"Another kitten?" Jase said, still cradling the first mud kitten to his chest, warming it. And my heart.

"It's the orange kitten," I said, wiping mud off him as best I could before handing him to Jase.

"Hey little dude, we've been looking for you." Jase held a kitten in each hand and kissed each on the top of its tiny little head.

*Gah.* If he got any more adorable, my ovaries would never recover from all the exploding.

We watched as Stella retrieved three more kittens, five in total. All of them were coated in mud and freezing cold.

"Holy shit, Stella."

The dog looked up at us, tail wagging.

"Yeah, sweet girl," I said, petting the dog, who'd kept everything but her paws and belly from getting muddy. Unlike me. "You did good."

I looked up at the sky, eyes squinted against the Colorado sun. We had maybe thirty minutes before the light would fade on us, along with the temperatures. When I'd started out this afternoon, I'd planned on a simple walk to and from the island to rescue a dog and maybe an orange kitten. Now, we had a dog, more kittens than hands, and a tenuous trek back to my SUV.

"We need to figure out how to get off the island. Any ideas?" I asked, turning towards Jase. What I saw made my mind go blank and my panties throw themselves on the ground at his feet in supplication.

Jase had removed his mud-coated tee, turned it inside out, and was placing the kittens in the middle. He tied the four corners together into a rough-and-ready kitten transportation hammock.

It was an ingenious idea, but unfortunately for his ingenuity, his abs were currently holding center stage. Although his broad shoulders and that rock-hard chest were definitely in the running for Most Impressive Male Part, and I very much wanted to be the trophy.

"Fuck it," I finally said before grabbing his face and kissing the hell out of him. He stilled for about zero point two seconds before placing his free hand behind my head and joining in the fun.

"Wait," he said, pulling away just enough to talk. "You sure?"

"Code foraging for mushrooms," I replied, hoping he'd understand.

"If that means what I hope it means, you're about to get very muddy," he said, right before plunging his tongue into my mouth and sliding his hand down my shorts to grab my ass.

*Yes!*

I moved my hands down those strong shoulders to his chest. Coarse hair trailed through my fingers as I ground my hips against his rock-hard cock.

Somewhere in the background, my brain registered that there were kittens mewing and a dog barking, but all I could hear were the groans he made as I continued to rock against him.

Stella barked again, this time pawing at our legs.

"Holy Klingons," I gasped. What had I been thinking? I hadn't. Not really. I'd been reacting. To all the ways Jase continued to show up. For Stella. For the kittens. For me.

There was no way I would not get hurt if he ghosted me again. That ship had sailed right down Harmony Creek.

Right along with my self-control, apparently.

"We need to stop," I finally said, stepping back and shivering from lack of heat from Jase that had been searing its way into my body.

"What brought that on?" Jase asked, panting. "Not that I'm

complaining." He slid his hands down my backside and squeezed, making my clit throb and my vagina ache.

"You," I said with more honesty than I'd been prepared for.

He grinned, then kissed me softly and took my hand.

"Let's get these guys home," he said, that word landing like a ticking time bomb on top of my heart.

*Home.*

I nodded as I tried not to panic when it didn't make me want to run away, but run *towards* something. Towards him.

*Spock help me.*

# JASE

itten number five, squeaky clean," Molly said, handing me a kitten that looked more like a wet washrag than a feline.

I held the kitten against my bare chest as I wrapped it in a towel. My shirt had been too coated in mud to salvage, and I hadn't wanted to dirty one of Molly's volunteer shirts she offered me if we were just going to get wet and dirty cleaning up the animals.

I marveled at the efficiency Molly had shown in getting the kittens cleaned in the giant wet room she used to bathe all the animals. If I'd known she had this, I might have spared myself the humiliation of using my own shower these past few months. A space so small I couldn't lift both elbows at once without smacking them on a wall.

This one was plenty big enough for me. And Molly. Together.

Tug Junior was starting to stiffen as I thought of the many, many ways I could make use of this space with Molly. Under the showerhead while I pinned her against the wall. Splayed out in front of me on the platform she used to wash

Stella so she didn't have to bend over. Oh! Bent over the platform while I drove into her from behind until her screams echoed off the tiled space.

*Mew.* The tiny kitten pulled me out of my wet fantasy and back to reality. Unfortunately, my, ahem, reality, was now very, very obvious.

I let go of one side of the towel so it draped in front of me.

*You're here to help, not get all pervy. Get it together, Tug. Sharp kitten claws. Dog drool. Larry. Mrs. Kowalski in a bikini.*

That did it.

"Everything okay over there?" Molly asked as she gathered up the sopping wet towels.

I cleared my throat and kept the towel hanging in front of Tug Junior, who was definitely not okay. He wanted to be let out to play.

"Yep, all good."

*Mew,* tattled the kitten.

Molly looked up, her golden eyes ablaze as she took in my still bare chest. Her tongue flicked across her bottom lip, causing my dick to jump. *Down, boy.*

I gently placed the kitten in the kennel with its four clean siblings and made sure the latch was closed before turning back to Molly. I'd planned to ask if I could follow her home and use her shower, volunteering to scrub her clean, hopefully with my tongue.

Molly put a dry blanket in an empty carrier before securing Stella inside it and turning to me. From the way Molly looked at me like she wanted to eat me for dinner—*yes, please*, Tug Junior volunteered—I was ready to fall on my knees right here in the wet room for my appetizer.

I could make sex in this giant shower work. And if it didn't, I'd try again at her house. And keep trying until she was screaming my name as she came on my face.

"You're still muddy," Molly said.

"You're wet." Her shirt clung to her chest, her nipples poking through the material, making me want to suck on them.

"You have no idea." She'd muttered it, but I heard it loud and clear and lost the battle of the boner. Tug Junior wanted out. I tried to adjust my shorts, but there was no room left. TJ wanted out *now*.

"I can finish cleaning up if you want to go home," I said against the protests of my aching cock.

Molly looked at my crotch and shook her head. "Wouldn't want you to slip and fall because you got lightheaded." A smile tilted her lips.

I swallowed, trying to make my mouth work, which was hard to do considering all my blood had left my brain and rushed south. "Wouldn't want that."

Jesus, I could barely string together three words. She was right, I would be a tripping hazard.

She walked up and stopped inches from me, her chest rising and falling. Her tongue darted out to wet her lips and my dick jumped again.

Sliding a hand down my shorts, she cupped me. "I can help with this," she said, right before she dropped to her knees and slid my shorts down my legs.

The sight of her golden eyes as they tilted towards me looking hungry, nearly brought me to my own knees. Dear god, I was going to blow my load before we'd even begun.

She wrapped one hand, then the other, around my cock, squeezing softly. Somebody groaned. Probably me, but I wasn't sure. In my defense, my brain had checked out the minute Molly had pumped me up and down, making me harder than I'd ever been.

"You like that?" she asked.

Before I could answer her, she swirled her hot, wet

tongue around the tip, making my knees buckle. I planted a hand on the wall to steady myself.

"Fuck, Molly."

"I take that as a yes," she chuckled as she slid one hand between my thighs and cradled my balls.

"Yes. Jesus, yes, a hundred times yes—*oh!*"

Molly opened wide, and I felt her tongue dragging as she lapped me from root to tip.

"Again," I begged.

"Mmm," she moaned, complying. I was dizzy with need and the strain of holding back. I was seconds from coming in her mouth, and I very much wanted to feel her come on me first.

*.426, .414, .387, .378.*

Molly paused, one hand still gripping my base while the other continued to massage my balls. "What are you doing?"

At least that's what I thought she said, since she still had my cock in her mouth.

"Reciting my batting averages, starting with the most recent."

"I… um… huh?"

I cupped her cheek with the hand that wasn't trying to keep me upright. "You feel too good, Molly. I don't want to come in your mouth."

She blinked and released me with a *pop.*

"What if I want you to?" She licked me like a fucking ice cream cone.

"Jesus, Molly. I'm trying to make this last." And make it good. She'd had a hell of a day, a hell of a month. I should be the one down on my knees, making her see stars. Not standing here while she made me feel like a god.

Taking my hand off the wall, I tucked her hair behind her ear. "Come here."

"But—"

"You feel amazing, but I want you to come on my cock more than I want your mouth wrapped around me. And I might freeze to death if we have to wait twenty to thirty minutes for that to happen because you drove me over the edge with that fantastic mouth of yours."

Molly chuckled as she leaned back on her heels. "You make a fair point."

Standing, she reached up to steady herself. I held out a hand for her to grab, but before she could, her heel slid out from underneath her.

"Oh, shit!" she yelled, arms and legs flailing.

The whole thing played out in slow motion before me, like a throwdown at home plate. But instead of being in control of the play, I was helpless.

Her legs flipped up, one arm slapped my stomach, catching the top of my dick as she struggled for purchase—*oomph! That was going to hurt once I had time to think about it*—and her elbow slammed on the tile floor.

"Fuck me," she muttered.

"Hey, you okay?"

I kneeled down before her as best I could with my shorts still wrapped around my ankles and Tug Junior complaining about the dick smack. My bad knee groaned in protest, but Molly might be hurt so it could damn well take a number. So could TJ, who was protesting the abuse to his manhood.

Molly groaned, sitting up and examining her elbow. "Ow."

"Is anything broken?" I held her arm while I tilted it back and forth, checking for breaks.

"I don't think so," she answered, letting me move her arm.

*Huh.* Molly was letting me take care of her. She was either really hurt, or else she was starting to trust me with more than just her orgasms. Based on the movement in her arm, she wasn't seriously injured, which left only one option.

Score one for me.

"But Jeff will never let me live down another sex injury," she added.

"Sex injury?" I barked out a laugh as I put it together, remembering how I'd tweaked my knee. And the lump on my head. "Oh, my god. What's wrong with us?"

Molly giggled. "For starters, we apparently can't have normal sex."

"Who wants normal? I'm fine with a few sex injuries."

Molly laughed in earnest. "Same. Wait. Did I just slap your dick?"

"Um, sort of?"

She covered her mouth with her hand, eyes wide. "Oh my Spock, I'm so sorry." Reaching out like she was going to grab it, she stopped short, disappointing both me and my dick. "Is it… okay?"

Despite the assault, Tug Junior stood tall and ready to step back up to the plate. *Way to take one for the team, TJ,* I mentally high-fived my dick.

"We're fine," I said. Or at least I tried to. My plan had been to punctuate the sentence with a deep and meaningful kiss to get us back on track. The track being the quickest way to get Molly to come on my face before I buried myself inside her.

Instead, my shorts, which had been stretched tight against my ankles as I'd been bending down, chose that exact moment to speak up. *Riiiiiip,* they went, tossing me backwards as I lost my balance. Tug Junior and my back both protested the sudden shift in altitude.

"Oh holy Klingons," Molly whispered right before she burst into a fit of giggles. The melodic laughter was punctuated by the occasional snort as she rolled to her side, holding her stomach with both hands.

I chuckled. It had to be quite a sight. My bare ass pointing heavenward, my dick still half hard, leaning against my stomach while my balls swung in the breeze.

Molly wheezed, wiping tears from her eyes. "I can't," she hiccuped.

Bolstered by her infectious giggles, my own laugh grew until I could barely breathe. Tug Junior was bouncing up and down on my abdomen, which just made me laugh harder.

Molly pushed herself up and, still giggling, crawled over to me. "You okay?" she said in a wheezing gasp.

It took me a minute to catch my breath. I nodded. "Yeah," I said, rising to a sitting position and kicking one leg out of the shorts. Torn right down the middle.

Molly sat next to me and rested her head on my shoulder. A simple gesture, but one that sang out to every lost and unsure corner of me, singing I was right where I belonged. Next to her.

"We should clean up," she said, not moving.

"Probably. Or, hear me out. We don't."

Molly's head swung up to look at me, hunger and a little mischief swirling in her eyes. "What do you have in mind?"

"Something much more fun," I said as I brought my mouth to hers and kissed the hell out of her.

43

## MOLLY

oly Klingons, did this man know how to kiss. I expected frenzy and heat and impatience. But he kissed me like he had all the time in the world. Like he wanted to savor the moment. Savor *me*.

His hands held either side of my face. The rough skin from years of playing baseball scratched at my skin, but I didn't mind. How could I mind when he held me like I was the most precious thing on the planet?

He moved his hands, tilting my face to deepen the kiss, and swirled his tongue—*oh my Vulcans, yes!* I tried to adjust, but he kept me pinned in place while he continued his demonstration of how talented his mouth and tongue were.

Not that I was going anywhere. No siree. I was in it for the long haul. I'd earned whatever orgasm—or *orgasms*— were headed my way. With skin and bones. And sore abs.

The interlude of uncontrollable laughter that caused the sore abs had been unexpected. But it was also… nice. I could be myself around Jase. He got me in a way no one else did. Not even my best friends.

They loved me but they didn't worship me. Right now, Jase was worshipping the hell out of me.

A grin I couldn't have stopped if the fate of the planet and everyone on it was at stake overtook my mouth.

Jase pulled back an inch. "You good?"

"So good." I pulled his head back into mine and sucked on his lower lip. A growl that was part hunger and part feral horndog escaped his mouth right before he pulled me so I was sitting on top of him.

I wrapped my legs around him and ground against his thick cock. How he was still hard after the fall and the slap—*holy shit, had I actually slapped his dick?*—and the laughing was a feat of magic. I was planning to ride the hell out of his magically inflatable dick all the way to Orgasmia, the magical land of happiness.

A giggle escaped me as Jase's mouth traveled down my neck, licking, sucking, softly biting.

"Something funny?" he murmured, his lips still paying reverence to my neck.

"No," I said, rocking my clit against his magic stick and giggling again. Orgasmia, here we come!

"I guess I need to try harder if you're so easily distracted."

He had no idea, but I wasn't about to say no to an A-plus effort on his part.

His hand slid around my backside, grabbing and kneading my ass.

"Why do you still have clothes on?" he asked.

I looked down. *Huh.* Look at that. I was still fully clothed. While my personal chauffeur to Orgasmia was completely naked.

Vulcan gods, he was a gorgeous male specimen. Even after a few years of not playing professional ball, he was still all angles and muscles. His abs bunched as he held me in place, sucking on the tender spot between my neck and collarbone.

"Mmm…" I moaned.

"Clothes. Off. Now," he said, biting down on my shoulder and leaning me back so I was laying on the floor, with Jase hovering over me. I lifted my head off the ground so he could pull my shirt off. My bra went next. The cold tile bit at my back, the coolness a welcome relief for my hot skin.

My fingers, which were shaking with need—*same sister, my vagina commiserated*—fumbled with the button to my shorts. Stupid jean shorts. I should take a page out of Jase's book and just wear disposable, tear-away clothes from now on.

In a move more tender than the heat from his gaze might otherwise suggest, he moved my hands and unbuttoned my shorts. He bent and pressed a kiss to my belly button.

*"Fuuuck,* that feels nice."

He grinned against my stomach. His lips continued to pepper my stomach with soft flutters while he slid my shorts and panties down my legs, just far enough to give him access, but not far enough for me to wrap my legs around him.

He placed a kiss on my sex, and I bucked. He swirled his tongue, and I bucked again.

"Keep that up and you're in danger of getting a black eye," I warned, trying to shimmy my shorts down further so I could kick them off.

"Another sex injury?" he said against my clit. "Worth it."

Before I could laugh, he sucked my clit and my pussy clenched as I shot off the ground like a fucking rocket. Stars shot across my vision as the climax shook my entire body like I was riding a rocket straight to Orgasmia.

Jase flattened his tongue and licked me from bottom to top, flicking my sensitive bud. And I might have just come a second time. It was hard to tell since I hadn't stopped coming from the first round. "Holy fucking Romulans," I cried out.

He continued lapping at my folds, giving me a soft reentry to reality. I was still panting, my eyes barely open, when he pulled my shorts and panties all the way off and rolled over, taking me with him.

Straddling him, I glided up his rock-hard shaft before I leaned down and kissed him. The taste of me on his lips damned near brought me to a third orgasm.

"Shit," Jase said, stilling.

Not the reaction I was expecting. "What?"

"I don't have a condom on me."

*Oh.*

The responsible thing would be to stop and try again once we had condoms. But I didn't want to stop. Or be responsible. I really, really wanted to feel his magic dick inside me.

"I'm on birth control." I kissed his jaw. "And clean."

"I'm clean, too." He took my face in his hands. "Are you sure?"

I'd never been with someone without a condom before. As much as I loved sex, I loved being safe more. But I was safe. With Jase. I knew that, as much as I knew I needed to feel him inside me.

"I'm sure," I said, lifting myself just enough to center myself on his cock, and began inching my way down. Down, down I went on the rocket ship to bliss, until I was fully seated, so deep I could practically feel him in my throat.

"Molly," Jase whispered reverently as I rocked back and forth, his cock stretching my walls in all the right ways.

Best. Ride. Ever.

"Ride me harder, baby," he answered.

"Did I say that out loud?"

He chuckled, thrusting up into me. My head dropped

back from the sensations I was feeling. Everything, all at once. It was too much. And not enough.

*More.* I needed more.

"Take what you need," Jase answered.

Not wanting to disappoint, I lifted and slid down as Jase drove up, slamming into me.

"Yes," I said.

"More," he mirrored before lifting me and slamming me down again. And again.

Vulcan gods, I was going to come a third time and there wasn't a thing I could do to stop it. Not that I wanted to.

My climax spiraled up, up, up in time with the pace Jase set. My hands curled on his chest as I tried to keep up. A scream erupted from my mouth as my orgasm slammed into me, followed quickly by Jase's own, punctuated by one last thrust up and a deep, guttural grunt.

My arms refused to keep me upright another second, and I collapsed against his chest, which rose and fell as we both struggled to catch our breath. His arms wrapped around me in a giant hug as he showered my head with kisses.

*Holy fucking Klingons.*

If there was an award for the best orgasm ever, I was in the running. If there was an award for the best orgasm *giver* ever, Jase and his talented tongue and magic dick were taking home an ensemble award.

A sigh escaped me as I lay there, tucked into his arms, Jase still inside me. He was warm and strong, gentle and loving, with every touch. I wanted to stay here forever.

Wait, not forever. Just until I caught my breath and my limbs worked.

*We might be okay with forever,* my heart whispered.

*Especially if he keeps giving us monster orgasms,* my vagina cheered.

*Big fan of monster orgasms,* my ovaries agreed.

*Knock it off down there*, I replied, but not disagreeing. I could totally see a future where Jase and I did this many, many more times.

The orgasms, not the hugs.

*Maybe the hugs, too*, said my heart.

Yeah, maybe the hugs, too.

THE RISE AND FALL OF JASE'S SOLID CHEST SOOTHED MY muscles, which were a puddle of post-sex satisfaction. The temptation to fall asleep to the rhythm was strong, but the desire not to be caught naked in the shower room by one of my volunteers—or worse, Jeff and Tyson—was stronger.

I flattened both hands against the cool, wet tile and pushed so I was sitting.

"Mmm. God, you feel good," he said, thrusting up slightly with a groan as he slid his hands up my sides and cupped my breasts.

"Is it possible to fuck the bones out of someone?" I asked, rocking with his slow rhythm.

He chuckled, the low vibration reverberating off me, making me tingle in all the good places. I may be short on skeletal structure, but the rest of my body was ready for round two.

*Woof*, Atlas said from the next room.

"What the—?" Jase asked, stopping his motions.

*Nooo…* cried my lady parts.

"It's just Atlas," I said, rocking back and forth on his award-winning dick that was inexplicably still half hard.

Wait. Atlas? He was supposed to be at home. Wasn't he?

I stilled.

"Yoo hoo!" Jeff yelled from somewhere near the front of the shelter.

"Oh shit," I hissed as I looked down at Jase, whose eyes were wide and his face frozen in an "O" that probably looked a lot like my own O-face, but with more terror and less sex-induced bliss. It was absolutely unforgiveable that they were going to catch me and Jase a third time. Was the universe pranking me, or trying to tell me I shouldn't be doing this?

"Clothes," Jase said, scrunching his abs to sit up, causing his dick to do something to my insides that made my vagina sing an aria.

"Oh, yes," I groaned.

"Molly? Did you say something?" Jeff said, instantly killing my libido.

*Focus!*

My tee was within reach, so I leaned over and grabbed it, tugging it over my head. I'd worry about my bra later.

Jase was sitting up, my legs still wrapped around him. Which is how Jeff was going to find us—*again*—if I couldn't convince my body to work. I reluctantly lifted myself off his joystick of happiness—*so long, Orgasmia, until we meet again*—and stood, naked from the waist down.

Spock help me.

Jase held out a long arm. My panties were dangling from his fingers.

"Thank you!" I said, plucking them up and sliding them on.

Inside out.

Just like my shirt.

But people who took express rides to Orgasmia in a doorless room inside a building where multiple people had keys couldn't be picky.

"Molly? Where the hell are you? You sound like you're in a cave."

If only. Caves were at least dark. The shower room was lit

up like a fucking NASA shuttle launch. It was so bright the International Space Station could probably see all our bits.

"Uh, just finishing up in the shower room. Be right out," I called.

"Why'd you tell them where we were?" Jase whispered. "And where the fuck is my shirt?"

I pointed to the corner. "In the pile of dirty towels, where you left it." Not that I'd been complaining.

"Shit. My shorts…"

The pile of red material formed a sad, wet lump to my right. I picked them up and his phone tumbled out of the pocket.

"Oops, sorry," I said, bending down and grabbing it.

"I've got it," Jase said, bending at the same time.

Our heads collided.

"Ow, fuck!" I cried out.

"Ow!" Jase said, much more quietly. "Are you okay?"

"Molly? What's going on?" Jeff's voice sounded closer. Too close.

Jase scrambled to pull up what was left of his shorts. The front looked more or less covered, but he turned around and —*hoo boy*—ass for miles. A delicious, well-toned ass, but that probably wasn't the look he was going for.

"You, uh, might want to—"

"What?" he asked, turning around, trying to see behind him. "I feel a draft. Is the tear big?"

"Um…"

*Wuf*, Atlas chuffed as he sauntered around the corner.

"Hey, boy," I said as I finally found my own shorts. They were soaking wet. *Drenched shorts are better than assless shorts, I thought as I tucked Jase's phone under my chin and shim-mied into them.*

"Just don't turn your back on anybody," I answered, taking the phone from under my chin and holding it out for

Jase, waking the screen. The background image was a drawing of the brewery sign. But that wasn't what caught my attention. It was the text message alert.

From Candice fucking Shoowater.

> Candice: I have something to show you. My place, tomorrow at 7

What. The actual. Fuck.

Numbness seeped through my limbs, drowning the post-orgasmic bliss I'd been feeling.

Why did she have his number? Why were her name and number stored in his phone?

*No, Molly, slow down. There has to be a logical*—no, fuck that. This was not happening.

I glanced at the screen again.

What was Candice going to show him?

"Thanks," he said, taking the phone from me and shoving it into his pocket without looking at it.

"Sure," I answered. My voice sounded like a flat balloon. Which seemed appropriate, given that's exactly what my heart felt like.

"Are you hurt?" he asked, running a hand over my head gently.

Yes, but it wasn't my head.

"I'm fine," my reply coming automatically.

Atlas leaned against my side and looked up at me, as if he sensed something wrong. I absentmindedly stroked his velvety ears. I should just say something. Jase probably had a perfectly logical explanation for why he was going to dinner with our mutual enemy.

Spock would tell me I was being illogical and letting my emotions rule. Fuck Spock. What did he know, anyway? The pointy-eared bastard hadn't met Candice fucking Shoowater.

"Hey," Jase said, rubbing my back softly and pulling me out of my spiral. "You still with me?"

I certainly had thought I was. I'd thought we were a team. That I could trust him.

But that text message… *My place tomorrow at 7.*

He told me Kenny didn't have any information about Candice's plans. Had he lied? Was he going to sell me out?

"Yeah, all good," I lied. "Just hungry. And thirsty."

"Okay, Molly Jean Sanders. What is the meaning—" Jeff stopped. "Holy shower sex on a stick. *Again?*"

I looked down. The tag on my shirt tickled my chin. Shit. Inside out *and* backwards. *Smooth, Molly. Real smooth.*

"What? No." I tried for casual cool, but the tightness in my throat made me sound more like a deranged squirrel looking for its missing stash of nuts.

Jeff eyed me. They knew I was lying.

"So… what's up?" I asked.

*What's up? Who was I, Bugs Bunny?*

Jeff looked over at the pile of muddy towels plus Jase's shirt, before taking in Jase, who was holding his shorts up with both hands, his rear end backed to the corner.

"You guys really should think about having sex in a bedroom sometime." They pointed at me. "I'm gonna want details, Sanders."

"Wine it out?"

"My house, thirty minutes."

"I'll, uh, just get going," Jase said, edging his way around the wall.

Yeah, he apparently had a date to get to.

The thought made me want to throw up.

Jase walked towards Jeff, holding his shorts together in the back as best he could.

Jeff smirked as Jase walked past them. "Way to hit that

touchdown, Tiger," they said, lifting their arm and swinging it down towards Jase's ass.

"It's not touch-*down!*" Jase said, his voice rising and his eyes going wide as the smacking sound of skin-on-skin reverberated through the space.

Jase stilled, Jeff's hand still on his bare ass.

"Oh. My. God," Jeff stage whispered, pulling their hand back. "Did I...? Did it...?"

Jase nodded slowly. "You did, and it did."

"I'm so sorry," Jeff said. "I didn't..."

"No, no. It's okay. It was an accident. I hope." Jase waved off Jeff and looked at me, red brightening his cheeks like a little kid who'd gotten into his mom's makeup kit. "I, um, am going to go... somewhere."

I pinched my lips together and nodded. I didn't know whether to laugh or gasp or apologize for my friend's accidental ass slap.

It was probably better Jase was leaving. Candice's text was still ping-ponging around in my head, and I didn't know what to do with it.

Walking up to Jeff, I put my arm around their shoulder. "You okay?"

They raised their face. "Dear baby Jesus, thank you for these gifts we have received this day," they whispered reverently, holding up their hand. "I am never washing this."

A giggle escaped my mouth. *Okay, fine, I giggle.* I couldn't help it. The night had taken a horrible turn on me, sure. But Jeff was having the night of their life.

Good for them. Someone should get a win today.

"Come on, Sanders," Jeff said, still holding their hand up, like the queen of England. "You still need to spill the tea. And I need to have my hand bronzed."

What I needed was a time machine so I could go back in

time and forbid my heart from ever glancing in the direction of Jase Tugwater. But I'd settle for wine with my besties. For now.

44

# JASE

*I* tossed my phone and torn shorts on the bed and dug around in my closet for something dry, and less breezy, to wear.

I grabbed a new pair of boxers, some jeans, and a Catcher's Box tee. The shirt was clean; the jeans were questionable. I sniffed them. They'd do.

Thankfully, Sam and Eliza were each too preoccupied with their own work to notice me slinking back to the Catcher's Box on my way back from Happy Tails with my ass hanging out. Eliza had sequestered a corner of the bar to take a call, and Sam hadn't shown his face after locking himself in the office doing… whatever he was doing.

Fully dressed, I grabbed my phone and swore. A text message from Candice stared at me.

> Candice: I have something to show you. My place, tomorrow at 7

What the hell did she want? I typed out a response.

> Me: Go to hell.

<delete> <delete> <delete>

*Diplomacy, Tugwater.* She may be a nightmare, but she was a nightmare we needed information about. Maybe this was a way to get answers for some of our questions.

> Me: Busy tonight. If you have something to show me, drop it by the Catcher's Box.

Not that I wanted her here. The amount of drama she created wherever she went rivaled Larry. But better here than being seen in a restaurant with her, looking like we were on a date.

"Blech," I said, shuddering.

"What's blech?" my sister asked me from the doorway, bouncing Edith gently on her hip.

The pale blond hair that both my sisters and I all had at that age stuck up on one side of her head. My niece's eyes blinked heavily. Must be getting close to bed time.

I looked down the hall for Landon.

"He's out like a light," Eliza said, answering my unasked question. "What's blech?"

"Blech," repeated Edith.

"A business thing."

"Sounds specific."

Eliza swayed back and forth while Edith rested her little head on my sister's shoulder.

I considered whether Eliza could help me with my Candice predicament. After all, she'd built her own business from the ground up, faced every problem thrown at her and found solutions for all of them.

But I doubted she'd ever encountered someone like Candice. I'd been all over the world and never encountered someone so single-mindedly spiteful.

"It's a brewery thing," I said.

She nodded. "Need help?"

"Nope. Got it under control," I lied.

Eliza's brow raised as if she could see right through me. Which she probably did. In my experience, big sisters had an uncanny way of seeing through the bullshit thrown by their little brothers.

"I'm here if you need me," she finally replied. "Well, not here." She gestured to the surrounding space. "As much as I loved seeing you and watching Sam be horrified by my little snot machines, I've got a redeye to catch. Need to get these snot machines home before Penn forgets he's married to the love of his life and Chloe decides she doesn't need her mommy anymore."

As if either of those things would happen. Her husband adored her. And Chloe was the greatest kid on the planet. Along with the two currently in my brewery.

"You're right," I answered, smoothing Edith's hair and earning a small smile from the little girl. "You're highly forgettable."

"Uncle Jase is a meanie," Eliza said to Edith, tickling her belly and eliciting a giggle from the little girl.

"Meemee," Edith repeated.

"That's right, baby girl," Eliza said before turning back to me. "Seriously, I'm here for whatever."

"I know," I said, nodding. And I did.

Even if Eliza hadn't ever come across the kind of vindictive meanness Candice specialized in, she'd likely have some expert advice for me. But I wanted to prove to myself that I could do it. Just like Eliza had. Just like our sister Evie was doing with her DIY television show. Forging a path for ourselves.

Once upon a time, my path was baseball. Now I was on a new path. Wherever it led, I'd figure it out. Because there was no alternative. No room for failure.

Failure meant losing everything. Losing Molly.

I would not fail.

"Okay, little brother," my sister continued, pulling me out of the thoughts in my head. "The kiddos and I need to hit the road if we're going to make it to Denver in time for our flight home."

"Need any help?"

"Everything's already in the car," she said, heading to the door. "But you can grab Landon and walk us out."

I WATCHED AS MY SISTER AND NIBLINGS DROVE OFF INTO THE sunset. Literally. The last thing I'd said to her was to watch for deer on the side of the road. Not I love you. Not drive carefully. Not text when you get to the airport.

Watch for deer.

Dear god, I was starting to sound like Oscar and Bruce Lewandowski. This small mountain town was getting under my skin.

And I didn't hate it.

*Ding.*

I pulled my phone out of my pocket and cringed.

> Candice: On my way

That was quick. I looked at the office door. Sam was still here.

> Me: I'm on the patio. Come around back.

That was going to have to do. I just prayed that Molly was still at wine it out with Jeff and Tyson, and that Sam was too preoccupied crunching numbers and blowing up my business plan to worry about what I was doing.

I poured myself a pint of Junior's stout, tentatively named the Double Play, and headed out back, flicking on the patio lights as I went. The sun had set, bringing a coolness to the air that reminded me I was over eight thousand feet above sea level. The crispness bit at my nose and fingertips as I sipped my beer, enjoying the quiet of the night.

A quietness that was interrupted less than five minutes later with the squeak of the patio gate. I made a mental note to pick up some WD-40 the next time I was at Stuff's. If I could find it.

Candice sauntered into the yard, wearing a royal blue tank and a white tennis skirt that was just long enough to not be indecent. Her blond hair sat in a high pile on her head, and bright pink lipstick stained her mouth. The whole thing came across as trying too hard.

She might have been showing off miles of legs, but it was the cardboard tube she held in her hand that caught my attention.

"Jase," she said, all business.

*Bleat!* yelled Larry from her pen next door.

Candice jumped. "Jesus, that fucking goat."

Biting down on my smile and making a note to give Larry an empty bag of my hops for her to destroy later, I pointed to the chair across from me. "Have a seat."

"Thank you," she said, lowering herself demurely into the seat and making a production of crossing her legs.

"What was it you wanted to show me?" I asked.

"Your future," she said, a cunning grin stretching her pink lips.

"My future?" As I said it, an image of Molly sitting next to me while a gaggle of kids—with her dark hair and my blue eyes—ran around the yard. Servers carried my beer and food while weaving in and out of the crowd, who were enjoying the Colorado sunshine on my patio. A space full of friends and family. Full of love.

I could see it clear as day.

Candice took a poster-sized paper from the tube and unrolled it in front of me, sweeping an arm in front of it like a game show host. "Feast your eyes on the future of Harmony Springs."

A tad dramatic, but I couldn't deny my curiosity.

As I looked over the sheet, the blood in my veins ran cold. It was a high rise, of sorts. It looked to be ten stories, at least. Which in this town was the equivalent of an eighty-story skyscraper in New York. Metal and glass and harsh angles looked back at me from the paper.

It was a beautiful building. Just not here.

"What's this?"

"Harmony Towers," she answered, grinning like a snake about to swallow a mouse.

"Harmony Towers?" What the fuck was Harmony Towers, and why was it sitting at my table instead of a Denver suburb where it belonged?

"A multi-use building, with modern, state-of-the-art condos for sale on the upper floors. Lower floors will be fitted for retail and restaurants—or breweries," she said, cocking an eyebrow at me, making me feel dirty for even listening to this absurd plan.

"And where, exactly, would this tower go?" I asked.

Candice grinned like a shark about to attack. "Right here."

"Here? Like, where my building is?"

"I already have almost all the signatures I need for the council to vote on this idea next Tuesday."

"Almost all?" Christ, I had a week to figure out how to stop an out-of-control freight train.

"I just need one more," she said, pinning me with a stare. "Yours would do."

A burning roiled through my gut, up my chest and into my head. "You can't be serious."

"It would be a mistake to underestimate my level of commitment to this project," she said, looking every bit as serious as she claimed to be. "Think about it. The flagship Catcher's Box Brewing Co. here, in Harmony Springs, anchoring my flagship Harmony Towers building."

"Flagship?" Not that I hadn't thought about it, but she was years ahead of me in terms of plans.

Nodding. "Your beer. My buildings. We could build a franchise empire."

Jesus fucking Christ. I wanted to believe this conversation was nothing more than a fever dream, but the dread knotting up my gut told me it was real.

"Over my dead body."

She shrugged a shoulder, as if my death might be a mere inconvenience. "This is just the start of my plan to modernize this nothing little town full of small-town nobodies."

"These small-town nobodies are my friends." I clenched my jaw so tightly I practically whispered the words.

This was madness.

These hard working "nobodies" had supported my business. Embraced my entry into small-town life. They shared their gossip with me. Treated me like a local, instead of some big-time celebrity. Except Jeff, who still acted a little starstruck around me, but that probably had more to do with having seen—and touched—my bare ass than the size of my bank account.

Who the hell was Candice to think she was better than the rest of them?

"This is happening with or without you," Candice spit out. "You can't stop it."

"Watch me," I challenged.

I had no fucking idea how, but I *would* stop it.

For Molly. For the life that we could have.

The scraping of metal on cement at Happy Tails caught my ear. I needed to check Larry's pen before I turned in for the night.

Candice stood, squaring her shoulders. "I can promise you one thing."

"What's that?"

"You'll never regret working with me."

Candice rolled up the hideous plan and stuffed it back into the tube. Raising her chin, she looked at me and smiled. "We'd make a great team, Jase." Without another word, she walked out, hips swaying, flicking a dismissing hand over her shoulder.

I shook my head. "A partnership with Candice," I said before finishing my beer. "What a great fucking idea." *Not.*

*A*re you sure that's what he said?" Tyson asked as he refilled my wine glass. I didn't remember drinking it, but as long as someone kept filling it, I might stop the flood of feelings threatening to overwhelm me.

I'd practically run to Tyson's after watching the horror show take place in Jase's backyard. After Jeff and I had left Happy Tails, I couldn't remember whether I'd locked the back door. With kittens in the shelter, I didn't need Larry deciding they needed to be free range again. So I'd popped back to double check everything.

That's when I saw the patio light on over at the Catcher's Box. I stepped outside, thinking I would invite Jase to wine it out at Jeff's.

Then I heard it.

*A partnership with Candice. What a great fucking idea.*

"Or maybe it was someone else?" Jeff asked.

"Some other former pro baseball player who just happened to be sitting in the brewery yard at nine o'clock at night, letting Candice fucking Shoowater woo him with her business plans? Sure. Why not?"

Atlas picked up his head as my voice rose a full octave.

"I think what Jeff means," Tyson countered, his voice level and soft to my rising agitation, "is that maybe you misunderstood."

Maybe. *Maybe.* But I'd also seen that fucking text Candice sent to Jase.

"There was nothing to misunderstand. I was right there. I heard him say… it." Spock help me. I couldn't even bring myself to say the words again. I'd barely choked them out the first time I'd told the story.

Tyson stood and topped off Jeff's glass, then his own, his calm demeanor defiantly stepping on my last nerve. I didn't need calm. I needed rage. Why didn't they understand that?

If I were a Klingon, I'd just swing my bat'leth around and behead anyone who dared to disrespect me.

Unfortunately, I was human, and beheading was frowned upon on Earth.

"I still don't get why you didn't just ask him?" Jeff asked. "I mean, he saw you, right?"

Cupcake, one of the Fishers' two Chihuahua mixes and the oldest of the Fisher pack, stood on her hind legs and placed her tiny front paws on my leg. I obliged, picking up the dog and plopping her in my lap.

"I might have been hiding," I said into Cupcake's fur.

"You hid?" Jeff asked, their eyebrows threatening to shoot off the top of their head.

"I panicked."

My friends blinked at me.

"What? I went out there to invite Jase to join us and he was there… planning to sell me out. To *her.*"

The thought of Jase teaming up with Candice turned my stomach into a cesspool of revulsion. But more than that, it meant he thought his business was more valuable than mine. More valuable than what we could accomplish together.

It was all too much.

"I don't know," Tyson said, sipping his wine. "That doesn't exactly sound like Jase."

"What do we really know about the guy?" I countered. "He's a big, fat superstar. Why wouldn't he team up with someone more successful and beautiful than me? He's used to getting whatever he wants whenever he wants."

Like getting in my pants. And heart.

And I fell right into that trap. Giving him exactly what he wanted until the next best thing came along.

"I agree with my perfect, insightful husband," Jeff said, earning them a glare over Cupcake's sweet, frosted face. "He might have lived that lifestyle once upon a time, but I've sen how that man looks at you. He only has googly eyes for Y-O-U." They punctuated their sentence by poking my arm with their finger.

"You can sleep with someone and still want to throw their business under the Candice bus," I said, rubbing my arm, hating their pointy fingers.

"Sorry, I just don't see it," Tyson answered, earning him a glare.

*I felt like the Oprah Winfrey of dirty looks. You get a glare! And you get a glare! Everyone gets a fucking glare because no one is taking my side! Glares for all of you motherfuckers.*

Okay, that wasn't very Oprah-like.

"It doesn't matter," I said, putting Cupcake back down on the floor. "It's done. He's made his choice." Her little paws click-clacked back over to the pack, where she settled down in between Atlas and General. A giant dog sandwich. Probably wasn't a safer place on the planet. I wanted to be Cupcake right now.

"Why don't you just ask him what Candice wanted?" Jeff asked.

"Pish," I answered before draining my glass and holding it out for a refill.

"Then text him," Tyson said, causing me to frown while he refilled my glass. Which usually made me smile.

But smiling was for people who didn't get betrayed by people who were supposed to have their back.

"Smoke signal?" Jeff suggested over the rim of their glass.

I rolled my eyes.

But the words hit. Were they right? Should I talk to Jase? What would I even say? *Hey, saw you talking to Candice. Are you sure you want to go into business with the worst human being in Colorado and possibly the planet and evict me from the only tether I have to my dead mom?*

I already felt like an idiot for trusting him. There was no way I could allow him to make me feel pathetic, too.

I had far too many feelings swirling around inside me. It felt like a swarm of bees. Emotional bees, buzzing and stinging and hurting.

Emotions sucked.

"What do you need, sweetie?" Jeff asked, pushing my wine glass towards me as if more wine might be the answer.

It wasn't *not* the answer.

"What I need is logic. I need Spock."

"It's okay to have Big Feelings, Molls," Tyson said, pushing the plate of cheese and crackers my way.

I plucked a cracker off the board and tossed it in my mouth, not tasting it.

"I don't have Big Feelings," I assured them. "That would be illogical. I can sleep with a man without involving my heart." Weak little organ that it is.

"Even Spock had feelings," Tyson pointed out unhelpfully.

Smarty Pants Fisher thought he was so smart. But Spock knew how not to feel his feelings. How to use logic to overcome all the confusion and nonsense that came with those pesky emotions.

So why couldn't I?

"I… I just can't, you guys. I can't do this right now."

"Oh, Molls," Jeff said, hugging me with one arm while they chugged down the remnants of their red with the other. "You get to feel whatever you're feeling, even if it's anger."

"That's just it," I said, twirling the stem of my wineglass between my finger and thumb. "I'm not angry. I'm…" *Heartbroken.* "Disappointed."

That was the right emotion when I'd probably been half in love with him, only to find out that he hadn't really cared that much about me, wasn't it?

*Only half in love?* my heart asked softly.

*We loved all the sex,* my vagina unhelpfully added. *We want more!*

*No more sex. No more love,* I warned before gulping down half the wine in my glass.

*Boo!* they both said.

Jeff and Tyson shared a glance that suggested I'd just said all that out loud and didn't believe me any more than I did.

Atlas, sensing my distress, groaned as he lifted his hefty frame and plodded over towards me, laying his head on my lap. I rubbed one silken ear while I watched as Tyson topped up my wine for the forty-seventh time.

I'd be sleeping on their couch tonight. There was no way I'd be able to safely walk the few blocks between here and my house, even with Atlas to lean on. Disappointing.

Great, now I was disappointed in myself.

"Disappointed is… new for you," Tyson observed, placing the empty bottle on the counter behind him. "Not very logical."

That could be the name of my fucking autobiography. *Not Very Logical: The Molly Sanders Story.*

I took a healthy gulp of wine. Tyson could have poured me a glass of motor oil and I wouldn't know the difference at this point. Maybe that was a good sign. It meant I was finally approaching maximum numb. Like maximum warp speed, except with wine instead of dilithium crystals.

"Nothing logical about falling in love with someone who can't love you back," I hiccuped.

"Uh…" Jeff said, their glass frozen halfway to their lips, eyes wide.

Tyson smiled.

"What's the matter with you?" I asked, my brows scrunched in agitation. At least I assumed my brows were scrunched. It was hard to tell.

I patted my cheeks. Yep, numb.

One body part down, the rest of them to go. *Heart, get on board the numb train!*

"Where there's love, there can be forgiveness," Tyson said like a fucking cryptic weirdo.

*Fuck love and fuck forgiveness.*

Which, from the looks on my friends' faces, I'd said out loud.

*Good. Fuck forgiveness.*

"So you said," Tyson said.

*Huh, still thinking out loud.*

"Yep," Jeff said.

There was a better than even chance I might not survive the hangover tomorrow. But that was Tomorrow Molly's problem.

Right Now Molly just wanted to stagger to the couch without stubbing a toe or throwing up. And to stop the fucking ache in my heart.

I rubbed at my chest. "I think I need to go lay down now," I said, tossing back the rest of my wine in one large swallow.

"We'll tackle the rest of this tomorrow," Jeff said, helping me to my feet while Tyson wrapped a steadying arm around my waist.

"Nothing to tackle," I said, leaning on Tyson and keeping a hand on Atlas's back for extra stability. At least my dog wouldn't leave me. Like that unworthy man I'd unwittingly given my heart to. "If Jase has decided to partner with the Sleaze Queen, then I've made my decision, too."

They shuffled their way to the living room, where I collapsed on the couch, wrapping a quilt around my head. I was done with Jase. Done with dreams.

Candice could fucking have them both.

"You don't really mean that," Tyson whispered as he kissed my forehead.

I didn't. But I wanted to.

## 46
## JASE

*O*h, come on, you temperamental she-devil."

I wiped the sweat from my forehead as I tossed the monkey wrench onto the floor. I pulled my foot back, ready to give Rosita a swift kick to pull her out of her mechanical temper tantrum, but stopped myself before I did any damage. Rosita held my flagship brew. It wasn't her fault I was in a mood.

After Candice's brief visit last night, I'd decided to do a soft opening of the Catcher's Box ahead of my planned opening. Which meant the Catcher's Box Brewing Co. was officially opening for business the day after tomorrow—four days before the town council meeting that would decide my fate. And Molly's.

Candice couldn't close what was already open. I hoped.

When I'd called Sam this morning to tell him the news, Sam had informed me he was on his way back to Denver this morning to catch a midday flight back to Chicago. He had some "non-Tugwater business" that needed his attention.

Which was the worst possible timing in the history of timed things.

So now I had to figure out how to open a week earlier than planned. All by myself.

I also tried texting Molly to tell her what had happened, but she was MIA.

"Rosita, baby," I cooed, rubbing the hammered steel with my hand like soothing an upset lover before bending and picking the wrench off the floor. "I'm sorry, but we do not have time for a meltdown. We've got beer to brew and two businesses to save, and we can't do either unless you get your shit together and fucking do it."

"You always talk to your equipment like that?"

I jumped at the unexpected voice. A male voice.

Not Rosita. Not that Rosita could talk. But if she could, I'd always imagined she'd have a sultry, smoky voice. Like a jazz lounge singer. Or my Great-Aunt Tilda, who, every Christmas dinner, told the story of the time she had an affair with a Cuban man during the Bay of Pigs Invasion and took up cigar smoking to remember him by. She claimed she smoked a Cuban cigar every day, right up to the day she died. At 103 years old.

Tyson appeared around the corner. "I tried knocking, but you didn't answer."

"Yeah, sorry. I'm a bit… preoccupied."

"I got your text message." Tyson pulled over a three-legged stool and sat.

"And?" I asked, tweaking the sanitary valve that didn't need tweaking, but I'd already gone over everything that could be wrong with Rosita, so I was starting at the beginning.

I'd texted Tyson when I couldn't get hold of Molly. I'd hoped for a text back, not a visit.

"Molly's hurting," Tyson said.

"What? Where is she? What happened?" I twisted the wrench in my hands, the questions tumbling from my mouth. Molly was hurt. I'd strangle whoever was responsible with my bare hands. As soon as I knew who'd done it.

I pulled my phone out of my pocket to call... who? The police? The hospital?

"Who hurt her?" I asked Tyson, all but pleading for an answer. I couldn't help Molly without answers.

Tyson stayed silent, watching my every move closely, like a teacher who was trying to decide whether I would suffer detention or get to go to recess. Given the way I was struggling not to squirm under Tyson's gaze, I was really glad I didn't have him for a teacher growing up.

"You did," he said softly.

I stepped back, the quiet statement knocking the literal breath out of me. "I... what?" I searched Tyson's face for some sign he was joking, but didn't see it.

I thought back to the last time I had seen her. Just last night. She'd been adorable in her inside-out tee and soaking wet shorts. I'd been, well, bare assed and put in my place by Jeff. Everything had been fine.

Hadn't it?

"I don't understand," I finally admitted. "What did I do?"

"Are you really going into business with Candice?" Tyson answered.

I dropped the wrench, almost hitting my foot, the clatter of metal on cement echoing through the space.

Ignoring the wrench, I turned slowly, clenching my fists, until I was facing the man who had clearly lost all his fucking marbles if he thought even for a second I'd consider getting into bed—metaphorically or otherwise—with someone as underhanded and cruel as Candice. "Where the hell did you get an idiotic idea like that?"

Tyson cleared his throat. "Molly overheard you talking to Candice last night. She said you said something about a partnership?"

"She was there?" The noise I'd heard and thought was Larry. It was Molly.

"Wait. It's true?" Tyson looked gutted.

"What? No. I didn't…"

I'd been so pissed that Candice would want to turn this town on its head and bulldoze over its residents and their hard-earned dreams. That's all I could remember. Had I said something as Candice left that led Molly to think I was agreeing to a partnership?

"What *exactly* did she hear?" I finally asked.

"That you said a partnership with Candice was a great idea."

"Oh. *Oh.*" The lightbulb clicked on over my head. "I did."

"You said that?"

"Yes. But no." I remembered now. I thought I'd mumbled the sarcastic comment under my breath, but my temper must have been pushing those words to the surface more forcefully than I'd remembered.

"I don't understand," Tyson said.

Right. Which meant neither did Molly.

"I said that. But I didn't mean it. I was being sarcastic."

I forced myself to stay calm as Tyson eyeballed me, the calculating look making him look more like a discerning principal than a stern teacher. The last time I'd been this thoroughly measured, I'd been a rookie starting my first game in the majors. The first batter had nearly made me shit my pants.

But I held his gaze, just like I was holding Tyson's now. I may be a puddle of nerves on the inside, wondering if Tyson would believe me, but damned if I'd show it.

Finally, Tyson nodded. "I believe you."

*Victory!*

"But I still don't understand," he continued.

I didn't have time to explain. I needed to get in front of Molly and explain.

Except... why wasn't Molly here? Confronting me? Reading me the riot act? "Why are you here?"

"I knew there had to be some sort of explan—"

"No. Why *you* specifically? Why isn't Molly here?"

"You hurt her."

"Exactly. Why isn't she here yelling at me? Telling me to get fucked? Why is she hiding from me?"

I was yelling, but Tyson didn't shy away. He was shaking his head.

"She needed some time this morning to... process."

Process? What the fuck was there to process? I wasn't going into business with Candice. And Molly needed to understand that. Understand that I'd never, ever do anything to hurt her. I loved her.

"I need to talk to her, Tyson."

I needed to convince her I wasn't doing any deals with Candice. Even if I didn't have a solid plan for how to stop her. I had a solid first step, but had wanted to talk to her so we could figure out what to do next.

Together.

Tyson nodded. "You do. But not yet."

I reeled as if I'd been slapped. "Do not get between us," I ground out.

I considered Tyson my friend. Jeff, too, even if he was a little much sometimes. But if either of them thought for a second that I would just stand by while they kept me from Molly...

"I can see the wheels turning," Tyson said. "So let me just stop you. Why don't you tell me what's going on?"

"I need to see Molly," I reiterated through clenched teeth.

"And you will," Tyson answered, with the patience of a fucking saint. "But if you go in there all 'Hulk Smash!' and she's still processing, she's likely going to shut down on you."

Tyson was right. I didn't like it, but that didn't stop it from being true.

I wasn't good with subtle. I was definitely more Hulk than Bruce Banner when it came to fixing problems.

"So what do I do?"

"Why don't you start from the beginning and we'll go from there?" Tyson encouraged.

"I love her, Tyson."

"Have you told her that?"

I leveled a look at the man. "Of fucking course not. Do you think I'm stupid? She's not ready to hear it." Yet.

Tyson grinned. "Just checking."

I ran my hands through my hair and started pacing. "I'm in love with her. Everything I'm doing, I'm doing for her. For us. I need her to know that without it freaking her out."

God, it felt good to get that off my chest. Tyson stood there, listening, taking it all in. If he wasn't a high school teacher, he'd make a hell of a psychiatrist.

"So what's the plan?" Tyson finally said.

"I'm going to do a soft opening. This weekend."

Tyson's eyebrows shot to the top of his forehead. "As in the day after tomorrow?"

"Yes. But Molly comes first. Always."

Tyson nodded. "Okay, then."

We looked at one another as we let sit the gravity of everything I had just laid out.

"So what now?" I asked, rocking back on my heels.

"A soft opening won't dissuade Candice," Tyson said. "And I'm not sure it will be enough to show Molly you're serious, either."

I blew out a breath. Deep down, I knew that. But it was all I had. "If you've got any other ideas, I'm all ears."

"I think I know just the thing." Tyson grinned, a glint of mischief growing in his eyes. "But we're going to need some help."

"Help?"

Tyson nodded. "A lot of help."

"How much?"

"About a town's worth."

*I* popped a couple of over-the-counter pain pills into my mouth and took a deep swig of water. Two days after the Great Candice Meltdown and I was still hungover.

Served me right for letting Candice take up space in my head rent free like that.

All I had to do was march over and ask Jase what was going on. But noooo. I jumped right over all logic and common sense and straight into the hellfire of baseless conclusions. Conclusions that, upon further—and more sober—reflection, I knew were garbage.

Once upon a time, the King of Baseball might have been persuaded by Candice and the idea of cashing in on a more lucrative business plan. But Jase Tugwater, local business owner, neighbor who put up with Larry despite her many, many attempts to destroy his brewery, rescuer of muddy kittens and giver of the world's best orgasms?

That man was here to stay.

I'd woken yesterday morning to two of my least favorite things ping-ponging around in my head: a raging hangover, and the realization that I owed Jase an apology for something he probably didn't even realize I'd done. Placing the cleaned and refreshed litter box in the kennel next to the sweet orange kitten, I closed the latch. That was the last of the morning chores. I was officially out of things to do. Which meant judgment day was upon me.

Atlas stood from the corner of the room where he'd been napping and stretched. *Time to do this,* he seemed to say.

He was right. It was time. I could do this. All I had to do was walk over to the Catcher's Box, fess up to eavesdropping on his conversation with Candice, and explain how I thought he was going to sacrifice my business for the sake of his, and how much that had hurt because… because I loved him.

*Fuuuck.*

I loved him. When did that happen?

Probably sometime between the Sunshine Festival and orgasm number 287.

"Get to it, Sanders," I said, sighing as I shut the light off and walked to the front door, my dog trailing behind me.

*Yeah! We're ready for some hot makeup sex!* my lady parts shouted.

*We weren't technically fighting…*

*Tomatoes, to-mah-toes,* they responded.

I threw the lock on the front door and flipped the open sign to closed. But something made me pause. No, not some*thing.* Some*one.*

Someone was outside shouting. From the sound of it, many someones.

"What's going on?" I asked Atlas.

I leaned over the top of him so I could see out the big front-facing window, which was hard to do since I'd recently paid one of the high school art students to paint cartoon animals on it.

Peeking over the top of an elephant's ear—*I really should*

*have been more specific about* which *animals I wanted*—I saw Mr. and Mrs. Jenkins and their three daughters. A crowd had gathered around a circle of a dozen or so people marching, led by the Jenkins family.

Was everyone holding signs?

I opened the door, and a loud cheer went up from the crowd in a deafening roar. Then a familiar voice chanted through a bullhorn. "Hell no! We won't grow!"

*Jean-Luc Picard in a hot air balloon.* Who gave Jeff a bullhorn?

The Celebration of the Nation festival was about to get a major upgrade if Tyson couldn't convince them to give it back to whoever had given it to them in the first place—or pry it from their cold dead hands.

Jennifer Shuester, a retired school nurse, marched past me, holding a bright green poster board duct taped to a broomstick. "We believe in you, Molly!"

"Wait, is that—?"

Yep. Some inspired individual had pasted Candice's class president picture from senior year to the board with a big red circle around it and a line slashed through the middle.

Dale Dalton was carrying a sign with a skyscraper on it and the same big red "No" circle around it.

The one behind him, belonging to Wallace Stuff, simply read *Get your stuff at Stuff and Stuff.*

"What's going on?" I asked Wallace as he marched past me, dozens of his fellow friends and neighbors following.

"Hell no! We won't grow!" Wallace responded, which was repeated by the crowd, drowning out any chance I had to ask again.

Atlas let out a chuff as he wandered over and sat next to Tyson.

I zigzagged my way through the crowd, following him until I finally stood next to Jeff, who was shouting into their new toy. Tyson was next to them, holding an "Anti-Candi" sign.

"What the hell is going on?" I shouted over the protesters.

"They're here for you," said a familiar baritone voice from behind me. Shivers erupted up and down my body.

"Me?" I asked, turning towards Jase.

He was wearing an obnoxiously blue tee shirt that said *Save the Animals, Free the Beer*. It had my shelter logo and his brewery logo intertwined in a way that looked almost intimate. Like they were embracing. He was handing out shirts and smiling to the crowd as they circled by him.

Standing there, next to my friends, in the middle of the typical town chaos, he looked comfortable. Like he belonged here. With me.

"Why me?" was all I could think to ask.

"Because they believe in you." He handed the bundle of shirts to Tyson, who kept handing them out, and turned towards me. "Because *I* believe in you."

"Why me?"

Jennifer Shuester marched past again. "Because without you, I wouldn't have Meredith to keep me company."

Meredith was a stray adult cat who'd come through the shelter five years ago. It had taken almost a year before she finally found a new home with Mrs. Shuester.

Dale Dalton followed her. "And I wouldn't be out walking three times a day with Baxter. Gotta keep in shape for protests," he said as he disappeared around the circle.

Baxter was a one-year-old boxer that Mr. Dalton adopted from me this past spring.

Mrs. Allonsey yanked a shirt over her vintage Van Halen tee, causing a minor disruption in the progression of their circle. "And my sweet Sassy, may she rest in peace, was a godsend," she said, referring to the beagle she'd adopted from Happy Tails years ago, after my mom first opened it.

"I didn't do anything."

"You kept Happy Tails going after Belinda passed," Mrs. Jenkins said as she stepped out of line and gave me a quick hug before jumping back into the circle.

"And we stick up for what's right here," Mr. Jenkins added as he marched behind his wife. "If Candice thinks she can bulldoze this place to put up an eyesore, she can think again."

"Hell no, we won't grow!" the crowd continued to chant, which wasn't helping my second-day hangover any, but it was hard to be too upset about it. I had what looked to be most of the town, plus a few extras, tourists I'd seen in town before, chanting with anti-Candi signs in front of my building. *Who* and *how* didn't even begin to cover all the questions I had.

"Most of the town had no idea what Candice had been planning," Jase explained. "So we took it upon ourselves to inform them."

"We?"

Jase tipped his head towards Tyson.

"Once they found out," Tyson continued, handing a tee shirt to Oscar Lewandowski, who fisted it into the air, "they sort of organized themselves."

"Wow," I half whispered. "I can't believe I thought you and Candice…"

"Me and Candice what?"

Jeff shuddered and their bullhorn squelched, causing everyone to jump and the chanting to stutter to a stop.

"Sorry! Sorry everyone," they shouted into the horn. "Keep going! Hell no! We won't grow!" They punctuated their words by fisting the air.

After a couple of seconds, the crowd took up the chant and resumed their circling.

"Yeah," I said, swallowing my fear. This was my chance. I still wasn't completely sure what I was going to say to Jase, only that I very much wanted him by my side as we figured this out together.

*Come on, Molly. You got this.*

"I sort of... heard you guys the other night when you were talking. In the yard."

Jase nodded. "Yeah. Tyson told me."

"What?" I turned to Tyson, who was helping Oscar pull a tee shirt over Bruce's head. Atlas had been lulled to sleep by the chanting and was passed out on the sidewalk next to him.

"I wanted to be sure," he said with an unapologetic shrug. We were going to have a talk about boundaries after this. Right after I gave him a giant hug for being the *best* best friend.

"Molly, you have to know, I would never," Jase started as his phone dinged. He pulled it out of his pocket and stared at it.

"Everything okay?" I asked.

"Yeah, I think it might just be." He shook his head. "Later." Grabbing my hands, he blew out a breath. "Right now, I need you to understand how important you are to me. Candice is... she has..."

"No morals?" Tyson offered.

"No soul?" I added.

"Fake titties!" Jeff sang into their bullhorn, much to the delight of the growing crowd.

"Seriously, who gave Jeff a bullhorn?" I asked.

"*Save the animals! Free the Beer!*" Jeff shouted into their horn, stopping the mass from taking up a fake titties chant.

"I don't know," Tyson said, smiling fondly at Jeff, who was having way too much fun as the crowd director. "But when I find out, they will pay."

I looked around, unable to help the smile growing on my face. The town was here. For me. For Jase. For our weird little town.

They wanted to save their small town as much as I did. And with it, my shelter.

"Jase, I need—" I said.

"Molly, I'm sorry—" Jase said at the same time. "Sorry, go ahead," Jase said.

I shook my head. "You go first."

*Chicken*, my lady parts said.

He cleared his throat and brushed a hand down my arm, as if he was trying to make sure I wasn't going anywhere. But there was nowhere else I wanted to be.

"I'm really sorry, Molly. I should have told you she wanted to meet me, but I was just trying to figure out what Candice was planning."

"No," I said. "I'm the one who should apologize for thinking you'd team up with the likes of Skanks McGee. I just… lost my head for a second."

*Bahk, bahk*, my vagina clucked.

He grinned, a devilish look in his eye that said, I want to take you back to the shower room and fuck you against the wall.

*Okay!* cheered my vagina.

Instead, he dipped his head low and pressed a kiss against my jaw. "You're the only partner I want, Molly," he whispered in my ear.

Partner. In business? Or life?

It didn't matter. Okay, yes, it did. And I'd get there. I would.

But right now, right this minute, with this beautiful town rallying behind us, it didn't matter. What mattered was making sure Candice fucking Shoowater and her dastardly plans were finished. Once and for all.

I took a shirt from the shrinking pile Tyson was holding and yanked it over my head. "How do I get myself one of those signs?" I asked.

Someone handed me a sign. It said *Picketing is my Love Language*.

Close enough.

I began waving it up and down. "Save the animals! Free the beer!" I shouted, and the crowd cheered.

"Molly Sanders!" a voice screeched from beyond the horde. I looked over as Candice fucking Shoowater, the devil herself, slammed the door to her shiny black Mercedes, the scratches Larry had inflicted on full display against the bright sun. Bob Mulhoney exited the passenger side, much more cautiously.

*Here we go.*

"You good?" Jase mumbled out of the side of his mouth.

I nodded. "Let's do this," I said to Jase, holding out my hand for him to grab. Because if we did this, we were going to do it together.

"Fuckin' A," he said, intertwining his fingers with mine.

"Fuckin' A," I replied, nodding.

Candice wouldn't know what hit her in the fake titties.

48

# JASE

*I* stood hand-in-hand with Molly, a larger crowd than I honestly expected behind us, booing as Candice stalked forward. Let her try her best. I could conquer the fucking world right now, with Molly by my side.

"Oh shut up, you country bumpkins," Candice snarled, shoving shoulders aside as she marched through the still-booing mass. Bruce shook his sign at her. I was glad he had pants on today. I practically had PTSD from all the mornings I caught a ball shot of Bruce as he bent over to retrieve the morning paper wearing only a very short robe.

She snatched it out of his hand and attempted to throw it like a javelin, but it only waved around in the breeze before plummeting to the ground, stick first.

"Boo!" the crowd continued.

Jeff's bullhorn squawked, and they shouted into it. "Can-di sucks! Can-di sucks!" The horde took up the challenge, continuing the chant with gusto, no one louder than Molly.

"Can-di sucks!" Molly shouted, punching her sign in the air, which read *Picketing is my love language.*

I shook my head, grinning. When I'd agreed to Tyson's plan,

I thought the town would band together at a council meeting. Place a few posters in shop windows. Hold a bake sale.

This was a full-scale peace rally from the sixties.

*Sort of,* I thought as a sign declaring *I hate signs* passed by.

"What is your problem, Sanders?" Candice shouted, pointing a sharply manicured finger in Molly's face.

Anger turned my vision scarlet as I stepped next to Molly.

"I'm looking at her," Molly quipped, jaw thrust, one hand holding her sign down at her side. She might seem relaxed to the casual observer, but I saw the gold in her eyes swirl like a wildfire. She was coiled and ready to strike.

So. Fucking. Hot.

I angled behind her to adjust myself.

"Your little crowd of criminals is breaking the law," Candice said as Bob finally made his way through the crowd and practically cowered next to her.

"This isn't my crowd, and we aren't breaking any laws," Molly replied.

Well, Mrs. Allonsey was probably breaking a few fashion laws with her tie-dyed skirt, lilac purple trainers, and the bright blue shirt bearing the logo my niece had drawn for us yesterday. And Jeff was definitely breaking the laws of physics thanks to the bullhorn they found for themself.

But the rest were peacefully protesting in a private parking lot. No laws broken that I could see.

"You think this little demonstration is enough to stop progress?" Candice snapped. "You're delusional."

"That's enough, Candice," Molly replied.

Candice's eyes narrowed like an apex predator looking at its next meal. "I will dance when the wrecking ball smashes through the doors to your shelter."

"You wouldn't." Molly looked back at our building, some of her bravado wilting.

*No.* I did not go door to door like a fucking salesperson to rally this town behind her, only to watch her fold like a bad hand at a poker table.

"I think we both know I would."

I placed a hand on Molly's back and leaned down so I was right in her ear. Goosebumps broke out along her neck. Unable to stop myself, I placed a soft kiss just under her ear, grinning when she let out a small gasp.

"Get a room!" Jeff said into their bullhorn, as the ragtag mob cheered.

"You've got this," I whispered, ignoring everyone else.

She glanced up, her golden eyes hitting me right in the chest before she looked around at the crowd, who were still chanting "Candi sucks!" as they marched by. A grin slowly spread across her face.

I could feel her posture change. Hunched shoulders straightened. Drooped chin rose. An energy buzzed through her, electrifying her skin where I touched her.

"No," she said, facing Candice.

"What?" Candice's squawk was almost louder than Jeff's bullhorn.

"I… I said no, you're not destroying Happy Tails," Molly said.

"You can't stop me," Candice said, a threat dripping from her words.

Every molecule in my body vibrated, ready to protect Molly. But before I could say a word, Molly took a step forward. Candice stepped back half a step, the confidence on her face faltering.

"Yeah?" Molly challenged, taking another step forward.

*My warrior.*

Atlas stood, as if sensing the tension. Tyson nodded at her while Jeff grinned and held up two fingers in a V for Victory pose, while maintaining a death grip on their bullhorn with the other hand.

I surveyed the dozens of faces, recognizing some of them. Neighbors, friends, fellow business owners. All here for my cause. Mine and Molly's.

And the chance to protest.

More than a couple of residents had regaled me with stories of Harmony Springs' proud history of marching for a cause. According to Bart Stuff, the town's founding was rooted in a love of civil disobedience. Tyson confirmed later it was actually tourism, but apparently protesting was a close second.

Bart's brother Wallace had complained that the town hadn't had a good protest since winter before last, when Whinny Bottlesly had changed the background color of the Let it Snow Festival flyer from wintergreen to moss green without consulting anyone. I still wasn't sure why that required a protest and not a reprint, but Jeff had assured me it was a big scandal.

"Watch me," Candice answered. "When I'm done with you, you and your animals will be begging for handouts in Haven Falls."

A collective gasp rang out from the crowd.

"Too far, Candice," someone shouted.

I looked at Tyson and raised an eyebrow in question.

"We hate Haven Falls," he muttered out of the side of his mouth.

"Their football team has beat ours every year for the past ten years running," Wallace Stuff said as he circled past.

Rivalry. Something I understood.

Molly's face flushed. I normally loved seeing that on her, because it meant I'd done a thorough job at making her very, very happy. This was not a happy flush.

Her neighbors, Bruce and Oscar, nodded at her as they

walked by. A woman in a moo-moo holding a *No Candice Zone* sign held up a fist.

"Go get her, Molly!" someone shouted from the back of the horde.

"You've got this," I whispered to her again, linking my hand with hers.

She smiled at me, so wide and brilliant and beautiful, it nearly knocked me off my feet.

"You can't have my shelter, Candice."

"Psh," Candice replied. "I'll be doing this town a favor. That's all I'm doing here, looking out for the good of the town."

"Fake news!" someone from the crowd shouted. The rest took up the chant.

"You're not looking out for anyone but yourself," Molly said. "Everything about you is fake, right down to your... motives."

"Nice pivot," I said out of the side of my mouth.

Candice's face turned the shade of an overripe strawberry. "These are one hundred percent real." She grabbed a breast in each hand and tried to jiggle them. They were so stiff they barely moved. It was like watching someone try to move a couple of small, slightly asymmetrical boulders.

A thunderous cheer went up from the crowd. Jeff started chanting. "Boo-bies! Boo-bies!" The crowd pivoted and started chanting with them.

"Feel them," Candice demanded, turning towards a man standing next to her. The poor dude videoing their exchange fumbled with his phone, nearly dropping it. The scowling woman next to him slapped him upside the head.

"Girl, you know them titties are faker than the moon landing," Jeff said into their bullhorn.

"Fake titties! Fake titties!" the crowd shouted.

I could practically see steam coming out of the top of her

head. "Do something, Bob," she yelled at Bob Mulhoney. "Before I take my money and my investors—and my campaign donations—to Haven Falls. Let's see you try to win an election without me."

Bob's mouth, which had been silent through the entire exchange, puckered, opening and closing like a fish.

"Dad?" a voice called from the crowd.

Ginger Mulhoney stepped through as the swarm of protesters parted for her. Kenny was close behind her, a steady hand on her back.

"What are you doing here?" Bob asked his daughter.

"I was about to ask you the same thing," she replied.

I noticed the shirt she was wearing at the same time Bob did. *Save the animals. Free the beer.*

*Heh.* Take that, Bob.

"I'm providing for your legacy, pumpkin. Yours and your sisters'."

"By ruining the only place we've ever lived? That's not building a legacy, Dad. It's tearing it down." She gently laid a hand on his arm as Kenny draped a protective arm around her shoulder. "You don't have to do this. Let's go home."

"Go home, Bob! Go home, Bob!" the crowd chanted.

"Don't you dare," Candice said to Bob, seething. "You know what's at stake."

Bob looked back and forth between Candice and his daughter, seeming to weigh his options.

What the hell was he waiting for?

"This is a no-brainer, Bob," I said, crossing my arms and adopting the home plate stare down I was so famous for. Bob's throat bobbed in a nervous swallow.

"Please, Bob," Molly hissed. "Think of what you'd be doing."

Bob's eyes swung to Molly. Whatever he saw on her face,

it seemed to soften his resolve. I just hoped it was in the right direction.

"He'd be doing everyone a service!" Candice barked. "Wealthy tourists bring their money."

"At what cost?" I asked. "How many historical buildings and small businesses do you have to destroy before this town is little more than a carbon copy of the big resort towns?"

Red traveled from Candice's bulging bosom up her neck and mottled her perfectly made-up face. "You and your family will be fucking millionaires, you witless, spineless, simpleton," she spat at Bob. "Sack up and do what you need to do."

"That's a lot of money…" he said.

"Bob…" Molly said.

Was Bob really allowing himself to be swayed by Candice's empty promise of money? Sure, she could erect a bunch of shiny buildings. But there was no guarantee the money would follow.

"Dad, think about this…" Ginger said.

"I am thinking. I can make sure you and your future children don't have to worry about anything ever again."

*Hell. No.*

I took a step forward to give Bob a piece of my mind, but Molly stopped me by placing a hand on my chest.

"I've got this."

She took a step forward.

"Bob Mulhoney, you listen here." She poked a finger into Bob's weak-ass sternum. "You do this and I will make it my mission to interfere with every move you make."

Bob swallowed as she whipped her phone out of her back pocket.

"I know people, Bob. You like to wash your car every Monday morning, right?"

She swiped her phone on and typed something out. "I just

texted your neighbors to make sure they aim their sprinklers at your car every Monday night."

Bob's eyebrows shot up.

"You think you're going to make reservations at Angelo's for your thirtieth anniversary next month?"

Molly's thumbs flew over the screen in a whir. I peeked over her shoulder and grinned. She wasn't doing anything but typing gibberish, but Bob didn't know that. "Too late. I've already booked all the tables for the next three months."

Bob's lower lip quivered. "Penny," he whispered.

"That's right, Bob. What will your wife think of that?" She crept closer to Bob, a devious grin forming on her beautiful face. "You think you can just coast into being our next mayor?"

I loved chaotic Molly, surrounded by the pandemonium of her animals. I loved soft Molly, who gave me sleepy grins in the mornings.

But this clever, resourceful woman in front of me? Who was going to bat for herself and her town?

Sign me the hell up.

"Meet your new opponent." Molly held out her hand to a stunned Bob Mulhoney.

"Molly for mayor!" Jeff shouted into their bullhorn.

"Molly for mayor!" the crowd cheered.

*Wait, what?*

49

# MOLLY

*ait, what?*

"Molly for mayor!" the chanting mob continued.

What in Spock's name had my mouth gone and done? Mayor? Me? The woman who could barely remember to brush her teeth most mornings?

I looked at Jase, who was grinning, eyebrows arched so high they almost disappeared under his hairline.

*Mayor?* he mouthed.

*Fuck fuck fuckity fuck.*

Bob's mouth puckered and unpuckered like a fish as he turned around and faced Candice. "Take me home."

"Hell no," Candice replied. "She's bluffing."

Yes, yes I was.

Wasn't I?

*If we were mayor, we could have mayoral sex on the mayor's desk in the mayor's office,* my vagina helpfully added.

*Those are not things. Probably. Also, that's not a reason to run for mayor!*

"I… it doesn't matter," Bob sputtered. "I don't need this. I just want a peaceful retirement and a happy wife. No one disappoints Penny."

Candice scoffed.

"*No. One,*" he reiterated, eyes wide.

Candice scowled, but stayed quiet.

Ginger hugged her dad and placed a kiss on his cheek. "I'm proud of you."

"Good job, Bob!" Jeff said into their horn, and the crowd changed their chant to match.

Kenny squeezed Bob's shoulder. "Come on, Bob. We'll take you home."

The family walked towards the back of the parking lot and Candice rounded on me, eyes narrowed, boobs at full mast.

*Uh oh.*

I could feel myself shrinking under Candice's gaze, when a strong, muscled man braced against me. "You've got this," Jase whispered.

He kept saying that, but based on the fact I just threatened to run for mayor, I was pretty sure I did not, in fact, *have this.*

"And we've got you," he continued, pointing towards the crowd.

Tyson and Jeff stood facing me. Tyson had his arm around Jeff's shoulder. Jeff held their bullhorn like it was a precious package. Atlas was leaning against Jeff's legs, looking at me with complete adoration in his big brown eyes. The rest of the town, signs and tee shirts proudly displayed, filled in behind them.

*Huh.*

Maybe I did have this.

"Go home, Candice," I said with more bravado than I actually felt. Fake it 'til you make it, right?

"I'm not done here. If Bob won't run for mayor, then I will."

A collective gasp went up from the crowd.

"You wouldn't—"

"You sure you want to do that?" Jase interrupted.

Candice snapped her head in Jase's direction. "What are you talking about?"

Jase waved his phone. "I just got an interesting text from a friend. Seems like your investors might not all be on the up-and-up."

Candice paled as I looked up at him.

"Fozzy?" I whispered.

He nodded, a mischievous grin on his beautiful face.

"This is over, Candice. Go home," I repeated.

"It is so not over, Molly Sand—"

*Blehhht!*

The unholy sound came from behind me, a battle call to arms, as Larry charged from around the building.

The goat ran up to me and stomped her little hooves as we stood side-by-side, facing off against our common enemy.

A grin overtook my face. *You sweet, mischievous little demon.*

Candice took a slow step back, keeping a safe distance between her and the goat. Larry matched her with a step forward. Candice stepped back. Larry stepped forward.

They continued this beautiful dance filled with anticipation and dread and all the drama until Candice ran out of space.

"Oooh, this is just like watching *Real Housewives*, but with farm animals," Jeff squawked through their horn.

"Don't call Candice a farm animal, sweetie," Tyson replied.

"I'd watch that show," Oscar said.

A few more people nodded in agreement.

"Go get her, Larry!" someone shouted.

*Blet!* Larry answered as she charged.

"No!" I said, reaching for Larry.

"*Aah!*" Candice screamed as she turned and ran towards her car.

Larry jumped and twisted in the air, looking like a parkouring demon goat, as she cut off Candice's escape. Candice turned and ran down the sidewalk towards town, Larry chasing gleefully right behind her.

Atlas trotted behind them, probably to wrangle Larry back to the shelter when she was done with her fuckery for the day.

"Stay out of Candice's flower beds!" I shouted after him.

"Don't break a heel, Candi!" Jeff shouted into the bullhorn.

"Lar-ry! Lar-ry!" the crowd chanted.

I blew out a breath. "This won't be the last we hear from her," I said to Jase.

Jase nodded. "Yeah, but with the town against her, and Bob no longer in her corner, I think we've at least earned some breathing room." He kissed my temple, making my stomach swirl in happy somersaults.

"Enough for you to open the Catcher's Box," I said.

"Enough for you to expand Happy Tails and keep rescuing all the animals."

Shit. The animals. "You'll totally run Happy Tails while I do the mayor thing, right?" I asked Jeff.

"You know it, sister," they said, holding out their fist. I bumped it with my own and smiled.

"We did it," I whispered. "We fucking did it."

"You did it," Jase said, wrapping my face in his hands and kissing me.

"Get a room! Get a room!" everyone around us chanted.

Jase smiled against my lips. "This town sure knows how to protest for a good cause," he said.

I looked around at the mass of people, who very much looked like they didn't want to go home. If the Let It Snow festival from two years ago was any indication, they could go for days if left to their own devices.

"They're having fun," I said. "Who knows when the next opportunity to get out their signs and march will happen?"

Jase laughed as I took a second to let everything sink in.

I'd stood my ground to the biggest bully in Harmony Springs. The person who'd gone out of her way, time and time again, to make me—and everyone else she encountered —miserable.

And I had just shut her down. With a little help from Jase. And my town. And my goat.

"Holy lady goat balls, we did it," I said loudly, shaking my head.

"In your face, Titties McGee!" Jeff shouted.

"Titties McGee! Titties McGee!" the crowd mimicked.

"No, no!" Jeff corrected.

"Give me that," I said, marching over to Jeff and wrenching the bullhorn from them.

"Attention everyone!" I shouted. Okay, maybe it was hard not to yell. "We did it," I said in a much more normal-sounding voice.

The people around me erupted into applause, whooping and whistling, but no one made any move to leave.

"You did it."

Dozens of faces all turned and looked at me. "I, well, thank you. For your support today. And over the years with Happy Tails. Your pets are all so lucky to have found you all. And I'm lucky you keep supporting us. You guys are... my family."

A few people clapped, but most were looking around like they were trying to decide whether to take up marching again. Why was I rambling? *And who the hell gave me a bullhorn?*

"You took it from me," Jeff replied.

*Ah, still thinking out loud. Oops.* Time to wrap this up for good.

"So I guess I'm running for mayor." More people clapped. "And as soon as I figure out what all that entails, I'll make it official. But in the meantime…"

I looked around. This was my town. My town. Fuck yes, I was running for mayor. And I'd be the best damned mayor they've ever had.

*And have sex in the mayor's office!* yelled my vagina.

Because I had a support system. A family. Mostly composed of misfits and weirdos, but they were *my* misfits and weirdos.

"You can, you know, go home now. Or something."

People looked at one another, not sure what to do.

"Go home. To your homes."

Jeff whipped the bullhorn out of my hand. "Watch and learn, rookie."

They cleared their throat and squawked the horn. "Attention good citizens of Harmony Springs!" they bellowed. "You have done your civic duty. Well done. You are hereby released from service."

Confusion filled the sea of faces.

"Oh, for the love of…" Jase said, taking over the bullhorn. "If you all go home now, I'll give anyone who shows up on opening day a free beer!"

The crowd let out a hooray and broke apart.

"Sam's gonna love that," I said, laughing as Jase closed his eyes and swore.

"We should organize another protest soon," Mrs. Allonsey said, spinning her sign.

"Agreed," nodded Bruce. "We should start a Monthly Protest Club."

"Dibs on president!" Mr. Jenkins shouted.

"You can't call dibs on that," Bruce grumbled.

"Can and did."

A monthly protest club? *Jean-Luc Picard help us.*

A few people stopped to shake my hand.

"Well done, Madam Mayor," Bart Stuff said, slapping me on the shoulder.

"You've got my vote," his brother Wallace said.

"Oh, I… thanks."

*Sweet baby Spock.*

"Madam Mayor," Jase said, standing next to me, bumping my shoulder gently. "Got a nice ring to it."

"You think so?" I said.

*WE'RE GOING TO HAVE MAYORAL SEX!* shouted my all my lady bits at once.

"I do," he nodded, his eyes flicking down to my lips.

I had to crane my neck to see him this closely. My heart skipped as those bright blue eyes hit me with all the intensity of someone who had my back. And he did. He'd reached out to the community for me. And they had come running. With signs and shirts and chants. And votes.

Like the weird little town they were.

I fucking loved this town. I fucking loved this man. And he deserved to know.

"I love you," I said, reaching up and wrapping my arms around his neck.

"I love you," he replied, purring as I ran my fingers through the back of his hair.

"I said it first," I said.

Chuckling, he wrapped his arms around me, pulling me closer as he leaned down and kissed me. His lips were warm and strong and soft and tasted like peppermint. Peppermint was now my new favorite flavor.

He teased his tongue across my bottom lip, inviting me to open. Who was I to argue? I deepened the kiss and my nipples broke out into song with my vagina joining in the harmony.

"Ahem," called a distant voice, so far away that it barely registered.

*Ignore it*, my ovaries said.

*Ignore it*, my vagina agreed.

*Rub me harder*, my nipples demanded.

I slid slowly up onto my tiptoes to comply.

"Ahem," boomed the voice through the bullhorn.

Jase pulled back—*boo!* cried all my lady parts—and hid a smile in my hair as I turned to eviscerate whoever had disappointed my vagina.

Tyson stood before us grinning, while Jeff rocked back and forth on their toes like someone who had a secret.

"What?" I bit out, breathless and frustrated and wanting very much to just get Jase back to my house and out of these clothes and into bed. Or on the couch. Or the floor. Whatever was quickest.

"Mayor, huh?" Tyson asked, still grinning.

"So it seems," I responded.

"Deadline to enter the race is next week," Jeff said.

"And?" Seriously, couldn't this wait until after I had an orgasm? Or three?

"*And* we've got some work to do if you want your name on the ballot," answered Tyson.

I smiled at Tyson and Jeff. My best friends, who'd stood by me through all the ups and downs. Nursed me through my mom's death. Helped me at the shelter even when I was too tired to ask for help.

And today. They'd been here, helping me win a future for

Harmony Springs. For themselves. For everyone who called this weird little town home.

Jase squeezed my hand, and I turned my grin to him.

This new path was going to be a lot of hard work, but with these people by my side—who loved me as much as I loved them—and the community behind us, I felt ready for anything.

"Yes," I answered Tyson. "And I promise to get right on that. As soon as I'm done here."

Grabbing the back of Jase's head, I pulled him towards me and kissed him like I had all the fucking time in the world.

Being mayor of Harmony Springs might be in my future, but I had more immediate plans.

*Woo hoo! Multiple orgasms, here we come!* my vagina celebrated.

I softened the kiss. "Let's go home," I whispered, continuing to pepper Jase with gentle kisses.

"I'll follow you anywhere, Molly," Jase said. "Now and always."

# EPILOGUE

## JASE

*Seven months later...*

"I can't believe I let you talk me into shower sex," Molly bit out as she stumbled into a pair of charcoal slacks and tucked in a silk ivory-colored blouse. Jeff had recently dragged her to the city to shop for more "office friendly" clothes since pretty much everything she owned was nerdy tees and cutoff shorts.

The effect was startling. Dressed down Molly was sexy, complete with kitten poop on her sleeve. She didn't have to try to turn me on. Just being in the same room as her got my attention.

But Mayor Molly was grown-up hot. Who knew I had a thing for office attire?

"We were supposed to be at city hall five minutes ago," she said as she fluffed her sleeves, clearly still not quite used to being in something besides cotton.

I grinned, digging around in a moving box generically labeled *clothes*, which is where I hoped my ties had landed.

Pulling a gray silk tie out of the box, I whipped it around my neck. "I'd say I'm sorry, but I'm really not." How could I be, when I'd made her come three times—once with my mouth, once with my fingers, and once with my cock— before the hot water ran out?

*High-five, Tug Junior!*

"Me neither," she grinned, stepping around another moving box. Atlas wagged his tail from our bed, where he'd taken up residence when we'd tumbled our way into the bathroom a half hour earlier. "But I will make you pay when we get home."

Home. I was *home*.

I'd moved into Molly's house last weekend, but we hadn't had time to unpack yet. She'd been busy with her campaign, which I still didn't understand, since no one was running against her. Something about the residents threatening to follow through with their plans to form a monthly protest club and use Molly's campaign as its first target if she didn't run "a full and fair campaign."

And the brewery had been taking up all my spare time. Tourist season in Harmony Springs was practically year-round thanks to the series of festivals hosted by my adopted hometown. After the Sunshine Festival, I'd had to gear up quickly for the Celebration of Our Nation Festival in July. Then came the Summer Blues Festival in August, the Batten the Hatches Festival in early September, and the Color Me Fall Festival to celebrate the turning of the leaves. We'd barely gotten through the Holiday Kickoff Festival last month, and in a few weeks, the Let It Snow Festival was happening.

You'd think the town would suffer from festival burnout, but it only seemed to energize them.

Molly shoved a box to the side and opened a drawer to her—*our*—dresser. "We really need more room." She side-eyed me.

"I know. Soon. I promise."

She rolled her eyes, which was the same reaction I got every time I gave her that response. I couldn't help that it was the same response my contractors gave me every time I asked them when my house would be done. It must be contractor code for "whenever they finally pulled their heads out of their asses and got the permits they needed from the county."

Too bad my land wasn't within the town limits. I could probably get the permits issued tomorrow if I promised Molly I'd do that thing with my tongue again that had made her go hoarse in the shower this morning.

*Heh.* I might do that anyway.

And now I had half a boner. *No time for an encore, TJ.* My lady had an acceptance speech to give.

"What are you grinning at?" Molly asked as she dived into the closet and started tossing shoes behind her. "Where the hell are those brown suede booties Jeff gave me for this outfit? They're going to kill me if I lost them."

"Maybe Larry ate them," I joked.

"Oh, my Spock. Do *not* joke." Her eyes had gone wide as she looked at me over her shoulder, her sweet ass positioned just perfectly for—

"We do not have time for round two, Tug."

I blinked and realized I'd been palming my hard-on. Oops. "That's fine," I said. "Because I'm going to have sex with the mayor tonight."

She glared over her shoulder, but her eyes had darkened. She wasn't angry. That was pure lust.

"Does *she* know that?"

"Oh yeah," I replied. "I've got something special planned for her."

She glanced at the alarm clock on the bedside table, and then slowly walked towards me.

*Oh, hell yes!*

Dragging her fingers lightly over the tie that was still hanging around my neck, she tugged at it and pulled me towards her. "Maybe we can—"

"Yoo hoo!" Jeff hollered from downstairs, causing Molly to jump in surprise.

Her head knocked against my bottom lip.

"Ow, shit," I said. Or tried to, but my bleeding lip made it a little hard to enunciate.

"Fucking dammit, they have the worst timing on the planet," she grumbled, rubbing her head as she took two giant steps away from me before glancing at my crotch. She raised her eyebrows. "You, uh, are showing."

I grabbed a dark tee shirt from the bed and pressed it to my mouth with one hand while I adjusted myself with the other. "Serves them right for refusing to use the doorbell," I mumbled through the fabric as I started subtracting my batting average from my slugging average for each year of my career to get TJ under control. "Your head okay?"

"You mean the new tooth mark I have in my skull? Yep, just add it to the list."

I chuckled. The list of all our sex injuries was impressive. And one hundred percent worth every bruise, cut, and sore knee.

Jeff stomped loudly down the hallway. "I'm giving you plenty of time and notice of my not-so-sudden appearance," they shouted. "So I'd better not see any lady bits when I pop my head into your room. Jase, you're free to be as naked as you'd like."

"Baby Spock on a rocket ship," Molly muttered. "We're fully clothed!"

Jeff popped their head into the doorway as promised, and winked at me. "Maybe next time, muscles."

"No, thank you," I responded, looping the end of my tie around to knot it. Thankfully, Tug Junior had complied quickly. Not too surprising, given how much action he'd been getting lately. Molly and I had christened every room and surface in the house. And a good chunk of the shelter. If the health department weren't so picky, we'd probably take a good run at the brewery too.

"I won a bet with Tyse to see who got to drag you out of your sex den so you can accept the election results," they said, leaning against the doorway. "So get your cute little tushies in gear. You've got fans to appease!"

Molly looked up at me, caramel eyes bright and wide. "I can't believe I did this."

"I can," I said, my voice low, pride practically bursting through my chest. She'd been taking care of this town long before I had arrived. It was about time they recognized her for it. Plus, did I mention, sex with the mayor? The next six years were going to be h-o-t. I hoped Tug Junior was up for the challenge.

"Come on. Let's go before we scar Jeff for life." Molly laughed as Jeff's face blanched.

I took her hand in mine and smiled down at her. "After you, Madam Mayor."

# EPILOGUE

## MOLLY

$\mathcal{I}$t is my greatest privilege to introduce your new mayor. Molly Sanders." Frances Cobb, the outgoing mayor, beamed as she shook my hand. "Congratulations, Molly. Your mom would be over the moon."

"I hope so," I replied, the words sticking in my throat as I choked back tears. Everything I'd done in the last few years had been for my mom. Taking care of Larry, despite her efforts to thwart me at every turn. Expanding the shelter. Taking care of the people in my town.

It might have taken a stand-off with my nemesis to shove me into the spotlight and the mayor's race. But as I looked out into the sizable crowd of my fellow residents, I could see how it was inevitable.

Jase squeezed my hand as Frances handed me the microphone. "Knock 'em dead," he told me. "Not literally. We want them to vote for your reelection."

"What makes you think I'm going to do this again?"

He bent down until I could feel his lips brushing against my ear. "Besides all the sex we're going to have in the mayor's office?"

I felt the heat burning my cheeks, and he chuckled, his breath blowing the hair around my face that had come out of my ponytail. "Because this is where you belong, Molly."

Turning my face, I kissed the fuck out of him. I couldn't help it. This man had stood next to me as I stumbled through my campaign. Believed in me more than I did. Showed up for me, every single day.

*And gives us all the orgasms!* my vagina cheered, as Jase's hands wrapped around my back and pulled me in tight.

*Yay for orgasms!* my ovaries agreed, when Jase slid his tongue across my lips and angled his face to take the kiss deeper.

*We love the sex!* my nipples added, as I felt the hard length of Tug Junior, hero of the afternoon, against my stomach.

*Simmer down, ladies. We're in public.*

"Get a room!" someone who sounded like Jeff yelled from the crowd above all the whoops and hollers.

Shit. We're in public.

I broke off the kiss and snickered as Jase angled his hips behind me.

*Let's go have sex in the mayor's office!* my vagina yelled.

*There's plenty of time for that,* I replied.

I took the microphone and cleared my throat. I'd practiced this speech in the bathroom mirror at home and to the animals in the shelter so many times I should have been able to recite it in my sleep. But looking out at the crowd, at all these people who were here for me, who voted for me, standing in a room decorated with all manner of snowflakes, snow people, and twinkle lights, because the Let It Snow Festival kicked off in a couple weeks, which I was now in charge of, as the incoming mayor.

Nerves hijacked my brain as I forgot how to word. "I, uh, thanks. For voting. For me."

Tyson was there, smiling up at me while he rubbed Jeff's

back, who was studying my outfit, which they picked out specifically for today. "The ivory brings out your eyes," they'd told me, as if that was a thing I worried about.

Brooklyn was also there with a group of seniors, including Mrs. Kowalski, who was wearing a bright pink shirt with my face on it. I looked like I was mid-sneeze.

"Where'd that photo come from?" I asked before I remembered I was still holding the microphone and the question went out to the entire crowd.

"I took it when you were stuck in that tree," Mrs. K replied while Bennie nodded next to her, in a matching shirt.

Dear Spock, how many of those had she made?

"Awesome," I answered and cleared my throat again. "Look, I had a whole speech planned, but I can't remember it right now, and, uh, Larry ate my notecards. So, we're having a celebration party at the Catcher's Box in an hour. I hope you all can come so we can thank you properly."

Jase leaned over my shoulder. "We have a new brew just for this occasion. Your first pint of Molly's Political Porter is on the house."

"Holy shit, Sam's gonna have you murdered in your sleep," I said into the microphone. I really needed to put this thing down.

"He'll have to get through you and Atlas first," he replied.

"And us," Tyson said.

"And Larry," Jeff added.

"We love Larry!" someone shouted.

"We love Larry!" the crowd answered as they chanted their way out of the room. "We love Larry!"

"I can't believe I lost my bullhorn," Jeff said, a frown on their face as they turned to leave with the crowd. Tyson looked up at me and winked. *You're welcome*, he mouthed.

"Thank Klingons for small miracles," I said. "I still don't know who gave Jeff a damned bullhorn."

"Yeah," Jase said, placing a hand on the small of my back. "About that…"

I sucked in a breath. "You didn't."

"Officially? No."

"And unofficially?"

"Are you asking as my girlfriend? Or my mayor?"

"Yes."

A deep chuckle reached the center of my core, igniting that flame that seemed to be never ending where Jase was concerned. He looked so fucking good today. I mean, he looked good every day, as my vagina could attest, given the number of times we've jumped him since we got together.

*Mmm, you know that's right,* my vagina agreed.

But today, he was… everything. His sandy blond hair was combed back, his face freshly shaven. And the dark gray shirt and pants, with his matching tie, which Jeff didn't even have to pick out for him because he just knew what made his eyes pop and what would match my outfit. I was out of my league, but I didn't care. He was mine. And I was keeping him.

"I stand by my official statement," he replied, his sexy voice low and his hand over the top of the microphone so only I could hear. Not that the crowd could hear anything over all the chanting about my goat. "But I'll make it up to you tonight."

"I don't know how you're going to top the shower," I said.

"I have a few ideas," he replied, heat swirling in his crystal blue eyes.

*Picard, help me.*

*Bring it on!* cheered my vagina.

*Challenge accepted,* agreed the rest of my lady parts.

My poor neighbors. We were going to need to move if he got any more creative or motivated to see how loud I could come.

"Lock the door if you two are planning to have sex in

your new office, Madam Mayor." Jeff's face peeked around the entryway as they grinned at us. "I'll make sure everyone gets a beer."

"We're coming," Jase said quickly, turning to me, panic causing his eyes to grow as round as a pair of baseballs. "We've got plenty of time to break in your office. But if I leave Jeff in charge of the tap, Sam really will have me murdered in my sleep."

I nodded as I followed him out the door. "Right behind you. But I'm still holding you to your promise tonight."

"Tonight, and every night, Molly. I'm yours. For as long as you'll have me."

"Forever then?"

His steps faltered, and he turned slowly towards me, brows furrowed. "Molly Sanders, did you just propose to me?"

Oh, fuck. *Had I?*

"No! Yes. Maybe?"

I mean, it wasn't the *worst* idea I've ever had. And the thought of going to sleep in Jase's arms every night, and waking up in them every morning. Yeah, I could definitely see that happening.

"Then I maybe say yes. When you're ready."

I was going to kiss this shit out of this man again. Right after we kicked Jeff out from behind the bar.

# BEFORE YOU GO

$\mathcal{U}$m...

Wow. You're still here. I guess all I can say is, thank you! Thank you for reading *Harmony and Havoc*. And thank you for taking a chance on a new author.

There are definitely more stories floating around in my head about Harmony Springs and these characters, so stay tuned!

Here's the reason I'm poking my little head into the end of your reading experience. I'm not only a new author, but I'm an independent author. What does that have to do with you, you ask? What a great question. And the answer is a lot, actually.

You may not know this, but reviews are one of the best ways to help spread the word and reach new readers, so they can (hopefully) enjoy this book as much as you did.

If you have a few spare seconds in your day, would you consider leaving an honest review on whichever platform you purchased this ebook from? Or even Goodreads. Whatever your preference. I'm not picky.

And when you're done, go do something nice for yourself. Think of it as a little treat for doing a solid for an up-and-coming author.

Hugs,
Amy Draper

# ACKNOWLEDGMENTS

Where does one even start when you've finally reached that stretch goal you set for yourself all those many years ago to become an author? I guess at the beginning…

None of this would have been possible without the love and support of a truck ton of people, so get comfy, dear reader. This is going to be a ride.

Nathan, thank you for being that voice at home who tells me I'm killing it, even when I'm not. And for giving me all the quiet in the mornings while I thaw out. And for just being you. I love you and I'm so happy you slid into my dms all those years ago and I didn't delete your message. Because I've been indescribably happy ever since.

Mom, you probably don't know it because I haven't been nearly as vocal about it as I should have (I know, no one is more surprised about that than I am) but your quiet support is everything. Thank you for having the fortitude to raise a strong-willed child. I know I didn't make it easy.

Dad, thanks for all the book talks over the years. I miss our talks almost as much as I miss you.

Anna! My sister, my best friend, my ride or die. (Wow, sorry, that was overly dramatic.) Your constant enthusiasm and love for all these characters is second only to mine. On the hard days, it actually surpassed mine, which helped me push through. I dedicated this book to you because I truly believe you're the reason I finished it. *Thanks, sista!*

Wow, this is getting long. If you're with me this far, Spock bless you! Just a few more before the orchestra starts playing me out to a commercial break.

Ali, Toni, Rikki and Jessi, thanks for your excitement about this book and continually asking about it. Nothing like an eager group of supporters to keep you writing until you get to The End.

JP, thank you for reaching out that one dark day and extending a hand. You're more than just a writing coach and editor. You were a cheerleader and helping hand when I needed it most, and keep me accountable every week, which is no easy task.

J and Susanne, thank you each for making space for authors to be authors and develop their craft. This book started and grew under your respective tutelages and I hope it shows.

Kat, editor extraordinaire. Thank you for helping make my manuscript a shiny treasure I'll always be proud of. Thank you also for knowing the difference between hyphenated and compound words, because I, clearly, do not.

If you loved the cover even half as much as I did, you can thank Miblart. They didn't even blink when I asked them to add a goat and a Great Dane.

And to you, dear reader. Thank you for taking a chance on a new author. I hope I didn't disappoint.

# ABOUT THE AUTHOR

Amy Draper writes steamy small-town romances featuring rescue animals with attitude problems, coffee-fueled heroines who collect trouble like others collect shoes, and heroes who didn't know they needed saving until the right woman came along.

When she's not creating chaos on the page, she can be found at home with her partner (in life *and* in crime) having philosophical debates with their rescue cat about the merits of napping versus watching Hallmark movies (the cat usually wins). She loves being a big sister, slays at being an auntie, and knows she needs to write that next scene but is probably watching videos of ducks running with the volume turned way up, so she needs five more minutes, please.

At the end of the day, she's just trying to spread joy one spicy happily ever after at a time, preferably with a side of mayhem and a large glass of wine.

To follow ~~the mayhem~~ Amy's work or to sign up for her newsletter, go to www.amydraperauthor.com.

*P.S. Here's your big sister reminder to hydrate.*

www.ingramcontent.com/pod-product-compliance
Lightning Source LLC
Chambersburg PA
CBHW031737180726
48283CB00005B/1557